Also by Kyell Gold

Argaea
Volle
Pendant of Fortune
The Prisoner's Release and Other Stories
Shadow of the Father
Weasel Presents

Out of Position
Out of Position
Isolation Play
Divisions
Uncovered
Over Time
Titles

Dangerous Spirits
Green Fairy
Red Devil
Black Angel

Other Books
Waterways
Bridges
Science Friction
Winter Games
The Mysterious Affair of Giles
Dude, Where's My Fox?
Losing My Religion
The Time He Desires
In the Doghouse of Justice
The Silver Circle
X (editor)
Ty Game

Love Match

Book 3 (2013-2015)

by Kyell Gold

Dallas, TX

Love Match
Book 3 (2013-2015)

Production copyright FurPlanet Productions © 2020

Artwork © Rukis 2020
https://www.furaffinity.net/user/rukis/

Published by FurPlanet Productions
Dallas, Texas
www.FurPlanet.com

ISBN 978-1-61450-527-3

First Edition Trade Paperback 2020

Table of Contents

Part Seven: Challenger (2013)   9

Prologue (2015)   11

Chapter One (2012-2013)   19

Chapter Two   24

Chapter Three   37

Chapter Four   51

Chapter Five   60

Chapter Six   73

Chapter Seven   82

Chapter Eight   91

Chapter Nine   100

Chapter Ten   110

Part Eight: Overseas (2014)   121

Chapter Eleven   122

Chapter Twelve   131

Chapter Thirteen   141

Chapter Fourteen   156

Chapter Fifteen   170

Chapter Sixteen   190

Chapter Seventeen   206

Chapter Eighteen   224

Chapter Nineteen   244

Chapter Twenty   253

Interlude (2015)   262

Part Nine: Tiebreak (2015)   269

Chapter Twenty-One (2014-2015)   270

Chapter Twenty-Two   280

Chapter Twenty-Three   294

Chapter Twenty-Four   308

Chapter Twenty-Five   318

Chapter Twenty-Six   333

Chapter Twenty-Seven   348

Chapter Twenty-Eight   363

Chapter Twenty-Nine   369

Chapter Thirty   380

Chapter Thirty-One   389

Chapter Thirty-Two   408

Chapter Thirty-Three   430

Chapter Thirty-Four   447

Patreon   463

Acknowledgments   466

About the Author   467

About the Artist   467

About the Publisher   467

For my sister

Part Seven: Challenger (2013)

Prologue (2015)

bazinga1991
holy **** this match

enkari22
Does anyone have a code to watch on AAB Online?

smilinglikethedevil
jackal gonna take that fox apart

bazinga1991
this is ******* history yall

bazinga1991
if longacre is gonna grand slam hes gonna earn it this is amazeballs

tartframboze44
oh theres a grand slam? huh weird youd think the announcers would mentin it eighteen millin times

longacrelife
branden is bae

longacrelife
*braden

longacrelife
autocorrect

jeffreydean28
Tart they have mentioned it a lot

bazinga1991
cmon start the fifth set already

tartframboze44
* adds sarcasm detector to chat group

jeffreydean28
im rooting for nguwe because longacre has won enough,
time for someone else

bazinga1991
r u serious? history dude!!!

smilinglikethedevil
Longacre is a ****** anyway

emersonemeritus
Personally I dont want Longacre to get the Grand Slam
because he hasn't really earned it. The level of competition
is way down this year. When Palmer did it in 1966 he was
playing Townsend, who got a Grand Slam two years later,
he was playing two other Hall of Famers. Since Tempest
fell off a couple years back there's no truly great player on
the tour this year.

bazinga1991
you dont think hes earning it now? fifth set!!

overturnedonreplay
Totally disagree, longacre is just that much better than everyone else this year. He deserves the grand slam. I think nguwe will be a top ten player in a couple years.

emersonemeritus
The guy lost in the quarterfinals at Ursaria to Kingbury.

smilinglikethedevil
i mean f a g

smilinglikethedevil
his "gf" said they never slept together

tartframboze44
ffs its 2015

overturnedonreplay
I guess when Palmer won his grand slam he didn't lose any matches at all the entire year ever?

emersonemeritus
As a matter of fact he lost 15 times but he played 34 tournaments.

enkari22
I'm sorry, does anyone have a code to watch on AAB Online?

emersonemeritus
Longacre has only played in one more tournament than Palmer won.

overturnedonreplay
Level of competition wasn't as good in 1966.

bazinga1991
if I was up 5-3 and didnt win the set id be so mad, longacres gonna win 6-0

emersonemeritus
Are you seriously saying that? The athletes weren't in as good shape as they are today but relative to the field there was a lot more parity. Look at some of the other guys playing then.

overturnedonreplay
Look at the guys playing now! NGuwe is from a whole other continent, half the players are from all over the world. Palmer mostly played against people from Oceania, Europe, and the States.

bazinga1991
oh man that ace! here comes a love game!

truepattruecolors
Nguwe is a dick hes lived here for like seven years and didnt want to become a citizen? He shouldnt be allowed to win the states opnen.

truepattruecolors
Nguwe is a dick hes lived here for like seven years and didnt want to become a citizen? He shouldnt be allowed to win the states opnen.

truepattruecolors
Good, longacre! Get that sand dog

enkari22
Lunda has more rainforest than desert. There's some dry areas but you're thinking of the Sahara.

truepattruecolors
Jackals = sand dogs

tartframbozen44
thought this channel was moderated smh

dominicpettit
This channel is being moderated. I've already tossed one person for making a slur, and species slurs won't be tolerated either. Truepat, this is your first warning.

tartframbozen44
if species slurs arent tolerated just ban him

tartframbozen44
or her

emersonemeritus
Plus the tournaments were way smaller back then so it was only the best players. You didn't have hundreds of guys showing up.

bazinga1991
yeah longacre 1-0! service break service break come on!

tartframbozen44
i dunno looks like longacre's lagging a bit, he's waiting to place his shots, nguwe had more energy that first game just longacre got two aces by him. cant count on aces the whole match, this one might be tight

overturnedonreplay
Totally agree, longacre is panting more than nguwe too. We'll see how nguwe does on his serve but I think this one will go 6-4.

jeffreydean28
Yeah come on nguwe!

bazinga1991
hey any foxes inhere not rooting for longacre?

gordonpolkherov
Yo.

bazinga1991
what why dude?

gordonpolkherov
It's not just about species, Nguwe is the better story.

overturnedonreplay
Better than a Grand slam???

gordonpolkherov
Kid here from another country who earned everything he
got vs rich kid who had everything served up on a plate?
Yeah better story.

bazinga1991
longacre is from a rich family?

gordonpolkherov
Google his Wikipedia page. Mother is a top exec at Kaleido
Publishing, father sells multimillion dollar mansions in
the northeast. He has been to private school all his life and
went to Palm Gables and parents paid his way through
early years of the tour. That fox was born with a whole
silver place setting in his muzzle.

bazinga1991
they said nguwe went to palm gables too

gordonpolkherov
He did but he went on a scholarship and Longacre went on
his parents dime.

overturnedonreplay
That doesnt mean longacre isn't talented. You cant just
buy your wa into grand slam finals. Cub works harder
than anyone in the game. I bet he didnt' sleep with his gf
because he didn't want to take the time away from tennis

dominicpettit
Careful.

overturnedonreplay
Im not speculating on whether hes gay! I just said he probably didnt take time from tennis!

enkari22
I'm sorry, does anyone have a code to watch on AAB
Online?

dominicpettit
Stop asking for someone to give you codes or I'll have to
ban you, kid.

enkari22
I'm so sorry. I'm in Lunda and I want to see this match
very much only our television set is broken. I went to the
library but they won't let us turn on the television at this
time so the only way I can see the game is on the computer, but I can't find a place where I can watch it.

gordonpolkherov
Oh dang.

bazinga1991
ill pm you, theres some streams you can get to

dominicpettit
Enkari, send me an email and I'll see if I can get you a channel. I'm PMing you my address.

enkari22
Thank you all so much.

emersonemeritus
Go Nguwe, way to hold serve! Guess it won't be 6-0.

overturnedonreplay
Nobody who knows anything thought it would be.

bazinga1991
**** you dude

Chapter One (2012-2013)

Aliq's family invited me back to spend Christmas and New Year's with them. I didn't have Marquize and I didn't have Ma, and Ori was an ocean away. Braden wasn't exactly the kind of friend I was going to spend holidays with, and anyway he was an ocean away too, training for the Ocie Open (when you're top 50 in the world you get invited to the majors). Anyway, Aliq's mom had semi-adopted me into her soft white fluffy family—let me tell you, there's nothing quite so warm as a bunch of arctic foxes in their winter coats sitting together on a couch watching Christmas specials with hot chocolate—since I had, after all, gotten the news about losing my mother while a guest in her house.

They also got snow, which wasn't exactly a novelty to me at that point, but I'd never really gotten into snow the way they did. Like, literally. Two days after Christmas it started snowing in the evening and didn't stop until sometime in the early morning, so we woke up to a foot and a half of sparkling white as far as we could see and the sound and smell of great diesel plows trundling along the road pushing it into piles almost as tall as Aliq's mother was.

I would've been happy to sit with my chocolate and look out at the weird, beautiful sight, but Aliq and his parents ran out and plunged into it. I followed, cautiously, until Aliq lobbed a snowball at me. That wouldn't stand; I gathered up some of the cold fluff, packed it as tightly as I could, and missed him by a mile.

"You can hit a tennis ball into the corner of the court from fifty feet away," he taunted me, tossing another.

"Give me a racket and I'll hit your left ear," I yelled back, packing another snowball in my paws. This one at least hit his tail as he dodged it, and the game was on.

But arctic foxes have more padding in their paws and under their fur than this tropical jackal, so the cold seeped into my paws and feet long before they were ready to come inside. I hesitated on the doorstep, snow clinging to my fur and drifting to their welcome mat. I didn't want to track the wet into the living room, but I couldn't figure out where else to go. So eventually I hopped to the nearest bathroom to towel off.

I needn't have worried. When the arctics came in, they brushed each other's paws and tails right in that welcome-mat area, making a big pool of damp, and then they grabbed towels from a closet I hadn't thought to check and dried themselves off. Their fur still showed damp in spots, but none of them cared much.

"What did you think of your first snowball fight?" Aliq asked me as we sat down to lunch.

"Fun," I said. "I think I need to warm up to it."

They liked that, all of them laughing. His father explained my joke back to me—"A ha, but if you warm up, you'd melt it!"—and I laughed back. We played in the snow a little more, but it still chilled me too fast to stay out for long. That was fine; I enjoyed curling up by the bay window and watching the crisp sky brighten with fantastic colors over the wintry landscape as my friend and his family built snowfoxes and forts, had battles (at one point several neighbors joined in and fought off a furious barrage of snowballs from an army of teens), and also in the course of things shoveled their walkway and driveway.

Christmas was a big celebration: Aliq's family celebrated Hanukah but enjoyed the secular (a new word I learned) aspects of Christmas much more elaborately than Ma and I had. They sang carols, they had Christmas hats, they told Christmas stories that Aliq's grandmother (on his mother's side, because he called her "Grandma Tikkit" and his family's name was Loize) had told them from her home in the northwest, before they moved east. They made a huge dinner not unlike our feasts, and that was the point where I missed Ma the most. She would've loved all this, I thought, and I was quiet for a good half of the meal. It was a mark of how well they knew me by then that Aliq made one attempt to get me to talk, and his mother diverted the conversation immediately. After dinner, she took me aside and asked me if I wanted to go to church. I considered it, but it would have been too lonely.

And after New Years, it was back to tennis. We set our sights on Wimbledon this year, at least to be invited as a doubles team, because we'd gotten invitations to two top circuit tournaments in the spring. So we didn't really want to play the Challenger tournament in early January, but Lochen told us that most of the top talent was, like Braden, in Oceania, so we had a better chance to win this one, and a win was a win. Reluctantly, we decamped for some city in the south and left the snow behind.

By this time the rhythm of tournaments was as familiar to me as a family ritual. I was comfortable with air travel and getting to and from the airport; I knew the locker rooms and courts and in some cities the best cheap eats nearby; I knew more and more of my fellow players and more and more of them knew me. Aliq and Danver and I were greeted in the locker room with fistbumps and tail wags, especially at this tournament, which was mostly the 100-200 ranked players. We talked about those other guys in Oceania where there was a heat wave and hid our envy with talk about how terrible the weather was there.

Danver was his usual chatty self, telling us at length about his Christmas holiday and the numerous hookups he'd had during it, the usual mix of 90% exaggeration (probably) to 10% truth. We resumed our practices with only a little rust, as though the last tournament had been the previous week.

Aliq and I lost in the finals but that was still a good outcome for us. You get points on the circuit based on how you did the year before, so anytime you get a better result, you gain points. We'd made the round of sixteen in 2012, so this got us a bunch of points, and I remembered how I'd celebrated upon getting my first hundred.

In singles I didn't do quite as well, losing in the quarterfinals, which was only one round farther than I'd gotten the previous year. I was mad because the first part of this year was going to be a lot of tournaments I hadn't done well in, so I would have great opportunities to make up points. Toward the end of the year I was going to have to defend my points and I'd have a harder time earning more.

It was better than losing points, Aliq reminded me. "Not as good as earning more points," I said.

He laughed and elbowed me. "Look at you, all unhappy about getting to the finals and quarters."

"In a small tournament."

"You didn't think it was so small last year."

"I was at 316 last year."

He elbowed me again; Aliq was still sub-250 in singles. "Don't go getting too good at singles and abandon me in doubles."

"Nah, never," I said. A moment later I remembered all the times I'd told Marquize I'd never abandon him. But it would be different with Aliq. We weren't dating, for one thing. And Aliq was way more committed to tennis—no, that wasn't fair. His commitment to tennis more closely matched mine. We weren't going to argue about that. Mostly, though, I told myself, it was the dating thing. We were good friends and nothing was going to mess that up.

We watched the Ocie Open with Danver and Sean the following week when it got to the round of 16. Each of us had played against one of the players in nearly every match, so we spent a lot of the time comparing notes and the rest of the time studying their play during the match (which meant that Sean, Aliq, and I tuned out Danver's incessant commentary).

Braden got a favorable draw when Malic was upset in one of the early rounds, so the cross fox ended up playing the #57 player in the world instead of the #2 player. Still, he was playing great. "Braden could win this thing," I said after he won his quarterfinal match to go to the semis.

"Hah," Danver said. "You're just saying that because he talks to you."

"No, seriously." I pointed my muzzle up at the screen. "You seen his unforced errors? He's made like six this match, it's crazy."

"Six?" Aliq poked my shoulder. "You mean sixteen."

"That's what I thought. No. Six."

"Crazy," Sean said.

"It's not enough to cut down on your mistakes," Danver pointed out. "You still gotta beat the other guy. Unforced errors is a bullshit stat anyway."

"Still," Aliq said. "If he can keep it to six a match, jeez."

He didn't, as it turned out; his semifinal was an ugly five-set win over a muscular bear named Townsend where he made thirty unforced errors (though honestly a lot of what they called unforced errors in that one were just great shots by Townsend). In the final, he faced the #4 player in the world (Eumon, a squirrel, which finally made Danver shut up) and made him look like—well, me—and won in a fourth-set tiebreak. It was a fantastic match, I thought, especially after the semifinal.

I watched the whole trophy presentation ceremony and three thoughts went through my mind, in approximately this order: One, I wanted to hold that trophy one day. Two, I was happy Braden had won it. I'd only met Eumon twice, and both times he acted dismissive because I wasn't top-50. He was fast enough that once he got his erratic shotmaking under control, he was a force on the court, so I studied his film for lessons but I stayed away from the player himself.

And the third thought I had was that Braden's smile looked tight, his body language as tense as though he had another match to play. His tail curled upward so nobody really remarked on it, but I'd seen that tail loose and relaxed, like it should be when a match was over. He didn't radiate relief. He radiated worry.

Chapter Two

W hy, exactly, was I worried about the moods of Braden Longacre? It wasn't a tennis thing, because otherwise I would've shared my observations with the other guys. I liked to think it was concern over someone who was becoming a friend. But there was more to it too, because Braden was the first person I knew fairly well who'd won a major tournament. I had watched dozens of people hoist a trophy, and they'd all seemed ecstatic to me to various degrees. But I'd never talked to them. I'd never watched them over the course of a conversation the way I had Braden. Maybe they were tense and worried as well, but they expressed it differently. So I worried that getting to the top might not be the goal I thought it was, that winning a major might mess me up the same way.

After a night of sleeping on it, though, I woke up refreshed and with the resolution that Braden's issues were his own and that when I won a championship, I was going to hold it up as high as I could and smile so wide my muzzle might split in half. I visualized it over and over, myself standing in Braden's place, and nothing in that picture made me worried or tense. I would be sad that Ma wasn't there to see it, but in my vision, Ori was, because I'd managed to get her paperwork sorted out and she'd come over to the States. And Marquize was there too, smiling for me.

I didn't talk to him through the holidays, but I did text him on and off during the tournament, just updating him on my status, and he did the same back. After the Ocie Open, I texted him to see if he'd watched, and he texted back, "#1 asshole," which I took for a yes. I wasn't about to waste thumb energy convincing him that Braden was more complicated than that, so I replied that if that fox could win a major, so could I. We had gotten to the point that I wasn't going to say that he could win a major, and he wasn't going to argue with me about it. Which was progress, of a sort.

The next tournament, I waited to see Braden in the locker room, but he didn't show. Nobody knew where he'd gone, either. Townsend, who ended up being the highest ranked player at the tournament, engaged me in a nice conversation the upshot of which was that it wasn't unheard of for a player to take a break after a stressful tournament. He was a little surprised that Braden had, because he was young, but Townsend did recall that Braden hadn't been very talkative after their match; he'd congratulated the bear and then headed out to do media work. "Some guys," he said, "you play a major semifinal, they don't mind a little talk afterwards. But some guys want to go start prepping for the final right away. I guess. He even left his phone in his locker after the match."

He sounded a little wistful. I didn't think he'd ever been to a major final (I was right; he went to his first one later that year). Even though Braden had leapfrogged him, though, he didn't seem upset at the fox. "He was great," he said. "I beat him once and he beat me once last year, but this year he was really dialed in."

"It happens," I said. At least leaving his phone off might explain why Braden hadn't responded to me. But I didn't want to spend too much time worrying about that. Through my wins both with and without Aliq, I was making a dent in the money I owed Lochen, not to mention climbing the rankings, so I figured I'd focus on playing the best tennis I could, learning from Coach Keely when he had the time, and practicing every single day. My workout regimen with Aliq was paying off, too; I was noticeably less tired at the end of long matches, and when we measured velocity, my forehand had gained a few miles per hour.

I didn't feel like I was changing much about my game, but I continued to study the other players diligently. Now I was able to break down someone's game pretty easily, though I still had only moderate success using that information on the court. Aliq picked up on some of my study habits and I picked up his workout habits and we started to communicate really well during our doubles matches, which, probably not coincidentally, we started winning more of.

My singles success, growing slowly but steadily (Coach Keely assured me), came from familiarity with my opponents and my added strength and conditioning. "But how do I get good enough to be in the top ten?" I asked him once, which I now realize sounds like I thought he was holding back some magic secret of tennis that all the top players knew.

"You keep practicing," he said. "You're still thinking too much about your backhand, and your forehands could use more topspin, and you're still not patient enough from the baseline. Your serves are good but could be more varied, and your return game is quite good but you could improve your footwork. So you keep working on all those things, plus a few more, and you'll be playing top ten players before you know it."

"I'm already playing them," I said, thinking of Braden. "I want to beat them."

He laughed. "Rocky, you're not even nineteen yet. You know anyone who was beating top ten players at nineteen? Give it another year or so. You're making a living now."

Not a good living, it was true, not enough to hire a coach full time nor pay off my manager. But it was a living, which was a better place than I'd been financially a couple years ago. So I grumbled to myself and practiced as hard and often as I could. I begged off more nights out with Danver and Sean because by the end of the day I was so exhausted that all I wanted to do was collapse into bed and review my shots and serves from that practice with my eyes closed, looking for the places where I could improve.

It was March, the week before my birthday, and Aliq and I had collected one more tournament win while I kept up my steady pace in singles. We weren't regularly going to the second-tier tournaments, let alone the majors, but the invitations from the Challenger tour came a lot more often. "Remember playing qualifiers?" Aliq said to me once.

"We will when we start going to majors," I said.

He touched his muzzle and pointed to the sky, a gesture I'd learned meant "from your lips to God's ear." "I feel a lot better about that now," he said. "We're getting better. You're getting stronger."

"And we've got a ways to go still."

I was still thinking about that conversation a little later when my phone rang. I thought Marquize might be calling to wish me a happy birthday a bit early, so I smiled as I picked it up. He didn't say, "Happy birthday," though. He said, "Rocky, I wanted to tell you in person. I'm quitting tennis."

For a moment I thought I hadn't heard properly. "You what now?"

"It's too much work and I'm not getting any better, and there's—you know, there's other stuff. I mean, stuff I want to do."

"Like what?" I couldn't imagine anything I would want to do more than tennis, and I was trying.

"Ah, I dunno, like...there's a country club here. I can hang out and give tennis tips to people."

"You get paid for that?"

A beat. "Well, I could do some gardening, too."

"Sounds like you already have a job at this country club."

"Yeah." He kept his voice low. "This friend of mine, Craig, he's a bobcat and his dad is one of the part owners. I've been talking to him about quitting for a month now."

"A month?"

"I didn't want to bother you! You've been playing really well and you got a lot on your mind. And there wasn't really a time. I know, I know, it's my fault too. But I thought, and Craig thought, that I should really give it my all these last couple months to make sure I'm doing the right thing. And I am."

He didn't say, "I think," or anything. And whoever this Craig was, he was Marquize's new confidant. Honestly, I was mostly glad he'd found someone, because we weren't talking and I didn't know how he was getting on with the rest of the Futures tour now that he'd been on it a while. As we talked, he told me that things weren't improving for him and that Craig's country club had offered him a way out where he could still pay off his debt to Lochen, though he hadn't told him yet. I offered to help any way I could, and he thanked me.

"Hey," I said as he was preparing to hang up, "it's my birthday next week."

"Oh yeah," he said. "Happy birthday, Rocky."

For a week or so, I would think about Marquize a lot while practicing, while having dinner with Aliq and the guys, while lying in my bed alone at night. We had a couple days off between tournaments, so I went to a gay bar and picked up a cougar, and I found myself thinking about Marquize during sex as well. Not because the cougar resembled Mar; he was better-looking objectively, I guess, but didn't have the cheetah's athletic body. It was more because Marquize had stepped out of the life we'd shared and I was thinking about how firmly that cemented him in my past. And I was wondering if he'd let himself go, like this cougar was starting to (not that that made him unattractive, mind; just different).

(I had figured out by this point that the best gay bars for me to go to were on college campuses, because either they had a wristband policy for under-21 guys or they didn't check ID at all. Lots of horny 18-to-21-year olds went there and so did the guys who wanted to fuck them, so picking up someone was often as easy as making eye contact and raising a paw. I also dressed in tight t-shirts and shorts, which helped a lot.)

But I'd started to let go of Marquize and the past by the first week of the next tournament. Danver and I finished up a practice session, and when I went to gulp some Boltade I saw I'd gotten a call from a number I didn't know. The voicemail was an unfamiliar voice, but they knew me: "Hey, Rocky? This is Craig. Marquize's friend. I got your number off his phone, sorry to bother you but I'm a little worried. I called his manager and he doesn't know but I thought you might. Who's 'Frio'? It sounds like Marquize is in a little trouble with him but he won't talk about it with me and I just want to know how worried I should be."

Trouble? I puzzled over the call for a while. Gearing up for the tournament, I didn't have a lot of time, and I could've ignored the message. But the mention of Frio got my hackles up and I wanted to know more.

So I made time after dinner, walking around out front of the health food restaurant and pacing back and forth on the sidewalk. I can't remember the name of the town, but it must have been in the lower Midwest, because it wasn't cold but the breeze did have a bite to it, and some of the people walking past me had scarves around their necks. One fox had a light scarf over her ears.

Craig picked up quickly. "Hi, thanks for calling me back. Hang on a second." He muffled the mic and said something to someone, then there were quick steps and a door closing. "Okay," he said. "Sorry, I was chatting with Keez."

It took me a moment to parse that "Keez" was Marquize, and I had a flash of irrational anger: that's not his name. But this guy knew him differently than I did. Maybe "Mar" wasn't around anymore. Now he was "Keez," this guy I didn't know as well. "No problem," I said. "I'm just done with dinner so I have a few before we head back to the dorm."

"I thought you stayed in hotels."

"Sometimes. There's a college campus near this tournament and they've got a dorm facility for visiting athletes so our manager arranged for us to stay there. Saves some money."

"Right, right. Keez talked about owing a little money still. That sucks, having that life and coming out of it in debt."

"So what's this about Frio?" I asked.

"Oh. Right. Yeah. So, uh. It relates to money, you know, I guess. Like, he was being all secret about a couple phone calls, and I don't care, he can call whoever he wants, but it was the way he was acting, y'know, like he was doing something wrong. So I asked him about it and he said it was about money, that's all, and he was taking care of it, so I thought it was his manager. But he, uh, he left his phone out after and I happened to see the name he'd called, and it was 'Frio,' so I was curious."

I was curious too now, not only about why Mar had been on the phone with Frio, but about who Craig was that he was looking at Mar's phone and calling his ex (did he know I was his ex?) to ask questions about who he was calling. The answer, of course, was obvious, but almost-nineteen-year old me avoided it, because I didn't want Marquize to have found someone else so quickly when I was having more or less anonymous sex in bars.

Of the two things, I was really more curious about Marquize's call, and though I hadn't really thought about it then, I realized later that one of the things I was likely worried about was whether he was still doing stuff with Frio. And if he was, then he was fucking over Craig the same as he'd done to me, and I didn't want him to get away with that. Right at that moment, though, I was just puzzled. Mar hadn't ever said anything about talking to Frio; in fact, he'd insisted that he was done with that asshole pedophile. So I told Craig that Frio was our old coach, and I didn't know any reason that Mar would still be talking to him.

"Okay," Craig said. "Hey, don't tell him I called you, but I really appreciate you talking to me and not just telling me to fuck off. It's real mature."

"Sure," I said. "Hey, be a good friend to him, okay? He's a good guy."

"Uh…yeah, I will, thanks."

We hung up and I stood there for a moment thinking about the things that I'd learned in that ten-minute conversation. Then I went around to rejoin Danver.

But it ate at me the next couple days. As I realized that Craig was Mar's new boyfriend—sorry, Keez's new boyfriend—I became more and more sure that if something was going on with Frio, I'd want to head it off before Craig had to learn about it on his own.

I wished I had someone like Ma to give me advice on how to handle the situation. I couldn't really ask any of the guys because then I'd have to make up a story about my ex that made him a girl, and I'd have to figure out how to talk about Frio and all the rest of it. I sent Braden another message, not because I thought he could give me advice but because the situation reminded me that I hadn't heard from him in a while.

That wasn't going to be the answer. But should I just call Marquize? What would I say? Craig had asked me to keep our talk secret. I couldn't bring myself to call Frio, and what would I say to him anyway? Where would I start?

Two days after the call with Craig, Aliq got a call from his mother as we were getting ready to practice, and I said, "Hey, can I talk to her when you're done?"

It was impulsive, but I didn't want to take it back. Mrs. Loize had always been nice and understanding, and she only knew about Ma, nothing else about my life really. I thought she'd be perfect to ask advice from.

(I didn't take into account then that of course Aliq would have told her everything he knew about me.)

Aliq flicked his ears back but brought them up again quickly. "Sure," he said. "Hang on, Mom, Rocky wants to say hi to you."

He gave me the phone, hanging around in earshot, which annoyed me but was totally understandable. If Ma had been alive and Aliq had wanted to talk to her, I would've wanted to know what he had to say too. So I worked at how I would word my question while we exchanged greetings and I made small talk about how the tournaments were going.

Finally she asked, "Did you just want to say hi, dear?"

"No," I said. "I—can I ask you some advice? It's a little personal."

Aliq, perhaps reassured, said, "I'll see you on the court," and left the changing room.

"Of course," his mother said.

"Okay. Um." I took a breath. "So I had a really big fight with a friend of mine last year. About—about some stuff he was doing that I didn't think was right. And we're still kind of talking to each other, but—one of his new friends called me and it sounds like he's talking to the guy, uh, the guy with the stuff, you know?" Ugh, I was starting to channel Craig with his stammering conversation. "So I know it's none of my business, but if he's doing stuff again then do I have a responsibility to tell the new friend about it? Or should I confront him directly? I don't know what to do here."

"Oh, honey." She breathed slowly over the mic. "Is this—stuff he's doing, is it illegal?"

"No." Well...it had been the first time he'd done it. It wasn't anymore. "It's just...not the right thing."

"All right. Well, if it was illegal, or if anyone you know is doing something illegal, you have to report it to the authorities, you know. Otherwise it can get you in trouble too, if people know that you knew about it."

"No, I'm pretty sure it's not illegal."

"Then…it depends on your relationship with this friend. If you think it would be better coming from you, then call him directly. If you're not really good friends with him anymore, then—no, you know, you should try talking to him first. If he doesn't listen to you then you should call his friends. But if you think something not right is going on, then you should do something about it."

I didn't say anything, digesting that, and she said, "Wait. Will it hurt your career? That's important too. But no, you should always do the right thing, Rocky."

"Thanks, Mrs. Loize," I said. "I think I'll call him."

So the day after the next, when I had a little time to myself again, I called up Marquize. Asked him how the country club life was going, and he told me he had his first tennis student. "She's terrible, Rocky, really bad. Like I didn't know where to start. I kept asking her to do things she couldn't figure out, and she was getting frustrated with it and she quit last week. I felt really bad. But today she came back and said her wife told her she should give it another chance, and I told her I was going to try to tailor my lessons to her better."

"Uh huh," I said. "That's great. Hey, have you talked to Frio lately?"

I counted five breaths before he replied. "No. Why, have you?"

One lie to expose another? Or should I give away Craig's secret? I didn't owe him anything, but Marquize was the one behaving badly. I opted to keep Craig's secret for a little longer, at least. "He called me last week and mentioned he'd talked to you."

Three breaths this time. "Oh yeah. I guess I talked to him last week."

"Did you mention me?"

"No! You don't think I'd—"

"I don't know what to think, Mar. You said you were done with Frio. So…what?"

It might be hard to remember the early days of our friendship, but this tension, the secrets and problems between us, that I remembered well. "What did he call you about?" he parried.

"Don't change the subject."

"Oh," he said, "it's okay for you to have secrets from me but not the other way around?"

I almost admitted then that I'd been lying, but then I imagined him saying, "So how did you know I'd called him?" I'd have to make up something or else give up Craig's secret, and I'd already lied to protect Craig. So I made up something plausible. "It was about you quitting," I said.

I didn't expect his response. "Fucking hell," he snapped. "I told him not to bother you."

"He wasn't ever much good at listening," I said.

"I guess not." He was quiet. "Wait, so...so you know?"

"I wouldn't be asking you if I did."

He talked slowly, working it out in his head. "He called you about me quitting, but you don't know what it's about? What, did he just offer you the money and not tell you how to make it?"

"Money?" I asked, startled, and then said, "Yeah, that's right. He said I could make money, and I told him I didn't need any and didn't want to talk to him."

Marquize's voice took on a warning tone. "Rocky. Don't bullshit me, not about this."

Oops. I sighed. "All right, look. Craig called me. He heard you talking to Frio or something, he didn't want me to tell you. But he's worried about you, and I am too."

"That fucking...that's none of his business. It's over now anyway." He paused. "And you lied to me."

"Just about Frio calling. Craig didn't want—"

"So what do you owe him? You'd lie to me to protect him?"

"Hey," I said. "Calm down. I came clean. You want to join me?"

Eight breaths this time, hard ones. "No."

"Mar, come on. It's something about money, right? What's going on? You want me to call and ask Frio?"

"No!"

"All right, then."

The click of his claws came faintly through the speaker. He was pacing. "Craig doesn't have anything to worry about," he said.

"Do I?"

"No. How many times do I have to tell you?"

"A couple more, probably. But I promise you I'm going to call Frio if you don't tell me." A thought occurred to me. "Or his friend Gen who hired me back in school. I probably still have the number of the warehouse in my phone somewhere."

"Dammit, Rocky." I waited. "All right, but look, I was just doing it to help you out. To try to help you out. But then you didn't need my help, so…I mean, I didn't do it a lot. And technically—I don't think there's anything illegal about it technically. Like card counting."

"What? What's 'card counting'?"

"It's—you know what, Google it." He drew in another breath and let it out. "Frio bets on tennis matches. Any level. All I was doing was telling him a bit of inside information about, like, player health, where their heads were at, how well they knew each other. I mean, it's stuff you could look up. Mostly."

"Betting on who would win?"

"Yeah. And look, I never threw a match."

I knew what that meant; we'd bandied around the term back in Lochen's group. "Why would you throw a match?"

"Because he'd bet on the other person when I was favored."

"Oh."

"But I wasn't ever favored enough. I mean, he said that's when I could make real money, but he paid me for tips if his bets came out."

I thought I'd been prepared for anything; when I'd envisioned this conversation, it had been around sex, with an outside chance of drugs. Betting on tennis? Yeah, we'd been warned about it in seminars, but they made it sound like it was a few individuals here and there, not a school coach—former school coach—tapping his players for information and running a betting network.

And then I guessed why Gen was fine letting me have a job where I did nothing. If he was one of the guys who bet on Frio's games, that must have been worth a lot more to him than a few hundred a week.

"Wow," I said.

"I swear, I wouldn't have done it if you didn't need the money. I thought it might make things better between us."

And that made me feel like the biggest jerk in the world. "Sorry," I said. "I mean, thank you. For trying."

"Yeah, well."

"But Mar, with Frio?"

"Hey," he said. "I didn't have a lot of options open. No parents, remember? No way to make tennis pay off for me. I still owe Lochen a few thousand dollars even with Frio's money, and Lochen said I don't need to pay it but I'm going to anyway, because I don't want to owe anyone anything." His breath came in hard pants again.

"All right, all right. But you're done with it now?"

"I'm done with it now."

"So why did you call him last week?"

He sighed. "He was calling me again. Asking for the names of other players I thought might be helpful to him, might need money."

"Who'd you tell him about?"

"Nobody! Seriously!"

"Hey, I'm sorry," I said. "I don't know, maybe—" I was going to say something about how maybe that could make up the last few thousand he owed Lochen, but he didn't deserve that. Or maybe he did, but not from me.

"Nobody." Flat voice.

"All right."

I couldn't think of anything to say after that, and neither could he. I asked him about Craig and he said he was nice. He told me to tell him when I was in Pelagia and I said I'd check the tournament schedule. And he asked about Ori, so I told her she was staying with Raji's sister, in limbo while I tried to get her paperwork done.

After we hung up, I sat there in the park across from the campus where the tournament would be held. Was there any way I could apologize to Marquize? Did I actually need to? He'd cared about me, I knew that, and he'd been willing to do a lot to get our relationship back on track. I'd known that too, at the time. It hadn't made a difference then. Was there anything I could do about it now?

He seemed happy with Craig, or at least content, and I didn't particularly want him back. His way of going about helping me didn't really jibe with what I wanted in a boyfriend anyway, admirable though his intentions might have been.

So that was that; he'd helped Frio get an edge in some bets— illegal bets for sure—and had been paid for it. It was distasteful and probably part of it was illegal, but it was over. There wasn't anything I could do about it now.

I still wasn't happy as I walked back to campus to meet Danver and the other guys for dinner. I had a nagging feeling that I was forgetting something, like in that dream where I'd go into a match against someone and realize I'd forgotten to watch any film of them. The feeling lasted throughout dinner until it faded with the need to keep up with the quick back and forth of conversation.

That night I watched film of the guys in my side of the singles bracket, studying them in preparation for my session with Coach Keely. As I watched them I thought about Marquize relaying film session information to Frio, and I felt a lot less forgiving of him, even though he'd done it for me. I'd never asked him to—well, maybe I'd asked if he knew of any way to make money. I couldn't remember. But if he'd told me what he was planning, I would've said no, I don't want Ori to come home at that price, I'll figure out another way.

Which is probably why he didn't tell me.

Chapter Three

I kept in touch with Ori, calling at least once a month and usually more. I hated calling her, because every time I called, her "Hello?" rang with hope that I'd say that she could start packing to come to the States, and every time I had to say that I didn't have any news.

Once I got past that, though, I loved talking to her. She was back to helping at the Muslim refugee center and that gave her nights purpose; during the day she did a little work cleaning up for some local businesses so that she could pay Sarya for her meals.

Sometimes she would mention a male, usually someone from the refugee center, but occasionally one from a business she worked at, and our conversation would go like this:

"Daro?" I would say. "Is he the bat-eared fox you mentioned on the last call?"

"Probably," she would reply. "We worked together two weeks ago as well."

"So are you seeing him outside of work?"

"Oh, Ro. I don't have much time outside of work."

Just about every time, the soft evasion. I let it go. After all, if she were coming to the States, she wouldn't want to form any close entanglements. And if there were another reason, that was her business.

Other times we talked about Ma. We'd gotten over the grief, mostly, by April, but we didn't want to forget her. So we passed her back and forth: when one of us had done something, the other might say, "Ma would have liked that." It was our way of keeping her alive, I suppose.

Usually I called her, because my schedule was less predictable. This time in early May, though, we were in the middle of a tournament and she called while I was at practice. When I got back to the hotel room and called, she didn't even say hello. "Ro," she said, panting as though she'd run a great distance. "I've been sitting here waiting for you to call."

"I'm sorry," I said. "I'm just done with practice. What happened?"

She sucked in a breath. "You know the jackal Ma was dealing with to get me free of the marriage?"

"Laurent?" I'd talked to him a few times, but he'd made it clear that he had no interest in helping Ori get to the States unless there was money in it for him.

"Yes." The silence stretched out.

"What about him?"

"I ran into Kamina yesterday," Ori said.

"Ori, you need to finish one story before you move on to another."

"This is all one story." She made a "tch" noise. "She wasn't very happy to see me. She said, 'I would've thought your no-account father would have gotten you out of the country already.'"

My ears, already up, stiffened. "What?"

"Laurent's our father."

I felt as though I were on one of those TV shows Paulie used to watch, where they film unsuspecting people as they tell them bizarre things. "No," I said. "Our father died in a war."

"He didn't," Ori said evenly. "That's just what Ma told us."

"Have you talked to him?"

"No, but Kamina told me. She said he ran out on us because he had another family and Ma made him choose between them and us. I don't know why he picked the other family, but Kamina said he worked in the government and he could have supported all of us, but Ma didn't want that."

Having multiple wives was less common in Lundara than in the rural areas of Lunda. I hadn't ever thought about how Ma's Christian upbringing might conflict with her culture because everyone around us was Christian. But if Laurent had been a jackal from a nearby village come to the government through a relative or friend, and he wanted to have another family elsewhere… "I'm going to call him," I said.

"Maybe you should wait."

"For what?" I paced to the window and looked out at brick buildings and a parking lot. "When will it be better to ask why he never even tried to see us? To ask why he wouldn't say he was our father when we talked to him last year? What's going to happen to make that easier?" I wanted to go back to the tennis courts and smash serves from one side to the other. "It was bad enough when we thought he'd died, but we got used to that. Now he's alive and what are we supposed to think?"

"Kamina said that since Ma's gone, there's no reason we shouldn't know."

I could see Kamina's long muzzle set in a smirk as she said that. With all her worries about money, of course she would have thought Ma an idiot for giving up a husband who could support her, even if he had to split his affections. "I hate to say it, but for once she's right. No, I'm going to call and tell him he has to help his daughter. He owes us."

"Ro."

"What?"

"Do you think he doesn't know we're his children?"

The question stopped me. "Of course he knows," I said, and then I thought about it. If he knew, then me calling him wouldn't do anything to spur him to action. "I want him to know that we know."

She made another "tch" noise, and I said, "You knew what I would do when you told me, didn't you?"

"Yes, I suppose. But I also knew you'd talk to me a little bit about what we should do."

"All right. What should we do?"

"I was hoping you'd have ideas."

I snorted. "My best idea is to call him. If he's not doing everything he can right now, then maybe knowing that we know will help. If he is, then…I don't know."

"Kamina said something else."

I stopped and listened. Ori was so quiet that I could hear Sarya's cubs in the background, off in another room. Finally she said, "She told me that he was the one who told Ma to tell us he'd died."

I sat on the phone listening to my sister breathe, thinking about a father who'd wanted to cut ties so drastically. "I guess that's one more thing I can ask him when I call," I said.

I was going to call him right away, but when I hung up I had a text from Danver telling me where to meet for dinner. My stomach growled, and I thought it'd be better to get some food in me before I confronted my delinquent father.

At dinner we talked about our upcoming matches. I stayed quiet through the whole thing, imagining what I'd say and what he might say. Heck, I was trying to wrap my head around the concept of having a father at all.

"Rocky." Danver snapped his fingers in front of my nose.

I turned to the squirrel. "What?" He, Aliq, Sean, and Caboll were all looking at me. "What?" I repeated to the group.

"Cab asked what happened last time you played LeFevre. Did you not hear? You played him back in December, didn't you, or was it November? I said you won but Cab thought he remembered you had some trouble with him. Are you feeling okay?"

"I'm fine," I said, and addressed the rabbit. "LeFevre—Gallic rabbit, right? I've played him twice. Lost in 2011, won last year. Two sets but there was a tough stretch where he broke my serve and I had to hold off a set point two games later. Won in a tiebreak."

Reciting the match stats had the effect of jarring my mind back onto the tennis track where it belonged right now. Caboll nodded at me. "What's he improved since then?"

I'd watched the video of his matches from a couple tournaments ago. "His serve's the same. Backhand's the same. He's better with his crosscourt forehand than he used to be and he goes for it more often now. Still comes to the net a lot but protects it better. Still vulnerable to a good passing shot."

As I recited, I relaxed. Caboll turned a buck toothed grin on the others. "See, I told you Rocky was just planning his match."

"Yeah," I said. "Sorry."

"That's why he's highest ranked." Aliq punched me in the shoulder. "Can't relax even at dinner. What about Polli and Lavin?"

I didn't know our upcoming doubles opponents as well, but I knew enough for Aliq and I to review what we'd worked on in practice that day and what we needed to remember on the court the next day. Danver grumbled something about all work and no play, but we ignored him.

I knew that I'd have to confront my father, but I'd forgotten for the moment that the path to getting Ori back was for me to win enough to become famous. Not for the last time, I was grateful to my circle of friends for setting me back on the path I needed to be on. I wouldn't call my father until after the tournament, when I could spare the energy to deal with him.

* * *

I won my singles match and the next one, then lost in the semifinals. Aliq and I made it to the finals, where we lost in a close three-setter. I was going to call my father then, but I kept rehearsing what I was going to say and being unhappy with it, so through the few days of travel and getting set at the next tournament site, I didn't call him. After a while I realized that if I waited until the tournament opened, I could put off calling him for another week or two.

But also, when I got the tournament draw, I saw something else that distracted me: the name "B. Longacre."

I wouldn't have expected him to show up at this tournament. The Gallic Open was a month from starting, and the top players were all over there getting tuned up on clay courts. But here was Braden at a States tournament, not a small one by any means but not one where you'd expect to see the winner of the Ocie Open.

I checked out the Internet and found several columns speculating on what had happened. One said he'd suffered an undisclosed injury in the process of winning the Ocie; another said it was a nervous breakdown; a third said there'd been a fight with his manager. All of them had evidence to back up their theories, but none of them had anything convincing.

If Braden was going to be at the tournament, I could go see him. We weren't in the same side of the bracket, so we wouldn't play unless we both made it to the final, but I knew where he'd be practicing.

So did everyone else. When I saw the crowd around one of the practice courts, I knew who it had to be. I didn't want to be just one of the guys in the crowd, so I left for my own practice and figured I'd catch up to him in the locker room. There, though, a big stocky wolf stood between him and the rest of the room, like a bodyguard or something. Guys tried to talk to Braden like you do in a locker room and the wolf would hold out a paw and say, "Mr. Longacre would like some privacy," like it was a mantra. My friends and I wondered how he'd swung that, because normally only players are allowed in locker rooms. I guess when you've won a major and the tournament is thrilled to have you there, they bend rules.

By the second day, everyone had figured out to leave him alone. I happened to be coming back from my practice when he was dressing for his, alone at his locker with the wolf standing beside him casting glares around the area. When I walked up, I got one full force, along with the mantra, but I'd timed it so that the cross fox was facing me, having just pulled on his shirt.

I met his eyes and waited. The wolf unfolded his arms and let them drop to his sides, where his powerful biceps were less impressive but the huge paws more than made up for it. "I said—"

Braden raised a paw. "It's okay, Jan," he said. "I know this one."

The wolf's ears flicked back when Braden spoke and then leveled a finger at me. "Keep it short. Mr. Longacre doesn't have all day."

The cross fox looked annoyed, but that was his default state. I assumed that if he didn't want to talk to me, he wouldn't have stopped the wolf from chasing me off. In the annoyance and everything else, he looked extremely normal. His fur had been recently trimmed close, and the shirt he'd put on fit closely as well. His scent was just as I remembered, no trace of bandages or anti-infection ointment or anything like that.

"I just came over to say hi," I said. "I never congratulated you on the Ocie. I watched the match, though. It was great."

"Thanks." His annoyance didn't lift much, but again, that was par for the course.

"If you want to grab a drink sometime, let me know."

He nodded. "Yeah, I will. If I want to."

That was pretty clear, so I raised a paw and went back to my locker.

I won my first match the following day and stuck around to watch Braden play his. It was while I was watching him that I remembered that day in Palm Gables when he'd played me and Marquize and thought about how much had changed since then. Some things hadn't, though. He was still better than me, and we still shared some borderline traumatic memories of school.

I sat up straight in my seat. I'd gone to Braden when I needed money, and he'd warned me vehemently to stay away from Frio. Was it possible that he knew what Frio and Marquize had been doing?

Was it possible that he'd been doing it too?

Nothing he did on the court revealed the reason for his absence from the tour. He moved so precisely that I was sure if I were watching him on TV with one of those tracking programs that shows the trajectory of each ball, it would show that he'd gotten most of his shots in a few clusters of about two feet across. Maybe just one foot across; they were that tightly bunched. His opponent couldn't do anything against him and he won 6-0, 6-2. I think he only lost those two games in the second set because he was a little bored.

I watched him with the same rigid set to my posture, but inside I kept turning the possibility over in my mind. If Braden had been helping Frio…or even if he just knew about what Frio was doing… what could I say to him? What would he say to me? Probably tell me to mind my own business.

Honestly, a big part of me told me I should leave it there. Braden was a major tournament winner and he had a lot going for him; he could for sure handle whatever was going on in his life. What's more, he wasn't exactly the kind to reach out a paw and ask for help, nor even welcome it if offered. Marquize had once said, "If he was on fire and you dumped water on him, he'd growl at you for ruining his clothes." I didn't think that was too far off.

But I kept thinking about his demeanor after the Ocie, about his flat affect in the locker room. We'd gotten close, shared a moment over a Coke in a hotel bar, and now it was as if that had never happened.

You don't have any responsibility to him, Ma would say. Fuck that guy, Marquize would say. But neither of them knew him. So really, I had to ask myself what I would say.

And that's how I ended up back in the locker room walking up to Braden. "Mr. Longacre," the wolf said, but apparently recognized me, because he left it at that.

The cross fox looked up, eyes still flat. "I said I'd let you know," he said.

"I know. I'm sorry to bother you again," I said. "Only one of my friends got into trouble with Frio, and I'd really like to talk to you about it."

I watched his ears when I said that. They flicked, and his nostrils flared. He didn't ask what kind of trouble. He didn't ask which friend. He gave a curt nod and said, "You know the Palomar Hotel?"

* * *

The bar at the Palomar was not as nice as the last bar we'd met at: it was shiny glass and chrome all over, with huge glass panels separating it from the moderately busy hotel lobby. Braden chose a booth in the back corner and sat there staring down at his glass, swirling a red straw around the brown fizzy Coke.

He didn't talk, so I told him about Marquize and the illegal betting with Frio. And then I waited. He stayed quiet for a long time, long enough that I said, "I don't know anything for sure, but I remember you told me to stay away from Frio when I needed money."

If I hadn't been watching closely, I would've missed his nod. "And I did." I tapped my claws on the table, not sure what I'd do if he didn't say something soon. "So, uh, thank you for that. I didn't know what I was avoiding then, but I do now. At least, I think I do. So I think you know too."

He gave a minute shrug of the shoulders. "Nothing either of us can do."

"Is, uh." I had to gather a fair amount of courage before I could say what I was wondering. "Is he asking you to do something like that?"

Braden looked up at me. "Appreciate the concern," he said. "But there's nothing either of us can do. I'll have to deal with this on my own."

"I don't believe that." I took a drink because my mouth was pretty dry. "There's always something. People have to help each other out."

"You think so?" He picked the red straw out of his drink and flicked it across the table. I didn't wipe the drops of Coke off my paw. "You don't know the people I know. Nobody has to help anybody. You make a mess, you clean it up. The only thing that happens when you drag more people in is that more people get messy."

"I—"

"Stay naïve," he said. "It's a lot more pleasant."

I snapped my jaw shut. Then I got up, marched over to the bar, and swiped a pen out of the little stand next to the register. Armed with that and a white cocktail napkin, I came back to the booth and scrawled my phone number on the napkin. "There." I shoved it across the table at him, sopping up some of the drops of Coke he'd spilt. "You can call me anytime if you want to talk about it, or talk about—you know, the other thing—or talk about tennis. Whatever. I don't know what else I can do to help right now. Throw it away if you want, but there it is."

I turned and left the restaurant. When I got to the lobby, I looked back through the big glass windows. I could only see Braden's dark paw, but it rested on the white napkin that remained, whole and uncrumpled, on the table.

* * *

I knew I was in the middle of a tournament, but I was angry after the meeting with Braden, and maybe a little too motivated to prove that I could help someone. So I got out of the Palomar and fumed my way up and down the sidewalk, and then I got out my phone and dialed my father's number.

Over in Lundara, the sun must have just risen. But my father kept his mobile on him at all times and picked up when I called. "Who is this?" he asked in Kikongo.

I answered in English. "This is Rocky. I was talking to you about getting my sister Ori to the States."

"Ah. Oh yes. What can I do for you?"

"You could do more to help Ori get to the States, for one," I said. "I would think you'd be more concerned about your daughter."

He coughed, perhaps to hide his emotion, because his voice when he replied remained even. "And why should that be?"

"Because—because she's your daughter!"

"Ah, and we hold to blood, is that it?"

The expression was one Ma had used occasionally. "Blood is thicker than water," I replied.

"Ah ah." He snorted. "Let me tell you, I have a family. They call me Papa, they know me, they love me. I work to put food in their mouths, clothes on their backs, knowledge in their heads. Why should I take from them to give to this girl I barely know, who shares only her fur with me?"

"Why would you not? Don't you care about us at all?"

"Honestly?" He gave a short laugh. "No."

"You helped Ma get Ori away from the village, though."

"Heh heh. She paid me good for it. And Bompaka is an idiot. He deserves to lose a wife. I was sorry to hear what happened on the way back. But it sounds like you're doing all right for yourself, hah?"

"I'm doing fine," I growled.

"So why don't you think about helping out your old father, ah? Your half-brothers and sisters, your nephew?"

"Nephew?"

"Merope has a little cub this year. I should send you pictures."

I shook my head. "It sounds like you're providing for them."

"Look, you." He matched my growl. "I helped your sister, I risked myself for her, and now you ask me to do more, do more. When she gets to the States, what then? You send money back here? I don't think so. You don't think I'm your father any more than I think you're my son."

"If you help Ori get over here," I said, "I'll send you money. I promise."

"Promises don't feed the beggar," he said. "You send me money before I send Ori over."

"How much more money do you need?" I snapped.

His tone turned slick. "Same as before," he said.

"Another five thousand dollars?"

"Should be twice that," he said. "Much harder this time. Papers to sign, more people to pay off, official documents. I risk angering people."

I paced back and forth. "I don't have five thousand dollars."

"Ah," he said. "I'll be here when you do."

I hung up, still growling. My excuse was that I hadn't known he was alive, and what was his reaction when his son called him for the first time? To shake me down for money. He didn't even care. Of course, Ma had gone to see him the year before, so he probably knew all about me. And she must have forbidden him to call me. Or had he just not wanted to?

My hotel was only a few steps away, but I didn't feel like going to the room. The spring evening had cooled with the sunset, so I walked through the streets, avoiding the families with cubs out who seemed to be everywhere. Fathers carrying cubs on their backs, pushing strollers, holding paws, or deep in conversation with their teen children.

The town had a riverbank, but this one wasn't like the river in Lundara. The banks were bounded with concrete, the river held down by bridges. You could walk alongside it without getting mud on your feet, and you could cross it just about anywhere you wanted. There were rules here, and I knew intellectually that that didn't mean fathers couldn't run out on their families in the States. A couple of the players I knew had absent fathers. But it felt like there was a structure that was lacking back in Lunda, that if we'd been born in the States I could contact authorities and people could do things on my behalf.

Thinking about authorities reminded me that Lochen was working with friends of friends on Ori's case. The following day, maybe fired up by my conversation, I won my singles match in straight sets. (Afterward, Aliq said, "bring that same fire tomorrow and I'll just stay out of the way.") Because it was a morning match, I had a chance to call Lochen and ask him how things were going.

"Well," he said, as he always did, "it's a slow process, Rocky. I wish I had better news for you."

"I talked to someone over there who seemed to think he could move things along with money."

"Huh." He scratched his muzzle. "Do you want to talk to my friend?"

"Sure," I said. "Thanks."

His friend, a lawyer in Potomac, didn't have time until that afternoon, so I postponed practice with Danver and went to practice my serve by myself, blasting balls to the corner and the line and back to the corner, channeling my emotion into repetition and learning.

When the lawyer called me back, I was panting in the sun by the side of the practice court, gulping Boltade in between answers. "Mr. N'Guwe?"

"Call me Rocky." I tried not to pant too audibly. "Thanks for calling me back."

"My pleasure. I only have about fifteen minutes, but if you need more time we can schedule it. Why don't you tell me what you're concerned about?"

So I told him about my conversation with my father. He listened quietly until I was done, and then made a thoughtful noise. "Honestly," he said, "I wouldn't completely discount the possibility that someone in Lunda might be able to expedite paperwork through unofficial channels. Certainly in third world countries that kind of thing is common. But I'd also be very concerned about someone claiming they can provide that kind of service, because it's about five times as likely that they're not actually able to."

"You mean he's lying?"

"I don't know. Sometimes people overestimate their own abilities. I just know there have been numerous cases where someone has assured a client that a sum of money will clear away all obstacles, only to find that more money is needed, and more, and more. This person…" I hadn't told him it was my father. "May indeed have a path to expediting your sister's refugee approval. But I would advise against sending any money to him unless you have some kind of concrete proof that he's able to provide the service he claims he can."

"Like what kind of proof?"

"Oh…" He sighed. "I have never recommended that a client go this route. The official government route is slow, and I completely understand the frustration with it, but once it's under way, you have the backing of the States government. Even if this jackal can move your sister along in the process, anyone can hold her up along the way, demand another bribe, or in the worst case claim that her paperwork is fraudulent and have her sent back to the beginning."

"God dammit." I closed my eyes and leaned my head back. "Sorry."

He chuckled. "That's far from the most offensive thing someone's said to me on the phone. Mr. N'Guwe—Rocky—trust me when I say that things are moving along on your sister's case. Her name is on a list for review at the next opportunity. That doesn't mean her status will change, but she's at least in the system."

"All right," I said tiredly. "Thank you."

I had to go practice with Danver after that, and if my anger that morning had focused my play, my frustration in the afternoon hampered it. I hit well enough, but mechanically, and I let so many balls go by that the squirrel asked if I'd been injured in my morning match. I told him I was fine, but we called practice early anyway.

Aliq inadvertently gave me a path to follow that evening as we were prepping for our match the next day. "I'm sure glad to have you as a partner," he said, and I wonder now if he sensed my mood and was trying to bring me up. "I mean, I played doubles with other guys and there's times you just know they're gonna miss the next shot, you know what I mean?" His ears folded down. "I hope you don't get that sense with me too much, because I almost never get it with you. Like, every time it's your ball I feel like you're going to get it."

"No, I feel the same way," I said honestly.

"That's good." His ears came back up. "It's just so fuckin' frustrating when you see the ball you know your partner can't handle.

You're sitting there and you wish you could run around him and hit it for him, but you're stuck. Can't do anything. Most frustrating feeling in the world. At least if I mess up, it's on me and I can promise to do better."

"Right," I said, and my ears perked up too. "Doing something would be better than doing nothing, right?"

"Yeah." He tilted his head. "Wait, you look funny. What's up?"

"Nothing." I pointed to the film. "Thanks. I really appreciate it. Let's keep watching."

Chapter Four

Doing something was better than doing nothing. That kept running through my mind as I turned my idea over and over, examining it. There were so many reasons this was dangerous, so many reasons it would be easier for me to keep my head down and play tennis, and yet I couldn't let go of it. What would Ma say? I thought that she would tell me to be careful of where my good intentions led me. But as I imagined her saying it, she had that sparkle in her eyes that said she was proud of me.

I couldn't do anything about my father, not from here. I couldn't fly to Lundara. But there was another bully in my life, someone else who'd abused the trust placed in him. And Frio, him I could maybe do something about. He had in part driven Marquize out of tennis, he'd clung to Braden, who had won a major and then had disappeared. I didn't know whether that was linked to Frio, though he'd come close to admitting it was. If it wasn't, then Braden had two nasty secrets in his life and I didn't want to pity him that much.

And we'd all sat through that seminar when we'd come onto the circuit, about the criminals who bet on tennis, who sometimes tried to fix matches. If any of them approached us, we had to let the authorities know. I couldn't remember who the authorities were; I only knew that it wasn't the police or the FBI. I couldn't even remember the name of the person who'd given the seminar. At the time, Marquize and I had laughed about the criminals who'd bet on insignificant Futures matches.

I searched my email history and the web that night and found the name of the person who'd given the seminar. Reaching him was another matter. I didn't want to call Lochen, so I ended up sending an email to one of the people at the ATP and asking for the contact information.

Going to bed that night, I felt better. I was on the path to doing something. But with the lights out, satisfaction turned to worry. What if I was arrested? What if I got Braden and Marquize into trouble as well? What if I disqualified myself from tennis? I'd never get to a major, Ori would remain in Lunda. I'd have to go back to Lunda. Twice I almost got up to send a follow-up email telling them to never mind, forget about it, I figured things out on my own. But each time, I felt Ma warm at my side telling me to believe in myself, that she hadn't raised me to do the wrong thing. And after a little while, I finally got some sleep.

The morning brought a new match to prepare for. I had a couple bad lapses in my singles match, but my opponent wasn't sharp either, so I won in straight sets. In the afternoon, my fatigue got worse. After Aliq's talk the night before, I felt terrible whenever I missed a shot, and even worse when we lost the match.

"They're really good," Aliq said afterwards, and it was true that we were playing a team ranked #53 at the time.

"Sorry," I said. "I'm having an off day. I think we could've beaten them."

"You're still alive in singles," he said, and then I felt worse because he'd lost his singles match two days before.

"We'll do better next tournament," I promised him. "I didn't sleep well last night and it just caught up with me."

"Melatonin," he said. "Seriously. Let me know if you need it. When you're struggling to sleep, it works wonders. I have the canid formula so grab some anytime."

"Sure, thanks." I didn't want pills; I wanted a response to my email.

It was waiting when I checked next. The person who'd answered was very professional and didn't ask why I needed the info, but she'd replied and copied the seminar leader. Following that was an email just from him providing his cell phone number and asking me to call with whatever I wanted to talk about, promising confidentiality.

My nightmares of being banished to Lunda receded in the face of this reassurance. It was another hour before I found the time to call from my hotel room. I'd told Danver I needed privacy and let him assume he knew the reason.

The guy answered with a high-pitched "Hello" that jarred loose more memories of the pudgy raccoon at the seminar, of Marquize and I making fun of his voice. My ears flattened at the memory, but I tried to stay professional.

I told him that I'd attended his seminar and that a friend of mine had been asked to help someone betting on tennis matches. "He doesn't know I'm calling," I said, "but I know the guy who's asking him and I want to make him stop."

His voice got sharper and louder, as though he'd answered with his phone to his shoulder and was now holding it to the front of his muzzle. "What did you say your name was again?"

"Rocky N'Guwe. I'm number 184 in the world."

The click of keys. "Thanks, Rocky. I'm going to refer you to someone at the Tennis Integrity Unit whose job is investigating these kinds of things. Before I do, though, this is all off the record, okay?"

"Sure."

"He's going to press you to be involved. And involvement will disrupt your tennis career. I definitely want you to do what you can to help with this case, but I also want you to be aware that as far as the ATP is concerned, your obligation ends with you reporting the names you've heard and everything involved. As long as you're truthful about everything, and you didn't do anything wrong, we won't fine you or punish you in any way. You got that?"

"I got it."

"Okay. This number you're calling from, is this the best one to reach you?"

"It is."

"All right. He'll be in touch."

And that was the end of our conversation. That was how I took a step outside the court to do something.

It felt curiously anticlimactic. I'd imagined myself in a movie, with a gruff police lieutenant (probably a wolf; they were almost always wolves) on the other end of the line barking out, "This is just the lead we need to crack the case. You'll be a hero." Instead I got a middle-aged administrator, a referral, and a caution.

It didn't help me sleep that night, either. After dinner alone and an interrogation from Danver about my phone call (with a lot of suggestive winking), I lay back in my bed playing out how the movie of the next day would go. Would I get the gruff wolf this time? Or another administrator? Would they try to get me to be part of a sting operation (I remembered that phrase from a movie but had only a vague idea that it involved being undercover and catching criminals)? Or would he just take my statement, say "thank you," and I would never know how the investigation had turned out?

I barely even thought about my singles match, which as it turned out might have been a mistake. I was playing Alden Maric, #110, and despite the disparity in our rankings, I should've had a chance to beat him. Whether it was another night of disturbed sleep or my lack of focus, I dropped my first service game and that killed my confidence. I lost in straight sets.

That was the first tournament in 2013 where I finished worse than I had the year before. When I didn't get a phone call that day or the next, I started to wonder if I'd lost those ranking points for no reason at all. Maybe someone else had already turned in Frio and they had cross-checked my name against his. Or maybe they were investigating me and had found some reason in my past not to trust me. Did the Tennis Integrity Unit follow players around? Did they know about my hookups in gay bars?

That was when I stopped myself. Of course they didn't; a gay tennis player had won the Ocie Open this year. Nobody knew that publicly, but if they knew that about me then they knew it about Braden, too.

So I closed my eyes. Aliq's offer of melatonin hovered in my consciousness, but I was determined to get to sleep by myself.

The tournament ended and still I got no phone call. At least, I thought as Danver, Aliq, Sean and I boarded a plane to our next tournament, if nothing was going to come from this then I'd only messed up at one tournament.

And it was literally as I thought those words that my phone rang.

* * *

Avery Altamont of the Tennis Integrity Unit introduced himself with a soft voice that made me put a finger in my other ear to drown out the sounds of the people around me who were boarding the plane. "Is this a good time?" he asked.

"I'm getting on a plane," I said. "Can I call you back when I land?"

"Of course," he said. "My apologies for the poor timing."

"It's okay! What number should I use? The one on the cell?"

"No, that's a switchboard. Tell you what. How long is your flight?"

"Two and a half hours, I think." I put a paw over the mic and nudged Aliq. "How long is this flight?"

"I dunno," he said. "We get there when we get there."

"Two and a half hours," I said again to Mr. Altamont.

"I'll call you in four."

All through that flight I played out conversations with Mr. Altamont in my mind, so distracted that I couldn't even focus on the film Aliq was trying to review with me. "Who was that on the phone?" he asked finally.

"Just, you know, something with my sister," I said.

"Oh, cool." He folded the laptop's screen down. "What's happening?"

So then I had to invent some kind of story that sounded impressive without actually resulting in any movement on her case. I told him that the jackal helping us had started talking to the State Department and they were calling me to make sure he'd gotten her facts right. I felt bad at how excited he got and kept telling him that it didn't mean anything, that we were still far from getting her home, but his tail wagged. "It's gonna happen," he said. "I can feel it!"

The flight didn't even last two hours, leaving me an hour after we got to our motel to pace back and forth and wait for Mr. Altamont's call. Everyone else went out for dinner, and I was hungry but I didn't want to take his call in the middle of a restaurant. Aliq offered to wait with me and I snapped that I was fine, then felt bad and had to apologize.

After an hour of pacing, of sitting on my bed with my paws clasped between my knees and my tail flicking agitatedly, during which time I could easily have gone out and gotten dinner (I belatedly realized), my cell phone rang.

"Is this a better time?" Mr. Altamont asked.

"Yes, yes," I said.

"Good," he said. "Why don't you tell me exactly what's going on."

So I laid out the story as best I could without naming Marquize or Braden. When he asked, I said I preferred to keep them out of it.

"Ehm," he said. "That may prove difficult."

"It's a condition of me helping you." I was drawing a lot on movies for figuring out what to say in this matter. That wasn't really the best source—I knew that even then—but it was better than nothing.

"I see. The problem is, Rocky, that you can't lay out the conditions of helping us. You've alerted us to a problem, which puts you under a bit of suspicion, I'm afraid. If you won't give us more details, that leaves us with only one person to interrogate about the matter."

I thought about that. "If I give you the name of someone who's already quit tennis, will you promise not to go after anyone else? Especially if I can't prove they did anything wrong?"

"I can't make that promise," he said. "But if you can't prove they did anything wrong, they won't be in any danger."

"What if—what if the guy, Frio." I'd already named him. "What if he says something about either of them?"

"I'll be honest with you." Mr. Altamont's cotton-soft voice stiffened. "If we discern a pattern of wrongdoing on the part of a player, we're going to have to take action. But our investigation will also go farther up the chain, and that's where we're potentially more interested. It may be that players who were involved simply get watched more closely in the future. It's very hard to prove wrongdoing if it wasn't terribly obvious to us, and I haven't seen anything over the last few years that would fit the pattern you describe. So I'm inclined to say that your friends—I assume they are your friends—will very likely come out of this with no more than a stern warning."

"If it's hard to prove wrongdoing," I said, "how are you going to arrest Frio?"

"Ah, yes. Well, that's where you come in. Assuming you really do want to shield your friends and keep them out of the investigation as much as possible."

I perked my ears. "I do."

"Are you willing to approach Frio and act as someone who needs money to get him to bring you into his scheme?"

"I…think so. How will that affect my career?"

"Hopefully very little. But know that we'll be in touch with the ATP in case there's any irregularity we need to account for. We want to avoid that as much or more than you do."

I swallowed. "All right. What do I do?"

"Usually," he said, "these deals are done by text message using a particular service that destroys the messages a short time after they're sent. I'm going to send you an app you will always have running on your phone that will capture those messages along with time stamps, location data, and other things that will help us match the messages to the other person's phone. If you can establish his identity in your conversations, that will also be very helpful."

"But what am I going to say to him?"

"You're going to ask him how to make money. You're going to pass him information he asks for and you'll accept money from him."

"Will I have to throw matches?" If I had to, if there was no other way to arrest Frio, then I would, but I wanted to know for sure that there was no other way.

He paused. "As I said, we're going to try to avoid that," he said finally. "It's a big hassle because we have to nullify the match after the fact and nobody likes doing that. It's unfair to the other player, who was playing his best and got a victory he perhaps didn't deserve."

"That would suck," I said.

"Exactly. So we will avoid that if at all possible."

"All right. When do I start?"

"Ehm," he said. "I would like to meet with you in person first. You would be in Callowwood, is that right?"

"Yes." I thought at first that he had been spying on me already, and then remembered that he worked with the ATP and of course he would know what tournaments were happening this weekend. He probably even had access to registration databases and could look me up.

"How about if I fly out before the end of the tournament to meet up with you, and then we can see how things look. Sound okay?"

"Sounds fine," I said.

"Think about this. It will be a lot of work and a lot of commitment. It won't be something you can talk to any of your friends about."

"I know."

"This may drag on for months. Just because you get a couple conversations doesn't mean we have enough to go on. We might need you to keep going for a while."

"All right."

"I know this sounds like a movie. It's not. It's very real."

"All *right*."

"I'm going to give you this same talk in person."

"I'll be ready for it," I said. "And I'll tell you in person, I'm committed to this. This guy messed up my life and some of my friends' lives and I want to see him go down."

"We'll do what we can," Mr. Altamont replied. "I'll call you when I've booked a flight. And Rocky? Thank you for getting in touch with us. I know how hard players at your level work on their career and for you to be willing to sacrifice to make this happen says a lot."

Those words stuck with me after he hung up, while I was out eating dinner by myself (I resisted the temptation to make it a fast food dinner, though I had to walk by two places that smelled amazing before getting to the casual dining restaurant that actually served salads). I'd already told Mr. Altamont why I was committed to doing this, and he still acted as though it was some high-minded ideal of justice that was driving me rather than the much pettier revenge.

And here I think he and Ma would have differed. Ma would have wholeheartedly approved of revenge.

Ma would not maybe have approved so much of taking on such a big distraction from my career. Mr. Altamont made me wonder whether I would completely sacrifice tennis to see Frio come to justice. I didn't think it would come to that—even if it took months and I dropped back into the 200s, I could build myself back up again.

But what would Coach Keely say if I fell off? Would he drop me? Would Lochen drop me? I hadn't thought until that moment that the damage to my career might be permanent, and that persistent thought made that dinner a very long and lonely one.

Chapter Five

Those thoughts about what I might be doing to my career kept buzzing about my head as I composed the email to Frio. I didn't have his number anymore but I was pretty sure I remembered the email address he'd sent me messages from. I hoped it was still active.

Altamont came out in person before we left Callowwood and we had the same discussion we'd had on the phone, the neatly-dressed cougar in polo shirt and blazer leaning earnestly across the table at the restaurant to make sure I understood both the possible implications for me and the need to keep this secret from everyone. "You never know who else might be in touch not with Coach Young but maybe with the other people he's working with," he said, and I nodded, again considering that Frio might not be the guy at the top. I wanted him to be the great villain, but the way Altamont was talking, he might just be a third or fourth-level part of a bigger organization. I assured the cougar that I understood what I was doing and was prepared to go ahead with it. We talked about how to frame the email, but in the end he left it mostly to me because he said, "You know your relationship best." He listened to my idea of how to approach Frio and only contributed some guidelines for specific phrases to avoid.

I wrote the email a bunch of times and kept putting off sending it. The resolve I'd felt while talking to Altamont was harder to summon in the moment. But there was a point where I realized I wasn't going to change the email anymore, and I sat staring at the "Send" command. If you're going to do it, do it, I told myself, and so I did.

We had just arrived at another tournament. They blend together in my mind but I remember going out to a specific restaurant chain after I sent the email, so it must have been out west. I can remember the matches clearly, but not so much the places where they happened. Or rather, I remember each place, but linking it to a specific match is harder. I do know that Aliq and I won that tournament and that not long after, our doubles ranking climbed into the top 100. My singles ranking lagged a little behind; I didn't make the quarterfinals but I hadn't last year either, so I didn't lose any points. For all of 2013, in fact, I hovered in the mid-hundreds, good enough to get to the final eight of some tournaments but no farther.

Good enough, I hoped, to catch Frio's attention. It was only two days into the tournament that I got a reply from him. He was glad to hear from me, sorry to hear my money situation wasn't going well, thought I should talk to my manager. I had some good endorsement deals and could get more.

I replied that my manager had already done all he could and added a few lines that made me seem frustrated with him. Altamont had advised me not to say outright that nobody else could help me, but to make it sound like I'd tried many other avenues and come up short.

What I told him was that my sister needed thirty thousand dollars to get into the Union. Altamont had advised me that that was a good amount to ask for: beyond my current means but not unattainable. He was worried that it was too specifically perfect, but if I told Frio I needed a hundred thousand, that wouldn't work, and if it was only five thousand, there wasn't any reason I wouldn't be able to swing that, and ten or twenty thousand, while believable, might not be enough to get the kind of requests Altamont was looking for. And he knew I had to be desperate to contact him; I'd put that in the email too.

The more I wrote of the story, the more of myself I put into it. At times I had difficulty remembering that Ori's fate was in the paws of our State Department, not some shadowy figure (in my head it was my father) who wanted thirty thousand dollars. The fact that I couldn't tell anyone about it made it weirdly more real. Sometimes I caught myself thinking that telling Aliq and Danver about the State Department was the real lie (and it didn't help that I'd already lied to

Aliq about some other operation involved, even though I'd quickly gone back to him and said that that had fallen through).

Maybe it was that secret belief that convinced Frio. He sent me a message a little while later telling me that I should download an app named Clene from a website he'd point me to, sign up as a username that looked like a random combination of letters and numbers, and he'd get in touch with me through that.

Heart racing, I downloaded the app, registered the name, and called Altamont.

He directed me to a website with an app called TMC9. "Register it with the email address I'll give you, set it up to scan Clene, and it'll send the logs right to me through a secure VPN."

I didn't know what that was but he told me it didn't matter. Then he said not to call him anymore to be safe; he didn't think Frio would be watching me or tapping my phone, but anything was possible. So I sent him a screenshot of Frio giving me my username and then all I had to do was wait.

At our next tournament, Aliq and I made the quarters in doubles and I made the quarters in singles. See, I thought, my career's going to be fine.

But in my practices with Danver, even though I thought I was fine, the squirrel said I was off. I had been thinking about Frio, I guess, planning out what I'd say next and worrying that he wouldn't ever get back to me. And partly I was hoping he wouldn't get back to me and I wouldn't have to go through with any of this, but when I had those thoughts, I got mad at myself. I was doing a good thing here, and what's more, I was doing a necessary thing. It was not only the right thing to do, it was what I wanted to do, and nothing that was happening now was anything I hadn't known about when I agreed to it.

There were two things I hadn't counted on. One was that it was easy for me to say that I'd just play tennis and I'd worry about the Frio business when it came up. I had times of the day when I wasn't thinking about tennis—rare, but they were there. I figured I'd slot my Frio time into those spaces. But my mind didn't follow its own plan. I found myself not only thinking about the whole enterprise, but wondering how I would intentionally lose a match if it came down to it. Would I be able to?

Perversely, I decided that if I were going to do it, I'd want to be good at it. Altamont had been talking about players losing suspiciously. I didn't want that to happen to me even if the ATP knew why I was losing. People outside might notice, especially now that I was starting to be mentioned on tennis news and blogs. I didn't want some reporter posting questions about my integrity.

So after that tournament, while waiting for Frio's call, I used my practices to miss the baseline, to miss the center line on serves. I practiced shaking my head in anger. I didn't want to dump the ball into the net, because that was too obvious. There were a dozen other ways to lose a point. I had to be not too tricky with my shots, because if I let a point go on too long, my opponent might lose the point before I had a chance to. I didn't want to hit any obvious winners, but I also couldn't pass up any obvious winners.

I really hoped I wasn't going to have to throw any matches, because I wasn't any good at it yet. I only did it when practicing with Danver, because I'd also made a rule for myself that I wouldn't throw any game with Aliq involved. I didn't want to drag him into this after he and his family had been so nice to me. And Danver was sharp; he noticed when I was distracted and when I was trying to lose on purpose. "Practicing fancy shots?" he asked when I had missed the baseline by a good foot. "Your groundstrokes are off."

"It's sailing on me," I said shortly. After that I only worked on my intentional misses a little bit in each practice. I wanted to get so good that even Danver wouldn't notice, but I wasn't there yet.

* * *

Frio still didn't contact me that week, but I got a phone call from Ori. "I'm sorry I haven't called," I said. "Tennis has just been really busy."

"It's alright." She sounded sober. "I was supposed to have an appointment with the refugee official, but when I went to the office today there was no record of it."

"What? I'll call the guy we're working with—"

"No, I found out what happened." She sighed. "I asked, because I thought that I had mistaken the day. But the secretary said that someone called to cancel the appointment."

"Someone." My ears flattened. "Did she say who?"

"He."

"He who?"

"The secretary is a he. Yes, he said it was our father. Don't growl, Ro."

I hadn't realized I was doing it until she said that, and then I felt the vibrations in my throat. I stopped them. "How can he do that? He says he doesn't consider himself our father."

"I suppose the government admits he is our father. I don't know how they know. Or maybe they don't care."

"I'll call and tell them he's not, that he shouldn't have any authority to do that."

Ori sighed. "This is his country, Ro, not yours."

"The refugee program isn't Lundan. It's the United Nations, the Union of States. I can tell people to ignore him."

"You can try."

We talked a little longer, but not much, because I was itching to call Lochen's friend in the State Department. I thought that I could resolve the problem with that call, but to my surprise, he was not so sure. He agreed that our biological father who'd abandoned us and played no more role in our lives shouldn't be affecting Ori's status, but the problem was that the appointments weren't easy to come by, and his interference had delayed Ori's next one by another three months. Next time, he told me, who knew what our father might do? All he had to do was cancel that appointment too, and even with the pressure from the Union side, Ori might not get another appointment for a year. Apparently the U.N. didn't appreciate people wasting their time when there were so many in true need.

My sister is one of those in true need, I wanted to yell at him, but I knew it wouldn't do any good. So I thanked him for his time and called the only other person I could think to call.

"It's your son," I said tightly when he picked up.

"Ah ah," he chuckled. "My 'son,' now, is it?"

"Why are you interfering in Ori's life? You don't want to help her, don't help her, but stay out of it then."

"And where's the money in staying out of it?"

I tried to process that statement. "You want money to do nothing?"

"You won't give me money to do something, so what's a poor civil servant to do?"

"I don't think either of those words is right," I growled, the vibration back in my throat.

"Eh?"

"Never mind." I breathed. "So how much?"

"What did we say? Five thousand?"

"Yes." That was—not easy, but fine. I could get five thousand. Lochen's friend's friend wouldn't like it, but he didn't have to know.

"So now it's ten."

"What?"

"Cassava is cheaper at the beginning of the harvest than the beginning of winter."

That was a new one on me. I got the meaning quick enough anyway. "Where am I supposed to get ten thousand dollars?"

"Hey," he said. "Big tennis star. I see those dollars at the States Open, at Wimbledon. Get some of those dollars."

"I can't—" I took a breath. "You have to be invited to those things or be good enough to have a chance in the qualifiers. Like top 150. I might get invited this year but I'm two years away from having any sort of shot at it."

"Eh well," he said. "Ori is young."

"Just be a decent father for once in your life!" I yelled.

His voice turned cold. "I am being a decent father," he said. "I have cubs, I see an opportunity to provide for them. This may not happen again in my lifetime. Your half-brothers, half-sisters—"

"I know," I growled, and hung up the phone. I didn't want to admit how angry it made me that he was being a good father to his other family but not to us.

I didn't have a practice scheduled, but I had to burn off some anger, so I went to the gym and put myself through one of Aliq's harder workouts. At the end of it I was panting and still as angry as before, and the anger persisted into the next day, still boiling inside me when my phone buzzed.

I looked down at it and saw an unfamiliar notification and the message, *OK lets talk.*

For an instant I thought it was my father willing to negotiate. I brought up the program and saw the splash screen: "CLENE: Guard Your Privacy." That's when I realized what was happening. The window I opened had Frio's username on it and his message with a little timer counting down from fifteen. When it reached zero, the message vanished.

I took a breath to steady my fingers. Then I typed, *What's up?*

My words stayed on the screen for fifteen seconds, then flickered and disappeared. A moment later, another sentence appeared with another fifteen-second timer next to it. *I can help you with your money problem.*

I hoped Altamont's program was logging the messages like it was supposed to.

> *How? I don't want to do
> anything illegal.*

> > *Not illegal just answer a
> > few questions for me*

> *Is that what Marquize
> did?*

> > *At first ;)*

At first?
> *What about later?*

> > *Lets worry about later
> > later*

> *Let's worry about it now.*

I hesitated, but Altamont had told me to make it authentic.
> *I still don't trust you.*

> > *Smart ;)*

> *So what else did Marquize
> do?*

When he didn't answer, I went on.

*I want to know what's
down the road before I
start on it.*

> *Lets just say that a double-
> fault at the right time or
> a service break in the first
> or last four games of a set,
> stuff like that could be
> worth a couple hundred
> dollars to him*

Couple hundred?

> *At your level maybe a
> couple thousand*

*What's the questions
worth?*

> *Five hundred or so*
>
> *Depends on how the
> information pans out*
>
> *sometimes nothing.*

Nothing??

> *Come back with answers
> you'll make your money*
>
> *Your at a higher level than
> Marquize was*
>
> *Info worth more*

So where do I start?

> *Match between kirol and
> pak coming up tomorrow*
>
> *kirol looked injured last
> match, but nothing official*
>
> *Tell me whether he's
> actually injured and how
> bad it is*

That's all?

> *Thats all.*

It didn't actually seem that bad. I could do that. I didn't know Kirol well, but people talked all over the locker room and it'd be easy enough to go to one of the trainers for a massage and say something about Kirol to see if they had heard anything. Kirol was ranked #28, one of the highest ranked players in this tournament, and plus he was a brash, talkative coyote, so naturally everyone knew where he'd been.

And, Frio added, *I need it by tonight*

That was harder. I'd just finished our 2 pm practice, so I'd have to go around and ask people in the next few hours. But I wanted to prove I could do it. *Okay.*

Players like Kirol had their own trainers, of course. But they talked to the other trainers onsite, and so even the on-staff trainer, whom I had to wait forty-five minutes to see, knew something about what was going on with lots of players, even ones he hadn't treated. Luckily, it turned out he had treated Kirol, because the coyote had been injured during a match. The trainer wasn't going to tell me exactly what the injury was, but he described Kirol's grimaces and growls, even mimicking them, and I had a pretty good idea that the coyote'd pulled something in his leg, maybe a hamstring, and that it was pretty painful.

I felt quite proud of how I'd gotten the information so quickly. Then I thought about it more and my tail flagged. I was going to give someone information that would allow them to bet on Kirol's loss. It wouldn't really affect the game, that was true, but there was something distinctly unsavory about it. I wanted to talk to Altamont to remind me that what I was doing was for a good cause, but he'd told me not to call him, so I was stuck pacing back and forth. If Altamont didn't call to give me guidance before Frio's deadline (a nebulous "tonight"), I was going to have to go on his last instructions and pass the information on to Frio.

When seven p.m. came with no word from Altamont, that's just what I did. I opened the app on my own, and Frio was the only contact in it, so that was easy. I typed out what I'd learned.

A few moments later, the words, *Good boy :)* came across the screen. They flickered and then disappeared.

* * *

Kirol lost his match. I felt bad about it, as though I'd participated in some way. I had to remind myself that I hadn't done anything to affect the match; I'd only allowed someone to make money betting on it. Maybe. Somehow that didn't make me feel a whole lot better.

It would've been easier if Altamont had called to tell me I was doing the right thing. But he was staying away like he'd said he would, and I had to guess that I was doing okay. The uncertainty boiled over into other aspects of my life, though. Like one day at practice when Danver brought a case of Forge from his sponsorship (one that Lochen had been looking into for me but they thought the hyperactive squirrel was a better fit). This time he happened to have brought my least favorite flavor, the weird lime-kiwi blend that didn't go together and stung the back of my throat. Ordinarily I would've just drunk it anyway, or would've taken a water or a Bolt without commenting, but this time I stared down at the case and said, "Free is too expensive for this shitty flavor."

Danver looked taken aback and said, "You don't have to—" and then Aliq muttered something about my sister to him, and they left me alone. Which was the right thing to do but was also frustrating because I wanted someone to yell at me.

The next day I got a message from Frio wanting to arrange payment. Altamont had helped me set up an ePay account that he also had access to (and had warned me not to extract any money from), so I gave that info to Frio and he said the transfer would happen in a couple days. In the meantime, he asked me to keep an eye on a couple players at the next tournament, none of which I knew. I could do that, sure, and I tried to recapture the pride I'd found in getting information about Kirol, but the whole process felt even dirtier this time. I knew I was doing it to trap Frio, I knew that this wasn't really me, but I still had to ask the questions and type out the information. You're doing this to help Ori, I told myself, and then remembered that that was a lie I'd told Frio. Except it was a lie that had gained more truth since I'd made it up, and that was even more confusing. The reality of Ori's predicament shaded everything I was doing, and it was all confusing.

I stayed in a funk all the way to the next tournament, but an unexpected bit of news jolted me out of it. Lochen called me at seven-thirty in the morning, while I was dressing to work out on my own. Danver wasn't a fan of early morning workouts, so I grabbed my shirt and ran out into the hallway to take the call so I wouldn't wake him. My heart pounded because the only thing I could think was that he'd heard from his friend about Ori, some piece of news, something.

So I didn't really process what he'd said at first. "What? Ori's open to come to the States?"

"Rocky." His voice quavered, high-pitched, and he rolled the 'R' more than usual. "You're in the qualifiers for the States Open. You're going to Port City."

"I'm…" Port City? The States Open? Me? I tried to picture myself there and it wasn't working.

He went on to talk about logistics and travel, and it wasn't until he'd told me about the lodgings near the event that I said, "What about doubles?"

"You and Aliq got a wild card entry. I haven't been able to reach him; he must be working out."

"Yeah, he's at the gym." Ori and Frio were forgotten. All I could think was that I was going to play in a major. I was going to one of the biggest tournaments in the world, and I'd been invited there, I'd been asked to come because of how well I'd played. And how well I'd played with Aliq. "I'll tell him."

I pulled my shirt on and ran to the gym, where I found the arctic fox bench-pressing without a spotter. "Jeez," I said, momentarily distracted from my news. "Didn't you tell me never to do that?"

He hefted the bar back onto its rack. "I'm not pushing myself. This is just maintenance. But now you're here, can you get another pair of 25s?"

I brandished my phone at him. "We're going to the States."

Aliq sat up on the bench. "What? The Open?"

My mouth felt weird, stretched back because I was smiling so much. "The Open. I got into singles quals and you and I got into doubles with a wild card entry."

It took a moment for the info to sink in, just like it had for me, and then he whooped and jumped off the bench and hugged me. I hugged him back and both our tails were wagging. "This is the big time," Aliq said. "Next year maybe we'll play the Gallic or the Ozzie or even..." His ears splayed. "Wimbledon."

Aliq and his family adored Wimbledon, the traditions and pageantry of it all. But for me, it was the States Open. Not that I didn't also love Wimbledon, and had loved it growing up, but the States Open was my adopted country's tournament. I was excited to go there as a States citizen—sort of. I was technically still a Lundaran citizen, because Lochen said that had been advantageous for a number of reasons I didn't really understand, but he'd put the paperwork through for my permanent residency so I could have a Union flag and the abbreviation UOS next to my name like all the other Union tennis players.

Lochen couldn't fly out to be with us—he was traveling with his team and we were on the West Coast at the time. But he insisted on buying us dinner, so me, Aliq, Danver, Sean, and Caboll went out and Lochen called the restaurant to give them his credit card number. We had a great time with some great food, joked about sneaking Danver and Sean into the States Open, and generally extended the glow of pride Aliq and I felt at getting in.

We started the tournament with a renewed sense of purpose and drive and all of us did well in the early matches. When I got back to my room after the second night, I checked my email, because Lochen had said he was going to send me more details about registering for the States. He had, but I didn't open it right away, because above it there was an email from Braden.

Hey,

Good job getting into the States. See you there (if you make it out of quals).

-B

That was kind of cool and made my tail wag all over again. The last time we'd parted it had been on strange terms, me telling him I could potentially help him, but he hadn't been in touch with me since then. I didn't know how he knew about my invitation (at the time; I've since learned that those results get published to players on the tour), but at least he was looking and thought to send me a note when he recognized my name. I shot back a quick reply, casual, and went to bed with a smile on my muzzle.

I think that was the first night that I thought about Braden lying next to me as I lay in bed trying to sleep. I'd been very careful not to fantasize about him because he was so prickly and had insisted so much on keeping those parts of our lives separate. But this little note, inconsequential though it probably was, broke down a barrier. I knew what he smelled like and could imagine his weight in the bed next to me.

The funny thing was that even though I imagined him lying next to me, I still imagined him not letting me touch him. *What do you want,* I imagined him asking me, *to cuddle? You think that's what I do?*

I laughed, with a paw over my muzzle so I wouldn't wake up Danver. Of course Braden wouldn't cuddle, wouldn't want to be lying with me. He'd maybe want to have sex, but it wouldn't ever lead to anything. And so I imagined him getting up out of bed, waving down at me, and walking out the door.

I was still chuckling from that little fantasy when my phone buzzed. What a weird coincidence if it was Braden, I thought semi-foggily, and was looking at the message even as I was realizing how ridiculous that was.

The message on my phone was in CLENE. The text said: *Congrats. Ready to make some real money?*

I stared at it and then shut the phone off, lying back on my bed. Shit.

Chapter Six

I tossed and turned for about half an hour. When I rolled over and saw that it was just after 11 pm, it struck me that even though it was an hour past when I should be getting to sleep, out there the night was just beginning for some people. If I wasn't going to sleep, at least I could do something other than lie here.

Danver snored while I got dressed as quietly as I could and didn't wake up when I snuck out the door. Down the hall, I kept my toes up so my claws wouldn't click on the linoleum, and eased the door open to the stair. There was nobody watching us; we were all adults and our behavior was our own business. But I didn't want to wake anyone up and have them ask where I was going, or, worse, ask to come along.

At the base of the stair, the door was a large metal thing that I couldn't keep quiet, but it was far enough from the rooms that even after it clanked shut, my ears caught no other sounds from inside. Of course, at that point I was in the street and cars drowned out whatever small sounds I might have heard.

I didn't know if there was a gay bar nearby, so I picked a random direction and then consulted my phone. There was, but it was a mile and a half away. Did I want to walk over half an hour for the possibility of a blow job? There was a Happy Friday's just across the street.

So I sat at a cheesy bar and drank something that seemed equal parts sugar and water—they wouldn't serve me alcohol and I didn't ask—and I avoided conversation both from the bartender and from the female fox, the female marmot, and the male wolf who attempted to engage me. Mostly I thought about dropping out of the States Open until the Frio thing was done, which I really wanted to do because I didn't even want to pretend at messing anything up in my first major tournament. But I couldn't do it for two big reasons, the first being that the whole point was to catch Frio doing something, not to take away the chances for him to, and it would look extra suspicious if I dropped out of this huge opportunity for no reason. The second, of course, was that I couldn't do that to Aliq. He could find another doubles partner, maybe, but he and I were a good team and I knew he'd be upset if I didn't go with him.

Twenty dollars' worth of drinks later I felt a little sick, so I settled up and went back to the dorm. Nobody heard me come in that I could tell, and though Danver wasn't snoring when I came in, he started up right as I lay back on the pillow and closed my eyes. I sighed and reached for my earplugs.

The next morning, I met Aliq for our routine at the gym. We went through our workouts, spotted each other, and when we were gulping Forge (I'd nabbed a couple of Danver's free ones of a flavor I liked), he cleared his throat and said, "So, uh," and then stopped.

He wasn't looking at me. I had been thinking about Frio's text and I guess I'd been a little quiet that morning when he'd talked about going to the States. "What's up?"

"Oh, uh." He still didn't look at me. "You okay, *achi*?"

"Yeah, I'm fine."

He paused again. "I don't want to get all, you know, but you've been moody, and then we get this big news and you were happy for an hour or two and this morning it's like it never happened."

The last thing I wanted was for Aliq—or anyone—to start asking what I'd been doing with my free time lately. "I'm doing fine," I said. "I'm just, y'know, I'm nervous with my sister and all."

"Oh," he said, "did you get more news?"

"No." I hated my reflexive honesty sometimes. "But you know… going to the States Open…maybe that would help raise my profile. If we do well. And that could help."

"Okay." He scratched at the side of his muzzle. My hasty words didn't seem to have calmed his worry at all, because he took another drink and wiped his lips, still not looking at me, and then started again. "I got an email from my mom, uh. So I guess this friend of mine in high school, he got married last weekend."

"Cool."

He cleared his throat again. "To his boyfriend," he said.

I got a little chill of fear, but before I could say anything, he went on. "I think that's really cool," he said. "He's a great guy and I'm happy he found someone. You know, in high school he didn't date much and I felt bad when the rest of us went on dates. We thought he was just picky, but then he came out his freshman year in college. Met someone and they've been dating a year and figured it was time, and you know, it's legal now."

I didn't like making a big deal out of gay rights stuff, especially since marriage legalization had been right before that awkward meeting with Marquize. "Uh huh," I said. "That's great for him."

"So anyway, um." He gulped down some more Forge and tossed the empty bottle into the trash. "I thought it was cool, that's all. I mean, I dunno that I'd tell just anyone on tour but I thought I could tell you. You know."

"Why?"

He sighed. "Because you seem like a cool guy, Rocky. And I wanted you to know I'm cool too. With whatever. You know?"

Maybe it was because I was exhausted from practice and the physical fatigue was breaking down my emotional walls. Maybe it was because I thought about Aliq and his family taking me in over Christmas, being there when Ma died. Maybe it was Aliq's kind of charming roundabout persistence to get me to admit something to him. Whatever it was, I put a paw on his shoulder. "Thanks," I said. "I'm really glad to have a cool friend."

He smiled, and I went on. "Maybe someday I'll have some more stuff to tell you, but right now, you know, let's just focus on the States."

"All right." He grabbed his racket. "That sounds like a good plan."

We went back and cleaned up, and to my surprise I found my mood improving. Even though there was another message from Frio when I picked up my phone, the knowledge that Aliq was on my side and could be a future confidant gave me a little emotional lift.

Frio wanted more information this tournament and to plan for the States once we knew the draw. I told him that was fine, but he was offering less money for all the info I was going to provide.

It was five hundred last time. Why only two hundred for each now?

None of this is as sure as that

This is a lot of scattershot info

might pay off, might not

more sure the bet, more money

So I have to wait for a sure thing to come up?

Not necessarily ;)

I stood and stared at those words. I got what he meant pretty quickly, but it took me a while to figure out how I was going to reply. Finally I decided I ought to play dumb.

How could I find a more sure thing?

Maybe you dont find it

maybe you do something to make it

That was direct enough that I couldn't ignore it. And Frio knew I wasn't dumb, and besides, he'd told me about some of the things Marquize had done for him.

Are you talking about throwing a match?

Not throwing but maybe you double fault in one game

I tell you which one

Just a double-fault?

> *Yeah you can still win if*
> *you want*

> *That doesn't sound so bad.*

I paused.

> *How much?*

He didn't reply for a while, and I was worried I'd scared him off with the direct question. But then he came back right as I'd decided I was too hungry to sit in my room texting.

> *Depends on the*
> *tournament*
>
> *Thousand in a challenger*
>
> *Two thousand in*
> *champions*
>
> *Five thousand in a major.*

Five thousand? Just for double-faulting? That would be hard to turn down. He'd told me Marquize had gotten only a couple hundred but I guessed that was for the Futures circuit.

> *That's a lot*

> *If your interested I can*
> *tell you where it would be*
> *available to you*

I wanted to consult with Altamont. He'd told me that I wouldn't have to throw any matches, and I wanted to stick to that. But this wasn't throwing a match. This was just throwing a point.

> *Tell me*

The deal, Frio explained to me, was that he'd want to see me prove I could double-fault on command in a Challenger tournament before he trusted me to do it in the States Open. That'd be a thousand and then another five for the States if I did well. I could clear most of the thirty I needed in like three months, he told me. It took me a moment to remember that I should be happy about that, and fortunately we were talking over text so he didn't notice my hesitation.

The tournament he was talking about, in Hilltown, was the one I'd skipped the previous year when Ma died, so I didn't have any ranking points to risk there. I was supposed to double-fault and lose

my second service game in the second set of a match he would spec-
ify the night before. Losing a service game put me at a big disadvan-
tage in that second set, so if I were going to win the match I'd need
to break my opponent in the second set to even us up or else win the
first and third. Depending on who it was, I could do that.

I had two tournaments between now and then, and in the first
one, to my frustration, I did worse than I had last year. Only one
round, but the loss wasn't even on anything fluky like a net cord
or a bad call that I could shrug my shoulders at, and I hadn't been
practicing trying to double fault. I missed shots, my serve was off
all match, and the other guy was good. Still, I was mad enough at
losing this early, with the potential loss already decided in an upcoming tournament, that Aliq and Danver tried to calm me down that
night in Aliq's room while his roommate was out with his coach.
Aliq reminded me that we had to go out and play our quarterfinals
doubles match the next day. "I wish we could play it right now," I
growled.

"Whoa," Danver said, "Rocky, I've never seen you this upset.
Angry, I mean. It can be good for you, though. Take it out on Lowry
and Oliveira. I bet you can beat them this time."

"We almost beat them in March." Aliq, uncharacteristically,
didn't wait for Danver to take a breath before interrupting. "If I
hadn't fucked up my service game in the third set."

"It wasn't your fault," I said, although if Coach Keely had been
there to ask me, he probably would've said that Aliq's serve was the
reason we'd lost, and I'd have been inclined to agree. "I muffed a
couple returns."

"I put you in a bad position. But my serve's better. We can take
them."

Danver put a paw on both our shoulders. "I know you can," he
said.

"Hey," Aliq said, "Danver, you got any Forge left?"

"Couple," he said, "back in our room. What flavor you want?"

"Doesn't matter." The arctic fox grinned. "Thanks."

When he'd gone, Aliq grabbed my shoulders. "You gonna be
okay tomorrow?"

"Yeah," I said, a little startled. "I'm just mad at myself."

"Okay." He released me. "I didn't know if something else was bothering you or what."

It was; I'd been thinking about Frio and the match I had to arrange a double fault in, but I'd sent that to the back of my mind and I didn't think it was affecting me. What if it was? "No," I said. "Just had an off day and I didn't want to lose points here."

"You've got that tournament in August, so you'll make up a bunch there."

He couldn't know why that didn't help me. His earnest manner and wagging tail, though, did help me, and with an effort I forced myself to realize that he was trying hard to be a good friend, and what's more, that he'd sent Danver out of the room in case I wanted to talk to him about my secret gay life. I resolved to do that sometime soon. He'd been a good friend and he deserved to know the truth, once I'd figured out that I wouldn't just be telling him to make my own life easier.

Danver came back then with a bottle of blue Forge, which I think was supposed to be mixed berry flavor. He gave it to Aliq, who tossed it in his bag. "You're not going to drink it now?" the squirrel asked.

"I wanted it for my workout tomorrow morning," Aliq replied, with a subtle grin at me. "You rather I come wake you up at six for it?"

"I still don't know how you survive getting up at six a.m." Danver rolled his eyes. "But I guess it works for you guys, so go ahead with it. Just don't try to drag me into your 'early bird' routines. I know how much sleep I need and how much I can get, and it doesn't matter if I go to bed early, if I get up at six I have a lousy day."

The talk with Aliq had relaxed me enough that I returned his little grin. "All right," I said, "but I need to get to sleep now so I can get up and go work out."

The next morning, Aliq and I did our morning workout, abbreviated because we had to play a match later, and we split the blue Forge. I tried to be outwardly in a better mood so he wouldn't ask if I were hiding anything, and it seemed to work because he limited our conversation to our workout. We had our usual breakfast, went over our opponents and our strategy, and went out at noon for our match.

I'd funneled my anger from the day before into determination. Saying I was going to get to every ball was tricky when playing doubles, because I didn't want to poach Aliq's territory. But every ball that came my way was going to meet my racket, I promised. And once the game started, it was easy to settle into our familiar rhythm.

Aliq picked up on my energy, seeming to have an extra spring in his step as well. Whether it was subconscious or whether he had decided not to let me down I never asked, but he had a terrific serve that match. Lowry and Oliveira battled hard but we beat them in straight sets.

"Wow," the wolf said as we were shaking paws at the net. "What got into you guys today?"

"Rocky doesn't like losing in singles." Aliq grinned at me.

Oliveira, the maned wolf, laughed shortly. "Who does?"

"Good luck, you guys," Lowry said. "Hope you win it all."

We came close, losing in a tough third set in the final. By that time I was pleased enough with our progress that I didn't mind the loss as much. We'd gain doubles points and that was at least something.

* * *

At the next tournament, a small one, Aliq and I got to the semifinals, and I got to the semis in singles, improving on 2012, so I got more points in both doubles and singles. And then we had to go on to Hilltown, and the tournament where I was supposed to double-fault in the second set of a match.

Just before the tournament, I got a text from Altamont telling me that he was going to be observing my match. He didn't say more than that; I guessed it was so he could confirm that I'd done what Frio asked, as a supplement to the texts Frio and I had exchanged. I asked if he wanted to talk to me and he said no, he didn't.

So I was a little on edge, but I made sure not to let that affect my doubles play. It had occurred to me that if I lost in the singles qualifiers (this was the next to last tuneup before the States Open and a ton of guys were playing in it, so I'd been pushed back to the quals), I wouldn't have to face the dilemma of faking a double fault. Frio would be disappointed, but he'd pick another tournament. With the States Open so close, just two weeks away, it wouldn't be that one, and I'd be able to go there and play honestly.

But then that also meant months more of worrying about Frio. If I went ahead and did well at this tournament, hopefully they could go arrest him and I'd be free of him by the time we went to the States. The worry that I wouldn't be able to go to the States, or that I wouldn't be allowed back if I threw my match, kept surfacing in my head. I told myself that I'd promised Altamont I'd do a job, and that I was only nineteen. I'd have plenty of chances to go to a major. Still, I had trouble sleeping again that night and ended up taking some of Aliq's melatonin—which helped—for the rest of the tournament.

In the end, I did my best because that's how I play. I got to the finals of the qualifiers, and the night before my match, I got a text from Frio. *Tomorrow,* is all it said.

Chapter Seven

Altamont knew, because he was reading our texts. I spotted him in the crowd when I went out to warm up, and after that I had to battle to stop myself from looking over at him at every break. I was playing this hyena who'd dyed a blue stripe between his ears, someone I'd talked to a few times but never played before. And the refrain kept running through my mind: double-fault in the second set, double-fault in the second set. During our serving warmups, I wondered if I should practice missing the line or hitting the net. It would be good to have a little more confidence in my ability to double-fault on command, even though missing serves was pretty easy. On the other paw I didn't want anyone going back and looking at film of my warmup and seeing that I was missing serves the same way I'd double-faulted. Even though the TIU was on my side and understood what I was doing, even though I knew I wasn't going to face any penalties for this, I still worried about the press, the bloggers. There were people who broke down every shot and analyzed patterns, and what if they did that to me?

(It did not occur to me then that missing a serve in practice would be the perfect cover for missing it in a game; if your serve is long in practice and then long again during the game, people will say, "ahh, he was having problems with his serve all day." It was just that I was convinced people were studying me and looking for every little detail to analyze.)

In the end, I tried to hit the net twice, and hit it both times. I figured that was innocuous enough that I could get away with it. I wanted another half hour of practice, but then we were heading back to our benches and the match was set to start. I couldn't help looking at Altamont again. He was drinking something out of a plastic souvenir cup and checking his phone, just like half the other spectators. So I drank my water, ate my Coach Keely-approved energy bar, and focused on my breathing.

The hyena was good, ranked about ten spots ahead of me. He had either seen film of me or he was a quick study, because he handled my serve well and, more importantly, he was ready for my returns. We battled through a tight first set, but he was the one who broke my serve and won the set 6-4.

I served first in the second set, already so nervous that every time I didn't get a first serve in, my second was so careful that it was easy for the hyena to return. I fell behind love-30 in like a minute. I bounced the ball before my next serve, lecturing myself in Ma's voice to pull myself together. This guy wasn't that much better than me, I could do this. And sure enough, I served an ace.

Pretty soon I got it to deuce, and there I found the confidence to serve another ace, and finally won the game on a passing shot when he came to the net. For a second, I stood there and absorbed the win, and then I had to get ready right away for the hyena's serve.

That second game didn't go well, because I couldn't stop thinking about the next game and how I was going to have to double-fault. Well, I'd faulted on the first serve enough times, I decided. As soon as I went ahead and did that in this game, I'd go ahead and somehow—serve into the net, I guessed, because that was less suspicious than serving long. Too late, as we were walking around to change sides, I realized that if I'd played better in that game, I would have put off the moment where I had to intentionally miss a serve in this one.

I didn't look at Altamont but I could feel him there as I rolled the tennis balls around in my paw. I selected one, bounced it, and then took a look at where the hyena was (standard spot beyond the baseline). I tossed the ball into the air and—served an ace. Great, I thought, just great. Here when I needed a double-fault. But there was nothing to do except walk to the ad court and try again. I certainly wasn't going to serve four aces in a game.

The hyena returned my next serve—it was good—and we rallied for a little while before I came to net and finished him off. I wanted to get ahead in the game so I could lose a point and still have a chance to win it, but now my chances to do what Frio had told me were running out.

So on this serve I tried to hit the net. But somehow the ball cleared the net—I didn't even get a let—and streaked perfectly to the sideline. The hyena jumped for it and flailed at empty air with his racket. Another ace, and now I was up forty-love.

Crossing to the ad court, I talked to myself again, but this time in my own voice, not Ma's. I told myself that if I messed up this game, Frio wouldn't trust me or he'd insist I do something at the States Open, and that was more than I was willing to risk. We'd never arrest him and then all this risk I'd taken, all this stress I'd put myself under, it would be for nothing. Not to mention Frio would still be able to take advantage of Braden and who knew how many other players.

I tossed the ball into the air and slammed it down at the net as hard as I could. This time it clipped the net, bounced, and landed out on the hyena's side. That was one fault at least. And here was my chance to practice that serve just outside the line. I visualized, bounced, tossed...

And served perfectly, two inches beyond the service line. Double-fault. 40-15.

There was a stretch of about five seconds when I was smiling, and if any cameras caught that, I'm sure they were curious about it. But I could pass that off as a frustrated "doesn't that suck" smile, and a minute later I'd won the game, so maybe it could also have been a determined smile.

You might think that with that weight off my shoulders, I would go on to play fantastically and win the game, but all I did was hold serve that set and lose in the tiebreaker. I barely even cared. I'd be getting another message from Frio, and the evidence against him would pile up. Maybe Altamont could even arrest him after this and I wouldn't have to worry about the States Open.

"Tough luck," Aliq said after the match, "but silver lining, you'll be able to focus on doubles, eh?"

I was relieved enough to grin back and swat him with my tail. "Maybe I'll get lazy without more matches to play."

"Oh, then extra practices. Done." And before I could retort, he patted his backpack and said, "I've got lunch. See you out in the lounge?"

"Get out of here," I told him, and he hurried out, tail wagging.

How long would it take Frio to find out that I'd followed his instructions? I didn't want the message from him to come in while I was hanging out with Aliq, but I also didn't want to wait forever. After fifteen minutes, I couldn't dawdle any longer; my tail was twitching and my feet were tapping, so I went out to meet Aliq.

And of course it was then, in the middle of eating, that my phone went off with Frio's message. I picked it up to answer it, and Aliq hesitated. Of course I knew it was rude to answer messages while hanging out with friends, because we'd talked about that. Caboll did it often, but none of the rest of us made a habit of it. There were exceptions for family, of course, and Caboll's girlfriend, but in general we didn't really have a lot of other friends messaging us all the time.

Frio's messages would vanish as soon as I read them, but they wouldn't vanish if I didn't read them. So I looked at the CLENE notification and decided he could wait until I'd finished my lunch, and I put the phone back down.

"Something about Ori's case," I told Aliq.

"You can get that if you want," he said.

I shook my head. "If it was important, they would've called."

I liked the feeling of making Frio wait. My feet tapped with excess energy, but I was also feeling good about having prioritized Aliq over Frio. That felt like the correct way to live my life.

So after Aliq and I were done, I picked up the phone and called up the app. Frio's message hung there for a few seconds.

> *Good boy :) time to get*
> *paid*

I exhaled and typed back.
> *Let's do it.*

> *So I guess I owe you a*
> *thousand*

Sounds right.

> *Ok look for it in your account soon*
>
> *Want to make five at the states?*

I paused over that one. I couldn't consult with Altamont, but he would want me to continue to play along. I hoped by the time the States rolled around, Frio would be under arrest and I'd be out of this whole thing. Still, it took some effort for me to get my fingers to type back.

I don't have to lose?

same deal

Then sure.

> *Awesome*
>
> *Ill be in touch*

The message flickered and vanished, and then there was no trace of it on my phone. But Altamont had it, I hoped. I wanted badly to call the cougar and ask if he had enough now, if I was going to have to ruin my first appearance at a major open because of this job I'd taken on. Viewed in that light, was I crazy to have done it? I hadn't known about going to the States when I'd signed on, but should I have told Frio that the States was off limits? Then I wondered if he'd gotten suspicious, knowing how much tennis meant to me, that I'd given in so easily.

Aliq and Sean were going out to watch some of the afternoon matches, but I told them I wanted to get in some more serving practice—the only thing I didn't technically need a partner for. Aliq offered to come but I told him I'd see him at the gym in the evening. "Don't tire out that serving arm," he said, and grinned as he left.

So I grabbed my equipment and headed for one of the designated practice courts, hoping nobody would be using it at this time. But as I approached, I heard the rhythmic twang and thwack, twang and thwack, like clockwork, of someone practicing his serve. Just one person, I thought, so maybe I could practice opposite them.

I came out onto the court and saw a dark-furred fox in tennis whites on the deuce side tossing a ball and hitting it, tossing and hitting. He glanced my way but didn't stop as I circled the court to give him space. Center line, middle of service box, sideline, back to middle, then center line. Over and over.

"Hey, Braden," I called as I got to the ad side of the opposite court. "Mind if I serve across?"

"Go ahead," he called back without breaking his rhythm.

I plunked down the hopper of tennis balls and started my own serves. They weren't as rhythmic or precise as Braden's, but then, I was trying to settle down my mind's chaotic whirling. I imagined an opponent standing in different places on the court and decided where I'd serve to unbalance him. Center. Sideline. Center. Center again, because he'd be expecting me to go sideline.

Braden ran out of balls before I did and crossed to the other court. I picked up my carrier and crossed to where he'd been, and as we approached each other, he said, "Want to hit a few?"

Some people stood or sat around the court, including Braden's bodyguard-wolf and a smattering of spectators. Anything Braden did was an event now. But nobody was likely to make a big deal over him practicing with some 145th-ranked jackal, I hoped. Nobody had really reacted when I came out onto the court.

"Uh, sure." I gestured. "Just let me pick up the balls."

A red wolf was picking up his, but nobody'd taken charge of mine. Braden snapped his fingers at the ballboy and said, "Collect his when you're done with mine."

"Yes, sir," the wolf said, his tone mild, but I noticed the flattening of his ears.

I waved. "It's fine, I'll get them."

Braden grabbed my arm. "You've got to start acting like a star if you want to be one."

His hazel eyes stared into mine. I nodded. "I know," I said. "But it's no trouble. I can do it just as fast and then we can start sooner."

He rolled his eyes and released me. "Fine."

For whatever reason, I was grinning to myself as I hurried over to pick up the stray tennis balls. I didn't get all of them, just the ones around the court, but it felt good to be doing the work. I knew Ma would have approved, and as much as I'd been starting to like Braden, it was nice to annoy him when he was being a dick.

The practice was fun, both for us and the spectators, who looked a lot more engaged than when we'd just been serving. We started casual but the rallies quickly got heated, almost as intense as a real match. Neither of us overexerted ourselves to get to shots at the edge of our range; we clapped and said, "Nice shot," more often. But I had to work harder than I did with Aliq to keep up with Braden's practice level.

There was something predictable to Braden's game. I couldn't put my finger on it at that practice, so I didn't say anything then, but I remembered that the last time I'd played him, I hadn't been able to figure out any cracks in his game. At this practice, I couldn't either, but I found that my guesses about his shots were right more often than I expected. Maybe it was just practice, maybe he wasn't fully committing himself the way he would in a match.

Whatever it was, it took my mind off Frio for the day, and then I met the guys for dinner and Aliq and I did a short gym workout. I didn't tell them about practicing with Braden.

Altamont still hadn't contacted me the next day, but also Frio's payment hadn't gone through, so I tried to put all that aside and worry about playing a tennis match. Aliq and I started strong, and despite a shaky patch in the beginning of the second set, won in straights. "Hey," he said. "At the States Open we're going to have to play more sets. Three, maybe four or five."

"We're in shape," I said. "We can do it."

"I know." He grinned. "It'll be weird not having the match end at best of three, you know?"

We won the next day, too, still with no word from Frio or Altamont. I focused on practice, film, and tennis, and almost forgot about the rest of the stuff going on in my life. In the quarterfinals, we won in three sets, and it was after that that I got a call from Altamont.

The cougar's soft voice was even, but he started right in without pulling any punches. "Rocky, you may have to withdraw from the States."

"What?" I'd walked outside the building where we were practicing to take the call, and now I hurried over to a bench and sat down hard on it. "Why?"

"When the payment goes through, we'll have all the evidence we need to move forward, and we're going to need you to testify that the communications we have came from your phone."

"Why? You have it, you have all of his and mine, and…my phone number, and…"

"Someone else could have been using your phone." He spoke gently. "We also need your testimony about how you got involved, all of those things you told me at the beginning of this."

"But…I already told you."

"We need it under oath."

I sighed. "Aliq's going to kill me. Wait—I told you I don't want Marquize or anyone else implicated in this."

"That's fine," he said. "You can say 'a friend' if you want."

There didn't seem to be any way I could express the emptiness in me. "Can't it wait a couple weeks?"

"Here's the problem," he said. "There's likely to be gambling on the States. If we catch him beforehand, we can intercept a lot of it. We won't have an opportunity like this until the next major."

That was the Ozzie Open, four months away. "I don't want to wait until then. But couldn't I just fly in for a day right before, then go back?"

"Maybe." He sighed. "But bureaucracy being what it is, I can't guarantee that the schedules will line up and we need to get this done as fast as possible."

I had one last desperate idea. "Can't my testimony wait until after?"

"It weakens our case without it, is all. And you might need to rebut claims Coach Young makes once we arrest him. I'm sorry, Rocky. If it's any consolation, I'm sure you'll be invited to a major in 2014."

If Aliq didn't dump me for skipping our first one. "What if the payment doesn't come through until after?"

"Well…" He hesitated. "Then you'd be under obligation to him to compromise a match at the States Open that we don't need you to. Would you rather play a false match or not play at all?"

I hated when he put it like that. "Fine," I said, and put down the phone. For several minutes I sat there with my paws clasped together, head bowed so the sun beat down on my ears. I couldn't figure out how I was going to tell Aliq.

Chapter Eight

Because I couldn't figure out a good way to tell Aliq, and with the faint hope that something might come up that would allow us to play in the States Open, I didn't say anything. After all, we'd already bought our tickets to go, so there wasn't any point in canceling them. And there might be a miracle. You know, I'd been down a set and a break and still come back to win the match.

The hiding my stuff with Frio was over, at least. He stopped texting me until we got closer to the States, and Altamont wasn't going to text me until the money came through, so I didn't have to hide my phone to have conversations or think too much about whether I was cheating the game of tennis. Weirdly, I still practiced intentionally faulting on a serve. I liked the idea that I had that much control over it, and after all, if I could convincingly land a serve an inch outside a line, couldn't I also land it an inch inside that line?

Still, going out to dinner was a little awkward when everyone talked about me and Aliq going to the States. We were the only ones of the group who'd been invited, and every time someone said they envied me or said it was going to be so cool, I got a flush of guilt and couldn't really respond to it. I got better at changing the subject and keeping my ears from going flat, at least.

We had one more tournament, a Challengers one, before heading to Port City for the States Open, and it was after the opening round there that I got a call from Ori.

As soon as I picked up, I felt guilty. I'd gotten so caught up in trapping Frio that I'd forgotten what the aim of my fake cheating was, and I'd gotten so mired in self-pity over not going to the States Open that I hadn't thought to call Ori. So when she called, I excused myself from dinner, saying, "It's my sister," and hurried outside into the warm muggy air to talk.

"I got an appointment again, Ro!" Ori sounded breathless, as though she'd run to tell me the news. "They had a cancellation tomorrow and the officer called me to see if I could come in."

"That's great!" My hackles went up, though. "Don't tell anyone. It'll get back to Dad."

"No, I know." She sounded like I'd told her not to try to breathe water. "He called me after hours and said he would see me personally. I told him that I would definitely be there and not to listen to anyone else."

"Good."

"I think he knew what I meant too, because he said not to show up too early. I think Dad has people in the office who might call him when I come in. But I hope if I have the appointment and the papers are filed that he won't be able to do anything to me after that."

"Don't underestimate him," I said. "He's still waiting for me to send him ten thousand dollars so he'll probably do whatever he can to protect that."

"I know." She said it softer this time. "Thanks, Ro."

"Maybe I can call and distract him or something? Tell him money's on the way?"

"You'd better stay out of it. If I'm lucky, I can go to this appointment and get through it before he knows I'm there. Then there won't be anything he can do."

I still wasn't sure, but Ori's logic seemed sound. Plus if I followed her advice, it meant I didn't have to deal with my father. And as much as I wanted to take out my frustrations on someone, my rational brain reminded me that he could turn around and continue to make life difficult for Ori. That was the last thing I wanted.

So I wished her the best and hung up to spend the next day worrying about whether she'd get her appointment. Fortunately, being in the middle of a tournament meant that my life was structured and dominated by tennis, tennis, and more tennis, and even though I couldn't stop thinking about the States Open, either, I turned my fixation around so that I was determined to do the best I could in this tournament. And at least for that day, I won both my matches.

Ori called in the middle of my singles match, so I called her back from the locker room without even waiting to clean up. "How'd it go?" I asked.

"I think it went well." Today she sounded calmer. "We talked for half an hour, not even, and he said he thought I was a good candidate."

"For refugee status to the States?"

"Not quite to there yet, but to Gallia or Anglia maybe for a couple years. Then it would be easier to get to the States."

"I guess that's something. Then I could come visit you for the Gallic or Wimbledon next year."

She laughed. "Are you going?"

I hadn't told her about the States. And now, should I? I wasn't going to go, but that wasn't official yet. And I'd been invited, which was a big deal. The news about me not going could wait. "I got invited to the States Open," I said. "Aliq and I are going for doubles and I got in for singles, too."

"Ro, that's amazing! I can see you on TV?"

"I guess. If you get the channel that gets the qualifying rounds. Not many carry that."

"I'll ask around. Oh, I'm so proud of you!"

And that was somehow the worst thing of all. I hung up the phone a few minutes later and cleaned up from my match, and when I went out to meet up with Aliq, I took him aside.

"Hey." The words weren't coming easily. "I, uh, need to talk to you."

"Yeah, what's up?" His smile faltered as he caught my mood. Aliq was good like that. "What happened? Something with your sister?"

"No, no, she's fine. Actually, she got an interview and it went well, so we're optimistic. But look, that's not—" I sighed. You would think that after so many years of drama, I'd have a better idea of how to deliver bad news. But it was hard to look at his worried eyes and perked ears and know that the next thing I said was going to hurt him. How had Marquize done it when he had to tell me his news?

His was worse and was ruining a deeper relationship. But he'd done it and so could I.

I took a breath. "I can't go to the States Open."

His whole expression changed, but it wasn't anger; it was worry. "Why not? Wait, did you get hurt? What's going on?"

I shook my head. "I'm not hurt. I…I have a conflict. I need to call Lochen and tell him to cancel too."

Now the worry was shifting into anger. "Conflict? What kind of conflict? Your sister?"

"No, I—it's private. I can't tell you about it."

If I'd been able to tell him, he'd understand, I was sure. But I couldn't, and there wasn't any way for him to know, not yet. By the time he did, it might be too late.

His ears flattened and his brow lowered. "You didn't find out about it until just now?"

There he had me. I could've told him days ago. "I wasn't sure—I mean, it didn't get confirmed until, like, just recently. I didn't want it to be true. I was trying to get out of it." All half-truths, safer than the full truth except not really. "If you want to find another partner, it's cool, I understand."

"Yeah, well," he said. "Little late for that, isn't it?"

"I'm sorry."

He shrugged, turning away from me. "I guess it's not something you can control. It's cool, we'll get another invitation next year."

"Of course we will. Hey, thanks for being cool about it."

He half-turned back. "I know you're as disappointed as I am."

"Yes!" This wasn't a lie. "I've been looking forward to this forever."

We walked back to the dorms in silence, and it wasn't until we were a block away that he asked, "When are you going to tell the rest of the guys?"

"Let me call Lochen first." I sighed.

"Don't let him push you around."

"You kidding?" I leaned against the wall right next to the door. "Talking to you was the hard part. Talking to Lochen will be easy."

I'd intended that to be like a testament to our friendship, but he didn't really respond other than to lift a paw to me as he went inside.

Lochen took it much harder than Aliq had. I spent about ten minutes going, "No, I can't tell you. No, I can't get out of it," over and over again. I promised that I'd be able to tell him pretty soon.

"Is this another girl thing? You told me about the last one and it's no big deal."

"It's not a girl thing," I said. "Trust me, it's a—it's a thing. I'm not allowed to tell you."

He finally let it go and let me get off the phone. That's when I got the notification that Frio's payment had been deposited to my account. I stared at the numbers and felt a rush even though I knew I wasn't going to be able to use the money. Then I put the phone away and went out with the guys.

Dinner was kind of tense because it was preceded by me telling them about not going to the States Open. None of them took it as badly as Aliq did; the arctic fox stayed quiet, ears down, throughout this conversation.

Sean just said, "Huh."

Danver got over his surprise pretty quickly. "Whatever it is must be pretty important if you're gonna skip the States. I get that you can't tell us now, but maybe later? Or whatever, I mean, you don't have to. Everyone's got private stuff. Hey." He pointed at me. "It isn't that you were worried about your first major, is it? Cause I mean, you don't have to worry. You're the best in our group. I know you'll kick ass at the States."

"Hey," Sean said.

We all stared, because we rarely interrupted Danver, and the jaguar almost never did. "It's not nerves. It's private. Let him be."

And that was the end of it. For that meal, anyway.

I still had to finish out the tournament, and despite all the complicated events going on around us, Aliq and I won again in doubles. This thawed our relationship a little. "Cool," he said. "I know we can both play upset."

"I wasn't worried," I lied. And he gave me a quick nod, with maybe a hint of a smile. I guess that was all I could hope for at that stage.

After the match, I was working out a sore hamstring muscle when my phone buzzed—a call, not a text. The number was Altamont's, and I was so eager to hear from him that I picked it up before I realized I shouldn't talk to him in front of the trainer who was working with me. "Hi," I said. "Sorry, I'm in the training room."

"It's all right," his soft voice said, sounding more relaxed than I'd heard him in a long time. "We tracked down Coach Young and worked with the FBI to place him under arrest. Illegal gambling, illegal money movement, and so on. We're scheduling his hearing so I'm going to be sending you a plane ticket for Sunday night." He paused. "So that if you make it to the finals, you'll be able to play."

"Thanks."

"Get back to your training," he said. "Look for the ticket to come by courier tonight."

"All right. I guess I'll see you in a few days."

"Rocky?"

I held the phone to my ear as the trainer worked on my leg. Altamont went on. "I know this has been difficult and an inconvenience for you, but you've helped us out a great deal, not only to catch one person but also to get a lead on many more. We owe you a lot."

"You're welcome," I said, but what I thought was, *And you're still asking me to do more.*

But the really annoying part didn't come until the next day. We'd won our doubles match in the morning, my hamstring seeming fully recovered. In the middle of lunch between that match and my singles match in the afternoon, Altamont called again.

"I wanted to make sure that the tickets arrived," he said.

"They did." They were safe in my suitcase in the dorm room. It felt strange to be going somewhere different from everyone else for the first time in—ever. It might not have been that weird if there weren't also all the bad feelings between us.

The cougar said, "Good," and I was about to say something like "see you then" and hang up, but he went on. "Things are going very well so far. Coach Young is cooperating, sort of."

"Sort of?"

"He maintains his innocence. He says he was just a go-between and never made any arrangements himself. We haven't told him about your involvement yet, but he told us he'd passed information along to you."

"What? Just like that?" My fur prickled. "Did he figure out that I was the one who got him arrested?"

"Oh, no. He's giving us lots of names. Covering all his bases." The cougar laughed.

Now my fur was prickling for another reason. "Lots of names," I echoed. "Like, other people he's given money to."

"And taken money from. Those are the ones we're most interested in—oh." His tone changed as he figured out my concern. "Yes, well. I did say that we couldn't guarantee that those other names would be kept out of the record. He said them before we could stop him, really. Anxious to shift the blame to anyone else."

"No no no," I said. "No, that was—you promised me."

"Rocky, I'm sorry, but—"

"I did that to help them!" My voice got a little away from me. I reined it in. "I wouldn't have done it otherwise."

"You've done a good thing," he said. "We can't always control everything about a situation."

Marquize had already left tennis, but Braden's career, ruined? Because of me? Sure, I could blame Frio, and largely, I did, but I was the one who'd precipitated this exposure. Guilty warmth flushed my ears and cheeks. "You can control this, though."

"It's in the official record. I'm sorry." Altamont didn't sound sorry.

"It doesn't have to stay there, does it?" My mind spun. "You can get it expunged, or redacted, or…" I wasn't sure of the right word, even after years of movies.

"I'd need a really good reason to do that," he said, now shifting into annoyance. "More than just you not wanting your friends to get hurt."

"Not ruining someone's life isn't a good reason?"

"These people made bad decisions, Rocky. They ruined their own lives."

"All right," I said, and an idea came to me. "All right. Here's a good reason. If you don't, I'm not getting on that plane on Sunday."

My threat—I didn't think of it as a threat at the time, but looking back on it, there's nothing else I can call it—was met with several seconds of breathing. "I'd urge you very strongly to reconsider that position."

"I guess you have the rest of the week to answer," I said. "I'll call you Sunday if I haven't heard from you by then."

"Rocky—"

"This isn't negotiable." I knew that line from movies. He stayed quiet. "If you won't do the right thing, then you won't do it without me." That didn't come out right. "I won't be a part of it, I mean."

A long, frustrated sigh. "I will see what I can do. But if I can't, I really hope you will fly here to provide your testimony anyway."

"Talk to you Sunday," I said.

My heart raced as I hung up. I'd been scared, and somewhere in that fear and anger at Altamont I'd spurred myself to talk to him like I'd never thought I could. I paced back and forth under the overcast sky, staring at my silent phone and muttering things like, "you promised!" and "liar!" I must have looked like a crazy person.

Then I finally registered that I was staring at the time on my phone and I remembered that I still had a singles match to play.

I tried to use the anger and fear as motivation, but honestly, the farther I got from the phone call, the more fear there was. Fear is not a good emotion to carry into a tennis match; I'd learned to harness anger, but fear was different and it made me careless with my shots. In a quarterfinal match, this cost me a victory I probably could have had.

Frustrated, I called Ori again because I had nobody else to talk to, but she was out. So I walked around on my own until I got shaky from hunger, and then I stopped to eat something. It wasn't great—a burger on a thick bun—but at least I had enough presence of mind to get a salad with it instead of the steaming pile of greasy fries I kind of wanted.

Sleep would bring peace, I hoped, and indeed, when I woke the next morning I was more tired than anything else. But the day brought another complication with it: pouring rain. Aliq's and my doubles match for the day was postponed, and there was an official tournament announcement posted at the center that if the rain persisted into the next morning, the final matches would be held on Monday rather than Sunday.

"Good thing our flights out are on Tuesday," Aliq said. "I mean, not that it matters to you."

When I didn't respond, he said, "Hey, sorry. Let's practice, okay?"

But I wasn't mad at him. He was right, after all. I was thinking of the ticket back in my room. Maybe it wouldn't be a problem. Maybe we'd lose one of our next two matches and wouldn't have to play in the final. Maybe Altamont wouldn't call back and I wouldn't have to go. Maybe it would stop raining.

We woke the next day to the same constant, driving rain.

Chapter Nine

Now I had a dilemma. I'd already let Aliq down once. Assuming Altamont came through and we made the finals—neither of which was a given—I would have to either keep my promise to him and let Aliq down again, or keep my friendship with Aliq, which was already frayed, and give up all the work I'd done to convict Frio.

That's what my teenage angst-ridden mind was telling me as I stared out at the rain. I wondered if I could convincingly cost us the quarterfinal or semifinal match. Yes, I was planning ridiculous things like this, and they seemed not only sensible at the time, but possibly essential.

Aliq and I did finally play our match that afternoon when the backlog of the schedule allowed. We had worked out together lightly in the morning, warmed up together in the crowded indoor gym, and it might have been my imagination, but he didn't seem quite as angry with me as he had been.

During the match, there were moments I spotted, times when I could have missed a shot, cost us a game. Every time the thought crossed my mind, I couldn't do that to Aliq. And every time but one, we won the point. I don't know that those points made the difference, but we also won the match.

"Two more to go," Aliq said in a pretty happy dinner group afterwards. Sean was in the other doubles semifinal, but as we kept reminding him, we'd beaten him and his partner the only time we'd played, so we weren't worried about facing them in the final. Some of it was bravado, but honestly that was the least of my worries about a potential final.

At least the clear weather persisted into the next day. Sean lost his semifinal match, but Aliq and I won ours. My flight was scheduled to leave at eight pm, but I didn't say anything. If Altamont didn't call, I wouldn't be heading to the airport.

At quarter to four, my phone rang with his number. I picked up, dreading what he was going to say. Either he'd be telling me that I was going to get on a plane, or he'd be trying to talk me into testifying even though he couldn't guarantee the safety of my friends. So I took a deep breath to calm my nerves and said, "Hello?"

"I've got good news for you, Rocky." He didn't even bother saying hello, and his voice wasn't soft and soothing like it had been in the past. The words came out crisp and businesslike. "I've managed to strike a deal with the FBI that will keep your friends out of Coach Young's testimony. Okay?"

"Great," I said, and remembered to add, "Thank you."

"So I'll see you tonight?"

"The TIU isn't going to take action against any of them?"

He took a moment to answer. "No."

"That's great news. Thank you. You know, we were all victims of Coach Young."

"I know. So? Tonight?"

I took a breath. "So here's the thing, actually. I'm playing in the doubles final."

"Yes? That was today, right?"

"There was a weather delay. They're playing it tomorrow."

The cougar made a small, amused noise. "The one time I don't bother to check the results. All right. I'll make some calls and have your ticket changed to tomorrow night."

"Wait. Really?"

"Of course. You have to play the final, Rocky. Good luck."

For once, it seemed, my conflicts had been resolved without a huge amount of drama and heartache. In the future, maybe I could just ask people to help me instead of worrying that I was going to have to arrange everything alone. I went off to finish the day with my first smile in a while.

* * *

We lost the final, but it was a three-setter and we were pleased with our performance in it. Overall, Monday was a pretty good day, even when I had to leave the guys to go to the airport. They were curious about that, too, but nobody asked any questions, probably knowing they wouldn't get answers.

I'd packed my usual bags, including tennis gear, even though I wasn't going to a tournament. Maybe there'd be a practice court or something. I decided I could afford a taxi to the airport, and even though I was alone, it was pretty easy to navigate the flight to Potomac. Sitting beside strangers was weird, but I put my headphones in and listened to some music, and they didn't bother me.

Altamont had told me that there'd be a car waiting for me but hadn't said how I'd find it. I went to baggage claim and got my bags and as I was looking around, uncertain where to go next, a cheetah came up to me, nearly as tall as I was. "Mister N'Guwe?"

"Yes?" I was reminded of Marquize for a second, but only a second; his voice was deeper and his build thicker. Then I noticed that he held a sign that had my name printed on it.

"I'm your driver. I'll take you to your hotel. Can I help you with your bags?"

And he took charge of the heavier bags and walked out to the parking garage. I followed him to a long black car so glossy I could see my reflection in it. "They sent a limousine?"

"It's a Town Car." The cheetah smiled and put my bags in the trunk, then reached for the ones I was carrying.

"It still seems like a big deal."

He opened the door and held it for me, still smiling. "You must be pretty important."

"I guess so." I got in and sat down on smooth leather seats, breathing in a clean citrus smell.

It took half an hour to drive to the hotel, during which I read up on the States Open. Braden was considered the fourth strongest on the male side; he'd skipped the Gallic and lost in the quarters at Wimbledon. I looked through the competition there and thought he had a good chance to win. It took a little more work to look at the list of people in the qualifiers, but eventually I found the list.

I knew most of the people on it, if not personally then by reputation. I charted a few possible paths for me, looking at the draw and imagining various outcomes. I could see myself getting into the main draw there…or this way. That guy had always given me trouble; if I played him I only had a fifty percent chance of winning. It looked like I could've made it to the main draw, if I weren't here putting Frio in jail.

Then I turned to the doubles side and looked at the draw. That was even more depressing. Aliq and I could've beaten a bunch of those teams and I felt sure we would've won at least two rounds. Maybe—with luck—we could've made it to the quarterfinals.

Making it that far was a big personal achievement, but it also meant a good payday. Losing in the quarterfinals would get us about half of what we'd gotten for the tournaments we'd won. Which would be great, added to the prestige of being in the States Open.

By the time I got to the hotel, I was pretty morose about the opportunity I was missing. Sure, there would be more chances, but this would've been the first. And it still felt unnecessary to me that they'd need me to fly all the way out here to the east coast to do what I could easily do over the phone.

I asked the cheetah if there were any instructions for the next day, but he said he was just a hired driver and he didn't have a pickup at this hotel. So I called Altamont when I got settled, and he told me I'd come in the next day to make a statement, and the day after that if we ran out of time. He also said the room was paid for and I could put any food expense on the room charge.

I dropped my bag on the single king bed, surveyed the green and cream-striped wallpaper and bland fuzzy landscape portraits, and went out to explore the hotel. The lobby restaurant, called "The Backyard Grill," featured mostly grilled steak and grilled chicken in various forms. The smells indicated that the main seasoning was salt and pepper. There wasn't much more of interest on the ground floor apart from a small fitness room.

This "slightly better than a college dorm" hotel reminded me of the one Marquize and I had first had sex in, which was another depressing memory, not least because it reminded me that I didn't have a boyfriend and that it had been a month since the last time I went out to a bar and got laid.

Back in the room, I checked the Internet to see if there were any gay bars in the area, but the closest one was six miles away, and even if I could get a cab there, I'd either have to go back to his place or bring him six miles out to this hotel, and if Altamont called early… no, I could wait. When this was over, I hadn't really thought about what I'd do, but maybe I could rejoin the team in Port City. There'd be plenty of opportunity there.

* * *

What I'd pictured when I thought about where I was going to give testimony was a big courtroom like in the movies, with an attentive jury, a court stenographer taking down my words, and a solemn judge in black robes looking down on me as I faced Frio to my right and Altamont to my left. I would glare back at the ferret as I condemned him with my words and he wouldn't be allowed to say anything to me.

It made me nervous, as I rode there in another Town Car, but nervous with a giddy anticipation. I'd get to tell him off, and maybe I'd throw in a few other things for good measure.

But when we arrived, Altamont met me at the door and shook my paw. "We're hopeful this will only take a few hours," he said. "Coach Young's attorney will be present but won't be allowed to ask you any questions. If she does, just ignore them. Both attorneys have to go through the FBI agent."

"Oh." I rubbed my muzzle and followed him along a chilly, Neutra-Scent-soaked hallway. "What if the judge says I have to answer them?"

Altamont laughed shortly and then resumed his serious demeanor. "There's no judge, Rocky. This isn't a trial. It's a sworn deposition. You're going to be in a little room with both attorneys, an FBI agent, and a notary, and your statement's going to be recorded. I've got it all written down here." He tapped the briefcase he carried. "You'll have time to read it through and then sign it, and then you'll read it aloud, and then the agent will ask you some questions if he thinks anything's unclear."

I said, "Oh, I see."

My ears must have shown my disappointment. "Did you think it was going to be a full trial? No, that's far more complicated than we need to get at this stage. He's already cooperating so we're confident we can get a plea bargain. And of course, the TIU just needs his statement about the other people involved." He held up a large paw. "The people above him, not the tennis players who were his 'victims.'"

I heard the quotes around that last word and felt the need to justify myself. "They're not going to do anything with anyone else. He was the one who got them into it."

"We'll see about that." Altamont sighed. "Once a cheater, always a cheater, I'm afraid. Except for your one friend who's out of tennis already." He gave me a sideways look.

"He was…" I didn't know how to explain Frio's hold over Braden and Marquize without getting into a whole other matter. "He was very charismatic in his own way."

We arrived at a door that was only distinguished from the other doors along the hallway by the number plate on the door that read "109." Altamont preceded me in and waved me to a chair set up with a mike on a stand. One person, a black-furred squirrel, sat at a small desk, and three more chairs remained empty.

"They'll be here soon," Altamont assured me.

"Aren't you staying?"

He shook his head. "Unfortunately, I have a lot of…" I wasn't even trying to hide how much I wanted a friendly face in the room, or even a used-to-be-friendly face. "Sure I will." He indicated the floor area near my chair. "I'll stand here with you."

"I'm sure one of the attorneys will let you borrow their seat." My attempt to be funny fell flat.

"If I get tired, I'll bring another chair in from down the hall." He waited until I was seated and then adjusted the mike. As he touched it, though, the squirrel jumped out of his seat.

"Please don't touch that, sir, let me make the adjustments." His jumpy manner, very squirrel-like, reminded me of Danver, but unlike my friend, he didn't say another word as he adjusted the mike with long, delicate fingers.

Altamont produced my statement, which was three pages long and took me about ten minutes to read through silently. In that time, the other two attorneys showed up, a lemur in a beige suit and a chubby raccoon in a dark blue one. Lastly, the FBI agent joined, and he looked right out of a movie: a slender maned wolf in an impeccable grey suit who sat, watched me carefully, and didn't utter a word.

The statement went through my experience in very dry, legal terms. Everything checked out factually, based (I guessed) on my conversations with Altamont and the texts Frio and I had exchanged. So at the end I asked Altamont for a pen so I could sign it.

Then I had to read it aloud, and that took about twenty minutes because I had to keep stopping to take drinks of water. When it was over, the raccoon and lemur took turns talking to the agent, and he was the one who'd decide whether to ask me questions to clarify my testimony. "How did you know to approach Coach Young?" was the first question.

"He'd offered me help at Palm Gables," I said, "and helped me deal with a phone bill. But also…" Here I paused. Marquize had suggested Frio, but I didn't want his name to come up. However, Frio had already told them about some of his other contacts; if he'd mentioned Marquize then maybe they would end up talking to him and if he remembered and told them…

I didn't want to lie, that's what decided me. "Another Palm Gables friend told me that Frio had offered to help him with money problems. I guess that's just what he liked to do."

They conferred, and I thought I heard the lemur ask the agent, "what friend?" But when the maned wolf turned back to me, all he asked was, "Had you discussed the possibility of earning money with Coach Young at any point prior to the first date mentioned in your statement?"

"No," I said. "Well, wait. My first year at Palm Gables I got a huge phone bill from talking to my sister, and he set me up with a warehouse job to help pay it off."

"And how old were you then?"

"Fourteen."

The agent made a note and then conferred with the attorneys. I caught the phrase "pattern of behavior," but they didn't ask about the warehouse job again.

The rest of the questions were easy, if occasionally asking me to recall details that I didn't have right at my fingertips. Finally the agent said, "No more questions," just under two hours total since I'd come in the building.

I got up, as did the attorneys, and the maned wolf stood casually between us until the attorneys had filed out of the room. The squirrel who'd adjusted the microphone notarized my statement, then took it with him and left in the company of the wolf, leaving only me and Altamont.

"There you go," he said with a sigh. "You're all done. I know it's been a burden on you and again, I and the sport of tennis greatly appreciate the sacrifice you've made."

"You're welcome." He had his paw half-out, so I extended mine and shook it. "Thanks for keeping my friends out of it."

He nodded. "If you want, we can fly you to Port City to see the rest of the tournament."

I considered that. "How long can I stay at the hotel?"

"It's booked until Friday," the cougar said. "If you need it extended, you can call me, but I'd encourage you to rejoin your friends as soon as possible. Put this behind you."

"You're probably right." I sighed. "I'll look up flights tonight and try to get out by Wednesday or Thursday."

"I look forward to watching your progress through the ranks." He smiled at me, the biggest smile I'd gotten from him since I'd arrived.

* * *

The hotel had cable, which meant that I could watch the States Open, an experience both exciting and depressing. My friends and I often gathered to watch the majors, and we joked about the time when we wouldn't be able to watch them anymore. Because we'd be in them, you see. And here I was with the chance to have been in one, and not only was I stuck watching it again, I wasn't even with my friends.

So that's probably why I called Marquize.

"You watching the States?" he said.

"Yeah." I wasn't sure how much to tell him. Altamont had said that there'd be some small public statement after the States Open, so I probably had to wait until then. "You?"

"On and off. I mean, I like it, but Craig keeps asking if I know any of the guys, or wants me to give him insights, so I watch it on my phone when he's working."

"How are things going with you two?"

He paused there, maybe trying to remember if he'd told me that they were dating. "Uh, you know, good, pretty good."

"Good." I sighed. "Hey, can you keep a secret?"

He snorted. "You should know that. Uh, I mean yes."

Knowing Marquize, I think that at first he was thinking about us being a couple, and then realized that I would think first of the secret he'd kept from me. I guess enough time had passed that the anger, though it flickered, wasn't visceral anymore. "They arrested Frio."

He sucked in a breath. "For the…"

"Gambling."

"Oh." A little disappointed, maybe.

"Better than nothing, though."

"Yeah. For sure. How do you know? I mean, why is it a secret?"

"Oh, I, uh, I helped. You really can't say anything about that. I think the arrest is going to be public in a couple weeks, but I don't know about…anyway, I helped catch him."

He was quiet for a little bit, digesting that. "That's awesome, Rocky. I mean, really."

"Thanks." And it really did help to have someone say that. "So you think Wilkerson can beat Xaili?"

We talked tennis for another twenty minutes, and it was a very normal and pleasant conversation. When I hung up, I lay back on the bed. Tennis was over for the night, so I turned it to a dumb movie, and within ten minutes I was asleep.

Chapter Ten

I never did see Frio all the time I was in Potomac. I didn't want to, but I also kind of did. Still, it never got to the point that I went and asked Altamont about it.

The cougar didn't call me until the day I was about to leave. Wanted to make sure I was okay, and to read me the small letter he was writing to my manager: "Dear Mr. MacDougal: I'm writing to apologize for taking Rocky away from the States Open. He was assisting the Tennis Integrity Unit in a very serious matter, and I'm pleased to say that his help has resulted in one arrest, many potential leads for future arrests, and in general has made the game of tennis safer and cleaner for everyone. You should be very proud of him."

"Thanks," I said. "Can you also tell him that it was your idea I not tell him?"

He laughed. "I'll do that. Enjoy the next week of the States. It should be a good one."

"Can I tell people about what I've been doing finally?"

He clicked his tongue. "I'd prefer you tell as few people as possible. I know the tennis world; this is going to get out. But the quieter we keep it, the easier it might be to do things like this in the future."

The flight to Port City lasted only a little longer than the punk-pop album Aliq had given me a few weeks ago. Listening to it made me wonder whether our friendship would survive this fracture. If I couldn't tell him what I'd done, would he think me unreliable forever? I would have to tell Aliq at least, I determined, and it'd be a secret we could have. He was my doubles partner and a good friend, and I didn't want to lose him.

Thus determined, I landed in Port City for the first time and immediately got lost in the airport. I'd counted on my ability to read signs and the general well-marked layout of public places to guide me around unfamiliar airports, but the Port City airport was over-marked, and I followed the wrong exit sign to a different terminal, and then had to find my way back to my original terminal to get my bag, and by that time the bag had been taken off the belt and put to the side, but I didn't know they did that, so I spent a few panicked minutes wandering around the bag claim area looking for anyone in uniform and wondering how I was going to replace all my rackets.

Finally, bag in paw, I grabbed a taxi to the hotel where my friends were staying and where, I hoped, there was a room for me. I picked up my phone in the cab to call Lochen and saw that I had a voicemail from him.

He'd gotten the letter. He went on and on about how proud he was, how if he'd only known I was working a dangerous undercover mission for tennis he wouldn't have been angry at all but he understood I couldn't tell him. It was nice at first and then I started to get uncomfortable as it went on. I mean, I'd heard the letter Altamont was sending him. It didn't say anything about…

"It's like you were on Mission Impossible!" He said that in the voicemail, and again when I called him. "How much can you tell me about it? Or did they close the file on it? Do I have to wait twenty-five years?"

I didn't know what would happen in twenty-five years. "No," I said. "It was very ordinary and I didn't use any 'spy gadgets'." I wasn't counting Altamont's special app, and in fact I didn't even think of that until after. "Sorry."

"It's still incredible." He drew out the rolling "R" in that word longer than I'd ever heard it. "I never had a client involved in under-cover work. Just tell me, was it about drugs?"

"No."

"Ah well. Still!"

I cleared my throat. "Do I have a room at the Carstead Arms?"

"Course you do. Danver's got a spare bed. Had an odd number of people and we didn't book anyone else. I didn't know you'd be coming but I can let him know."

"Sure. Do you know where they watch the tournament from?"

"Last week we went out to the matches, but tickets are harder to come by this week. I'm at the matches, Aliq is over by the doubles, and I think Danver is back at the hotel."

Probably trying to hit on ladies at the hotel bar. "Thanks," I said. "I'll drop my stuff off at the hotel and see who I run into."

"I'll call the hotel right now and put your name on Danver's room and then I'll call to let him know. See you tonight!"

I didn't see Danver, as it happened, but my name was on a room and so I put my stuff away and then turned on the TV to watch matches. I stayed there until Danver came back, and once again I was grateful for the squirrel's facility of conversation: he told me about all the matches they'd seen the previous week without once asking me where I'd been.

And when everyone else came back, clearly they'd all been warned as well. I realized it'd been probably a year since I'd seen Lochen in person; we did so much of our communication over the phone that my first thought upon seeing him was to wonder if he'd always been that old.

In any case, his happy personality remained the same. He hugged me when he saw me and his tail wagged I think the whole time we were hanging out that evening. "Since Rocky missed last week," he said, "I'll bring him to some matches tomorrow."

Nobody objected to that, and in fact they were all so happy to see me that I felt a little guilty about getting more perks on top of it. Even Aliq smiled, though he was pretty quiet.

When things had calmed down a little later, I asked if he'd take a short walk with me. We went outside into the warm, muggy night amid the smell of car exhaust and steak from the steakhouse next to the hotel. "I'm not supposed to talk much about what I was doing," I said. "But I can tell some people, and I want you to know."

Aliq's ears went back. "Ah," he said, "you don't have to tell me. I mean, I know it must have been important."

"It was," I said, "and I want to."

Over the next fifteen minutes I gave him a somewhat abbreviated version of what had happened. His amber eyes went round and wide and his ears folded back as he listened, and when I was done, he said, "Wow. That's…holy cow, Rocky. That's like, movie stuff."

"It's more boring than in the movies," I said.

"Doesn't sound like it." He opened his muzzle, hesitated, and then said, "There's just one thing I don't quite get. Why would he trust you so much after what, three years away from school? It doesn't sound like you were super close to him."

I remember that at this point we'd stopped next to a deli and the aroma of meat and cheese was so thick it made my eyes and mouth water. I'd already eaten but still wanted to stop in there for a sandwich. But instead I looked right at Aliq and said, "He hit on me in school and I never told anyone."

"Oh," he said, and then he thought about it some more and his ears went back. "Wait, like, hit on you like 'hey we should go out on a date sometime' or hit on you like grabbed your junk? Sorry, wait again, you were what, fourteen? Fifteen? Fucking hell. Why didn't you tell anyone?"

"Because," I said, "I was afraid…" And I didn't know how to say the next part, but he understood and I saw his understanding, and that made it easier. "I was afraid they'd think I'd asked for it. I was afraid they'd find out that I'm…"

He nodded. "So you are?"

"I'm…yeah." The third time, I got it out. "I'm gay."

I'd only told a few people in my life, so I was completely unprepared for Aliq to throw his arms around me and crush me in a hug. "I kinda knew," he said, "but it means so much that you told me. Anything I can do to help you, just let me know."

I hugged back and released him, and my tail wagged pretty hard then. "Thanks," I said. "I think I'm doing okay. But like, don't tell anyone?"

"Oh, shit, no, of course not." He gave a laugh that was more like a small giggle. "That's a lot of secrets for one night."

"Only two." I grinned back. "You have any secrets you want to tell me?"

He looked past me into the deli. "Yeah," he said. "We're not like, super-orthodox, my family, but we try not to eat a whole lot of pork.

With our diet and all it's easy. But right now I want a big mortadella sandwich."

I turned to the deli. "I've never had mortadella."

"All right. Come on in," he said. "We're doing this."

Look, it was probably just the night and the secrets and all, but Aliq and I took that immense deli sandwich over to a park and sat on a bench and each ate half of it, and that was the best sandwich I've ever had.

* * *

Watching the Port City matches with Lochen was a treat, and the only thing that could've made it better would have been to have Coach Keely there to give some more insight into breaking down the form of the various players. Lochen wasn't great at that, though he tried.

And in the afternoon, I got to see Braden play. There was no chance I'd be able to talk to him at this tournament. Even if I could use my status as a player to get into the locker room (I didn't think that players not registered could get into the locker room, though I'd never tried), I was sure he'd be mobbed by the press. As it happened, I saw him win a match to get into the quarterfinals, and from up in the stands I had a different view of his game.

As I watched, I imagined myself across the net from him, and as I had in the last match, I found myself anticipating what his moves would be. I still couldn't puzzle out how I knew that, but I absorbed myself in the problem so much that Lochen had to nudge me three times to ask if I wanted anything from the concessions.

I asked for a hot dog and away he went, leaving me to watch the cross fox on the sideline. Already up 6-3, 6-2, there didn't seem to be any reason for Braden to be concerned, yet he didn't look relaxed at all. I wondered if he still worried that Frio had a hold over him. Maybe he was supposed to double-fault during some match here, or do something else bettors could wager on, and he hadn't done it yet, or he had and was regretting it. I wanted to tell him that it was over, but I didn't want to do it over text. I'd wait until after the States

Open, at one of the slightly smaller tournaments where his and my paths intersected, and I'd tell him then.

That might be a long time to wait, though. I worried about it on and off over the next few days. Lochen took me to the quarterfinal matches, where I saw Braden lose to Milos Daryavic, a limber maned wolf who made a bunch of creative shots. Honestly, Daryavic was at the time the best player I'd seen in person, even though he hadn't won a major yet (and he would lose here in the final). I got to see a lot of his game that you couldn't see on TV, like the way his body shifted when Braden served. Not a lot, but I could see his weight move.

After that, I told Lochen other people could go to the semifinals and the finals. I was happy watching on TV now that I'd seen a few matches live. Lochen took me aside and said I had the most potential of the group and if I wanted to see more matches I should have priority, but that made me uncomfortable. I didn't feel like I'd earned anything yet. In fact, if not for me, Aliq and I would've been playing here. Never mind that more good came from missing it than playing in it. That seemed remote now that I was watching the best players in the world down there on the courts and hungering to be among them.

After Port City, we had a week off, which I spent up at Aliq's house. And while we were there, we got a call from Lochen. "Hey," he said. "Rocky, I've got some news that's going to mean a little extra work for you."

"That's fine. I'm just sitting around with Aliq." We were playing a video game, in fact, in Aliq's basement. The arctic fox had his ears perked up. "Can I put you on speaker?"

"Sure, sure. This involves him too."

"We have some extra work to do," I told Aliq, putting the phone on speaker and setting it down between us.

"Not Aliq," Lochen said. "Just you."

"Just me?" Aliq and I exchanged looks. He shook his head, not understanding either.

"See, you're going to have to take the States citizenship test," he said. "Because you and Aliq got an invitation to the Ocie Open and that'll make it easier for you to travel overseas."

"What?" I couldn't tell you whether Aliq or I said that, or if we both said it at the same time. I remember seeing the shock in his eyes turn to delight and thinking that it felt like I was looking into a mirror.

"You got in for singles, both of you for doubles. I'm going to book you in a few tuneups down there, so we'll fly down just after Christmas if that's okay."

"We?" Aliq pounced on that. "You're coming with us?"

"Can't let my best clients navigate a new country alone. Besides, I haven't been down in a while and it's good for me to go around the majors and see if anyone wants to change representation."

"We're going to a major? For real?"

Lochen laughed. "You thought the States was a one-time thing? Rocky, I'm booking you into the qualifiers for Champions next year. You're going to a lot of majors."

"I know, but…" I gulped. "When do I have to take this test? Do I have to study for it?"

"Probably, but I'm sure you know most of it already. This is a formality—honestly, if you'd waited another two years to get good you'd be a de facto citizen anyway. But we can't hold up your career for a formality, so I talked to my friend and we've got you set to take it over the Thanksgiving holiday. Where are you going to be?"

I looked a question at Aliq and he answered. "He's going to be here. Outside of Freestone."

"Great. I'll set up the test for Freestone, then. I'm sure they have a center there. Then we'll have to get you an expedited passport, should be no problem, and you'll be set to go first week of January."

"Just like that?"

"Just like that." He chuckled. "I'll send you some resources so you know what to study."

Aliq already had his phone out, and at this he held up a page that said, "Citizenship Test: What You Need To Know." I grinned and gave him a thumbs up. "Thanks," I said to the phone.

There were a few other things he wanted to tell us, while I sat on the couch and Aliq paced back and forth, tail wagging. When Lochen finally hung up, I stood up and Aliq threw himself at me with a huge hug, slapping me on the back.

"We're gonna go to every major next year!" he said.

"And the year after, we're gonna win one."

"You bet." He stepped back and gestured to the stairs. "Come on, let's go tell Mom!"

So we ran upstairs and told his mother, who hugged us both. I hung back as they called his father, because I had a wave of missing Ma very badly just then and I didn't want to spoil the occasion with sadness.

But later, I tried to call Ori. I didn't get through then, but a few hours later, at midnight, she called me back.

"I don't have any more news, Ro," she said.

"But I do." And I told her my news.

"Ro!" The delight in her voice set my tail to wagging. "I knew you'd get to another major and I'm glad they didn't waste any time. You deserve it."

"You don't know that." I relaxed back on the bed, smiling. "You haven't seen me play."

"No, but I hear about the results and I can check your ranking on the computer now, did you know? You have a page on the tennis site."

I recalled vaguely that someone had told us that would happen, but I didn't go check it that often. "Do they say nice things about me?"

"They list your tournament wins. You've won more doubles than singles."

"But still not that many of either."

"The wins will come."

"Not at the Ocie." I laughed. "But it's going to be a good experience. A whole new country! I'll have to study up on them."

"Study up on your own first," Ori said.

She was right, of course. After I hung up, wagging still from hearing her voice and having good news to share with her, I went right to the study materials Aliq and Lochen had found for me.

A lot of it I remembered from Palm Gables Civics, as Lochen had thought, and the rest of it seemed pretty easy to get through. The idea is that there are a hundred possible questions, which they give you the answers to, and the examiner will ask you ten of them at random. They're things like "What is the law of the land?" (The Constitution) and "Who is the head of the executive branch?" (The President). We also have to know who our president, senators, and representatives are, which means I needed to research those names for my declared residence, still in Pensa.

Aliq helped, and I was heartened when he said, "Whoa, I don't know half this stuff either. Glad I was born here."

"No kidding," I said, and he looked up with splayed ears.

"Hey, you're gonna do fine," he said. "Look, if it comes down to it, I'd rather have someone like you here—"

"I didn't mean that." I held up a paw. "I just meant it'd be a lot easier if I'd been born here."

"That's what I'm talking about, though." He spread his paws. "There's people who get angry about immigrants and stuff but look, you went through so much to get here, you're working so hard to stay here, and I just meant I'd rather have you here than some idiot who was lucky enough to be born here. Like me."

I laughed. "You're a good guy. I'm glad you were born here. And I'm glad I can finally be legit a States citizen. It feels really good, you know?"

"As long as you know the answers to the questions." He tapped the screen. "Let's go through a few more."

We had two more tournaments before Thanksgiving and I got to the semifinals in one of them. Aliq and I won that one in doubles too, adding another to our pages, I supposed. The other one didn't go as well, but we were playing against tougher competition and were proud of how far we got.

And then Thanksgiving came along and I had an amazing meal with Aliq and his family. By this time, I felt very much at home there, so much so that I didn't even mind the one minor drawback that I couldn't exactly go out to gay bars and hook up. Aliq did ask me about going out once, because he now understood what I was doing the one or two nights I went off on my own during tournaments, but it felt like I'd be guiding him around as a tourist. Besides, I wouldn't be able to wave and say good-bye if I did meet someone who wanted to take me home. Honestly, I was getting used to having sex on average once every two weeks, and I kept active enough that I didn't often find myself "achin' to bust a nut," as Danver apparently often did.

On Black Friday, while Aliq's parents braved the shopping malls, he drove me down to the citizenship test. I kept my eyes squeezed shut, but there were only two moments where his driving made me fear for my life, and then we were at the Homeland Security office. We waited about an hour and then my number was called.

Lochen had helped me fill out my application for naturalization, and the questions about my background were brief. Lunda was apparently not on the list of countries that raised flags. And when I talked about Ma's death after she worked to bring me over, my examiner, an elderly female skunk, made a choking noise and said, "Well, let's go right to the test." To my relief, she asked me ten easy questions. I didn't even have to worry about pronouncing the name of my representative, though I could've spelled it if pressed. When we were done, she said, "Congratulations," shook my paw, and told me there was a ceremony scheduled in an hour where I could take the Oath of Allegiance.

All of the work I'd done up until the ceremony had been very paper-heavy and felt more like homework than anything else. But the ceremony got me very emotional. Twelve of us stood in front of a judge who gave a short speech on the responsibilities we were accepting along with the privilege of calling ourselves States citizens, and it hit me that I was changing something about myself. "Where are you from?" people had asked me, and I always said, "Lunda." Now, perhaps, I would be able to say, "I'm from Lunda originally but now I'm from here."

We repeated the oath after the judge, and maybe it was just emotion, but a wave of warmth washed over me as he said, "Welcome, citizens."

We all shook paws and hugged after that. "I have waited three years for this," one female raccoon told me. A tall red deer said he'd feel more stable in the business he owned. A husband and wife rat couple hugged their kit, who'd been born here, they said, and now they knew they'd be able to stay with her.

And I thought to myself, one day I will stand in this room and listen to Ori take the oath, and I'll run up and hug her when it's done. I belong here now, and I know she does too.

Part Eight: Overseas (2014)

Chapter Eleven

Aliq and I didn't win our last tournament of the year, but we performed well enough to boost our points a little, keeping our team in the top 100 of doubles teams worldwide at #89 to end the year. I hit that milestone as well, the result of getting to the semis in that October tournament, and I ended the year at #98. Again, Aliq's mom asked if I wanted to go to church for Christmas and I was tempted, but I also didn't want to impose on them and I didn't know any of the churches around. A year farther removed from Ma's death, I felt more comfortable talking to her about how Ma and I had celebrated, and she suggested I tell the family as well.

So on Christmas morning, I sat at the breakfast table and told Aliq, his parents, and his aunt and uncle about the celebrations back in Lunda, the all-day pageant and the food, and then about our celebrations in Palm Gables, the simple decorations and the Christmas ham and the visits to church. I got a bit emotional, even though it had been over a year since Ma's death, and at the end of it Aliq's mom hugged me and said she would go out and find a nice ham for dinner once the supermarkets opened.

And they surprised me with a gift; I hadn't thought to get anyone anything, and Aliq and I had talked about it only enough to agree that we wouldn't exchange presents. But his parents had gotten me a little e-book reader like Aliq had, and a $50 credit to buy books on it. "You're going on a long plane flight," his mother explained, "and the battery on this will last longer than your phone."

It was sweet of them, and something I honestly hadn't thought about. I guess I knew the flight would be fifteen hours, but I thought I'd sleep or play games or something. I remembered mostly sleeping on the flight from Lunda, watching movies for a bit, talking to Ma and asking her over and over what the States would be like. One of our neighbors, a raccoon (I think? I remember his mask, but he might have been a ferret), asked where I was going and I told him proudly that we were moving to the States.

So I asked them for some recommendations, because I didn't know what books to read, and they picked out two for me. Then I looked for one about Lunda and found a science fiction book by a Lundanese author, which wasn't something I'd known had existed. Becoming a States citizen had nudged me to remember that I came from a different country, and that when it came down to it, I didn't know a lot about that country.

Aliq was reading a novel about a community of arctic foxes that moved from the north down to Taysha, and he said it was really good, so I bought that one too, and that didn't leave me with a whole lot of credit. It wasn't until the following year that I would discover that there were a whole lot of e-books selling for a dollar, or even free, so as we prepared for our trip down to Oceania, I had exactly four books to last me.

The week between Christmas and New Year's was spent with a good deal of packing and preparation. Aliq's father got more and more worried as the year drew to a close—not that he would say he was worried, but he took to poking his head into whatever room we were in and saying things like, "Hey, Aliq, did you remember to pack your knee braces?" His mom was also worried, but I didn't know until Aliq told me that she didn't usually hug him that often.

"You go away for months out of the year," I said as we were walking down to the closest tennis courts we'd found.

"This is to the other side of the world, though." He grimaced. "We're not big travelers. Our family vacations were anywhere we could drive in a day."

"I didn't travel much once I got to Pensa." I bounced a tennis ball on the sidewalk. "But I've loved seeing the country and I'm excited to get to see more of the world."

"Me too. And hopefully Gallia in the spring, and Anglia in the summer."

"Back in Port City in the fall."

We hit around, dreaming our dreams of getting into the majors, and our excitement stayed at a high level up through our trip to the airport. We flew out of Freestone to Crystal City, and from there we'd go on to Bourkeville, where the Ocie Open was located, so it would be a six hour trip followed by a fifteen hour one. There were plenty of movies on the flight to Crystal City, so I started the Lundanese book as we were taking off and then put it away to watch adventure movies the whole flight. During our three-hour wait in the Crystal City airport, though, I took the book out again and this time got engrossed in it, so much so that even when we were in the air and the much larger selection of movies was available, I kept reading the book until I finished.

It was then that I became aware of how uncomfortable our seats were. Aliq had been shifting around for a bit, watching his movies, and both our knees were drawn up. It didn't help that the people in front of us had reclined their seats all the way back, leaving us almost no room. We checked and saw that the people behind us had also reclined, but we still felt bad about putting our seats back. When you fly frequently, you learn how intrusive it is to the people behind you to recline your seat, so you try not to do it. It's easier on short flights than long ones.

Lochen, sitting with us, had put his seat back immediately. "You're young," he said. "You have the luxury of being uncomfortable."

But still, Aliq and I were both well over six feet tall, and the seats were not designed for that. On domestic flights, we'd flown often enough that we sometimes got upgraded to first class, but the upgrade on this flight would have cost money. So as we tried to arrange ourselves, Aliq leaned over to me. "On the way back," he said, "we tell Skinflint there to upgrade us to business class."

Our manager, whom we'd thought was asleep, flicked his big fox ears. "This trip's already costing us twenty thousand," he said. "You make more than thirty over that and we'll fly back business class."

* * *

So we disembarked in Bourkeville with moderately stiff legs, high hopes, and a modest goal—after all, we were getting almost fifteen thousand just for showing up for doubles. If we won two doubles matches, we'd get thirty-six thousand. I was getting three thousand six hundred for playing in the first round of qualifiers, and that payout more or less doubled at each round. So for getting to the qualifying final, I'd make fourteen and a half thousand, and if I won that match, I'd get thirty and secure us comfortable seats on the way home.

Before the Ocie, though, we had two small tuneup tournaments to play, both Champions tournaments in different cities. At the first, both of us came out slow in our doubles match, jet lag beating us before we'd even stepped onto the court. Fortunately, my singles match wasn't until the following day, when melatonin had given us one extra good night's sleep, and I was able to win that match and another the next day before falling to the world #40 two days after that.

It was just after that match that three people approached me in the locker room as I was sitting down, composing myself. I looked up, and it took me a moment to recognize Braden. His entourage was different here than it had been in the States, but they had the same forbidding demeanor.

I knew Braden was here, of course. He'd played opposite me once and I'd seen him in the locker room multiple times, but we hadn't spoken, nor exchanged anything more than a nod. But now he came up and asked, "Hey, you got a minute?"

I spread my paws. "Nothing but time until next week."

"Heh, yeah." He waved to the kangaroo and fox—no, maned wolf—behind him. "Give us a minute, guys."

They retreated back to the room outside the locker room. "No witnesses?" I joked, even though a few guys I knew were changing and talking just across the room.

Braden didn't laugh. "They don't need to hear this." I waited for him to sit next to me, but he remained standing, one paw rubbing his muzzle. "I heard you did some work with the TIU."

My skin got hot and my fur prickled. The "no witnesses" comment didn't seem as funny now. He could for sure get in a few good punches before anyone could come to help me. "Uh…yeah."

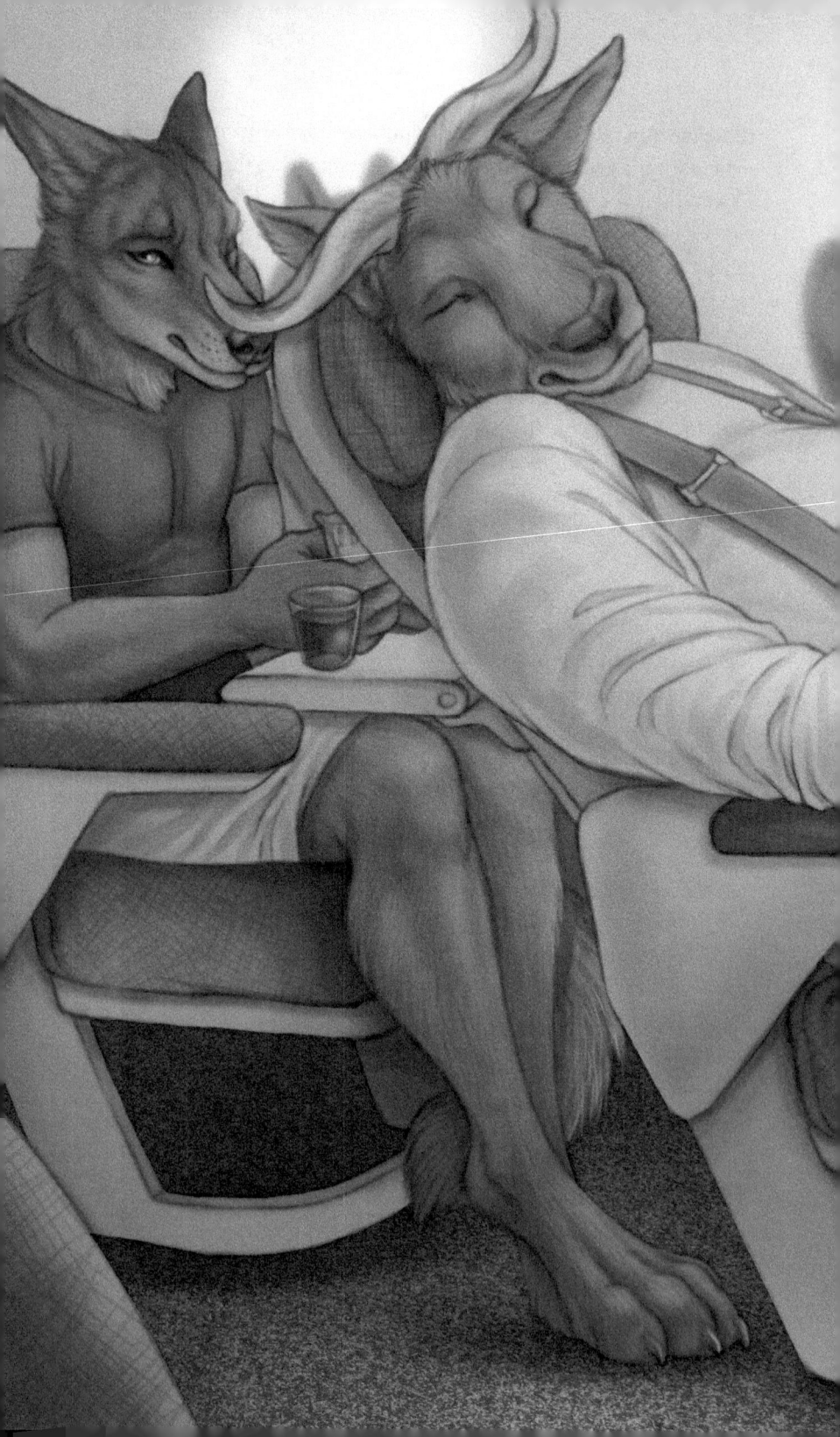

"They called me. I'm being fined for 'activities counter to the interests of tennis.'"

"Hey," I said. "I'm sorry—"

He stopped me with a raised paw. "Nothing's being reported about it. They said that *he's* been arrested and his operation stopped, and they understood that I was under some coercive obligation but still I did things I shouldn't have." His eyes drifted to a point above my right ear, perked as it was to listen to him. "They're right. I'm happy to pay the fine and get it over with."

"Oh," I said.

"You free for dinner?"

The invitation came brusquely, and only then did he drop his gaze to meet mine. "I, uh, I don't have plans. I mean, I'm here with my—" I shook my head to clear my thoughts. "Yeah. Sure. Uh, are they," I nodded toward the locker room entrance, "coming too?"

He grimaced. "Nah. You got phone service here? Number still the same?" I shook my head. "Okay, jeez," he said. "You need to get on an international plan."

"Never needed to before."

"There's a place on the other side of the park called The Tea Club. Can you find it?"

"Sure." Everyone spoke English here and I'd been finding my way around easily.

"Seven o'clock?" I nodded, and he raised a paw again. "All right. See you there."

The Tea Club had this old Anglic style to it, aged wood and polished brass and old timepieces and ship's instruments on the walls, the kind of place that you might imagine sailors came home to a couple hundred years ago. When I commented on the décor, Braden glanced around as if noticing it for the first time. "I came here last year before the tournament," he said with a low growl. "I like it because it's got all these small rooms and shit and it's hard for people to get a picture of you."

We were in a booth, but with solid dark wood walls behind each of us. The only view anyone had into the booth was from the side where the waitress came to take our order. When Braden leaned back against the booth, I didn't think anyone would be able to see him from outside. He thought that too, obviously; he stayed back against the wall for most of our dinner.

The other thing I remember is that that place didn't have air conditioning, so I spent the evening panting lightly. Braden, somehow, didn't, but all he said was, "You'll get used to the heat."

We talked about the upcoming major, a little about the competitors we knew, and then the conversation lagged. "So," I said, "how big was the fine?"

"Nothing I can't afford." His eyes slid sideways and then back. "Nothing that isn't worth what it means."

"Knowing that guy's locked up?" I guessed, counting on my own experience.

He canted his ears to one side. "I was going to say 'freedom,' but that's also good, I guess."

"Freedom?"

His ears slid further back and his eyes narrowed. "What did you end up doing with the TIU?"

"How did you hear it was me?" I countered. "They weren't going to publicize that."

A smile fluttered around his lips and then vanished. "I know people who know things. I asked around."

"Oh," I said, "Well, my friend Marquize—the cheetah—" Braden nodded. "Got caught up with him." I had to pause, feeling again the twinge of guilt. Marquize had done it for me. "And I was fed up. Just tired of this guy fucking up my life and the life of everyone I cared about. So I ratted on him, and the TIU asked if I'd pretend to need money so we could catch him in the act. And, uh, we did." I spread my paws. "That's it."

"Must have been a little rough," Braden said. "But exciting. Spy kinda stuff?"

"Kinda." I grinned. "There were moments. But I had to miss the States Open. That sucked."

He frowned at that. "You were invited to a major and you skipped it?" He was playing with his fork, tapping the wooden tabletop and tracing the grain of the wood, but now put it down to give me his full attention.

"I wasn't going to win," I said. "There'd be others."

"Of course there'll be others. But being in a major, the spotlight, the crowds...you need to get used to it. So you'll do that here instead of there. Not that it's not sometimes okay to skip a major," Braden went on, "but the States...travel's cheap, you're the home country."

"Officially now," I said with some pride, and told him about the citizenship test.

"Congrats." But he looked bored with it.

So I went back to the TIU case. "It was just timing. They needed my testimony right when the Open was happening."

"Well." He studied his fork. "I appreciate it, because I don't know if I'd have skipped my first...first?" I nodded. "First major. Just to put some dick in prison."

"Seemed important to do." I wanted to tell him that I had asked them not to publicize his involvement, but that felt like bragging and things were going well anyway.

So we had our dinner and moved back into talking about the people on the tour. It was casual and fun, and Braden shared some stories of people who reminded me of other people I knew. I asked him how things changed when he won a major, and he scowled. "For one thing, there's an entourage now. Mostly they're fine, but sometimes I need to ditch them. Like if I want to have a quiet dinner alone. And then there's paparazzi. It was so weird the first time someone randomly took a picture of me and it got published in some blog online. Now I'm used to it. Still annoying, though."

"I can imagine." Though really I couldn't.

"You won't have to imagine for long. Couple years, it'll happen."

I glowed a little inside but acknowledged the comment with a quick, "Thanks."

When the waitress brought the check, Braden snagged it. "I'll get this," he said. "You're still starting out and this trip is expensive enough."

"Thanks." I leaned back. "It was good."

"It's fine." He gave his card back to the waitress with the check.

"Excuse me." The willowy thylacine leaned over. "Are you Braden Longacre?"

Braden nodded, his ears going back. "Who's asking?"

"Couple gents outside." Her accent was thick. I liked it. "Asked if there was a young cross fox and if I'd let them know when he was coming out. Had their cameras with 'em."

The fox gave me a look, eyebrows raised. He pulled out a few bills and peeled off a hundred dollar one. "Think you could sneak us out a different door?"

The thylacine took the bill and pocketed it. She ran his card through the processor she carried with her, and when Braden had signed the receipt, she said, "Follow me."

She led us past the bathrooms and through a small kitchen. "They might be lookin' at the back door," she explained as she waved us through, "but the owners live above the restaurant and this hall-way here goes up to their apartments and out..." She shut the door to the kitchen behind us and pivoted to her left, where she threw back the lock on a thick wooden door. "To the park."

"I'll go first," I said, and took a step out. I didn't see anyone loi-tering on the street, let alone anyone with a camera, so I beckoned Braden out.

"Thanks," he said to the waitress, and then hurried out onto the street with me. "You might want to head back a different way if you don't want to be caught in a photo."

I was going to say that it was fine, but then I realized it was a hint, and decided to take it. "All right. Thanks for dinner."

"Yeah. Like I said, I appreciate what you did. And...how you did it. Could've been a lot worse for me."

I tilted my head. "Well," I said slowly, "I didn't think it was fair that any of the people he sorta-blackmailed should be ruined any further."

His ears stayed back, but the hint of a smile played around the corners of his mouth again, and this time it stayed. He gave me a quick nod, and then pulled his hood over his head and hurried around the corner.

Chapter Twelve

We flew down to Bourkeville soon after that, where Aliq and I prepared for our first major. From the hotel Lochen had booked, we walked about ten minutes through the heat to get to the complex, two entire city blocks adjacent to a large park. What intimidated us was not the size of the grounds—Port City's were bigger—but rather walking into the registration area, in a large hall with huge posters of past champions. We got our passes under the gaze of Doppel and Indiro, staring out past their rackets, and walked down to the locker room past the glass case that contained the singles and doubles trophies we'd be playing for. Aliq nudged me and we slowed down to look at them, which caused Kieran Lubovic, the fennec, to pat me on the shoulder and say, "One day, mate."

I figured Aliq and I could do pretty well in the doubles, especially since we didn't have to play through a bunch of qualifying rounds. He served as my practice partner during the singles qualifiers, the first one of which would be played the day after registration.

The tune-up tournament had been rough because of the heat and the jet lag, but it had been two weeks since then. Still, when I went out for my first match, the temperatures were approaching 38 C (100 F), and the heat felt more intense than I was used to from summers in the States. We were surrounded by attendants and taken care of better than I'd been at any other tournament I'd attended—there were piles of fresh, clean towels; there were people to take the dirty towels; the locker room smelled fresh and clean and not like disinfectant; a hundred other little things that made me feel important. My opponent, native to Oceania, seemed unfazed by the heat and the pampering and rolled over my lackluster game in the first set.

The prospect of going home without winning a single set at my first major panicked me. Come on, I told myself, I'd dealt with heat before, and the court was the same as every other court I'd played on. So I drank a good deal of water during the break between sets and got one of the attendants to bring me an ice cube to hold on my tongue. That kept me cool and refreshed, and my serve responded in the second set. I won that one and the third, and then realized that the match wasn't over. I was up two sets to one, which in every other match I'd played in my life would be enough to win. Here, I had to go back out and keep playing.

What motivated me in that fourth set, besides wanting to win, of course, was the knowledge that if I lost, I would have to play yet another set. Fortunately, my opponent wasn't good enough to force a fifth, and I won the match. It was just a qualifying match, but it was a win at a major tournament. I found that as I packed up my equipment, I couldn't stop smiling.

Aliq and Lochen met me in the locker room to celebrate. "Hey," Aliq said with a grin, "three more wins to business class."

* * *

Two more days, two more matches. I played a rabbit from Oceania and a red panda from Kathma, and though the panda took me to five sets, I beat them both. The heat didn't bother me and I was enjoying playing to the crowds. Every time Aliq and I practiced, he gave me encouraging advice, and though Lochen spent the days walking around giving his card to players in the qualifiers, he found time to tell me how well I was doing.

With the benefit of hindsight, I know that I got cocky, but at the time I felt like I'd been ranked too low for months, not realizing that a lot of the qualifying field at an international major is made up of people around or below my level who play the equivalent of the Challenger circuit in their home countries, players I never see. So in effect the qualifying rounds of a major sometimes feel like the last few rounds of a Challenger tournament. I'd won Challenger tournaments, and I was doing well here in the qualifiers, but I wasn't prepared to face Sanjay Tarraga, a Tasmanian devil (a "tazzie," the locals called them), in the finals.

Sanjay served as well as anyone I'd faced, and it took me most of the first set to figure out his rhythm and patterns. He didn't seem to have that problem with mine, making all of my service games competitive. He broke my serve on a beautiful cross-court stroke, and I couldn't gain any traction on his serve. I'd get it back into play most of the time, you understand—I'm a good returner—but I always seemed to be a step in the wrong direction when we started to rally, and he remained in control of the point, moving me around the court. I play good defense, but you can only keep that up for so long.

After losing the first set 6-3, though, I found my footing. I spent the break thinking about the points I'd lost, the rallies where I was forced into defending. There, I thought, and there, and there. Feet to the left six inches, back toward the baseline more to give me an extra half-second to react. I closed my eyes and visualized the movements, saw myself making them over and over, and went into the second set more confident.

I would've won that second set if not for two net cord bounces. The first one happened in my third service game, when Sanjay had been returning as well as I had. I'd hit a great lob that he had to sprint to get back to, and I'd run up to the net anticipating a weak return. But he wasn't dumb; he hit the ball hard, and I had to lunge to one side to get a racket on it. He had no chance of getting back to the net, so I tried to tap the ball over, and it hit the net, wobbled, and fell back on my side. That made it 30-40 instead of 40-30, which didn't cost me the game, but I smoked an ace past him on the next point that would've won the game if I'd gotten the bounce. Instead we went to deuce, and after I'd won an ad point and been knocked back to deuce twice, Sanjay got the advantage when I sailed a forehand long and finished his service break with a great return off of my dispirited serve.

The second net cord bounce came with him up 5-4 and serving for the set. I had a break point at 30-40, and we'd settled into a baseline rally. I was trying to keep it to his backhand just as he was trying to work around to mine, so I hit it to the ad court sideline.

He stretched and stroked the ball back, right into the net cord. It bounced up into the air, and if it had landed on his side of the court we'd be even again and I could've hoped for a tiebreak or an outright 7-5 win. Instead, it came down—by one inch—on my side. I started running as soon as I saw the bounce, got my racket on the ball, but flipped it right into the net.

So I lost the second set 6-4. But this was a five-set match, so losing two sets didn't mean I lost. I was determined to take advantage of that chance, and I think Sanjay might have been affected by the heat in the third set. Whether it was my determined, aggressive play or the weather, or maybe that I was getting more used to his play, I got good looks on his serve in almost all his service games and broke him twice, making up for the one time he broke my serve.

I won 6-3 and went into the fourth set with renewed confidence. Sanjay recovered from whatever had afflicted him in the third, and the result was the best set of tennis I played in Oceania. We had a 34-shot rally, and one of the sequences from it made the blogs: Sanjay lobbed it over my head as I came in to the net; I ran back and flipped the backhand for what should have been a clean winner, but the tazzie somehow got there and flicked it at a sharp angle across the court; I sprinted and at full extension tapped the ball over the net; he ran up to tap it back; I hit it at him; he went for the lob again; I ran back to the baseline with plenty of time this time and hit it down the line; he lunged and got it back over the net; I was already running forward and this time he was too far to one side and I hit it to the open corner for a winner.

(What they said on the blog was, "Look at new States citizen Rocky N'Guwe showing off his chops down under! Look out for this jackal in 2014." I might have watched it a few times on the way home.)

We went to a tiebreak in the fourth and I won when Sanjay netted a forehand. So I felt confident going into the fifth set, but there the heat caught up to me. I'd drunk enough water, I was sure, so maybe it was the accumulation of all the previous matches, the five sets, or the fact that the sun had moved to be right on the backs of my ears. Whatever the cause, those tiny traces of fatigue I'd noticed in Sanjay in the third set now happened to me. One step slow here, one half-second slower turning the racket. Everyone has those sets—Braden had one at this very tournament, in fact, in the match he lost to DeSantos—and you just hope the timing isn't bad. Here it was: I lost the qualifying final in five sets.

"Good match," Sanjay said, shaking my paw, and I echoed the sentiment. Then he went off and raised both arms in the air, and I walked back to the locker room to the hollow comfort of Aliq reminding me that we had a doubles match in two days and we could still win ourselves a business class ride home.

We expected to win that one, but I wasn't up to form and Aliq, though he played very well, couldn't do enough to make up for it. So we lost to a pair of kangaroos who offered to take us out for a drink after and show us the town. Well, we didn't have any more matches to play, and the legal drinking age here was eighteen, not twenty-one, so we had a few beers. Both Aliq and I stopped when we got buzzed—neither of us strangers to booze despite being too young—but the roos got completely trashed. They put their arms around us and told us that it was a crime how the States society stopped us from learning how to drink at an early age, and then went on to complain about all the big cats coming to Oceania, "but you doggos are okay, we love you."

It was a fun night all in all, but as we walked home (after making sure that the roos got in a cab, both of them singing the fight song from a local rugby club), Aliq said to me, "I want to see their next match."

"Me too." I laughed. "Something tells me they'll be fine."

They were, winning in the next round before falling to the #23 seeded doubles team in the world. We didn't go out with them again, but they were always friendly to us in the locker room and whenever we met them at other tournaments. That was only at international events, though; they wouldn't come to the States until we were all four legal to drink there, they vowed.

* * *

Before our long, uncomfortable economy class flight back to the States, we had some business matters to attend to. Aliq and I went to as many matches as we could, because watching them live was better than on film, and the level of play was outstanding. Tickets weren't quite as hard to come by here as they were at the States Open, and as players we had access to tickets when the matches weren't sold out.

I still remember the final, where Alex Tempest won his fifth major over Li Xu, an athletic tiger with a nasty forehand. It wasn't a very good final—Tempest was heavily favored and won in straight sets—but all the same I was thrilled to be able to see it live.

When we weren't watching tennis or practicing, we were playing tourist in Bourkeville or being dragged to meetings by Lochen. With our tennis out of the way, he wanted to get us more endorsements, and he used that clip of me in the blog to woo some potential sponsors. "The future of tennis," he called me, omitting the "States" part for the international companies.

It was at one of those meetings that I got a rather large surprise. Lochen had set up a meeting with the people from One Two Three, the ones who'd put me in their international campaign and who'd been sending me shorts for a couple years now. The money from that expanded campaign had helped move along Ori's path to the States, and so when we all sat down around the polished wooden table, I asked Lochen if I could speak first.

The red fox nodded, so I addressed the marketing director, a portly pangolin in a trim blue jacket and skirt. "I just wanted to say thank you," I said. "I know it wasn't intentional, but your campaign from a couple years ago, the extra five thousand, that was really critical in trying to get my sister home."

She brightened and gave me that sort of smile that happens when you stumble across an unexpected piece of good luck. "I'm so glad! So your sister is home?"

I explained a little of Ori's situation, the different stages and how at every stage there were expenses, and she nodded. "I wish you much luck then. It's funny, though, that you thank us."

"Not at all." I thought that perhaps her English and my English were creating misunderstandings. "I know you didn't know about the situation, but you helped me solve one part of it."

"No," she said, "I understand that. I mean only that the campaign almost did not happen."

Lochen leaned in here. "Why not?"

She turned to her assistant, a lemur so tall that even sitting down the pangolin had to look up to her. "Zasha, help me remember. We had talked about this campaign for six months? Eight months?"

"Eight months, Ms. Ryamur." The lemur spoke so demurely that I had to focus my ears to hear her.

"Yes, eight months." The pangolin returned her attention to me. "We want very much to do it, but there is no..." She described a large circle with her thickly clawed paws. "Big center person."

"Superstar?" Lochen offered.

"Yes." She pointed. "Big superstar. We talked to six, ten, twenty players."

"Thirty-one," Zasha near-whispered.

"Thirty-one players. One Two Three is not well known outside the States. My job is to change that."

"Sales have increased sixty-eight percent in the last fiscal year," Zasha recited.

Ms. Ryamur beamed. "So I do a good job. But this campaign, what happens is that a superstar calls *us*. He had said no, now he calls back and says yes, he wants to do the campaign, but also he thinks we should include young players in the campaign."

I'd never actually seen the One Two Three ads. I just knew Lochen sent them pictures and video, and I kept getting shorts. I guess they'd all aired outside the country. "Ah, that's really cool," I said. "Who was it?"

"You, of course, and several other players. And he was even interested in how much we would pay you! We wanted three thousand but he thought five was more fair." She waved one of those thick paws. "He is the important part. The rest is small."

"No, I mean, who was the star?" I thought I knew; only one high-profile tennis player had known I needed money, had talked me out of the only way I could think of to get it. But I wanted to hear the pangolin say it.

She blinked at me, either not understanding my words or why I had said them. I explained: "I never got to see—this is the first time I've been out of the country."

"Oh!" She laughed. "Zasha, show him."

So the lemur pulled out a tablet and searched through it for a minute while I wondered why it wouldn't be easier for her to just say a name. But Zasha was good at her job, so I only had a second to wonder that before she turned the tablet around and showed me a short video with cheery music playing.

There were a bunch of young players, and there was my video, with me positioned so the logo on my shorts was visible. The voiceover was in a different language—Xaiqinese by the sound of it, though I was no expert—but they said "One Two Three" in English.

And there at the end was a cross fox in a One Two Three shirt, with a racket in one paw and a tennis ball in the other. "It's what I wear," Braden Longacre said, with foreign characters shining across the screen below him.

* * *

My meeting with One Two Three resulted in a new endorsement deal, better than the old one but still not spectacular. Getting into the first round of a major would carry some financial perks, but I had made enough of a name for myself that the company felt confident making me a larger part of their campaign. There were no campaigns planned in Africa anywhere, but jackals were also native to areas of the Middle East where tennis, and more importantly, athletic clothing, was popular.

I wanted to see Braden again, to thank him for what he'd done years ago, but I didn't get the chance. He lost in the quarterfinals and didn't respond to my text asking if he'd have time for a drink.

So I explored Bourkeville with Aliq and watched tennis with him and Lochen, and boarded a flight back to the States, wincing as we settled into the economy class seats. At least on this flight, the beaver in front of me only put his seat back for a few hours, and Aliq and I were both able to sleep.

I thought a lot about Braden and what he'd done. On the one side, it wasn't that big a deal to him. A company had approached him about doing an ad campaign; he'd called them back. But on the other side, he'd refused at first, so he must have had a reason not to do it, and he'd put that aside to help me. He'd given them my name and made sure they paid me the amount I needed. That showed a lot of thought and caring that I wouldn't have associated with him. And yet, was I wrong to make that assumption? Braden had gone out of his way to talk to me more than once, had come to Palm Gables even though Frio was there. Did he secretly help a lot of young tennis players? If not, what was special about me?

Maybe there was nothing special about me. Maybe Braden did nice things when he had the opportunity, and because I came from a poor background, I'd given him multiple opportunities.

Or maybe it was that we were both gay, had both suffered the attentions of the predatory ferret. I knew that shared suffering could create bonds, as it had between me and Ori, and me and Marquize to some extent, but all the suffering we'd shared had been remote.

I felt close to him though, and I'd sought him out for advice on multiple occasions. Perhaps he'd been responding to that?

There was no way for me to know for sure. So I turned on a movie and fell asleep in the middle of it, and when I woke up the flight attendants were bringing us breakfast.

"Now," Lochen said as we were tucking into the tiny omelettes (Lochen had brought extra meals because two athletes and a foodie could not survive fourteen hours on the "miniscule" meals the airlines served, but we'd eaten all the spare food by this point), "it's time to talk about your future, you two."

"Okay?"

He speared a piece of egg, bit it from the end of his fork, and swallowed it all in one smooth motion. "You and Aliq are making enough now that you've paid off your debt to me, and your income's going to keep growing. I think it's time for you to hire a coach to work with the two of you full time."

I'd gulped down most of my omelette already, but I paused with the last bite on my fork. "Really?"

"You won't be able to get a top tier coach, but someone who only has one or two other clients would be a step up from Coach Keely's telephone coaching."

"All right," I said, tail wagging against the seat.

"Fantastic," Aliq agreed, and bumped my shoulder, and the cramped seats felt a little more free.

Chapter Thirteen

Back in the States, I got hit with jet lag worse than on the trip. I'd wake up in the middle of the night and lie awake for an hour; I'd be dragging my tail all day long. Fortunately, we didn't have any tournaments for a couple weeks, so we kept the practices loose and made sure to get lots of nutrition. Lochen told us that we'd readjust, but Aliq and I were miserable for a week and it really felt like we'd be that way for the rest of our lives.

Change comes gradually. I slept through the night a week later and got up a half hour early, but I didn't think anything of it until Aliq and I were talking over lunch. By the end of the second week, I felt back to normal again, just in time to take a plane out to Mount Karouan, a couple hours north of Chevali, for our first tournament back and one of the last Challenger events I'd play.

Going to a major tournament had changed me too, in small but noticeable ways. Crowds at Challenger events hadn't intimidated me for a year, but now I looked around at the stands and remembered playing in front of rows of seats that rose twice as high (only in the qualifying final, which had been on one of the major courts). Three sets felt like a narrower margin to win, so I came out with fire, determined to put my opponent away in two. And I'd learned a lot from my matches, especially the match with Sanjay, that served me well.

I remember Mount Karouan specifically because I won that first tournament back. Not as impressive as it sounds, because a lot of the big competition was at a larger Champions event in Crystal City, but a win is a win, and I'd only made it to the quarterfinals there the previous year. Only one match, the semifinal, seriously challenged me.

What's more, Aliq and I got to the semifinals. He too had improved after our one match Down Under, though I think it was less about what he'd learned and more about a determination to prove himself. Unlike Marquize, when faced with a doubles partner outstripping him, his response was to work harder.

I know that's not fair. Marquize had his own life to live, and he actually called me when I was back from the Ozzie. We talked about tennis and about Craig. He sounded relaxed and happy, describing sailing with Craig and hikes and some political activism. The life sounded completely foreign from what he and I had shared and yet he'd fitted himself perfectly into it. When I tried to talk to him about tennis, I felt the same way as when I talked to Aliq's family, trying to explain basic parts of life we all took for granted. More than once, Aliq and I had exchanged a look and a smile whenever one of us was forced to talk about the tour, knowing we weren't explaining it adequately and unable to do any better. I'd never felt that with Marquize, but now that I was at a different level and he'd been away from the game for a year, that gulf became harder and harder to cross.

And yet there was something between us still. I couldn't put a name to it—more than friendship but not love. I hung up with a smile, glad he'd found a place in the world where he fit.

For my part, I continued to define my own place. I rose in the rankings thanks to my wins at the Ozzie, climbing to 81. I thought I would make it to 60 easily within a month, but the next few tournaments I played were on the Champions circuit, where I was back in qualifying, and though I made it to qualifying finals in each of them, I only advanced farther in one. Finally, at the first tournament of March, I got to the quarterfinals of a small Champions tournament, which boosted my ranking to 68.

That was in Bautista, on the West Coast, and as I sat in the locker room after my semifinal loss, a fox came up to me and wagged a dark brown finger. "Rocky. It's been a while."

I'd known he looked familiar as he came up to me, but it wasn't until I caught his scent that I remembered. "Nashan?"

He spread his arms, showing off the navy blue tie dotted with yellow over his canary yellow short-sleeved shirt. "In the fur."

It took me a moment to reconcile the business casual fox with the player I'd intentionally lost to years ago, playing out the tail end of his career. Then I grabbed the proffered paw and shook it with vigor. "How the heck have you been?"

"Not too bad." His grin widened. "Don't have to ask how you've been. I saw you at the Ozzie."

"That blog post?" My ears flicked back, pleasantly self-conscious.

"Not a bad rally. You should've won that match, too. Had a couple chances."

"I know." I told him about Lochen's promise to fly us back business class, and he laughed.

"Next time you'll get that business class seat." He sat down next to me as I sat on the bench, tossing my dirty tennis clothes into my duffel bag. "If you don't mind me asking, who's coaching you now?"

"Sure. Daffyn Keely. Just part time, though. We get together when he has time." I started to say that Lochen was looking around for a new coach, but stopped myself. I didn't know what Nashan wanted yet.

"At this point in your career," the fox said, with a speech that sounded practiced, "you should have someone full time."

I nodded. "Kinda looking to make that move."

"Thought so." He smiled. "I'm getting into coaching. Not many clients yet, but I have a lot of experience and I come pretty cheap at this point in *my* career."

"Wow." The duffel bag strap slid from my fingers and I turned to look him right in the eyes. "You gave me a lot of good advice back in the day."

"You've done pretty well with it. Not thrown any more matches?"

"No," I said, and then scratched behind one ear. "Actually, there's a story…" Not many players were in the locker room; my victorious opponent had cleared out, and everyone else was either out watching the other semifinal or long gone from the tournament. One ferret at the other side of the locker room was changing for practice, probably. "But I shouldn't tell it here."

"Free for a coffee?"

I gestured at the duffel and the dirty clothes in it. "Got nothing else to do now."

So over coffee, I told him in sketchy detail about the Frio thing. His jaw dropped. "Seriously? That's amazing."

"I just did what I thought had to be done." Months removed, it was easier to be modestly noble now that I'd played in the Ozzie and the sting of missing out on the States was eased.

"As your coach, I would've been pissed. But as a former player…" He shook his head. "You took a big risk."

"Skipping the States? It'll come round again."

"Of course it will." He waved a paw. "I mean that you could've gotten caught up in the scandal. I wouldn't trust those TIU guys farther than I could hit a tennis ball."

"You can hit a tennis ball pretty far."

His ear flicked. "Not that far."

"Anyway, they were cool. Laid everything out for me and it all worked out."

"Mmm." We were on an outdoor patio with static noise curtains around it, but still he kept his voice down. "I'm glad it worked out."

"If you'd talked to them, you wouldn't have been worried."

"Maybe so." He smiled. "Either way, I still admire you for your commitment to doing the right thing. Now I really want to coach you."

"Still?"

"Sure. Find a player with good character and talent? Don't let them go. With some coaching—which I can provide—you can be a top ten player within, hm, two years."

My first reaction was to perk up my ears, but the giddy rush of hope didn't last longer than it took to make that motion. "Now I'm not sure I should believe you."

"Don't trust my eye for talent?"

"You're trying to get hired," I said. "You'll tell me anything I want to hear. A year would be too short and I could fire you right after. Two years gives you time to become entrenched, to promise me 'just a little longer' if it doesn't happen."

The corners of his mouth stretched back. "You've grown a lot in a couple years. I rest my case."

"I'm going to have to talk to my manager," I said.

"Of course." He winked. "Remind him that I pointed you to him in the first place. We haven't talked in a year or more."

But the thing was, even as we parted ways I was thinking about having him as my coach. I felt comfortable with him and he'd be cheap, and those were the two things I valued. I didn't know how Ma would've felt about him, but she hadn't liked any of my coaches.

So I called Lochen and asked.

* * *

Lochen was against hiring Nashan. "He hasn't coached anyone. You need someone proven who can take your career to its full potential."

"And how much will someone like that cost?" I countered. "Nashan can devote time to me. He's seen my game and I'm comfortable with him."

"You can afford it if the coach is part time."

"And Nashan would be almost full time."

"Almost?"

"Full time, he said full time. I was just hedging."

"So he doesn't have any other clients."

"I guess not."

Lochen sighed. "You can find a better coach."

"You don't know how good he is. He's just starting. He could be great."

My manager was silent. "And he's a red fox," I reminded him. "And your friend."

"We were friends years ago, and species isn't everything," he grumbled. "Do you trust him?"

"I—I think so."

"All right," he said. "If you're sure you trust him, I'll set up an interview with him."

And then I wondered, how could I be sure I trusted him? Our most significant interaction had been the time he'd yelled at me for slacking off so he could maybe win one last tournament. That had left me with a good feeling about his respect for the integrity of the game, as well as his ability to analyze someone's game just from watching them. Granted, most of my connection with Nashan was emotional, and while I remembered the views I'd had of his naked body, I also remembered he was married. You're not hoping something will happen, are you? I asked myself. No. Probably not.

"Set up the interview," I told Lochen. "And I'll set up a time to talk to him again myself to be sure."

The prospect of hiring a full-time coach felt like growing up to me, like taking another step on my way up. I'd miss Coach Keely, but he'd never felt as close to me as my friends who played every tournament with me, or even as close as Lochen, who'd started my career and helped me with personal matters, like when I needed to get tested at the clinic.

I told Aliq about Nashan, and though he had his own reservations, he was more excited than Lochen was. "My mom has a couple coaches on a list for me to look at," he said, "but a lot of those are aspirational, you know? The guy who coached Tempest, and Doppel is still coaching."

"Doppel the rat?" That brought back conversations with Paulie talking about the great old matches from the late 70s. "That'd be amazing."

"Maybe." Aliq grinned. "I mean, yeah. But why would he spare the time for a couple newbs? And if he has the time, if other guys aren't beating down his door, how good can he be? I kinda like the idea of a guy who just retired, who knows the modern game, and who's starting out so he's got a lot of investment in his first clients."

"You'd hire him too?"

"Oh sure. I need a new coach too, and it makes sense for us to have the same one, doesn't it?"

It did, I thought. "I'm going to interview him again. Why don't you come along?"

His tail wagged. "You think we could have him before the Gallic?"

I blinked and grabbed his shoulder. "We're going to the Gallic?"

"Oh, uh, I think so." He grinned. "Lochen told me he wants to call us about it tomorrow so I assume we got an invitation. We did okay, right?"

"Yeah, but it's a clay surface. They always tweak the rankings based on their surface."

"So what could it be about?"

Neither of us could come up with anything. So the next day, before practice, I went over to the hotel room Aliq shared with Caboll and we called Lochen.

The first thing we told him was that Aliq was also interested in Nashan as a coach. "That's fine," Lochen said. "I was going to suggest it anyway. And while we're on the subject, did you guys get along as roommates at the Ocie?"

"Sure." "Yeah." We spoke at the same time, turning to look at each other.

"If you want to start rooming together on tour, I can set that up. You're already going to different tournaments from some of the others so it'll be easier to do it that way anyway."

"Like the Gallic?" Aliq said it just before I could.

Lochen chuckled. "That's what I wanted to talk to you fellows about. Aye, that's coming up, and you haven't been invited to join, but I suspect you could get in as a wild card if you go."

"Cool!" I said, and we fist-bumped.

"Lutèce," Aliq said. "I've never been and always wanted to go."

"But I'm not sure that's the best thing for you."

This stopped us, our smiles frozen. Aliq spoke first. "Why not?"

"To be honest, we covered expenses at the Ocie, but not by much. And with all the tuneups and travel, it was a very good experience, but you're making steady progress at the American Challenger tournaments and I'd like to see that continue. I think next year maybe you'll be ready to do the international circuit, or maybe the year after, but I don't want to rush it."

We stayed silent. "It's your money," Lochen said, "and if you want to go, I'll arrange it. You want some time to discuss it?"

"Please," Aliq said.

He gave us some information about our flights for the next tournament, another Champions one that the other guys weren't going to, and then left us alone. We sat there in Aliq's room, Aliq on his bed and me on Caboll's, and for a few minutes we didn't talk, both of us thinking. "If Lochen says," I began.

"Yeah." Aliq nodded. "I really want to go to Lutèce. I mean, one of the reasons I wanted to play tennis was to see the world, and so far we've only really seen the States."

"We've got a lot of career left." I tapped my paws together. "We'll get to Lutèce for sure. Just maybe not this year."

He rubbed at his whiskers. "All right, then I guess we'd better practice to make sure we get invited next year."

* * *

A few days later, in the evening after my first match of that tournament, I got a text from Braden. It just read, *Dinner?*

So I responded yes and begged off dinner with Aliq, which was easier now because he assumed I was running off to a gay bar. Knowing how Braden liked his privacy, I couldn't tell Aliq that that's who I was meeting, even though I felt guilty about keeping it secret from him.

Braden picked the place; he was the one most worried about privacy. The little dark Sonoran restaurant behind a strip mall set off my warning alarms as I scanned the half-empty dining area, the gaudy decorations, the peeling sign out front. But the moment I stepped in, delicious aromas of beans and spicy sauces flooded my nose and for a moment I stood there, a bit tipsy. Then I spotted a waving paw from a booth at the back and hurried to join Braden.

We ate chips and salsa and made small talk for a bit about the restaurant—one he knew from a visit a couple years ago—and then talked about the Ocie for a little. In a lull in the conversation, I cleared my throat and asked, "Was there a reason you wanted to have dinner?"

He licked salsa from his fingers and eyed me. "Because I was hungry."

"Okay," I said. "But why with me?"

"If you don't want to, you just have to say no." He picked up another chip. "I won't be offended."

"I do." I took a drink to give myself a moment. "That's why I'm here."

"Don't you go out to dinner with friends?"

That got my ears splayed to the side. "Are we friends?"

His eyes met mine. "Aren't we?"

I smiled. "I never like to assume. But I'd like to think we are."

He gave a quick nod. "I don't give out my phone number to just anyone."

"Also," I said, "I'd guess you don't call up athletic gear companies and insist they pay just anyone five thousand dollars."

He frowned. "They weren't supposed to tell you about that."

"The person we talked to didn't remember a whole lot about it. I'm not surprised she forgot. But I wanted to say thank you. It means a lot."

The fox looked away and then said, "You're welcome. Did it help with your sister?"

"Yeah. I mean, I'd won a tournament then, so I had money, but it still helped out a lot. And you didn't know, so it's still—it was really nice."

"Wasn't a big deal." He looked around at a bright red and green wooden lizard with golden diamonds running down its back. "It was a phone call."

"Still."

"And, uh." Beside the lizard hung a bright orange guitar. Braden examined that. "You told the TIU not to release my name. So that was nice of you, too."

Shoot, his contacts were thorough. When he didn't mention that in Oceania I thought he hadn't found out. "I didn't think your career should be derailed because of some sexual predator."

That jerked his attention back to me, eyes wide for a moment before he regained his composure. "You didn't even know if I did anything wrong."

I hadn't thought of that. "If you did, though—I mean, I talked to you. You hated him, but you kept going back. He must have had something on you, and I figured if you did anything, it was because of that. You're not—I don't think you'd cheat, ever. You respect tennis."

Braden nodded sharply. "I didn't. For the record. I didn't throw a match or even a point. I never took money from him. I just told him things when he asked, things I knew about players on the tour."

"That's fine," I said. "I didn't ask."

"Well, I don't know what your other friend did. But I never took money."

All I could think of in that moment was that Marquize had taken money, but he'd done it because he thought I needed help. "Sure you didn't," I said. "Did you ever *need* money?"

That startled him again. He sat back in the booth. "No, but even if I did…"

"You never have. So how do you know what you'd do if you did? What if you had a friend, a best friend, who needed help and you didn't have any parents or trust fund?" I didn't know what a trust fund was except that it was something rich people had. "Would you take the money then?"

"No." He tilted his head, ears flattened back. "I mean—no. I don't think so. I wasn't raised that way."

"Who was? How do you know, if you were desperate enough, what you'd do?"

"Hey." He met my eyes. "I told you, I didn't do anything."

"No, but you're implying that Marquize is weak somehow, or morally inferior or something, because he did. But you don't know what it's like."

"I'm not—" He stopped and gathered himself. "I didn't mean it that way. I don't know your friend and I don't know what he was going through. He shouldn't have done that, but he was trying to help you, so…" He shrugged.

I almost got up then and walked away, because his privileged attitude was like a burr in my tail, but the waiter came with our food and it smelled amazing, and also I was pretty hungry.

We ate in silence, and I started feeling better by halfway through the meal. "This is really good," I said.

"Told you." Braden glanced over. "Not too spicy for you?"

"It's fine." The pleasant tingle in my muzzle reminded me of some of Ma's cooking.

"I have to order it mild or else I can't finish it." Braden looked down at his plate. "That's what happens when you grow up in the Northeast."

I eyed the burrito he'd made his way halfway through and was now picking at. "Can I try?" He flicked his ears back, so I said, "I can just cut a piece off."

"Sure." He pushed his plate toward me.

His chicken burrito tasted a little bland, but there was still plenty of flavor. "It's good," I said, pushing his plate back. "Want to try mine?"

"No thanks. I've had it." He dug the filling out of his burrito with a fork. "Did you get an invitation to the Gallic?"

"No."

"You going?" His tail swatted the booth seat. "I can point you to a couple clubs. It's easier to hook up there. More discreet. And also everyone there is gorgeous, my god."

"Nah. Our manager thinks we should skip it. It's expensive to go over and we won't recoup the cost. We could use the time better here."

"Hah." He stared down at his plate and set his fork down, then dabbed at his muzzle with a napkin. "Managers are always about money. What about the experience? Go. If you play your way in as a wild card that's a great feeling."

I set my fork down as well. "Money's still important to some of us."

He leaned back, ears flat. "Ah, not this again."

"I'll go to the Gallic next year," I said. "For now I'm going to take my manager's advice, because I can't afford to go have experiences all the time."

Braden shook his head. "I didn't ask to be born into a well-off family."

"Neither did Aliq, but he doesn't throw his money around all the time and he understands what it's like not to have money."

"Who's Aliq?"

"My doubles partner. Anyway, I mean…" I realized I didn't know how wealthy Braden was relative to Aliq. I thought just having a nice house in a nice neighborhood in Freestone, which I'd been told was expensive, meant someone was well-off. "The point is..." He watched me, wary. "Just, like, don't tell me to do things like I have all the money in the world."

"Duly noted." He said it dryly. "I guess I'll take care of dinner, then."

"I can afford dinner."

"No." He held up a paw. "I asked you out, I'll pay for dinner. Don't worry. It doesn't come with any obligations."

"I didn't think it did." He might be prickly about his money for some reason I didn't know. What would Ma say? How would she handle it? "I really appreciate all you've done. It just seems like sometimes you think everyone should be able to do the things you can do, and we can't. And it's frustrating. Because you're a good person."

He'd put his credit card on the table and had been looking for the waiter, ears cupped toward me, but at that last sentence his eyes slid my way as well. "Am I?"

"Yeah."

The fox's paw tapped the credit card on the wooden table. "You seem pretty sure of that."

"Sometimes you don't act nice, but that's not the same. When it comes down to it, you do the right thing."

He thought about that while the waiter came over and took his card. "You don't know most of my life."

"Maybe not, but I can only judge what I've seen. Maybe you're a terrible person to everyone else, but around me you've been good."

We sat there with the smells of food and the low buzz of restaurant conversation around us. The waiter returned and gave Braden the check, and he signed it carelessly without looking at the amount. I was about to comment that he hadn't added a tip when he took two twenties out of his wallet and laid them on the table. As we stood, he said, "If you don't put the tips on the card, it's easier for them to manage it."

"Thanks," I said.

"I worked for tips at my dad's country club when I was twelve." He walked out of the restaurant, and I followed his white-tipped tail.

"I never worked in a restaurant," I said.

"My father thought it was important that I learn the value of work." He took out his phone. "Want to share a ride?"

"Sure. I'm just a few blocks from the tennis center."

He tapped a few things on his phone. "Ride'll be here in six minutes. Anyway, I worked for a summer. Everyone was polite to me because of who my dad was, and behind my back they'd say things about me." He flicked a large ear. "I guess you've heard things people didn't mean you to, too."

"Sometimes."

"I saw the other waiters, busboys, caddies, all being so obsequious to these people so they could get a little more money, a couple more dollars here and there. Then in the back room they'd talk about them worse than they talked about me. Me, it didn't matter how I acted; my dad's friends all tipped me anyway, even if I told them how shitty their golf swing was. But I never wanted to have to suck up to someone just to get a couple more bucks. I don't take money from my parents anymore, even."

"Did you get a scholarship to Palm Gables?"

"Ah...no. They paid for that."

"Mmm."

We didn't talk much in the car, not until the driver had left us in front of Braden's hotel. Then he extended a paw. "Thanks for coming to dinner," he said.

"Thanks for inviting me," I said, shaking. "I'd like to do it again."

"Really?" He raised his eyebrows.

I smiled. "Sure. Just because I think you're a rich jerk sometimes doesn't mean you're not a good person and a friend."

"That's a relief." He let my paw go and studied me. "All right. Let's do it when I'm back from Gallia."

"Good luck at the Open. I'll be watching."

"Good luck getting your ranking up." He turned and walked into his hotel.

The evening air felt refreshing on my muzzle. What an interesting evening, I thought. I had time to go to a gay bar if I wanted, but

I didn't feel like it right then. I just wanted to walk alone for a bit and think about this strange, fascinating fox.

* * *

Lochen had set up two other coaching candidates for me to meet with. I liked them well enough but neither one inspired the confidence in me that Nashan did. Both of them had other clients and invited me to ask around about them, but I knew a few of their clients and wasn't all that impressed with their play.

In retrospect, I know there are good coaches who can't scrape together top-tier talent to coach. Probably either of the coaches Lochen set up would have been fine, but at the time I most valued someone I could trust, and Nashan fit that criterion better than anyone else.

Aliq and I met with the red fox after those other two. Nashan had dressed in a suit and tie, and he smelled nice, a very professional mix of cade oil and lavender. I sat back while Aliq asked him questions, and Nashan handled them all very well. When Aliq turned to me, I'd already come up with a question or two of my own.

"I already know how you'd teach us on the court," I said. "I want to know how you'd handle things that would come up off-court."

His ears canted. "Off-court?"

"I've had a distracting year. I told you about some of it, not other parts." When I said that, Aliq's ears went back and I knew he was thinking about my Ma. "So when it comes to distractions, things about our personal lives…"

"Are you asking how I'd coach you to deal with distractions?"

"Kind of. But also, how you'd handle them."

Aliq stepped in. "Are you going to insist we go to worship? I don't attend synagogue and Rocky doesn't attend church."

"Oh." Nashan laughed easily. "I've seen everything out there on tour. I don't care if you worship. I don't care if you have one girlfriend or ten girlfriends or a one-night stand in every city. Hell, I don't even care if you have boyfriends. Your personal life is your life. Two things I care about." He held up two fingers. "One, no drugs. If people find drugs in your stuff or you end up fucked up somewhere, that reflects back on me. If you need to take even vitamin supplements, you check with me and we figure out if they're okay for you to take."

"No problem," Aliq said, and I nodded agreement.

"Two, you give a hundred percent effort. Whatever you have going on in your personal life is fine, like I said, but when you come to practice, when you come to play, you give it everything."

"That sounds great." I didn't want to tell him that I'd made up my mind the moment he'd said "boyfriend." He might not have been serious, but he'd said it without me bringing it up, and that made me so happy and confident that I couldn't imagine hiring anyone else.

Chapter Fourteen

I went about getting Nashan hired in a slightly sneaky way, by talking to Aliq first. He liked Nashan and didn't have any strong preference for either of the others we'd talked to, so I sold him on Nashan's virtues until I could be sure he'd back me up with Lochen.

As it turned out, Lochen didn't put up much of an argument. "If that's the guy you want, we'll go with it. I'll work it out and we'll see when he can join you," he said, and he didn't sound upset or parental or anything; I didn't get the feeling he was subtly hinting to me that I'd regret the choice but that I had to learn from my mistakes. He treated me like an adult who'd made a decision and knew what he wanted.

True, I had no idea how Nashan was going to affect my game, but I didn't know how any of those other coaches would either, and if I was going to be spending a lot more time with a coach, I wanted to be sure they were someone I wanted to spend a lot of time with. Kind of like having a boyfriend, I guess.

In the meantime, Aliq had given up on his singles to focus on playing doubles. Mostly this was because we were being invited to Champions tournaments as a doubles team, and while I was also getting invited for singles, he wasn't ranked highly enough. "It's okay," he said. "I'd rather play doubles with the big boys than singles at the cubs' table."

"You think I'm one of the big boys?" I laughed. "I'm nineteen."

"Almost twenty, and that's how old Tempest was when he made it to his first major final. You're one of the hundred best players in the world, and you're only going to get better."

I punched his shoulder. "You, too."

"Sure, in doubles." He laughed. "Anyway, I could fit a few Challenger tournaments in between our Champions events maybe, but honestly I'd rather take that time to get better. I think the only way I'm going to a major is in doubles; I just can't get my serve good enough to be a force in singles. You, you've got that lefty angle and plus you can do things with your spin and kick that I can do maybe some of the time, not reliably. All I'm good at is getting it in the box and then playing tennis, and that's doubles."

When I looked at it from another angle, I was giving Aliq the opportunity to go to Champions events that he wouldn't have had from just his singles, so I felt better about it that way. Besides, I enjoyed our doubles matches quite a bit. They weren't as exhausting as singles, physically or mentally. Of course they were still mentally challenging, but in singles, all the pressure was on me to figure out my opponent, to decide the strategy I was going to use and whether to change it—and if so, when and how. In doubles, Aliq and I could confer and come up with our best options, and only on rare occasions did we disagree.

We met up with Nashan at a Champions event in Yerba just before my twentieth birthday. Lochen went over the budget with us by Skype and I stared at the amount we were paying Nashan. Aliq noticed my distraction. "Too much or too little?" he said.

"I…I don't know. I have no idea what a coach gets paid," I said.

"Trust me," Lochen said, "he's getting paid very well for a new coach. This might be low, but I've included incentives for him based on your performance. And anyway, your new endorsement with One Two Three will cover his salary, and I've got two or three more deals lined up. Don't worry, you're both making a lot of money."

"Both?" Aliq's ears perked up.

"One of the deals I've got is for both of you, and I'm trying to get you into one of the others as well." Lochen sounded faintly smug. "Congratulations. And at this point you'd both better start thinking about traveling to Wimbledon, because that's going to happen more likely than not."

"Wait," Aliq said. "Why Wimbledon but not the Gallic? What's changed?" He slid a look my way. "Rocky's jumped like five spots, sure, but is that enough?"

Lochen laughed. "What's different is that Wimbledon is the one tournament the world watches. Even if we don't make our money back in prizes, as long as you two play the way I know you can, you're going to attract a bunch of attention. Attention becomes endorsements and endorsements become money. So we're going to start traveling more. And you two should both get on social media. That's another way to build your celebrity."

We exchanged looks. Neither of us had anything in the way of an online presence, though I knew Danver was on InstaPic and Caboll was on Scentbook, and both of them were on Twitter. Aliq kept in touch with his family through phone calls because his parents didn't use any social media at all. "Okay, so, uh…"

"InstaPic seems to be best. You can set up accounts with the other services and post to them…"

He said a lot more about it, but I kind of zoned out. Aliq broke in. "Can't we get someone to manage our accounts? I know some players who do that."

"Sure," Lochen said, "but it's better if it starts with you guys personally because then the people managing it have a good idea of what kinds of things you'd like to post and it feels more authentically you."

Aliq rolled his eyes and I shook my head. "I don't know what's authentically me." I gestured around. "Pictures of the hotel room? The practice court?"

Lochen smiled. "Something like that. And talk about your prep, the match you're looking forward to, stuff like that."

"All right, we can do that. We'll get on InstaPic this weekend."

"Speaking of this weekend…I thought you might like to get together with Danver and that group one more time before you move fully over to the Champions circuit. They're in Lake City, which is an easy flight from Yerba, so if you want I can give you an overnight layover there on your way out."

"Yeah," Aliq and I chorused. "That'd be cool."

* * *

We were at the gate waiting to board the flight to Lake City when I got a phone call from the lawyer who'd been looking into Ori's case. "Hang on," I said to Aliq as I hurried off to take it.

"It's good news," the lawyer said first. My heart jumped and my tongue dried up all in an instant and I couldn't think of anything to say to him. After a moment, he went on. "There's been a change in your sister's case. It looks like they've reassigned her destination to the States, so there's no more of this 'live in Deutscherbund or Anglia for two years.' They'll be hearing her case next week and I fully expect her to be en route to the States soon after that."

"Next week?" I croaked.

"Next week. This only happens when someone high up takes an interest in your case. Did you make any friends in government recently?"

Altamont's soft voice echoed in my memory. "Um, maybe like, last September?"

"Five months." He laughed. "Yeah, that timing about checks out. Even when government expedites something, it goes slow."

"Do I need to do anything?"

"Stay by the phone. I'll let you know as I hear things."

"And if the hearing goes well, then?"

"It'll go well. Even if you weren't making more of a name for yourself, dead boyfriend and dead mother and predatory father are a pretty ironclad case." He paused. "Oh. Sorry."

"It's all right." I pressed down on the stabbing of memory in my chest and took a deep breath, then let it out. "Ma would've wanted to get Ori back, so…"

"Right." The silence stretched on awkwardly. "So…when it goes well, it'll be a couple weeks, probably. Let me know where you'll be and we'll arrange the transportation then."

"All right." Around me, the public address system announced a flight boarding. I couldn't remember the flight number I was on but I thought it might be that one. And then I imagined Ori getting on an airplane in Lunda, landing in an airport very like this one, coming down a hallway and through security where I'd be waiting for her, and my eyes blurred. "Thanks. I think my flight's boarding."

"I'll keep you updated."

Aliq was gathering his bags, but when he saw me he stopped. "Good news?"

I dragged the back of my paw across my eyes. "Uh, yeah. I know I keep talking about my sister, but…they're actually going to have her hearing next week. It's scheduled and everything. And…she's coming here. She might be here by the end of March." Saying it aloud felt strange, as if I were telling him about a dream I'd had, but no, it was real.

He whooped and threw his arms around me, and I hugged him back. "So cool," he said, tail wagging. "I'm gonna get to meet her finally!"

"You and everyone." They were calling us to board, so I put my phone away and followed Aliq's wagging tail onto the plane.

* * *

Lake City sat in the mountains near a giant lake that we saw flying in, and we thought that's where the name had come from, but a plaque in the airport told us that Lake City had been named for a possum, Myron Lake.

As we collected our luggage, it occurred to me to call Lochen and tell him the good news about Ori. "That's fantastic," he said. "Hey, I'd like to get some publicity going around it. Remember that fox who did the article on you and the other African players? He's writing for tennis.com now and I think he'd be interested in a follow-up story. Then we can push it out to some mainstream outlets."

"Sure," I said. "My number's the same if he wants to text me."

I didn't think about it that much because right after that we met up with Danver and Sean and Caboll, too, and we went out to a Happy Friday's restaurant. We spent a couple hours talking about the last years and how they'd be seeing me at some of the Champions tournaments soon. The funny thing about the conversation was that they didn't envy my rise in rank or that I'd be playing against the top competition in the world as much as they envied the money

I'd be making (if I won enough; they assumed I would be winning enough). They envied Aliq, too, but none of them tried to convince him to give up Champions doubles to keep working on his singles.

We stayed out most of the night until the guys had to get to bed. Aliq and I had an early flight, but when we got back to our hotel, we weren't tired. So we sat up by the slot machines playing for fifty cents a spin and talking about the year ahead of us. Champions was intimidating; these guys we'd seen on TV were now going to be matched up against us. Both of us were excited about it, though. I hadn't played any of the players in the top ten at that point; Braden was #11 after having skipped such a large chunk of the previous year and was trying to rebuild his ranking.

"Down to my last spin," I said as I pushed the buttons one more time. "Ah, well, there it goes."

"I'm up two dollars." Aliq pushed the button again. When his digital wheels stopped, five matching raccoons in sporty evening wear flashed, not in a line, but in a W pattern that was apparently enough to win. "BIG WIN" flashed across the screen as we watched the numbers go up.

In the end, he cashed out with sixty-five dollars from his original ten. So he bought us ice cream at the front desk and we went back and ate it in our room. "Maybe you can play slots while I'm playing singles," I said.

He laughed. "I somehow feel like I won't win six times my investment every go. Besides, you're gonna be playing some epic singles, and I want to watch."

Lying back in my bed as I tried to sleep, the weight of expectations kept my eyes staring at the dark ceiling. What if I couldn't beat the top tier of singles? What if I'd already gone as far as I could? Braden said nice things about me but if I looked back objectively, he'd beaten me pretty soundly every time we'd met. Sure, I made him worry. I'd played players two hundred spots below me who made me worry for a few games in a match. But there was no question who was better in those matches, in either case. Where were those players now? Had they gotten better?

True, a few years ago I'd been losing to players I now beat handily. Not many, but there were a few who had definitely plateaued. By any measure, but especially by the most important measure (my ranking), I was improving. And I figured I would continue to improve. That thought helped me get back to sleep.

In the morning, my phone woke me. I grabbed it off the nightstand and answered without looking at the number. "Hey," an unfamiliar voice chirped. "Rocky N'Guwe?"

"Yeah."

"It's Streaks Fox, the blogger. Your manager said you had some news about your sister?"

"Oh. Yeah." I struggled to sit up in bed. "Sorry, it's early."

"I know. When I get a gig for NBC, I can call you at prime time, but your manager said you have a flight in two and a half hours, and I'd like to get this started today so I can do some corroboration. You know the deal."

"Right." I marshaled my thoughts. "So you want to hear about Ori?"

"Love to. Feel-good stories get lots of clicks and this is a great one. Let's start with how horrible it is back in Lunda."

"Uh." I had to think about that for a moment. "It's not all bad. I grew up there. It's just tough if you're not male, and worse for some species. Jackals I think have it a little worse than lions and hyenas, better than anteaters and foxes."

"My ancestors came from, well, not Lunda, but the other side of the continent. That's why I started writing about African players. And had to go down to Futures because there's only about a half dozen total."

"Hope your writing encourages more to come over and play."

"Hah." He had a short bark of a laugh that made me smile. "Your play is going to do that about a thousand times better than my dumb article. Sorry. It's not dumb. It's a very important article."

I chuckled. "I appreciate it, anyway."

"So okay. What happened to your sister?"

By the time I'd finished the story of Ori's engagement and Ma's death, Aliq had woken up, stumbled to the bathroom, and gotten dressed. "Want me to grab you something for breakfast?" he asked.

"Sure." I waved.

As it turned out, Streaks wrapped up his questions a few minutes later. "I'm going to call some people from Lunda. They probably won't call me back, but hey, I gotta try. Thanks, Rocky, you're a great interview."

"Thank you," I said. "I'm glad to help however I can."

"Don't get your hopes up like this is going to bring a wave of disadvantaged cubs over to make fortunes in tennis. It's a small step."

"Small steps make for big journeys."

"I like that. Can I use it?"

"Sure. It was one of my Ma's sayings."

He typed. "Sorry again. She sounds like a great jackal. Would like to have talked to her."

"Yeah," I said. "Me too."

And then we were done. I texted Aliq that I'd come down and join him, and we hurried through breakfast before catching a cab to the airport.

* * *

At Yerba, we got a message from Nashan that he was in the room adjacent to ours. We had barely thrown our bags on the bed when a knock came at the connecting door.

"Hi, guys," the red fox said when we opened it. No suit this time; he wore a yellow polo shirt and khaki slacks and carried a large binder stuffed with pages. "I got this whole plan here for you to look at."

"The whole thing?" I stared at the pages. "Today?"

He laughed and patted my shoulder. "No. Today we'll just go over the highlights."

"Are our workouts in there?" Aliq crouched down as if he could see the ideas between the pages.

"Lochen told me you're a gym junkie." Nashan tapped the binder. "I talked to a friend of mine who hit the gyms all the time on tour and he gave me a couple pointers about what worked for him. But I'm happy to let you keep doing whatever's working for you. I just thought you might want to have another input."

"Sure." When Nashan looked down, though, Aliq flashed me a look that said that he'd been doing his workouts for years and already knew what he needed to know. I flicked my ears back and tried to look both sympathetic and reassuring. Not sure how well that succeeded.

To give Nashan another chance, I said, "How about a nutritional plan? Is the one we had with Coach Keely okay?"

"Oh." The red fox put a paw on his binder and his ears went back. "Shoot. I was up all night the last few days and I kept feeling like I'd forgotten something. Yeah, stick with what you've got. I'm sure it's fine. I'll do some research."

"Okay, good." I tried to make a joke. "Glad we won't have to go buy a bunch of new food."

It didn't go over too well. Nashan opened his binder and went right to our workout schedule, and Aliq chewed on his bottom lip. But fortunately, the workout schedule was very similar to what we'd been doing. We'd planned to work out that morning, so he went with us to the gym ("I don't need to do this every time, just the first time to give you a chance to ask questions and give me feedback"), and it went pretty well. Aliq had some comments and Nashan made notes to change some minor details of the workout.

Afterwards, as we were cleaning up, I was still thinking about him having forgotten the nutrition plan, and Aliq was quiet, so I said that I thought we should give him a chance.

"Of course we will." He packed away his racket, seeming unconcerned.

"I mean, the nutrition thing was just an oversight and it's his first coaching job."

"Rocky." Aliq turned to face me. "He screwed up but he owned up to it right away. He didn't cover it up or say, 'Oh yeah, that's not important' or anything like that. I was annoyed that he didn't have a diet plan—seems pretty basic—but the fact that he came clean about it means a lot more."

"All right." I exhaled.

Aliq patted me on the shoulder with a grin. "Keep your ears up. I know he's your friend and this was your choice. It's only the first day. Let's see how it goes."

Where Nashan impressed us was the next day, when we started preparing for our opponents. He had a tablet computer with multiple folders of film organized by player and then date. "I subscribed to this service with my own money," he said. "Totally worth it. But now that I'm working for you…"

"Sure," I said. "Lochen will take care of it."

"Thanks." The red fox grinned. "All right. So here's your first doubles opponents."

"We know Lowry." I tapped the big wolf. "But he used to play with a maned wolf. Now he's playing with this fennec, I guess."

"They started playing together six months ago." Nashan called up footage of one of their matches. "Tasman, that's the fennec, he's a doubles specialist and he's a lefty, so pay attention to his angles. You'll have an advantage, Aliq, because you get to practice against a lefty, but remember they'll have the same advantage. You already know about Lowry, right: great forehand, weak backhand and no slice to speak of but good placement, adequate defense but you can catch him guessing. Tasman is a better net player than Lowry; his forehand isn't as good, but his backhand is better, so watch out for it. He's not as good a defender as Lowry— doubles specialists in general aren't going to be as good defenders as singles players, because they don't have to be."

Coach Keely had given us info like this, but then Nashan pulled up a point from one of Lowry and Tasman's recent matches. "Here," he said, "see, Lowry's back, he runs around to get a forehand on this, and he catches Vyler napping."

Both of us watched, rapt. "Tasman was blocking him." Aliq pointed.

"Yes, but also, Vyler's expecting the backhand. He recovers pretty quickly, but that fraction of a second takes some pace off his shot, and Tasman puts it away easily." Nashan looked up at me. "You're a better defender than Vyler, Rocky, but I've seen you fall into the trap of thinking you know what your opponent is going to do. Often you do. But a canny opponent, and you're going to be facing more of those, will go against type. Don't assume you know your opponent's next shot. Know their tendencies and wait for your observation to confirm it."

"Right."

"For singles, we're going to work on your return of serve."

"Oh. Okay." I'd always thought that my return of serve was one of my strengths.

He smiled. "Your return is great for doubles. It's a touch conservative for singles. You can be doing more with it, especially on the ad side. We're going to work on that. Your net play is excellent and as I mentioned, your defense is good. Your serve is pretty good, but there's room for improvement. And we can always work on your mental game. Here, want to see my breakdown of you guys?"

We glanced at each other. "Yeah," Aliq said.

So he brought up two-page long reports with links to video of various points that illustrated the things he wanted us to work on. We sat there for almost two hours with him as he went through our play in detail. Coach Keely had done this piecemeal, here and there, but always it had been, "here's one thing to work on this week." He'd talked about doing a full report, but it was always going to be later, when we'd hired him full time. He'd never given us an exhaustive report, and when I told Nashan that, his eyes widened, and then he nodded.

"I'm a little surprised, but not much. He's done very good work with you, but there are little gaps here and there. We're not going to change much, but we're going to work on patching them up and adding a few weapons to your arsenal. I'll be honest with you: you're at a point where you won't get much farther in singles without improving your topspin backhand and seeing if we can't add a little more power to your forehand."

"I'm helping him add muscle in workouts." Aliq punched my arm.

"Good, that's what I was going to suggest."

His breakdown of Aliq took less time because he was only evaluating my friend's doubles play, but still the arctic fox's tail wagged eagerly at the end of it. Then he guided us through a practice, which felt to me (and Aliq, I confirmed later) more sure than Coach Keely's guidance. Nashan had taken the time to study us thoroughly and it showed.

That evening, as Aliq and I shared dinner at the hotel, we talked eagerly about our future with Nashan. "I take back everything I said," Aliq said. "He's smart."

"You didn't say all that much."

He grinned at me. "I take back the stuff I thought and didn't say, too."

"Coach Keely said my return of serve was good." I pushed peas around my plate with a fork. "But Nashan made some good points about improving it."

"We'll see if it works. You gonna eat that?" Aliq reached over and speared one of my carrots when I didn't answer and then chewed it noisily. "You've got a few matches this tournament to make some changes."

I don't know whether it was Nashan's changes to my game or the fact that he was physically present for each match, one of the first to talk to me afterwards, but I played really well that tournament. It helped that most of the top players had already gone over to the Gallic, so we were seeded #2 in doubles and I was seeded fourth in singles, my highest seed yet. We won doubles and I came within one set of winning singles, losing 3-6, 7-6, 5-7 in the final to a player five ranks above me.

We both felt that those results spoke well of Nashan's coaching. He had a way of preparing us with a positive smile that gave both me and Aliq confidence that we could win the match. And after our losses—well, after my one loss, he started with the list of things I'd done really well and moved on after a short time to places where I'd lost crucial points. "We have some things to work on now," he told me, still cheerful. "This is all fixable."

"Cool." I wagged my tail.

"Now," Nashan said. "About the post-match interview…"

He gave me more pointers on how to talk to the media on the way back to the hotel. And there, Aliq and I thought we were going to talk about the next tournament upcoming and our trip to Anglia for Wimbledon, but Nashan surprised us. "The next couple weeks are the Gallic," he said. "Did you guys ever watch majors with your coach?"

"Lochen took us to the States, and we sat on some matches with him at the Ocie."

"All right, good. I was thinking we could park ourselves and watch some of the early rounds. These are players you'll be facing sooner than the top tier and we'll be able to watch their games live. You up for it? Aliq, it'll be more singles than doubles because it's harder to find the doubles televised. Sorry in advance about that."

"It's fine," Aliq said. "It's all still useful to learn."

"Sure is." Nashan reached out a paw. "Now, I know you guys can't drink, but I wanted to get you something to celebrate our first tournament together—I mean, beyond the checks you got. So…"

He reached into his bag and brought out two slender boxes. Each of us opened one to reveal a tablet computer. "Oh," Aliq said. "Cool."

"I know." Nashan grinned. "You could buy one if you wanted. But I put some stuff on here. You've got access to all the film I have on them. We've got a workout tracker, and there's a backup one if you don't like the one I picked. There's a nutrition guide, too. I went and looked that up after you asked about it. This program and the workout one sync with your phone, so you can enter what you eat and how much you work out on your phone and the program here will pick it up. And the calendar you were using is on there. I got Lochen to help me set you guys up. So it's all done, you can play with them as much as you want. Oh." He took mine, as I'd just turned it on. "The code for both of them is 0-5-1-0-1-4 because I bought them a couple days ago, but you can change it if you want." He logged in to mine and gave it back to me. "There's also a book reader app if you want to listen to books."

Aliq had already opened the workout tracker; I looked at the folders and folders of film. "That's awesome. Thanks!"

"Yeah." Aliq's tail wagged like mine did.

"Well, you know what they say." Nashan was smiling. "You can always buy someone's respect."

We both looked up at him. "Kidding," he said. "Nobody says that. But I hope you get some good use out of them."

Chapter Fifteen

Watching the Gallic Open with Nashan was a different experience than I was used to. Sure, with Lochen we analyzed the matches, but for the most part he let us watch and then quizzed us afterwards. Nashan spoke up during some of the points to say things like, "Now see where Longacre keeps pushing Ferrera to his backhand. Ferrera's got a good backhand, but it's better when he has time to set for it, and Longacre's trying to put more pace on the ball to get it there a bit faster. It's sort of working, but on the slow clay court, it's going to be tough. I'm not sure there's a better strategy, but in his place I might try mixing up his shot selection. He's letting Ferrera get used to it and anticipate his shots." And just as he said that, Ferrera (a stocky Corsican hare) stepped around a shot that landed too short in the court and smashed a forehand that Braden had no chance of getting to.

I felt like I learned a lot during that tournament and I came away from each viewing excited to get back onto the court. Aliq and I had some practices together, but it wasn't the same. And when we weren't practicing, we were working out. Aliq had tried Nashan's app and he didn't like it, but I convinced him to give it another couple weeks. These two weeks were ideal to start a new routine, because that would give our muscles time to acclimate, and for sure after the first two days my legs and arms were sorer than they'd been since I started working out with Aliq. He didn't have quite the same problem, but then he was just in better shape than I was and he wasn't boosting his workout as much.

That Ferrera-Longacre match was in the semifinals, and Braden lost it. The announcers talked about how he hadn't been able to regain the confidence he'd had in the Ocie Open, or maybe it was that clay wasn't his surface, or maybe it was that at that Open, many of the higher seeds had been knocked out early by upset or injury. Whatever the reason, they talked about him as a brilliant but flawed player, and one of the commentators said, "The right coach might be able to set him straight, but it's so hard to find that person."

"True enough," and they went on to talk about a player who'd poached a coach from another player and the tension it had caused between them. That comment stuck with me, though, and I thought about how much Nashan had done for us in just two weeks. I hoped it would continue and that we'd found the coach who'd take us to the top.

After the match, I texted Braden and said that I thought he'd played well. And then I forgot about it because he was probably asleep by then and that evening I got a phone call from Ori. I took it out in the hall of our hotel, because Aliq was in the room watching film and trying to concentrate.

"Ro," she said, her voice trembling. "I have a flight."

"When? Oh my god, Ori, are you serious?"

"It's in two weeks, a flight from Lundara into Port City. Once I'm there..." She ruffled some papers on her end. "I have to report to the States Immigration office for my green card and paperwork and then they said I can go wherever I like. I'll have a counselor to help me find a job, although I'm not sure what skills I have. They suggested teaching or social work, but I don't know, I hadn't even thought that far ahead. What do you think?"

"You'd be great at anything," I said. "When does your flight land? I'll come out."

"Are you sure? You won't be playing?"

"Doesn't matter. I'll pull out. Aliq will understand."

She laughed. "Ro, don't pull out just because of me. Buy me a flight to wherever you are and I'll come to you."

"No. I want to be there when you get off the plane."

"Well, all right. But if your coach says you have to play, I'll understand. Anyway, it sounds as though they'll have me there most of the day. Oh, Ro. I can't believe it's happening finally."

"Me neither. In just two weeks, Ori. Two weeks!"

"I know!"

"What do you want to do first?"

She laughed. "Hug you. After that I don't care. I want to meet your partner and watch you play a tennis match and go to sleep without wondering what will go wrong next. I want to go to a diner like in that movie and eat a piece of pie. I want to go to a club and go dancing. I want to do anything else you want to show me."

"I'll tell Aliq and we'll think of something," I promised.

I hung up feeling as giddy and happy as if I'd just won a major. When I went back into the room, my tail wagged so hard it smacked the doorframe, and Aliq looked up from the tablet. His ears perked and he smiled. "Good news?"

So I told him, and he jumped up from the chair and ran over to hug me as if we'd just won a major, his tail wagging as hard as mine. He even insisted on calling his parents so I could tell them the good news.

I thought it would be quick, but his mother talked to me for twenty minutes. She asked a lot of questions about Ori and about Lundara and the process, and she asked if I wanted them to drive down to Port City to meet up with us. "It's no trouble," she said, "and we'd love to meet her."

"That's okay," I said. "I think I'll be flying in."

"Of course. Just let us know, it's no bother."

Aliq grinned when I gave the phone back to him. He said his good-byes and then said, "She offered to drive down, didn't she?"

I nodded. "But I was going to fly out. I mean, it means missing the next tournament. If you're okay with that."

He hesitated—and I noticed that he hesitated. But his ears came up and he recovered quickly. "Yeah, of course! She's your sister. I'd fly to Port City with you if that's okay."

It sounded good to me. But when we called Lochen to talk about it, he hesitated too. "If it's really what you want," he said, his voice echoing around our hotel room, "of course we can withdraw."

"My sister's coming home!"

"Yes, yes, of course, it's wonderful. But we can easily put her on a plane to Pinewood. That'd cost less than you pulling out of the tournament." When I didn't say anything, he went on. "And it's just an extra day or so. She'll be safe. Rocky, this isn't the Futures or even Challenger anymore. You're on the Champions circuit. Skipping a tournament—if you're not injured, it's a big deal. You need points, and frankly the money wouldn't hurt either. All the big names are back and you need experience against this competition."

I paced back and forth, staring at the phone, then turned to Aliq. "You think your mom really meant it about coming down to meet Ori?"

His ears perked up. "Sure. You think Ori would mind?"

"She's staying with her—with a friend's family. In Lunda, it's not uncommon for families to help each other out. I'm sure she'll be fine with it."

Lochen, from the speakerphone, said, "That sounds like a terrific idea. So you'll stay in the tournament?"

"Yes." I met Aliq's eyes and smile. "We'll stay in."

* * *

Aliq's parents responded to our request to meet Ori with a great deal of enthusiasm, resulting in me spending another half hour on the phone with his mother being interrogated about Ori's likes and dislikes. I also had to talk to Lochen and someone in the State Department again to arrange Ori's flight, because her documents weren't processed yet, and it was difficult to book a flight without proper States ID, which she wouldn't have until she landed. With my permission, Lochen hired a Port City lawyer to expedite the process, which only cost me a couple thousand dollars. There had been a time when that couple thousand dollars would have felt like an insurmountable obstacle; now, between my doubles and singles, the money came more easily—as Lochen had predicted, playing in the tournament was a better use of my time.

I had to play in the qualifying tournament in Pinewood, though it would be one of the last times I did. I won a spot in the draw, won my first match on an unseasonably warm spring day, and won my first doubles match with Aliq as well.

Braden had responded to my text with a thanks and a note to the effect that Gallia was boring and disappointing, and I presumed that meant not only for the tennis. He was at Pinewood, too, so while Aliq and I were taking in a ladies' doubles match on our afternoon off, I texted him to say hi. He had the evening free, so I asked if he'd want to grab dinner and he said sure.

"Going out for dinner tonight," I told Aliq.

"Sure," he said, watching the match.

We often liked to watch other matches when we weren't playing. It's helpful to see other players live. The ladies weren't ever going to come up as opponents, but we could learn from their style, though I suspected that Aliq's interest in the ladies' matches was less about tennis than mine was. Still, it was nice to watch tennis and analyze the game without having to think about playing those players one day.

I always kept an eye on the ladies' draw anyway in case Kim's name came up. I knew she'd made it to the Challenger tour and was doing well in doubles there, but we hadn't managed to meet up yet. Nobody else in my class from Palm Gables was even close to where I was now. In fact, I thought I was closer to Braden than Bret, still struggling on the Futures tour, was to me.

* * *

As per usual, Braden knew a good restaurant with discreet seating. This one was a brew pub, dark wood and the smell of hops throughout, with partitions around the booths that surrounded the larger open area. We came in through a back door that let us flag down a waiter, who took a twenty from Braden and led us to a booth in the corner. The cross fox sat with his back to the main room and his jacket hanging from the post behind him to further hide him. I didn't worry as much, but his paranoia was contagious, so I hid back in my own corner, though I didn't have a jacket to hide myself with. One more thing I learned from Braden.

"So tell me about Gallia," I said after we'd ordered, when he seemed reluctant to start the conversation. I still wasn't used to Braden Longacre asking me to hang out with him, but it was less strange than it had been. Despite that, I couldn't shake the feeling that whenever he asked me out, he wanted something, and I never quite knew what it was. Last time it had felt like he wanted companionship—maybe the same feeling I'd felt when I sought him out after having problems with Marquize. There was nobody else on the tour that we knew of who could relate to what we were going through.

He slid a finger up and down his iced tea glass. "What, the tournament?"

"Whatever."

"You saw the match. Tell me about it."

His eyes challenged me. So I cleared my throat. "Seems to me you were trying to hit through Ferrera, and on clay that doesn't work as well."

He snorted. "Tell me something I don't know."

Stung a little, I took his bait. "You're not mixing up your shots enough."

That brought his ears all the way up. "What do you mean? I mix them up plenty."

"Yeah, but…" I searched for how to say it. "I haven't watched all your matches. But you seem to have patterns to your shots. Something like that. I'll watch and there's a lot of times when I'll know what you're going to do next because I've played you and I've seen it. I haven't put it down into writing or anything like that, but I get that feeling."

His fingerpad made a squeaking noise on the damp glass, and he stopped rubbing it. "I'll ask my coach about that," he said slowly. "Thanks."

"What did you think of the tournament?" I asked when he seemed to drift off into his own world.

"Let me ask you something." He leaned forward, out of the shadow of his jacket. "How do you decide how to mix up your shots?"

"I don't know," I said. "I just go with whatever feels…" I stopped, thinking about it. How did I decide what shot to hit in the moment? It was often a split-second decision.

"Don't say 'whatever feels right,'" Braden growled.

"That's kind of what it is, though." I raised my left paw and mimed hitting the ball. "Sometimes I look at where the other guy is and I feel like I know what the right shot is."

"You don't study the correct moves for certain situations?" He took a drink of tea and wiped his muzzle, leaning back. "How do you prepare for an opponent?"

"We study them." Maybe this was what he had asked me out for, though for a major winner to be fishing for tips from a player in the fifties seemed odd. Still, this might be one of those traits people talked about with champion tennis players: always looking for new things to add to their game. I wasn't sure how much I should be telling him about my preparation, but I could remain pretty vague. "You look at their tendencies and you prepare for a strong backhand, for instance."

He leaned forward again, animated. "So if you're playing a strong backhand guy—Colluvic, say—you avoid his backhand? That's it? What happens when he starts overplaying to the forehand and teeing off on your groundstrokes?"

"Obviously, you mix it up to keep him honest."

"How much? When?"

"I don't keep track of those sorts of things. I get into a rhythm and my game flows from that. I don't make decisions like 'if I hit this approach shot he'll get a good look at a backhand pass,' at least not all the time. A lot of the time I just...play."

"You internalize it." He nodded and rubbed his whiskers.

"What does that mean?"

A slight smile. "It means you absorb the lesson without having to think about it. Coach says I should be trying to do that more myself." He tilted his muzzle. "Where'd you learn to do that?"

"I don't know that I did." I spread my paws. "That's how I've always played."

"Hmf," he said. "Lucky, then."

"I guess so."

At that point the waiter brought our meals and derailed the conversation. Braden's rather intense questioning about my tennis skills was interesting to process but also a little exhausting, so I took advantage of the break to shift the topic. "How about outside the tournament?"

"Oh." He lowered his voice and looked away. "You know, Lutèce is usually pretty good. Bar scene, I mean. I know a couple places. But this year I took a cab and some reporters followed me, so when I got out by this bar and noticed them, I had to go across the street and pretend I was just walking along the river, and it wasn't a great neighborhood. Lucky thing about Lutèce is there's a tourist thing every hundred yards, so I found an old church and pretended to be really into it. If you see a piece about my love of old architecture, that's what it's from."

"So you didn't get to…" I waved. "At all?"

"Once." He shrugged. "It was fine. What was annoying was all the back and forth in the hotels."

"The hotels?"

"The male and female players stay in the same hotels, so if straight people want to hook up, it's just…go up two floors, go down the hall, stuff like that. Reporters hang out in the hotel but you can avoid them pretty easily. It's if you go offsite that it's a problem."

"Huh."

"Anyway." He gave me a lopsided grin. "Enjoy your relative anonymity while you got it. What's going on with you?"

"Oh. My sister's flying here in a week. Well, she's flying to Port City in a week and then she has to go through a lot of paperwork and then she's getting on a flight here."

His ears perked up. "That's great. I thought that happened a while ago, though."

"It takes so long." I explained the bureaucracy while he finished his burger. "So I keep thinking it's going to happen and now finally it really is."

"Awesome."

"And thanks again," I remembered, "for your help. With the money and everything."

"Glad it worked out," he said. "She's coming to the tournament?"

"Yeah. Her first time in the Union. I can't wait to see her."

He asked me a little more about her, which led to me telling a couple more stories until I was worried I was boring him. But his ears stayed perked and he listened attentively. "If she's around," he said, "bring her to dinner next time. But…" He gestured between us. "This other stuff we talk about…that's between us."

"Oh, sure."

"She knows about you?"

I smiled. "Yeah, I told her all about me and Marquize. She's fine with it."

"Cool," he said.

This time he let me split the check, and as we walked out, he said, "There aren't really any good bars around here, either. Sometimes it sucks having to depend on bars."

I nodded, but I was still thinking about Ori. "That's what was nice about Marquize, though we were underage for a lot of it and that made it more complicated. If I didn't have Ori to talk to, I'd have been pretty miserable."

His tail swished beside mine. "I appreciate having someone to talk to too," he said.

When I got back to the hotel, Aliq wasn't in our room, but I wasn't ready to sleep yet. We hadn't made a lot of friends on the Champions tour, but Lowry, the wolf, had told us to text him if we wanted to play video games any night. So I got out my phone and texted, and he told me what room he was in. I went up there and knocked, and he was there with Tasman, the fennec he played with, and two other guys. One of them, a swift fox with a killer backhand but a relatively standard forehand, I'd recently beaten in three sets. "Palomar, right?" I said when I came in.

"N'Guwe." He shook my paw and grinned. "Grats on qualifying."

"Thanks," I said, and sat beside him while Lowry and Tasman played a round of some racing game.

Palomar and I talked tennis and life for a bit until it was our turn to play, with Lowry and Tasman interjecting from time to time. The swift fox had been born in the upper Midwest but moved to Chevali and had taken to tennis at a young age, much as I had. He was twenty-six now but still felt as young as the rest of us (me at twenty, Lowry at twenty-two, Tasman at twenty-three), and I could see from his easy, friendly manner why Lowry liked him. I ended up talking about Ori a lot and everyone there made excited, sympathetic noises, enough that I didn't worry too much about boring them, even though, looking back, I probably did a bit.

That canid group felt fun and relaxed, and I made a mental note to bring Aliq by to hang with them. They didn't have the same energy that Danver and Sean had, but looking back, I think it's because at this level, all of us were devoting so much of our energy to tennis that we didn't have a lot to spare.

* * *

Ori called when she landed in Port City from Aliq's mother's phone. I know it doesn't make any sense, but she sounded closer than she had on any of our calls across the ocean. She was healthy, she was hungry ("we're going to feed her, Rocky, don't worry," Aliq's mother assured me), and she was happy to be here.

"I can't wait to see you," I said.

"Me too, Ro." She laughed. "The airport is so big! I'm glad Mrs. Loize is here, or I'd worry I'd get lost."

"Yeah, the signs don't really help." My throat threatened to close, because I knew exactly that feeling and that connection was a stronger marker than anything else that my sister was here, she really was here. "I got lost too."

"And so many different languages! I was ready to speak English, but everyone around me was speaking something different. I stood next to a fennec in white robes and a family of aardvarks in black t-shirts with a white design of the world on them and they were all speaking to each other and I couldn't understand any of it. There aren't more people than in Lunda—not in the airport anyway— but so many different kinds. I keep smelling someone and turning around to see what species they are."

She promised to keep me updated on her progress ("we'll get her a phone," Aliq's mother sang in the background) and on the flight, when it got booked. So I got Mrs. Loize's phone number and after we hung up, I called Lochen to give it to him so he could coordinate with Ori until she got her own phone. "Also," I told him, "can we add a phone to my plan for her?"

He promised to arrange it all, laughing at my excitement. He wanted to be around to welcome her as well, but he had to be at a tournament for his team. "I'll meet her soon," he promised me. "After all, we're going to have to get together to plan your Anglia trip."

"Anglia—" I understood right away. "Wimbledon?"

"Uh huh. You're in the main singles draw, you and Aliq are a wild card in the doubles draw."

I whooped and looked instinctively around for Aliq, but he'd gone out to get us dinner to eat in the room. "When are we going?"

"I'm registering you for some tuneups, like in Oceania. We're looking at having to go right after this tournament. Next year if you do the Gallic, you'll just stay over there and it'll be easier."

I wondered why Braden hadn't stayed over. He was surely doing Wimbledon. As the Pinewood tourney went on and I won more matches with and without Aliq, I had a few chances to talk to the cross fox, but nothing in private until the semifinals. Braden had cruised through the tournament and won his match, and I was just getting ready for mine. The guy he'd beat hustled it out of the locker room, and my opponent was over on the other side, and there weren't many other guys around. In fact, Braden didn't seem to have a bodyguard anymore, or if he did, he wasn't bringing him into the locker room. So I went to the fox and congratulated him and he wished me luck, and we grinned at each other, knowing that if I won, we'd be meeting in the final.

"So why'd you come back for Pinewood?" I asked. "You're heading over for Choner, right?" That was the first tune-up I was in.

"Yeah." He leaned against his locker. "I know it disrupts the schedule to come back over, but my parents wanted to see me and it's a better chance to make up points than just missing a tournament."

"Won't you miss out on defending…whatever one you're skipping over there?"

"Lankerham. Yeah, I didn't play it last year, so no danger there."

He sounded clinical and bored, as though it wasn't even a big deal. I guess flying around all over the world can get boring when you do it so often. "Well," I said, "it was good to see you. Hope to play you tomorrow."

He grinned again and held up his fist for me to bump it. "Good luck," he said.

I guess he's no charm, because I went out and lost in three sets. It was a good match, and I'm sure Ori wasn't on my mind during it. It was more that I hadn't gotten where I wanted to be with my topspin backhand, but Lomber—a kangaroo rat—was hitting my backhand pretty good and I was trying to mix it up. I'd learn from that match; Nashan made sure of that. We'd have to find someone to practice against who could hit backhands like Lomber, but that wasn't my problem.

When Ori got her new phone as promised, we talked almost every day. After the excitement of her arrival, she'd collapsed and slept for a long while. It wasn't just jet lag; she told me that Port City overwhelmed her if she stayed out too long. But for short stretches, she loved seeing all the different people and the stores Mrs. Loize took her to, and the immense buildings that towered over her.

I told her I was in a smaller town and she wanted to come see it, but her processing was taking longer than expected. As we got closer to the flight that would take us over to Anglia, I worried that we'd leave before I got to see Ori. I asked Nashan if we could stop over in Port City and see her, if it came to that, but he'd already bought the tickets and he assured me that her paperwork would be done in time.

Two days before we had to leave, I got the call from her that her paperwork was done. She did a good job of controlling herself, while I ran back and forth across the tennis court. I wanted to call Lochen right away, but she said she'd already been in touch with him.

"I'm getting in tomorrow morning, Ro. I'll be in Pinewood at nine. Can you be there?"

"Of course I can be there." I almost dropped the phone. "You think I'd miss it?"

"Lochen said you'll have to leave the next day, but he'll get me a hotel. How long will you be gone?"

I had to think about that one. "When Wimbledon ends. July, I guess."

"At least we'll get to be together for a day."

"I'll figure out some places for us to go. Can't wait."

"Me, neither."

So I found myself at the Casterton International Airport the next morning standing outside the passenger arrival area and wagging my tail as hard as I ever had. On a Monday the airport was moderately busy, but full of wolves, deer, foxes, rabbits, and squirrels. No jackals except for me. A few arctic foxes apart from the one at my side.

Aliq was almost as excited as I was, or at least his tail was wagging like mine. We both kept looking at the arrivals board and then at each other, grinning. "Hey," he said, staring at the board. "It landed! Look, it's in."

"I see!" My stomach was turning loops and I had to clasp my paws together. They felt warm and damp, so I wiped them on my pants and then clasped them together again. How long had it been? Six years? We'd said good-bye outside the Lundara airport and now we were at an airport again. I wondered if her tail was wagging as hard as mine was.

Passengers started coming through the doors in a clump. A pair of snowshoe hares, a brown bear, a timberwolf toting three cubs. Every time a canid came into view, my heart jumped, and then settled down again when I didn't see the distinctive coloring of a black-backed jackal.

And then a canid shape approached the door, a female shape nearly as tall as I was in a long blue dress. Her muzzle was tan and black and her ears stood up straight and narrow, and she walked with a determined stride. Aliq turned, but didn't say anything because he saw that I saw her, and a moment later, her eyes locked on mine and her tail set to wagging up a storm.

We ran toward each other across the cool slick floor and met under the "Passenger Meeting Area" sign in a tight, fierce embrace. "You're so big," I said. "You grew so big."

"You too, Ro!" She pressed the side of her muzzle to mine.

Her scent overwhelmed me. Different, more mature than I remembered, but still uniquely Ori. "I can't believe…" And then I couldn't say any more, and I couldn't let her go. That was okay, because she wasn't inclined to let me go either.

Other passengers streamed around us. I don't know anything about them, because my eyes were closed and my nose was full of Ori.

It seemed like perhaps the entire plane passed us by. Only stragglers remained in the hallway by the time I stepped back and touched my nose to hers. Her eyes were shiny and I think mine probably were as well.

She wasn't the little sister I remembered. Only six inches shorter than me, her muzzle and ears fully grown into adulthood. Her eyes, a soft liquid brown, held mine, and I said the only thing I could think to say in that moment. "You look just like Ma."

The moment I said it, I worried it was the wrong thing, but Ori smiled and her eyes glistened, and she hugged me again.

* * *

There were a million things about the States that I wanted to share with Ori, but with only twenty-four hours until Aliq and I had to leave for Anglia, I couldn't figure out which to do, or even any of the things to do. Aliq, who introduced himself to Ori with a bow and a gentle shake of the paw, suggested we go to Starbucks to get a drink after getting Ori's one suitcase, and even though Ori had been to her first Starbucks over in Port City, she was still thrilled by the flavors and wanted to try them all.

When we talked about Lunda, Aliq hung back, but we didn't touch on any subjects that would've made him feel awkward because those same topics would've made us sad. We talked about Sarya and her family without mentioning Raji, and we talked a little about our father without mentioning Ma. But mostly Ori wanted to tell me about the little things that hadn't made it into our phone conversations. I knew about the new hospital that had been built, but not that Ori had walked through its halls twice and smelled only medicine and antiseptic; I knew that Sarya had gotten Ori a new dress, but not that she'd bought it from a wildebeest trader from Mzansi, a country that hadn't traded very much with Lunda while I was there. I drank in all those little details, and in turn told her about my tennis life, and that's where I pulled Aliq back into the conversation. Though I'd told Ori about my itinerant life many times, she still didn't seem to grasp that we lived much of the time in hotels, flew around enough to be gold on two different frequent flier programs, and didn't even have the shaky stability she'd had living with Sarya. Or rather; we had it but found it in different places than the permanence of our surroundings.

When I called for a cab to take us back to the hotel, Ori's eyes widened. "Isn't there a bus?"

Aliq laughed, but only for a moment when he saw she was serious. "Oh, hey, me and Rocky make enough to pay for a taxi. It'll only be like thirty bucks for the three of us, and that's not that much more than the bus, plus we don't have to schlep your luggage all over the bus."

"'Schlep'?"

"Carry, he means." I picked up Ori's bag as a binturong waved a cab to a halt in front of us and the driver, a zebra, hopped out to open the trunk. I gave him the bag while Aliq opened the back door for Ori.

I rode with Ori in the back; Aliq asked if he could ride in front and the zebra said, "Of course, of course." When we got in, Ori wrinkled her nose at the thick chemical air-freshener smell but didn't say anything.

I pointed out some of the buildings I knew as we passed them, and the zebra joined in, filling in the many gaps in my knowledge. "You are new to Casterton?" he asked.

"I'm just arrived in the States." Ori had been showing me her temporary green card, and now rubbed her fingers over it.

"You are tourist?"

"No. I'm moving here to live with my brother."

My tail thumped against the seat, and then, as the zebra quizzed Ori on where she was from, I thought about what it would practically mean for Ori to live with us. Would she share a room with

Nashan? With us? No, she'd have to have her own: another expense. Lochen didn't seem worried about that, but for me it was a small stress. Taking a cab instead of the bus was one thing, but adding half again to our weekly expenses?

"Where is home?" the driver asked.

Ori hesitated and looked at me. I blinked. "We're going to the Courtyard on Hood Parkway."

"Yes, I know hotel, but where is home?"

I chuckled and leaned back into the seat, meeting Ori's eyes. "Home is wherever the next tournament is."

"That feels very lonely," Ori murmured. "Isn't there a place you go when you're not playing tennis?"

"I'm always playing tennis."

"Freestone," Aliq interjected. "That's where my family lives, and Rocky comes home with me sometimes. Ori can come too."

That brightened my sister's expression. "Your parents are lovely," Ori said.

Then the driver wanted to know what we meant by tournaments, so we told him about being tennis players, and that took the rest of the way to the hotel.

When we got out, Ori said, "Was that supposed to be...some kind of fruit?"

"Cherry," Aliq said. "That's what it said on the air freshener, anyway."

"Fresher? It was terrible. Even if he smelled bad, I'd rather smell him."

I couldn't help smiling. "I agree," I said, "but not everyone does."

Aliq went to our room while I accompanied Ori to the hotel room Lochen had reserved for her. He said he'd asked for rooms as close as possible, but we still had to go one floor up from ours. Once we were alone and the door closed, Ori asked me about Marquize, and I confessed I hadn't talked to him in a while. "Do you have any other friends?" she asked.

"Some of the other players," I said. "Plus I've got friends from Palm Gables and from the Challenger tour that I keep in touch with. Danver and Sean still email us and sometimes we talk on Skype."

"That's good." She walked around the room and went to the window, looking out at the sunny day. "And…anyone closer than a friend?"

I shook my head. "Not since Marquize." I didn't quite feel right telling her that I occasionally went out to gay bars for one night stands, so I just said, "I'm working on my tennis mostly now."

"That's good." She wandered from the window to the bed and fingered the soft cotton sheets. "So what should I do while you're over in Anglia for a month?"

"Well…I thought of a few things. You could go stay with Aliq's parents if you want. Or you could stay here. It's not bad for a month's stay, and Lochen gets a good deal. I mean…really, you could go anywhere in the country you want. I guess you just can't leave until you get your permanent card."

"No." She sat down on the bed and curled her tail around her hips. "Ro, I want to do something useful. I don't want to sit in a hotel room and I'm tired of staying with other people's families."

"You could explore another city, is what I meant. Pelagia is pretty, and Port City is huge. Crystal City is—"

"Is there anything you need done?"

I blinked. "Well, Lochen and Nashan take care of most of the tour. I could ask if maybe you could help one of them out."

"I want to stay with you, but I don't want to just hang about. I want to earn my way."

"Ori." I walked over and took her paw in mine. The bright sunlight lit her muzzle and the sight filled my heart. "I worked the last six years so I could bring you over here. If you don't do anything but be here with me, that's enough for me."

"Thank you, Ro." She smiled back. "But it might not be enough for me."

"Then spend a month getting used to the States. Walk around, explore, see what you'd like to do. You can do anything. There's charity work like you did in Lunda."

She laughed shortly. "It's hard to go from having no options to having all the options. But thank you. Maybe I will do that."

We talked a little while longer without resolving anything. I left her to Lochen's care, with a phone and his number and mine programmed into it, and he promised to explore possible careers for her, especially looking at one she could do while traveling around with me. He also assured me that we could afford the extra hotel room. "It'll be tight for a bit," he said, "but the One Two Three money helps greatly, and if you do well at Wimbledon there will be more."

Honestly, I had only the vaguest idea of how much money I had. I used a credit card for most things, and I could use it to get cash as well. Sometimes I looked at the account balance, but Lochen had told me that money was going in and out of it all the time for fees and such, so I couldn't use that as a sense of how much I could afford. I also knew that he had some of my money in other accounts. So I relied on Lochen to keep my income up and expenses down. Once a year he sat down with me and went over the figures, but there were a lot of numbers and every time I asked him, "So how much money do I have?" he said that income was fluid and he couldn't really assign a number to it. But every year he smiled more when he said it, and every year the "ask me before you buy anything that costs this much" number went up (this year it was "more than a couple hundred dollars").

Saying good-bye to Ori was hard, but not so hard because I knew she'd be safe and I'd be coming back to her in a month. I promised to call now that she had her own phone, and we hugged. She promised to call Lochen and that she'd tell me when she got situated.

And then Aliq and I were on a plane, watching movies and dozing off, and we landed fourteen hours later in Londinium with Nashan. He'd been there before, and neither of us had, so Nashan took it on himself to show us around. He told the taxi driver to take us by the famous cathedral and Parliament buildings on the way to the hotel, and Aliq and I admired them through heavy-lidded eyes.

We were going to be staying in Londinium for one night before driving north and meeting with some other players for the tuneup tournament, partly because we wanted to sleep off our jet lag. The hotel beds were small, like they'd been in Oceania, but the rooms were even smaller. Nonetheless, they were comfortable enough to send us right to sleep (though that might have been the jet lag).

The next morning, I woke to the ringing of my phone. I saw the international number and thought fuzzily that it was Ori, but the voice that jarred me to full wakefulness was my father's.

"I see that you've gotten your sister to the States without paying me my money, and that you've abandoned your family to become a citizen of this new country. I suppose your new States friends think they can violate Lundan tradition, and you went ahead and let them. Well, let me assure you, Rochi, that I will get my money."

"Your money?" I said. "*Your* money? What did you do to earn it? Walk out on a family nineteen years ago?"

"I gave you life," he said.

"You walked out on my life." He started to say something, and maybe it was because I'd just woken up, or maybe because I was still excited from Ori being safe, but I said, "Shut up and listen to me. My father died in the war. As far as I'm concerned, you're a con artist and you and Kamina have ganged up to try to extort money from me. You've failed. You've lost. So walk away. Because I have a family to protect too, and if you come near me or Ori again, I swear to God I will spend five thousand dollars, or ten, or twenty, to make sure that you get fired from your job and have to beg on the street for money."

He didn't say anything, so I said, "Is that clear enough for you, Laurent?"

There was a series of clicks, and then nothing. I hung up the phone feeling curiously numb. I'd made up the thing about the con artist, but it occurred to me that it might not be false. It didn't matter whether it was or not. The important thing was that I'd stood up for myself.

Chapter Sixteen

I didn't tell either Nashan or Aliq about my father's call, even though I was proud of how I'd told him off. I hadn't even told either of them that he was still alive. As far as I knew, Ori was the only person outside of Lunda who knew that, and I was happy to keep it that way.

Anglia felt less foreign than Oceania to me, though Aliq and I had a harder time understanding people once we were out of Londinium. Nevertheless, there was something charming about the small towns of Anglia, and once the people realized we were there for the tennis tournament, they were very friendly and helped us through any misunderstandings.

We recovered from our jet lag and made it through the tuneup tournament, just missing the quarterfinals in doubles, while I got through the qualifiers and two more matches in singles before losing to the world #20. I lost on basically two points in the third set, one a mental mistake and the other a bad double fault, one of those things that rarely happens—but it does happen. So I felt pretty good about my level going into the big tournament as we set up in a tiny hotel room half a mile from the tennis center.

Nashan ran us through a lot of film, as we were getting used to, and gave us physical and mental exercises for practice the next day. I had singles and doubles, so I got twice the work Aliq did, but I viewed it as a challenge and enjoyed the feeling that I had work I could do to improve, especially the next day when we walked around the tennis center for inspiration. There were plaques commemorating the great champions, and after admiring them, Aliq and Nashan and I walked around from court to court remembering the exciting matches that had taken place on each one. The famous Centre Court had hosted every final, but there had been earlier round matches on many others, and we went through them for about forty-five minutes before finally settling down on the practice court we'd been assigned for the day.

I ran into several people I knew there, including the swift fox Palomar, who was going to be in the qualifiers like me, so we compared notes. Lowry was there with Tasman, on track to meet me and Aliq in our third match if we both got that far (we would both be favored in our first match but not the second), so we arranged to grab dinner with them.

Braden was there too, and he and I had a pleasant chat in public, which I hadn't thought would be a big deal. When I walked back to the practice court, Aliq said, "Chummy with Bristlebutt?"

"Bristlebutt?"

"Ah, that's what Teresa calls him. She says he doesn't have a lot of friends on the tour."

He walked out to the baseline to practice serve, but instead of going to the other side of the court, I followed him. "Wait, who's Teresa?"

"Oh, uh." He'd bounced the tennis ball and now held it awkwardly. "She's a doubles player—you know, Teresa Sandleford. Arctic fox, we watched her play a few times."

"Oh," I said, searching my memory, and then I saw his ears back and said, "Ah. So when I go out to bars, you're dating Teresa?"

"Not dating." He bounced the ball, which only momentarily distracted me from his grin. "I mean, we've been talking a bit, but she's top ten in doubles and you know, we're just cracking the top 40."

"So?"

"Well, that matters." He scuffed his paw across the grass of the court. "She's not Jewish, but she's an arctic fox, and how many arctic foxes are you gonna meet on the tour? I think there's only like ten of us."

He'd told me a while back that he was expected to marry a Jewish arctic fox and have a family, but that he could probably put that off. "So would your family be okay if things work out with you guys?"

He shrugged. "There's lots of Jewish kids marrying sh—non-Jewish girls. I think if I really wanted to marry her, we could work something out."

"Do you?"

He held up his paws, which happened to be holding his tennis racket and ball. "Hey, we just started talking. But I kinda wanted to tell you about it."

I laughed. "Okay, well, keep me posted. I don't know if I can help, but I think your mom likes me and Ori."

He grinned back. "It's a long way away and we've got a lot more important things to worry about. Get over there."

We had a good practice and a good dinner after that with Lowry and Tasman exchanging stories about the tour. Tasman had been to Wimbledon and knew a good quiet pub, but as he and I had matches the next day (he was in the qualifiers too), we decided to save it for celebration or drowning sorrows.

On the way back to our hotel, Aliq and I talked about how the wolf and fennec were good guys, and about how hard it was to make friends at this level. Everyone had been through the same things, but everyone was tightly focused and had already made their friends in a few tournaments. You had to find someone like Lowry and Tasman, who'd broken in at the same time you did, or else get introduced some other way. "So how'd you get in with Longacre?" Aliq asked.

"Oh, uh." My mind raced around. "We both went to Palm Gables, you know, and we had the same coach there. He kind of connected us."

"Doesn't seem like the kind of guy who'd take time out to mentor a kid."

"No, but I guess...I don't know, I played him tough the first couple times we met, so maybe he respects me? I haven't really asked."

Aliq laughed. "It doesn't seem like he respects anyone. Well, maybe that's not fair. I mean, he respects people but he doesn't want anything to do with them. But I guess there's exceptions everywhere." He paused and lowered his voice. We'd gotten to the hotel and stopped just outside the doors, and I couldn't see or hear anyone else around. "You're not...dating him, are you?"

"No!"

"Sorry. I just didn't know—"

"It's okay." I pushed my way into the lobby, where only the night clerk, a dormouse, raised his head to us as we entered. "I'm happy to talk to you about stuff, but you know, if I'm dating someone else and they want to keep it a secret, then it's not mine to tell. You know?"

His eyes widened and he nodded. "I didn't think of that."

We got into the elevator. The doors closed, and I pressed the button for our floor. "But," I said in a low whisper, "I'm really not."

* * *

Tasman and I both won our first qualifying matches, and Palomar did too. This was my second major, but it felt more real than the Ocie to me. Of course I'd seen Ocie matches, but this was Wimbledon. It was close to our time zone in Lunda, so we could see the matches live as they happened, and in any of the old tennis specials the center had had, a Wimbledon match featured prominently. The Ocie Open to me had felt distant from the world of tennis because of the plane flight and the foreign country, but here I felt for the first time that I was on the world stage. Part of it might have been that it was my second major, and so the feeling that I really belonged here was only just beginning to kick in for me. Whatever the cause, I was jittery enough to have my serve broken in the first set of my first match, but my opponent, a possum from Oceania, as it happened, wasn't good enough to capitalize, and I won in four sets.

Nashan's training helped greatly. It wasn't that he was necessarily smarter than Coach Keely; it was that he was present and spent all his time getting to know my game. Between matches he kept me focused and gave me techniques to help shore up what he thought were my weak points. I used them effectively in the second match and won again in four, and then won my third qualifying match in straight sets and the qualifying final in five. Tasman played in another qualifying final and lost, which he said was just as well because he was starting to prepare for doubles matches.

I was doing that too, practicing with Aliq and then doing a whole other session of singles practice. Aliq practiced with me, but mostly as a returner and volleyer; he wasn't working on anything in particular with his singles play. I went to sleep frazzled the night before my first round match but woke so excited and ready that I could barely force down two eggs for breakfast.

Once I got on the court, I channeled that excitement into focused play the way Nashan was teaching me. My opponent, an antelope ranked thirtieth in the world, hadn't had to play four qualifying matches to get to this one, but he looked like he could've used more practice. I played aggressively to his forehand, because his strength was his backhand, and pinned him to the baseline with deep groundstrokes because he loved to come to the net. I don't know what he was feeling, but he seemed frustrated by this and made several mistakes before he adjusted. That plus some lucky breaks gave me the first set 6-2, and that rattled him. He took one set from me when I got overexcited and lost a service game, but I beat him in four, and had visions that night of being one of those players on a hot streak, the first unseeded player to win Wimbledon.

Aliq and I won our doubles match the next day, feeding that unreal dream, but the following day I ran into the number nine player in the world, a dingo who had an answer for every shot I made. Nashan had told me not to worry overmuch about his net game, but he ran up to the net every other point. I tried to keep him pinned at the baseline like I had the antelope, but he had an excellent groundstroke game and mixed up his shots with cross-court winners that stymied me. I lost 6-2, 6-3, 6-2, and the only thing I could be proud of was that I hadn't given up in the third set even though the match was clearly out of reach by then.

Nashan patted me on the back for that. "He's not that much better than you," he told me. "You'll get there, and sooner than you think."

Aliq and I did a little better in our doubles play, getting to the third round and playing a tough match that we lost in five sets. In the post-match meeting with Nashan, Aliq said that he thought we were getting the rhythm of best-of-five matches, which was something I'd been thinking as well. They play differently; in a best-of-three you don't have to keep back as much of your strength because you're not going to be playing more than three sets no matter what. But a Grand Slam match could potentially go two more sets—that's almost like playing two matches in a best-of-three.

Nashan said that was good, and that he was going to push us a little harder in practice leading up to the States—we all expected that we'd go to that, and I was excited to get to play there—and for two hours we went over the mistakes we'd made and the things we would be working on over the next few months. As always, he left us with encouraging words about the path we were on. "Now," he said, "we've got another week over here. We can get to see some of the matches, and we'll watch some of them here, but it's also important for you to go out and have fun."

"Lowry and Tasman are out now too," Aliq said.

I elbowed him. "What about Teresa?"

He laughed. "She's still playing. I want to go to her match tomorrow."

"I'll go along," I said. "You going out with her after?"

"We're not even dating yet." He grinned and elbowed me back. "But no, she said no dates while she's still playing."

"All right, then I'll root for her to lose."

"Hey," he said, "don't joke about that." But his tail flicked and he smiled. "She's probably not gonna win the whole thing, so it's only a day or two to wait if she wins, and I hope she does well."

But his ears were back just a bit, and I knew that there was something else going on. I wondered about his comment that rankings mattered. If Teresa did win more and more, would that create more distance between her and Aliq?

It might, unless he and I won more as well. We couldn't do that here, but we could compete at the States and at the smaller tournaments in between. With Nashan's help, we had energy and a plan to move forward that we both felt good about.

As it happened, Teresa did lose that match, but Aliq didn't go out with her that night. She wanted to hang out with her friends, and we were invited along, but Aliq said it was a half-hearted, "if you wanna come," and he sensed they'd rather be by themselves. So we grabbed Tasman and Lowry and had a fun night out at one of the pubs. The two of them pointed out to us that over here the drinking age was eighteen, so we could both drink legally. Even though we'd had beer in Oceania, we hadn't enjoyed it enough for it to be worth the calories on our nutrition plan. "Just because you can do something doesn't mean you should," Aliq said, and I agreed.

"All right," Tasman said.

"Honestly, the beer here isn't great," Lowry said, already halfway through a pint glass. "You're not missing much."

It was funny, I thought, that people who didn't seem to enjoy drinking all that much were so eager to get us to join them. I'd tried beer and other stuff and didn't particularly like being buzzed, so I didn't feel like I needed to push further on to get drunk, which some of my friends (Danver mostly) had insisted was really fun. It helped, though, that Aliq thought the same. "I've had kosher wine," he told me on our way back. "It tastes sharp, even the stuff they give fox cubs. And that's watered down from the watered-down wine they make for foxes."

I told him about Marquize's birthday party where we had the rum and Cokes, and he said he'd never tried that. "But you were what, fifteen then?" I nodded. "Hah, we never had booze parties at my high school. Well, I mean, some kids did, but not me and my friends."

"I think some of the cubs did it more often, but that was the only time I was part of it."

He held out a fist. "Here's to being jock nerds."

I tapped his fist with mine. "Is that a thing?"

"Sure," he said. "We're nerds, but for tennis, so we have to stay in shape. Drinking isn't a part of that."

I thought about that. "Cool," I said. "I didn't realize I was a nerd."

* * *

We went to a few matches, including a quarterfinals match on the males' side that Braden was playing in. He gutted it out through four sets, but it was obvious that he was overmatched. His opponent, Li Xu (the tiger who made it to the Ocie final) had prepared well for him, getting a jump on most of his shots, and even though the tiger had a stretch in the third where he wasn't as sharp and Braden broke him twice to win the set, he recovered in the break and beat the cross fox 6-4 in the fourth.

That evening, Braden texted me, just, *Dinner?*

Sure, I said. *Where?*

Royal Plaza 2130.

His hotel room? Maybe he didn't know private places in Londinium. I sat staring at the message long enough that he texted, *That ok?*

Hurriedly, I wrote back, *Sure.*

But all the way there I wondered what I'd agreed to. There weren't many reasons a gay guy would invite another gay guy to his hotel room, and I couldn't think past the one glaringly obvious one. You're being silly, I told myself. Braden doesn't want to have sex. He's probably in a funk from losing and wants to chill a bit before going out. Or he wants to order room service.

Or maybe he wants to sleep with me.

In the elevator to the 21st floor, I thought about that. If it came to it, would I sleep with Braden? Working against that idea was that he was a prickly guy, temperamental, and this would add complications to our relationship that might distract me from tennis. In favor was that he had a good body, probably more experience than I did, was unlikely to want this to become an attachment or a relationship, I got along with him, and finally the fact that I hadn't had sex since a week or so before we'd left for Anglia, so it had been a month and just the prospect of getting laid was eliciting an unambiguous response right there in the elevator.

Braden, being a fox, could probably smell my interest if I didn't calm myself down, so I spent about ten minutes walking up and down the hallway thinking very hard about tennis and the match I'd seen until I felt I was in a fit state to knock on his door.

He answered in a t-shirt and sweatpants, with a quick nod when he saw me. "C'mon in. Hope you don't mind, but I didn't feel like going out and ditching the entourage so I thought I'd get room service. On me."

"Sure." I stepped into a room significantly nicer than the one Aliq and I were sharing. The one king bed, enormous, filled the back half of the room, and in the front half a small round table with two chairs bore a huge pile of tennis equipment, bags and balls and rackets. The room smelled clean though, and Braden had recently showered, to judge from the warmth of the bathroom and the matching scent of it and of his fur.

He'd already made his selection, so I took the menu and picked a few things that sounded good. Braden called the order down in his usual bored tone, and while he did, I went over and stood by the window. He had a nice view of Londinium a ways away, especially pretty with the sun about an hour from setting over the horizon. "Nice room," I said when he'd finished the order.

"It's okay. Comfortable." He came over to the window, but sat on the bed, which unlike every other surface in the room was clear of tennis paraphernalia.

I leaned against the cool glass of the window, facing him. The light coming through the window brought out nice highlights in his fur and his eyes. He wasn't looking right at me, which was very Braden; he often went off into his own thoughts. But this time his ears were back and his tail was curled with tension. I figured this was a good time to clear up the question that was on my mind. "So hey, was this just dinner, or…?"

He raised one eyebrow and now those hazel eyes, green in the light, focused on me. "You want it to be more?"

My sheath for sure did. I cleared my throat and tried to maintain eye contact. "I mean, if you want it…"

He grinned slightly, a hint of white teeth showing through his black lips. "Don't tell me you haven't been thinking about it."

I wanted badly to reach down and adjust myself, but I also knew that doing so would be a pretty clear signal. "On the way over I wondered why we were going to your hotel room."

"It can just be dinner if you want."

"What do you want?"

He leaned back on his elbows and gave a minute shrug, and then he reached down and deliberately adjusted his own sheath, knowing I was watching. "We're both gay, we're both here, so why not, right?"

"That's all?" I flicked my tail back against the wall. "Do you like me?"

"What's that got to do with anything?"

"I dunno, before I get naked with someone I…" I thought about what I was going to say. Honestly, the last dozen people I'd slept with I hadn't known more than an hour. "I mean, I'm going to be seeing you around, and…"

"Hey." He held up his paws. "I'm not asking you to be my boyfriend. I don't think either of us needs that. What we do need, both of us, is to get off once in a while and do it discreetly. And it's better with a partner than hitting your balls against a wall. So." His paws turned outward in a "well?" gesture.

I've had a lot of awkward moments in my life. That first day in Palm Gables, walking into a classroom with a bunch of other cubs, barely confident in my command of English. The first match I played at a real tournament. My fifteen-year-old classmates passing around rum at Marquize's birthday party. All of these were moments where everyone around me was experienced and I was in a new environment where I was expected to figure it out quickly.

This moment topped all of those. Braden was the only other one there and he had laid out exactly what was expected of me. The problem was that both decisions held potential pitfalls. Obviously, if I said yes to Braden, our relationship—friendship—was going to take a new turn that I was going to have to think a lot about. I had to factor in whether or not it would hurt my tennis game.

I was pretty sure Braden wouldn't be suggesting this if he thought it would affect his game, so maybe the same would be true for me. But Braden and I were different in many ways, and one of those ways was probably in the things that we let affect us.

On the flip side, if I said no, that would change my relationship with Braden too. Not that we'd been the best of friends or anything, but every time someone said that he was prickly or unapproachable I felt a little swell of pride. Not to me, he's not, I'd say to myself. Our friendship was something we'd built together that allowed me to see a different side of him, the side that wanted to help people and be loved. If I said no, he might back off and I'd lose the chance to get to know this unique, fascinating guy.

So either way I ran the risk of things changing. But one way I could maybe get to know Braden better; the other, I probably lost that friendship. Or at least it wouldn't get back to this point again.

I probably would've leaned toward yes anyway. But when it came right down to it, I was twenty years old and hadn't had sex in a month, and a pretty attractive guy—looks, fur, and smell—was offering it.

"All right," I said. "Sure. Makes sense."

He barely reacted. I got a nod and an, "Okay," and then he pulled out his phone.

I glanced out the window as though maybe someone in a nearby building might have seen what just happened. "So, uh…how do we start?"

The cross fox looked up. "Oh, I figured we'd wait until the food arrives."

"So after we eat?"

"No." He put his phone away. "Sex on a full stomach is gross. I just don't want to be interrupted by the room service guy. So once the food gets here, we can bang this out and then have dinner."

"Uh…" I scratched behind one ear. Again that awkward moment. But this time I brought experience to it. I'd been in a bunch of bars and I'd never run into the line "bang this out" from someone who was trying to convince me to sleep with him. "Look, I know it's not your thing, but if you want to do this, could you at least pretend to be looking forward to it?"

Braden raised an eyebrow, his ears perked toward me, and the corners of his mouth twitched. "What makes you think I'm not looking forward to it?"

"Well, you…" I gestured to the pocket where his phone was.

"Because I didn't come over and hug you? Tell you how hot you are? You know all that."

"Doesn't mean it's not nice to hear." He tilted his head, and I realized that I hadn't said anything either. "I mean, I think you're probably the hottest guy who's ever agreed to do anything with me. I'm pretty excited about it, and not just because it's been a month."

He laughed. "For you too?"

"Uh—yeah. Anyway, we're both in the life and it makes sense, like you said, but I'm also looking forward to it."

"Cool," he said. "Thanks."

I waited for him to return the comments, and he for sure had time to do it, but after about fifteen seconds there was a knock at the door and he got up to let the room service in.

The food all smelled great, reminding me I was hungry. Braden tipped the lynx who'd brought the dishes, the lynx left, and then Braden flipped the latch across the door.

"Okay," he said, walking toward me. "Here's my rules. The less talk the better. You do me first, because I know that I'll still be able to do you after I finish."

"I'll be fine," I said. "I know there's some guys who just fall asleep—"

He held up a paw. "Last rule: I know what I like. If I tell you to change up something, don't tell me you know it'll work if I just give it time."

"Do I get some rules?"

He stopped in front of his bed, his pants already unfastened. "As long as they don't conflict with mine."

"Okay." Now I had to think, because I'd only said that to show him that he wasn't the only one who could set up rules. I didn't actually have any, so I thought back to what I'd liked about the previous encounters I'd had. "Afterwards, you have to—we both have to say one nice thing about it."

He considered that and then nodded, pushing his pants the rest of the way down. "Deal." He wasn't wearing underwear. I stared and then tried not to stare, then remembered that the point was for me to look. Braden sat on the bed and leaned back on his elbows. "I like muzzles, but if you don't like guys coming in your mouth, you can finish me with a paw."

"Thanks." I stared down at his lap, at the creamy white sheath and the pink shaft sticking out from it. Then I looked up his t-shirt at the familiar muzzle and tried to keep in my head that this was Braden Longacre, whom I'd known about for years, whom I'd lost to a few times in professional matches, and that was his penis, and I was about to go down on him.

And it was fine, because I'd done this before. So I knelt down by the bed and I touched his sheath, ran my fingers along his length, things that other guys had shown me or that I'd discovered on my own. I cupped his sac, all the while listening for his reactions to figure out which things he liked.

He did get all the way hard, and I thought his breathing quickened, but I didn't get any other reaction until I slid my lips over his tip. Then he sucked in his breath and his legs tensed.

His legs deserve a special mention. I knew that athletes had great musculature; I'd seen it on all my friends. But I'd never been resting my paw on a tennis player's thigh while I blew him, except for Marquize, and Mar's legs were built for speed, not endurance. Also, Marquize had at least twice the body fat of Braden (that's not harshing on Mar, by the way, even though it sounds like it; Braden was insanely fit and had maybe 8% body fat, while I think I still was around 11% at that point, by Aliq's gym measurements). Even through the fox's fur, the steel flexing of his muscles pushed against my paw, and I pushed back, holding it down. He squirmed more but didn't tell me to stop.

His shaft wasn't anything special—except that it was his. Average length and thickness, very musky fox taste and scent. Clean, though, which wasn't true of all the ones I'd put in my muzzle. I was enjoying myself and clearly he was too, squirming harder and harder the more I worked.

But he didn't finish, even though his knot got big and full, and finally he gasped, "Use your paw."

It felt like giving up, but I lifted my head and wrapped my paw around his slick shaft and started pumping. "Tighter," he said, and

I obliged. Even with that it still took two or three minutes before he arched his back, clenched his teeth, and spurted all over my paw.

"Ah-huh. Ah-huh." He lay back, eyes shut, tail bristly.

"Was that okay?" I asked.

He snorted, still panting. "Have you ever had a bad orgasm?"

I laughed. "Point."

Braden lay back another moment, then sat up and gestured me to the bed. "Your turn."

Now came the point where I'd have to strip for Braden. I sat on the bed and started with my polo shirt, lifting it over my head.

"You don't have to take off your shirt."

I held it up and tossed it to the side of the bed. "I know."

He grinned and didn't say anything as I reached for my pants and pulled them off with my underwear in one go, kicking them over to join my shirt on the floor. Then I was sitting naked on Braden Longacre's bed with an erection that was pushing farther out of my sheath the more I thought about it. I jumped when he put his paw around it, and he gave me a wry look. "Settle down," he said.

I panted. "You don't like that I'm excited?"

His eyes widened slightly, and then he bent his head down to take me into his muzzle.

If being naked on his bed was arousing, watching Braden blow me was nearly surreal. I kept flipping back and forth between thinking, "He's just an attractive fox," and thinking about the other times I'd met Braden. If you'd told fourteen-year-old me that I'd be having sex with that arrogant cross fox six years ago—well, I'd have had a whole pile of questions.

He was pretty good, as blow jobs go, but—I mean, his blow job was a lot like his tennis game: technically proficient but also repetitive. He found a sensitive spot and then each of his strokes went there over and over.

It wasn't going to make much difference tonight. Unlike Braden, I got close within like two minutes and grabbed his shoulder. "Hey— huh—I'm—I'm gonna—"

"Mmmf." He nodded and kept going, and a moment later his tongue slid past that sensitive spot one more time and everything that had been building in me let loose. I cried out and then stopped myself from making a noise again, gripping his shoulder hard with one paw and the bedsheets with the other as I emptied myself into the warmth of his muzzle.

I fell back on the bed. Braden got up and went to the bathroom. I heard him run water, but I didn't know if he'd spit into the sink or not. He did gulp a glass of water and then went to the little table where the lynx had left our plates, sniffed, and then put his sweatpants on. "When you're ready," he said.

I relaxed in the glow for perhaps another half minute. It was also nice not to be stressed about getting home afterwards, the slight worry in the back of my head about how trustworthy the guy I'd just blown/pawed off was. And I'd be lying if I didn't say I was pretty excited about having had sex with Braden, as mechanical as it had been.

But I was hungry, too. So I got up and padded over to the table. Braden eyed me with amusement. "Going to eat naked?"

I returned his smile. "Should I not?"

He waved a paw, and I sat down. I couldn't say why I didn't want to put my pants on exactly; I just didn't quite feel like it. And after all, the food wasn't that hot that it would burn anything sensitive if I dropped it.

"So," Braden said, a few bites into his steak. "I've got my 'something nice.' When do we say it?"

I'd gotten halfway through my first lamb burger. Shoot, I'd forgotten about that already. "Oh," I said, "Now is good."

"Okay." He took another bite. "Go ahead."

I took another bite of the burger to stall for time. It was good, with a sharp yogurt sauce and mint leaves, but I couldn't very well say that the dinner was good. What had been really nice about tonight? I started with a feeling and pursued it as I spoke. "I know," I said carefully, "that this isn't a boyfriend situation or anything. But it is something intimate and we hadn't done it before, and I appreciate that you invited me. I had a nice time. I mean…it could've been awkward but it actually wasn't. So thank you for making this happen. I know it wasn't easy."

Halfway through my speech, he put down his fork and knife and listened. When I was done, he nodded. "It would've been harder if I knew any other gay guys on the tour. That I liked."

"Don't argue with my nice thing."

"I'm not arguing! But you're welcome. Okay." He grinned. "Here's mine: next time I'll take my shirt off."

I waited for the rest of it, while he waited for my reaction. "Um," I said. "So what's the nice thing?"

He pointed at me. "You just said not to argue with the nice thing."

"I'm not arguing! I'm asking how it's nice!"

The fox shook his head. "It's nice because I'm telling you I want to do this again. That I had a good time with you and I trust you, and all that, and we should do this again."

I picked up my lamb burger. "All right," I said, and took a big bite, thinking about that.

He must've thought my tone didn't sound convinced, because right around the time I picked up my second burger, he said, "Okay, fine. I don't mind that you're eating naked."

"What?"

"Is that nice enough? You have a nice body, and also the fur patterns." He waved a paw toward me. "I like looking at you. You take care of yourself and you're attractive."

My ears flushed. "Oh. I mean, once you explained the other thing, it was okay. I got it. You didn't have to—but thank you."

"All right." He bent back to his steak. "So maybe I don't have to come up with a new one next time?"

I couldn't quite tell because he was eating, but I'm pretty sure he was smiling when he said that.

Chapter Seventeen

B y the end of the dinner, I was semi-ready to go again, but Braden didn't seem inclined to, and we were having a good conversation about tennis and about the various international destinations I'd be traveling to on the Champions tour. "You've got to go to the Kuwait Open," he said. "They roll out the red carpet and there's a lot of great food around. Not a lot of clubs to go to, but whatever."

"If I go, though, and you go, I mean…"

He grinned. "It's a long way away. Let's see how things go. But yeah, maybe."

So that was when I discovered why I shouldn't eat dinner without pants. My paw was resting in my lap and just naturally went over to my sheath and squeezed a bit, and then thinking about having sex again plus the squeezing had an effect, and my paw was drawn to holding the warmth and hardness…I pulled my fingers away and put my paw back on the table. "When is it?"

"October-November, something like that."

"Cool. I hope Ori can come with us by then."

Talking about my sister would make my erection go down, I hoped, and it did. Braden asked how she was doing, and we talked about her for a bit. I asked about his family, but he just said, "They're all fine" and didn't tell me much about them at all.

Soon enough I put my pants on. "Thanks for having me over," I said, standing at the door with Braden.

"Thanks for coming," he said. "See you 'round."

And that was all the affection I was going to get from Braden Longacre. That was fine; I didn't really expect anything more than that. I left singing a song to myself in my head. It was a tune from one of my newer punk albums, one that had been caught in my head, but I changed the words around a bit. *I blew Braden and he blew me,* I sang, and after a bit I added another verse: *I got to see something no one else can see.*

I didn't know if that was true, but it captured how I felt in that moment and it kept me smiling, so I kept singing it.

Feeling good made me think about calling Ori, even though I couldn't tell her why I was happy, but it was late here so it would be later where she was—wait, no, she was the one farther west than me now. Even if it was eleven at night here, I could call her.

"My arm hurts," she told me when I asked how she was doing.

"What did you do to it?"

"Nothing! I have been going to the doctor's office and getting a new needle stuck in my arm every week. Distemper, parvo, rubella, measles, something called 'myxa-something or other,' I don't remember what but they assure me that I need to be vaccinated against it."

"You do."

"I know. But it hurts now."

I laughed. "More than when you broke your leg?"

"I was six! And that was an accident. They're doing this to me on purpose." She laughed with me, though. "But I understand the bus and the city and I'm getting used to the States, slowly. There's so much television to watch and people dress so fancy, but also sometimes not, and there are very rich places almost right next to very poor places." She sighed. "I miss you, Ro. We only got the one day together."

"I'll be back in a few days, once the tournament's over. Then we've got the whole States Open season, and after that you'll have your paperwork done and you can travel with me."

"Can't wait. Oh! I talked to Lochen the other day. He's so nice, and I love his accent. Where is he from?"

"Pike, I think? But his family's from somewhere else, I don't know where. Alba, perhaps?"

"I might ask. But he said that he wanted to talk to me about perhaps managing your twitter account and InstaPic or whatever it is. He says you're not doing very well with it, but he doesn't want to bother you because you're doing so well with your tennis. So it would help you if I posted pictures for you and little updates. You have fans, you know."

"I—I do?"

This is going to sound really dumb, I know. I played matches at Wimbledon and at the Ocie. There were crowds at those matches, people cheering for me, people who even asked for my autographs after matches. But that kind of thing happens at tennis matches. People show up, they decide to cheer for one side or another, or they just cheer for the match. They get autographs from the players because the players are collectively more famous than they are. But the idea that a few people were following me specifically, my career, my matches—that hadn't really entered my head.

Ori laughed at me. "Of course you do. You've been in commercials, you're almost in the top 50 in the world. You have fans. Not as many as, you know, Tempest."

"Tempest does commercials for expensive watches where he's half-naked." I'd masturbated to one of those commercials with the half-naked panther a few years back. Not my finest moment, but I still thought about it sometimes. Braden was handsomer, though.

"That could be you one day."

I coughed. "If you're asking my permission to run my social media, you have it. Go ahead. I'll be glad not to have to worry about it."

"Great! I'm really excited about it." I could hear the swish of her tail wagging. "I'll still ask you to take pictures but then you'll just have to send them to me and I'll post them."

"Fantastic." I'd gotten back to my hotel room. "Hey, I'll call when I know when we're landing."

"Lochen will tell me." She laughed. "I think he likes me because I'm not a tennis player."

"Good. All right, I'm gonna get some rest. You want anything from Londinium?"

"If you see something nice, but I don't even know what to ask for."

"Next year you'll be here with me."

"Can't wait."

Aliq was already asleep, so if he'd gone out with Teresa, it hadn't lasted very long. I undressed and lay back in bed, one paw on my sheath, thinking about the cross fox whose paws and muzzle had rested there just a little while ago.

* * *

Aliq and I palled around for the next few days, having a great time despite wishing we were still playing. I didn't tell him about Braden, and he didn't say anything about how things were going with Teresa, though he did go out to dinner with her again the night after the male semifinal. I thought about texting Braden; I knew he was still around because I'd crossed paths with him in the player-only areas, but though he'd waved to me, we'd both been talking to other people and we hadn't gone out of our way to talk. So I figured I'd wait for him to make the next move.

It was the day before the final in one of those players-only areas that this happened. They'd put out snacks and I was talking to Lowry—I think Aliq was off with Teresa, though I wasn't sure. Braden came up in the middle of our conversation and jerked his head to one side. "Rocky," he said. "Can I talk to you a minute?"

"Sorry," I said to Lowry, who said not to worry about it and went off to get more strawberries and cream while I followed Braden away. His tone had been neutral enough that this could either be "let's hook up again" or "we're through," and I'd never know until he actually told me, but I wasn't really worried that it would be the latter.

We went off to one side and leaned against a wall. "I'm staying around Londinium for a few days," he said. "In a hotel downtown. If you're interested, maybe you could stay a bit too."

"Uh, yeah," I said. "I'd like to. Have to change my flight, but…I can do that."

"If it's too much trouble…"

"No, no." Already I was getting excited about the idea of a few more days, no sneaking around—well, not as much. "I'd love to get in some more, uh, practice with you."

He gave one of those half-smiles that showed that he got my joke. "Most of my entourage won't be around. I'll send them ahead to the next tournament, and—"

His eyes flicked to a spot over my shoulder and his smile vanished. A moment later, a heavy paw landed on my shoulder and Ljubo Colluvic came into view.

I'm one of the taller players on the tour, but this black wolf looked down four centimeters at me with a broad smile. "Hey," he said, his light Slavic accent coming through. "N'Guwe, right?"

He stuck out his paw and so I grasped it in mine. I usually don't squeeze hard when I shake paws, but I do try to match the other guy, and Colluvic was squeezing. "Yeah," I said. "Colluvic, number five. I saw your quarterfinal."

Our paws stayed clasped a moment longer, long enough for both of us to feel that our grips were equally matched, and then the wolf let go with a hearty laugh. "Sorry you had to see that. One day I will figure out this bobcat, but I'm not the only one who has trouble. Longacre too, yes?" He stuck out his paw and Braden shook it quickly.

Chix Kalanada, Colluvic's fellow Kanatian, would be playing in the final against the tiger who'd beaten Braden. Neither of them was present, both likely practicing. "I haven't played him yet," I said, "but that serve is killer."

Colluvic shook his head. "I thought I'd seen enough film, but he's very good with it. You think you're ready, but, whoosh." He jetted his paw through the air. "Right where you cannot reach."

"You're good," I said. "Best backhand in the game."

"Hah." He pushed my shoulder. "You have a good forehand and backhand. Solid game, all around, not much weakness. Just need to get a little better everywhere."

"I'm trying."

"Ahem," Braden said.

Colluvic turned to him. "Yes, sorry to interrupt. I thought I heard you say you are staying in Londinium?"

I nodded and spoke up before Braden could answer, jumpy that Colluvic had heard more than that (even though we hadn't said more). "We're planning to practice a bit."

"I want to visit a couple tourist spots," the cross fox said smoothly, "museums and stuff, but I don't want to neglect tennis for a few days, so I asked Rocky to stick around and practice. He's never been to Londinium before."

When he talked about tourist spots, that's when I remembered that I would be putting off seeing Ori again. My heart sank, but Braden was right here in front of me, and I'd already said I'd stay with him. I couldn't back out now.

"As it happens," Colluvic said, "I have family visiting, so I am also staying after the final. If you'd like, I would be happy to practice with you. With you both," he clarified.

"Me, too?" I couldn't help the surprise, and my ears folded back even before Braden shot me a disapproving look. I knew I should be more confident in my game, but I wasn't even top 50 yet.

"Solid game," Colluvic said. "Tempest practiced with me a few years back when I was number 45, and told me to give a chance to some young player in the future, so." His smile stretched farther back than Braden's, showing more teeth and genuine joy. "This is the future."

"Of course," I said, again pre-empting Braden. "I'd be delighted."

"That'd be fine." Braden kept his ears up politely.

So we exchanged numbers and the big black wolf went off wagging his tail. Braden's ears went half-flat when he'd gone. "He's not gay," he said. "If you were thinking of a threesome."

"No," I said, though now I was. "I just want to practice with as many great players as I can. You and him."

"I don't want to practice with him."

"You don't have to." I gave him a smile that I hoped was as large and genuine as Colluvic's. "He asked me, too."

Braden stayed a little sulky, but I couldn't get over being asked to practice by a top five player. Aliq got that too, when I told him. "Dude," he said. "Change your flight. Practicing with Colluvic and Longacre? Yeah, do that in a heartbeat."

"Thanks," I said. "It's only for a few days." I regretted that I wouldn't see Ori, but I was sure she'd understand about the practicing opportunity, even if I couldn't tell her about the rest of it. I'd promise her lots of pictures.

"This game is about learning all you can." Aliq patted me on the shoulder. "I'm a bit jelly but I'll get over it. Man, think about getting those guys in that intimate setting for a few days."

I coughed and made sure he didn't see me adjust my pants.

* * *

The Wimbledon final between Kalanada and Li wasn't one of the better ones I'd seen. Li, the tiger, had his forehand working even better than when he'd beaten Braden, and Kalanada didn't have an answer for it. The bobcat kept trying to step around his backhand to go on the offensive himself, but when he did, Li himself found the open court to hit easy winners. Braden, I thought, had played Li the toughest of anyone in the tournament. It didn't help that the temperature hit 30 C that afternoon, and at match time was still a bit north of 25. Li didn't mind the heat, but whether from losing the first two sets or from the heat, Kalanada moved visibly slower in the third set. Even in the trophy ceremony, he was panting and gulping water.

Everyone cleared out pretty quickly after that. Braden and I stuck around as planned, and a pawful of other players did as well. By the Tuesday after the final, though, it was just him and me and Colluvic.

I'd worried that the big black wolf would be hanging around us all the time, but he disappeared during the day, spending time with family probably, and returned to the Wimbledon grounds in the evenings, which were the best time to practice anyway. The weather had held for most of the tournament, but the heat that had rolled in the last weekend stuck around. Braden and I went to the Gaelic Museum that first day and spent it all in the cool air conditioning walking through marble hallways dotted with history: paintings, sculpture, artifacts of old civilizations. At one point when Braden was off looking in another room, an old fennec came up to me and started talking about how the Colonials had stolen these treasures from the native people—he had been born in Masr in the country of Kumat, very near the three famous pyramids, and he said bitterly that if the "colonizers" had been able to do it, they would have brought the pyramids back here as well.

The conversation was more intense than I was expecting, but I felt for him. I told him about my home and the endless wars there, and he shook his head and said that my people were still feeling the pain of colonization. He asked if I and my family were doing well, with an unexpectedly genuine interest, and I told him I had just gotten Ori out. He clasped my paw and said I had done well, and then he wandered away.

I thought about that while Braden and I ate in the museum cafeteria, and eventually asked Braden what he thought about the Gaels and Anglians stealing cultural treasures. He shrugged. "That's how the world works."

"I know," I said, "but that doesn't make it right."

"Those ancient Kumatians," he said, "also took advantage of weaker people. Stole some things, used other people as slaves. So it is 'right' for them to have the treasures?"

"They're part of their culture, though. Their history."

He nodded. "True. The thing is, there's always going to be strong and weak, and it goes around in cycles. This country," he waved a paw to indicate our surroundings, "took advantage of ours, until we broke away from them. Now we're stronger and they're, well, they're still strong, but things are changing. In a couple hundred years, we'll probably have collapsed and someone else will be on top."

"So what do we do?"

He raised his eyebrows. "We enjoy being on top."

* * *

Colluvic met up with us that evening on the Wimbledon courts. After the tournament, the courts were open to the public for a limited time—not all of them, not Centre Court, but the outer practice courts. A few had been reserved for our use, so we headed for those initially. For a while we rotated, one of us practicing serves on one court while the other two hit back and forth on the adjacent one. I'd practiced against Braden before, so I knew more or less what to expect, and this time I had his "enjoy being on top" comment in my head. So I started mixing up my play, trying to jar him off balance.

To my surprise, I got him a little rattled. He sailed a couple forehands long and walked up to the net to talk to me. "Hey," he said. "We're just practicing."

"I know." I grinned. "I'm playing around. Having fun. Try it."

He shook his head like I was the one who didn't get it, and after another ten minutes of that he signaled to Colluvic to come take his place.

I'd never played the big wolf, but I'd seen a few of his matches. Playing him was a whole other experience: he bounded around the court with the energy of a squirrel but had an extra foot of reach, so it was immensely difficult to get anything past him. If you could fool him, you could wrong-foot him and then you could get something by him; otherwise you could try the way Braden played: precisely placed groundstrokes that I think bored Colluvic to the point that he made an error. He was really good, though—not as good as Braden at his best, I thought, but such an exuberant style of play that at the end of one rally we met at the net, both panting, both laughing. I glanced at the adjacent court and saw that Braden wasn't serving anymore, just watching the two of us.

While we practiced, a little crowd had gathered at a spot outside the courts where you could look through. After that last rally, Colluvic pointed them out to me. "Hey," he said, "if we get one of those guys in here we could play doubles."

Still laughing, it took me a moment to realize he was serious. "Really?"

"I do that sometimes," he said. "People take pictures and they get so happy about it. You can't do it all the time, but there's twenty people there, thirty? We could give one of them a thrill."

I thought about Ori and my social media. "Okay," I said. "I'm in."

Braden was harder to convince. "Absolutely not," he said, ears flat. "Bring in two people and you two play doubles."

Colluvic looked at me and shrugged, up for it, but I wanted to give it another try. "Come on," I said. "One game, then you can sit out and we'll grab someone else."

Braden shook his head, so I went on, "Let people get some pictures, like Colluvic said. It'll be good for your image."

"People will start to expect it," the cross fox said. "I don't want to do a nice thing once and have people keep asking me for it later."

I raised an eyebrow. "Maybe you'll like doing it and you'll want to do it again."

"Mmm." He started to shake his head, and I held up a paw.

"At least once and you can say you tried. Colluvic will take the rando as his partner and you can play with me. Okay?"

The fox stared for so long that Colluvic started to say, "It's okay…" and then Braden rolled his eyes.

"Fine," he said, and gave me a look that I couldn't quite figure out. "One game."

"Cool!" The big Kanatian wolf bounced off to let in a few of the spectators and figure out who was going to hit around with us.

"I just think it'll be fun," I said.

Braden gave me another look and then shook his head again, bouncing a tennis ball on his racket. "I haven't played doubles in a while. You have signals you use?"

"I don't think it's going to be that formal." I grinned and walked up to shake paws with the overwhelmed red fox Colluvic had chosen, an amateur player shorter than any of us but dressed in bright white tennis gear and with a racket bag.

"Thank you so much," he said. "This means so much. Is it alright if my wife takes pictures?" He gestured toward the small crowd who'd come into the courts to watch, and at first I thought he meant the female fox, but she wasn't holding a camera up. The polecat next to her, in a white skirt and tennis shirt, was, and so I supposed that was his wife.

"That's fine," I said. "Would she mind taking some with my phone as well?"

My phone could take pictures from the lock screen, so I wasn't worried she was going to go into my private stuff. The fox stuttered that that would be fantastic, and as he seemed more interested in Colluvic and Braden than in me, I walked over with my phone (and Colluvic's, at his request) and gave them to the polecat.

"Thank you for doing this," she said, her eyes wide as everyone around her patted her and made approving noises. "He loves watching you all, but Mr. Longacre is his favorite player."

"He's a fantastic player," I told her. "Thanks for taking pictures."

"If you need help..." The female fox and another spectator offered to take the extra phones so that the polecat could focus on her husband, and while they were sorting that out I went back to the court.

Braden waited for me on one side while Colluvic and the red fox stood on the other. "Just call it if you're going to get it," he said, "and move out of the way if I call it."

"Got it." I bounced some balls on my racket. "Hey, the guy is a big fan of yours. Maybe sign a ball for him after or something?"

The cross fox nodded, but distractedly, as though I'd interrupted him getting ready for a match. Which technically we were, but even when Colluvic and the other fox got into position, we didn't play very formally. We played points, but for example, when a ball landed near the line on their side, Colluvic just hit it back without arguing that it was out.

I had a lot of fun, not just watching this fox have the time of his life, but also playing with Braden. It wasn't the same as partnering with Aliq, not by a long shot, but the feeling of being on the same side as the cross fox was fun. We all three made a point of telling the red fox when he'd made a good shot, which wasn't very often, but he didn't seem to care much.

Braden and I won the game (to the extent that we kept score) and afterwards Braden excused himself. I forgot about the autographed ball because Colluvic grabbed another spectator to play doubles with us and I went right into another game with the red fox as my partner this time, against Colluvic and a badger who was significantly not as good as the fox. So we won, and afterwards the fox thanked me and then said, "I'm frightfully sorry, but can you remind me of your name? I know it's Rocky, but I don't know your last name."

"N'Guwe," I said, "and it's no worry. I know I'm not as famous as these two."

The fox smiled. "You will be," he said. "Twenty years I've been watching tennis. I know a champion when I see one. Would you mind very much if…"

At that moment Braden came up holding out a tennis ball. "Here," he said. "This is the ball you got that winner with."

The fox stared and then took the ball. As he turned it over, Braden's tidy signature in thick black marker became visible. "Oh my God," he said. "Thank you so much."

"Keep working at it," the cross fox said, and then walked off to gather up his things with Colluvic.

"He's pretty cool," I said, because the red fox didn't seem able to muster up words. His wife came up to him then and he showed her the ball. "Hey, it was nice meeting you," I said, though I'd already forgotten his name.

"Wait!" He held out the ball to me as his wife dug around for a pen. "Would you—would you be able to sign it as well?"

* * *

Because Colluvic wanted to have dinner, it was past ten o'clock by the time he went back to his room, and once we were alone, Braden said, "Want to come back to the room?"

I grinned at him. "Of course."

So we had sex again, with muzzles again, and this time, true to his word, he took his shirt off and lay naked on the bed beside me, tail fluffed out to the other side. I lay on my back, having just finished, still trying to recover my breath. "You can do amazing things with your tongue," I told him.

After a moment, he said, "That was fun today."

"Which?" I panted. "The museum or the tennis?"

"All of it," he said. "But I meant the tennis with that random guy. I haven't done anything like that in a while. Even with Colluvic. I have my practice partners and I don't usually go outside the routine. So thanks for talking me into it." He turned his head slightly to meet my eye. "That's my nice thing about you."

I grinned. "Going outside the routine can be fun."

"Yeah." He laced his fingers together behind his head. "Don't want to make a habit of it."

"You never know." I rested fingers on his bare stomach. He flinched but then settled back again. "Might want to keep doing fun things once you've tried them."

* * *

By this time, flying by myself didn't worry me at all. Braden was flying back the same day, but ten hours later, so I went to the airport on my own, navigated the big confusing mess of lines and security checks (three different ones), passport and ticket and boarding pass and security voucher, a weird thing we didn't have in the States that told the second security checkpoint that you had indeed passed the first one. Lochen texted me the morning of the flight to make sure I was on my way to the airport in plenty of time, and again to make sure I'd gotten through security with no issues.

After sitting at the gate for half an hour, we found out that our flight had been delayed, so instead of boarding in forty minutes, we'd be boarding in two hours. That drove me to a coffee shop where I sat with my tablet and looked over my matches from Wimbledon (Nashan's orders) for an hour, and then, because it was available, I pulled up Braden's semifinal match.

For ten minutes I watched his form, studied the way he moved, the way he anticipated shots. I watched his reactions and his shot selection, and his footwork, all of which was excellent. This was a guy who'd won a major, so how had that tiger caught him so off? After that first ten minutes, I got distracted remembering how he looked naked, picturing that, remembering his muzzle on me and the intimacy of lying beside him.

That wasn't productive, but it did get me embarrassingly aroused in the middle of an airport coffee shop, so I returned to studying his tennis form. I don't know what I thought I'd be able to find that he and his coaching team wouldn't, but I hoped I could come to him with some tennis tip. But he was so tightly precise in all of his movements that I couldn't find any flaws with it.

Two coffees later, our flight finally began boarding, and I traded waiting in a roomy coffee shop that smelled nicely of tea and coffee to waiting for twelve hours in an airplane. At least my current income allowed me to travel in the more comfortable business class, where I got reasonable meals and had my pick of movies to watch. Nashan would want me to watch film, but I'd already watched a lot, so I selected a few movies and leaned back.

The first movie was a romantic comedy, which was fun but also unfortunate because it made me wonder about me and Braden. We weren't boyfriends; he'd hammered that home. But also we had established that we weren't just going to be a one-night hookup. So where did that leave us? In the movie, the attractive coyote guy wants to date the coyote gal, but she doesn't want to commit to anything. "Can't we just do this," she says, gesturing to their tastefully hidden naked bodies in bed, "and not worry about everything else?"

"I can't help worrying," he said.

I wasn't sure how much that applied to my situation, especially since whatever this new relationship was had only existed for a week. But like the male coyote (who was pretty hot himself), I couldn't help wondering what would happen when we got back to the States. Would he limit our nights to once a tournament? Only after we'd both lost?

If I'd been on an overnight flight and the cabin lights were dim, my fellow passengers all asleep, I'm pretty sure I would've ducked into the bathroom to take care of some of the pressure my fantasies were creating. But everyone was awake, and between me and the bathroom sat a fox couple, so I kept imagining that I'd come out of the bathroom and both their noses would turn toward me, and then I'd have to hurry back to my seat and they'd be whispering about me for the rest of the flight. So I turned to a comic-book action movie next, and that relaxed me, and I only thought about Braden a little bit for the rest of the flight. Well, a little bit at a time.

After landing and going through Customs, I expected to have to get a taxi or ride share to the hotel Lochen had texted me, but to my surprise, Aliq and Ori met me at the airport. I dropped my bags to

hug Ori, still delighted to see her in person, and then I hugged Aliq, too. "You guys didn't have to come. I can get around on my own."

"She didn't want to wait." Aliq jerked a thumb toward Ori.

"Besides," Ori said, "Aliq said he'd show me a river that used to be on fire. But it looked very normal."

"Used to be," Aliq reminded her. "Like forty years ago. They cleaned it up."

"It would be more interesting if it were on fire." Ori smiled at me.

"Probably not as healthy for everyone, though," I said. "Aren't there pictures of it somewhere?"

"I showed her pictures!" Aliq held out his phone.

"In black and white," Ori scoffed, but smiling.

I picked up my shoulder bag, and Aliq grabbed my racket bag before I could. "All right," I said. "It's good to see you two again."

We kept chatting all the way back. Ori and Aliq had obviously spent the last few days hanging out, because they conversed easily and happily. At one point Aliq mentioned something about me coming back with a muddy tail, and I laughed until I remembered that that was something that had happened when I was nine. "Ori," I said, and she was already looking back at me, her ears half-down.

"I'm sorry, Ro, but it was a funny story."

Because Aliq was still chuckling, I said, "All right, I'm going to call your mother and find out something embarrassing you did when you were nine."

Coming back to this family reminded me that this was my life, and that any romanticizing of my relationship with Braden was at best adolescent wishing. What, did I think we were going to travel together on tour? The best thing I could do was leave my relationship with Braden where it was and focus my energy on moving forward in tennis.

That didn't stop me from texting him, *Had a great time in Anglia. See you in Cuyahoga.* But then I thought, what if he thought "see you" meant that I was asking for another date, pressuring him? So I changed it to "have a safe flight back." But he was already on his flight back, so did that make sense? I stared at it until Ori leaned forward and said, "Ro."

"What?"

"Where do you want to stop for dinner? I've asked you three times. Who are you talking to?"

"Nobody," I said, and hit Send.

Nashan met with us early the next morning. I hadn't slept well, but I was awake, if a little bleary-eyed, sitting next to Aliq as the red fox showed us film for our upcoming matches. "We're going to play a bunch of tournaments," he said, "leading up to the States Open, which you're pretty definitely going to. I've squeezed one extra in there because Rocky, I think you have a chance at breaking into the top 50 by the States, definitely by the end of the year."

Aliq squeezed my wrist. I wagged my tail and said, "That's fine, I can play more tournaments. And how about our doubles ranking?"

"Oh, that'll improve, too," Nashan said. "But it won't really change your seeding at the States."

I nodded and stifled a yawn, trying not to let Nashan notice, but of course he did. "All right," he said, "let's get you some melatonin this morning and see if we can't kick that jet lag before you have to play."

And then it was tennis, tennis, tennis. The melatonin didn't help that day because I didn't take it until evening, but I did feel more alert and energetic the next day.

It was a good thing that I didn't have to play in the qualifiers anymore, because otherwise I wouldn't have been able to change my flight. I watched some of the qualifying matches as a break from practice, looking over a few of the players Nashan thought were particularly talented and might end up in main draws. But mostly it was getting back to practices and routine with Aliq.

Ori came to our practices and took pictures which she posted on my social media. I only looked at InstaPic, but I really liked the tone she took with the posts. She posted as me, so it was a little odd to look at a picture of myself with racket outstretched and the message, "Getting into the swing of things again." And where had she learned to make plays on words in English?

The account got lots of likes and comments—my fans, I guess. I had a few thousand followers, but every day I picked up more. Ori and Lochen talked about the social media stuff, and I only occasionally needed to be included in those discussions, which suited me fine. I'd given Ori the pictures of me playing with Colluvic and Braden, and those had jumped my following by almost a thousand in just a week. Of course, Colluvic had a great social media "presence" (that's what Lochen called it), and Braden had over a hundred thousand followers even though his feed was "sterile" (Lochen again), so anything I did with those two was sure to help. "Keep spending time with them," Lochen said, and I said I'd do my best, trying not to think about the fact that Braden still hadn't texted me back.

Chapter Eighteen

I did see Braden later that week, getting ready for his match in the locker room. "Hey," I said, walking over to him.

He looked up with that wary look he always had, which melted into a smile when he saw who it was. "Oh, hi. How was the flight back?"

"Not bad." I shifted, tail wagging before I stopped it. "How was yours?"

"First class." He shrugged. "They didn't have many movies I hadn't seen before, so I slept a bunch."

"I still haven't seen most of the movies on planes, so I watched all the way back."

"Cool. Anything good?"

And we talked about movies for like ten minutes, and then he had to go play his match, so I wished him good luck. It was all very unremarkable and normal. I didn't ask him why he hadn't texted me back; we didn't set a time to get together. But I still walked away wagging my tail and telling myself I'd see him again pretty soon.

I won both my singles and doubles matches the first couple days, and for the first time Ori got to see me play. After the first match she watched, when I came out of the locker room, she ran up to me panting, her tail wagging. "Ro," she said, grabbing my paw. "I knew you were good, but you're *so* good!"

Laughing, I hugged her. Aliq, standing to one side, said, "You should see him when I'm not there to help him out."

When we both turned to him, the arctic fox winked. "He's even better."

"Nashan showed me some of his matches," Ori said. "But watching in person is different. It's so much more exciting!"

"I've been doing it for years now, so I guess it's just routine for me." But Ori's excitement did make a difference; my tail wagged in sympathy with hers and my heart sped up a little.

"I got some great pictures and here's what I posted about your win." She showed me her phone. "Already twenty-three people liked it!"

"Nice." I pulled my phone out and turned it on. "You're doing great."

"All right," Aliq said. "I got our dinner reservations and Nashan wants to go over film for your match tomorrow. You guys ready?"

"Yeah." My phone beeped with a message, so I listened while we walked out of the facility.

Aliq saw my expression as I hung up. "Something wrong?"

"No, it's weird." I called up Lochen's number. "Usually Lochen tells me when I have an endorsement."

"You're getting so many, maybe he just can't keep up."

I'd gotten Aliq to be my partner in one of the endorsement deals, and he liked to have fun teasing me about how many I'd done without him. At this point I was paying for a lot of his travel and hotel anyway, so he appreciated that. "Maybe. You ever heard of Wildtown Apparel?"

I left a message for Lochen while Aliq said he hadn't and Ori looked them up on her phone. "They're a small shirt company out of St. Clair, mostly they seem to have college hockey players and—what's the sport with the nets on the end of sticks?"

"Lacrosse?" Aliq took her phone. "Yeah, that's lacrosse."

"No tennis players?"

Aliq shook his head. "Doesn't look like it."

"Okay. Cool, I'll be the first."

I didn't think anything more about it until the middle of dinner, when Lochen called back. "What is this about Wildtown Apparel?" he asked. "I looked them up. You want to do something with them? Should be easy, they don't have any high profile sponsors really, but I'm not sure it'd be worth your time."

"No, they called to verify an endorsement or something?"

"What?" Lochen's affable tone sharpened. "Have you been going off on your own taking meetings?"

"No! I've been in Londinium, how could I?"

"You know how we're talking right now, Rocky? You can call people."

I rolled my eyes. "Well, I didn't."

"So how do they expect you to be doing something for them?"

"I don't know! Call and ask them."

He sighed, but even his sigh had a growl to it. "Fine. Forward me their message, then I'll have the number."

"Okay." I paused. "How do I do forward a voicemail?"

"I'll help you." Ori held out a paw.

"You'll help me? How will you help me? You've only had your new phone for three weeks."

She raised an eyebrow. "I haven't had much else to do for three weeks. You might be better than me at tennis, but you're not better at everything."

Aliq chuckled. "I was gonna volunteer, but I think it'd be funnier if she does."

"Ori's going to help me," I told Lochen.

"I'll take care of it," he said.

So I gave my phone to Ori. She found the message and forwarded it to Lochen. I watched what she did but I still didn't think I could do it on my own. That was fine; I had people around me who could.

I lost just before the quarterfinals of the tournament, but that was a good showing considering I lost to the #19 player in the world. Aliq and I got to the semifinals and gutted out a tough three-set match to secure a finals berth. Meanwhile, Braden was playing in the singles semifinal right after, so I didn't even change before I ran over to the other court to watch. I'd seen him win his quarterfinal match, precise and powerful as always, but here he was facing Li Xu again and something seemed off. The tiger danced around, mixed up his shots, and Braden got to most of them but the tiger had more energy. He beat Braden 6-4, 6-7, 7-5; Braden stayed with him most of the third set until he was serving at 5-6 and Li broke him.

Aliq had gone off to see Teresa, so I was on my own. I ventured down into the locker room a little after the match, but Braden had already changed and was out doing his media session. I listened outside the door as he deadpanned a bunch of the same questions you get after every match. "What went wrong?" "After the second set tiebreak, did you feel like you had momentum?" "At 4-3 in the third, you double-faulted. Do you think that was the turning point?"

Braden had flatly affected answers to all of these. "Li's a great player and he had it going today." "You learn that momentum comes and goes in this game." "I made a number of mistakes in the match. I don't think there was one turning point."

They were the phrases that Lochen and Nashan had worked on with me, and yet when Braden said them they felt lifeless, even more so than they'd been designed to feel. He sounded like someone sent by Braden to read the lines for him, someone who had no emotional attachment to them. When I did interviews after matches, albeit mine were shorter and less well attended, I always tried to give the phrases my own flair. Braden had no flair at all. Or maybe you could say that his lack of emotion was his flair.

I texted him when he was done with the press conference, just a quick note: *Dinner?*

It wasn't until I got back to the hotel and was talking to Ori that Braden texted me back. *Sure. Marriott 799.* So I told Ori I had a dinner meeting, and she asked if this was one of my "nights out" that Aliq had told her about. I said that it was and she told me to be safe as I set off, tail wagging in anticipation.

On the way there, my phone buzzed. I was going to ignore it, but when I looked at the number it was Lochen, so I picked up. "What's going on?"

"I found out what happened with Wildtown." He sounded grim.

"What?"

"Someone claiming to be your father called them and tried to set up an endorsement deal. He gave them your phone number to prove he knew you, but thankfully they waited for your permission to move forward."

I stopped dead on the street. "That might be my father."

"I thought he was in Africa."

"He was. He was trying to get me to pay him to help Ori out of Lunda, so he was pretty mad when we did it without him. He called me a few weeks ago."

"What?" Lochen's voice got sharper.

"Not threatening, just telling me he was going to get his money out of me. 'One way or another,' if I remember." I leaned back against a wall and shook my head. "It sounds like a threat, now I think about it. Anyway, I told him to get lost."

"All right." He was quiet for a minute. "Don't worry about it. Consider it handled."

"Thanks." I hung up and stared down at my phone. I still had my father's number in it. Maybe this was his way of getting me to call him again. Whatever it was, he could fuck off. I had more important things to do tonight. So I slid my phone back into my pocket and hurried on.

When I got to Braden's room, he greeted me in jeans and a nice collared shirt, but the shirt was open at the front to show off his chest and stomach fur. Momentarily distracted from my father, I put my phone away. "We going out?"

"If you want. I know a great chili place a couple blocks away." He stepped aside to let me in as the door closed behind me.

"Sounds great." He didn't make a move to button up his shirt, and my thoughts had already traveled back to my father and the endorsement deal, so when he walked over to the bed, I didn't follow.

When Braden clapped his paws together, I looked up. He'd already pushed his pants down and dropped one paw to curl around his sheath. "Come on," he said. "I'm hungry. Get your head in the game."

He smiled, tongue lolling out, and I realized that he was making a joke. Another Braden Longacre first. "Sorry."

"I'm the one who lost today. You still thinking about your match?"

I pulled my shirt off and tossed it to the ground. "First of all, no, and second of all, I've still got a doubles match to play."

"Oh, well, doubles." His ears went a little back, and I wasn't sure if that was because I was still alive in the tournament or because he didn't like doubles or something. "So why aren't you practicing?"

"My partner's out with his girlfriend or something."

"Or something?" He'd started working his paw up and down and had gotten halfway hard already. "Like maybe a boyfriend?"

"No, she's definitely a girl." I sat beside him on the bed and leaned over, reaching for his sheath, and he let me take it. "They're just dating and not sure where it's going."

"Ah." He leaned back on his elbows and watched me with sharp hazel eyes. "So what is on your mind?"

I'd gotten my finger and thumb around his shaft, rubbing and enjoying in a distracted way how it felt, knowing how much I liked being stroked and being glad that I could bring that to someone else. It was strange to have that feeling and also consciously be thinking about something completely other. "I can save it for after. My muzzle will be busy in a minute or two anyway."

He closed his eyes and exhaled, and I thought he was relaxing into my stroking. But in the next moment he said, "You just don't seem like one of those people who can put things away and not worry about them."

My ears went up. "I don't mind."

"As long as you keep your paw working and you don't take more than like three or four minutes."

I considered that. Braden shifted on the bed. "Also don't finish me in your paw."

"All right, all right." I took a moment to compose my thoughts. "My father, who I thought was dead until last year, is mad because I got my sister over here without paying him thousands of dollars, so he claimed to be representing me to a small apparel company. Fortunately they called me to verify it. But I'm worried I'll never be able to get rid of him."

One stroke, two strokes, three strokes. I kept going and he cracked an eye open. "Jesus Fox. I thought you were worried about your doubles match or something. Don't you have a normal life?"

I squeezed his shaft. "Does anyone?"

"I don't live in the middle of a soap opera." He closed his eyes again.

"Sure you don't have an evil twin somewhere?" I didn't know much about soap operas, but I knew most of the jokes people made about what happened in them.

His ears came up. "Pretty sure I'd be the evil twin."

I chuckled, and his tail flicked on the bed. "Listen," he went on. "That sucks, but your dad can't do anything to you. You control your life and whatever happens, you'll get past it."

Looking back, those words were as bland as the things he'd said in the media conference. If you take the words out of context, what do they really say? All they're meant to do is make you feel better without offering any specific solution.

But that's the thing. They're meant to make you feel better. And in that moment, they did. Just hearing Braden say, "You control your life," reminded me that I was here because I chose to be, that I could make people part of my life or not as I chose. "Yeah, you're right," I said. "All right, it's out."

"Good." He squirmed in my paw, his tail curling. "I'm ready."

So I bent over and took his shaft in my muzzle. He hadn't been kidding; he was ready. It took him only about a minute to finish.

I sat up and somewhat without thinking about it, gulped. He'd opened his eyes at this point and that got me a raised eyebrow, but no comment. "All right," he panted. "Your turn."

As I got my pants down, he knelt in front of me and looked up. "And no thinking about your dad. Just think about what we're doing. If there's someone else you like thinking about, think about them."

Someone else? I'd thought about lots of different people while jerking off, but not in a serious way. There were movie stars and singers, other tennis players (but I wasn't going to confess that to Braden), the occasional model from a catalog or person I'd seen on the street. But right now, it was plenty for me to be here in bed with Braden, or at least in bed with Braden on the floor reaching up to wrap his fingers, and later his muzzle, around my sheath.

When I'd finished, he got up to go to the bathroom as usual. I lay back, letting the rush fade from my body. My tail at times like this felt more sensitive than usual, so I stroked it idly with one paw and was still doing that when Braden came back out. "Get dressed," he said. "We're going for chili."

"I like that you noticed something was bothering me," I said.

"What?"

"That's my 'something nice.'" I pulled my underwear up.

"Are we still doing that?" He kind of rolled his eyes, but maybe with an amused smile. It was hard to tell sometimes.

"You don't have to, I guess."

"No, no." He watched me pull my pants up and fasten them. "You have a pretty good—a really good muzzle. And even when you've got a load of problems that would make me not want to get out of bed, you still give it your all. Tennis or, ah, anything."

He probably wouldn't have liked it if I gave him a hug, so I just got my shirt tucked in and wagged my tail.

I didn't care that we hurried out of the hotel into a taxi, or that we went in the back door of the restaurant and ate in a small annex off the main room. This was just life with Braden as I knew it. At his request, we didn't talk much in the taxi, so I was left with my own thoughts. I might have used the time to worry about my father, but Braden's confidence had helped me, so mostly what I thought about was where we were going for dinner and when I'd see him again.

The chili did take my mind off my problems. Braden challenged me to get the hot chili while he ordered the mild, and remembering our burrito, I did. This spice proved to be stronger, but not too strong for my palate, while his eyes watered after a tiny taste of mine. "Don't know how you can stand it," he said.

"It doesn't taste that bad to me."

Braden shook his head. "Never got a taste for spicy food. We had a menu of spices that varied from salt to pepper with almost nothing in between."

"Wow." I tried to imagine that. "Well, look, you can get accustomed to spice. Just, like…" A bottle of hot sauce stood on the table. I picked it up. "Don't use a lot of this, but toss in a little bit and see how it tastes."

He raised an eyebrow at me. "Go on," I urged.

His fingers closed around the bottle. I let it go, and he drew it close and uncapped it. Eyes on me, he sniffed it, drew back, then tipped it to his finger.

"Don't taste it," I advised. "Just a few drops. See how it changes the taste."

For a moment, I thought he was going to taste it just to spite me, but then he shook a few drops out into his chili and stirred it up. "If it's inedible," he said, "you're buying me a new one."

"Sure thing." I watched him take a spoonful, sniff at it, and then taste it.

"You didn't spit it out," I said. "So I guess it wasn't terrible."

He swallowed. "It was fine. I can't really taste any extra spice."

"Add a few more drops."

"I think this is probably enough experimentation for one evening." Braden shook his head.

I grinned and went back to eating the pretty good chili. Our conversation wandered around to tennis, as it inevitably did, and tonight Braden offered me a couple tips on my game. They were smart and well-considered, and I filed them away for further use.

Then there was a lull, and I wanted to say something to him that would be useful as well. "Hey," I said, "did you have fun today?"

"When?" he asked. "Before this?"

"At the tennis match."

"Tennis isn't fun." He took another mouthful of chili.

I considered that. "It is, though. I mean, when I play, it's exciting."

"It's exciting, but more like..." Braden thought. "More like exciting because you're finding out how your opponent is doing that day. How you're doing. If the ball is dropping for you then you'll win. If your opponent is getting the breaks then you lose."

"Yeah, but...I've seen you pump your fist after making a good shot."

"Sure. It's great when your strategy pays off." He folded his ears half-back. "But it's not so much 'fun.' I know what to do and most of the time I can do it. Sometimes the other guy knows how to respond and can do it. It's exciting finding out whether it'll work. But 'fun' is for something that doesn't have any stakes."

"Doesn't have to be." I grinned. "The way to defuse tension about the pressure in a match is to relax and have fun."

"You sound like my therapist now." He stared past my shoulder. "I could never get to that point. He gave me a lot of tips, but none of them ever worked very well."

"You should try them again."

"Tabled for another time." He took another spoonful of chili and savored it. "You know, I can taste a little bit of spice now."

I decided that this wasn't going to be the time to bring up his bland media days. I could table that for another time too, maybe one when he'd gotten the taste for a little more spice.

* * *

Xu played in the final against Philippe Dubois, a tenacious marten who was #4 in the world at the time. They battled for three exciting sets, Xu's power and shotmaking against Dubois's excellent defense and ability to prolong points. Xu won the first set 7-5, and then Dubois took the second 7-6 in a 12-10 tiebreak. Late in the third, on serve, Xu went more and more frequently for winners, with the result that he missed two forehands and Dubois got a service break in the fourth game. That was all he needed, as he went on to win 6-4.

Ori sat with me and Aliq at the match and kept taking pictures and typing. It was only in the second set that I thought to ask, "Are you posting things on my account?"

"Sure." She smiled brightly. "I posted the thing you said about Xu having one of the best forehands in the game."

"You—you did?"

She showed me her phone and there it was, a picture of the tiger lunging for a shot and my comment above it. "It's not a great picture," she said. "I'm trying to learn how to get better. Some of the other players have some fantastic pictures on their accounts. Hold on." She took the phone back, swiped with her claws, and then held it out to me again.

There was a picture of me, a pretty good action shot that looked like it was taken from courtside. The caption was, "Bright young talent! Keep an eye on this jackal."

"Whose account is that?"

She pointed to the profile picture. "Colluvic. This is from earlier in the tournament."

"Did you take that?"

Aliq grabbed my arm just then because there'd been a terrific point and I was only half paying attention to it. "No," Ori said as I focused on the action. "I told you, I'm learning. This was—I don't know, he must have told his social media person to get a pic of you."

"Huh, okay."

"It's a good thing, Ro. He has like ten times as many followers as you do."

"I know, I'm trying to pay attention to the match."

"Sorry." She was quiet for a moment, holding the phone in her lap. "Anyway, the point is, his media person takes good pictures and maybe I'll try to find whoever it is."

"Thank them for me," I said, and she said she would. And then I thought I should warn her about our father in case he tried to do something to her, so I reminded myself to talk to her after the match.

When it was just the two of us, I told her about the stunt our father had pulled with the endorsement.

"Oh." Her ears splayed and she looked wary. "What are you going to do?"

"Nothing. Lochen's handling it. But—"

"Good."

"But I kind of want to—"

"No." She rested a paw on my arm. "Ignore him. He wants your attention, and when he doesn't get it, he'll stop."

"You don't know him. He won't stop. He thinks we owe him something and he's just going to keep chasing it."

"I know him as well as you do," she snapped. "Let him run around after whatever it is he thinks we owe him. It doesn't hurt you."

"It hurts us if he tries to mess up my reputation. You should know how important reputation is. He thinks I owe him, even though I told him to get lost."

She took her paw from my arm and clasped her other paw with it, tapping her fingers. "I know he only wants money from us, and he's good at telling stories to try to get it, whether it's to you or to this company."

"Fortunately he didn't know that they'd check with me."

"That's what Ma loved about him, you know."

I shook my head. "She told you that?"

"Kamina told me. Not with those words; she said something like 'his honey tongue caught her and then he spit her out when he was done with her,' and I asked more about how they met. He used to come by the market and tell her all these great stories about his ancestors, all the wonderful things he was going to do, and then…" Ori shrugged. "I suppose when I came along, two cubs didn't fit in with his story."

"Ori!" My own troubles sailed away like a bad forehand. "You think his leaving was your fault?"

"Well? He stayed around after you were born."

"I don't remember him at all."

"Of course not. You were one when I was born."

"Which means I was three, four months old when Ma got pregnant again. Maybe he'd already decided he didn't want to be saddled with cubs."

"Plural."

"Or a cub, whatever." I took her paw in mine. "He didn't even know you. That has nothing to do with who you are now."

She squeezed my fingers. "But you see, Ro, I'd rather leave all that in the past where it belongs. Going to talk to him, confronting him, it's a part of our life that's done. Let it go. Let Lochen handle it."

I shook my head. "We thought it was done and it came back once. What if he challenges your visa?"

"He can't. It's all in order. And in a few years I can apply to be a permanent resident." She smiled and squeezed my fingers again. "Honestly, Ro. He can't do anything to us anymore. Let him be."

As often happened with Ori, even if I didn't want to listen to her advice, I knew with my head that she was right. That was another thing she had in common with Ma.

We spent a day packing up and traveling on to Hilltown, where the next hardcourt tournament would be, and Hilltown was where Aliq and I got our invitation and seeding for the States Open. I wasn't seeded in singles, but we were the #26 doubles team, which was the highest we'd ever been seeded. Our world rank was #30, but there were four clay court doubles specialists ahead of us, so they got dropped down in hardcourt rank.

Because not everyone played every tournament, we were seeded #19 at Hilltown, and for whatever reason—maybe the States seeding or maybe being completely recovered from our overseas trip—we played really well there and made it to the quarterfinals.

Singles was another matter. I hit a rough patch and lost to a player ranked below me, which I hadn't done in months. It wouldn't hurt my ranking, as I hadn't played Hilltown last year, but it certainly wouldn't help it as much as I'd hoped. If I'd gotten to the quarter-finals, I'd have a good shot at cracking the top 50, which would be nice for my endorsements and publicity. As it was, I was going to go up one or two spots, up to #55 maybe but no higher.

The day after my loss I got a call from Lochen telling me that Roque-Ferrand, a company whose cool-pack wristbands I'd been using, had offered me an official endorsement. Which was pretty cool, no pun intended; they were very light but stayed cool through a set. If you pressed your nose to them briefly and inhaled when you were heating up, they cooled you down and reduced panting. I knew probably a dozen other canid players who wore them; Aliq did too.

"Hey," I said as he was winding up. "Did you ever hear anything else from…"

"From?"

"My father."

"I told you, Rocky, it's handled. If you want to know more I can tell you, but you don't have to worry about it."

Did I want to know more? A little part of me did, but I remembered Braden's words. If I asked to know more, I'd be letting him back into my life. "Nope. I'm good, thanks."

After that phone call, I had some intense video sessions with Nashan, who also wanted to tell me not to worry about losing early to a lower-ranked player. But in addition to not worrying, he wanted me to work on the aspects of my game that had shown cracks in the loss. My return game stayed strong, but my forehand had been off, so we hit a lot of groundstrokes until I was tired of them.

Braden made it to the semifinals, winning his quarterfinal match the day before Aliq and I were going to play ours, so I was a little surprised to get a text from him that evening inviting me to dinner.

Match tomorrow

???

Doubles.

Oh, right.

Me too, so practice?

He wanted to practice with me too? I'd already made plans to have dinner with Aliq and Ori, but I could break those plans. He probably didn't mean it this way, but the idea of practicing with him was enticing. I didn't know how it would go and I was curious.

Also I hadn't gotten laid since the last time with Braden, so there was that.

I wasn't sure how to dress for a practice-sex-dinner date. Workout clothes with dinner clothes in a bag? Dinner clothes on, workout clothes in the bag? In the end, I wore my workout clothes, figuring we probably wouldn't eat dinner before working out, and they were easier to take off if Braden wanted to get the sex "out of the way" first.

I made the right call, it turned out. Braden came to his hotel room door in his white shorts and t-shirt, with his tennis bag over his shoulder. "Workout first," he said, "then relax, then dinner."

"Sounds good," I said, though he'd already let the door swing closed and wasn't looking for my approval.

We took a taxi to a college called Forester that had indoor tennis courts which Braden had gotten permission to use through someone on his team. When we got to the facility, a beaver in a forest-green shirt with a pine tree logo on it let us in, gave us a big bin of tennis balls, and pointed us to the courts.

As we loosened up, Braden said, "So I was thinking about making this fun, like you were talking about."

"Uh-huh?" I said when he didn't go on. He was hitting groundstrokes to the corner opposite me while I served to the corner opposite him.

"So how would you make this practice fun?"

The question caught me off guard. "Well, what do you consider 'fun'?" He stared at me. "Like, what else do you do for fun?"

He still didn't say anything, but he raised an eyebrow at me. "Okay," I said. "Besides that."

"I don't know. Watch movies?"

I hit another serve. "Didn't you ever play games with your parents?"

"They didn't play tennis."

I didn't think he and his parents would've played skip-stones, so I let that line of questioning expire. "All right," I said. "I used to play this game by myself." I tossed the ball and served it again, dropping it right inside the corner of the service box. "See if I could get it on the line every time."

He didn't move to toss the ball he held. "That just seems like work."

"Basketball was fun," I said. "You ever played?"

He shook his head, but that gave me an idea. "Okay, how about this. There was a game the guys played on the court called Dragon."

"I've heard of that." He perked his ears. "You have to match shots or something?"

"Yeah, so…" I put down my racket and mimed shooting a basketball. "Say I'd start. I'd make a shot from the foul line. Then you'd have to make the same shot or you'd get a letter. D to start, then R, then A. And the first one to spell the word gets eaten by the dragon, I guess, or they just lose or whatever."

"Okay, so…" He bounced his ball on his racket. "What shots do we make?"

"That's the fun part. You have to come up with crazy shots that you can make but you don't think the other guy can."

He nodded. "Sounds worth a try. Should we do it from across the net?"

"To start, yeah."

At first I was worried that the game wouldn't work. Braden went first and hit a serve down the T, so I did the same. Then I bounced the ball on the service line and hit a drop shot, and he did the same. We traded shots like this five or six more times. He seemed to be enjoying it, but I was getting bored. "Okay," I said, "Bounce on the service line, drop shot to the sideline."

He watched me sharply. "What happens if you can't make the shot?"

"Then you get a chance to make it, and if you make it, I get the letter." I bounced, spun the drop shot away, and it clipped the sideline.

The cross fox didn't say anything, just nodded and bounced the ball on his own service line, then bounced it again. And then he sliced his racket under it, lifted a drop shot—and shook his head immediately, even before it landed well inside the sideline.

"All right," he said, "I get a D."

This was about a month before Aliq had to explain to me what "D" was shorthand for in slang, and later I would tell Braden. This would lead to exchanges like, "You get a D." "Maybe later, if you're lucky." "You saying you don't want a D?" "I'll keep my own D, thank you."

But for now, at this time, there was just the feeling that I'd made a shot that Braden couldn't. And it was his turn to come up with something inventive that I couldn't do.

"All right," he said with a crafty, foxy smile that I didn't remember seeing on him before. It was like a long time ago when he'd argued a ball on the sidelines with me, but devoid of the arrogance that I most associated with him. It was, I would come to learn, the look of Braden having fun.

Somewhat to my surprise, and I'm sure Braden's, I won the game of Dragon, D-R-A-G to D-R-A-G-O-N. "You're good at trick shots," he said, panting, as we left the court.

I didn't tell him why that was, why I'd practiced hitting so close to the line for weeks and months in case I one day had to throw a match or a point. I just said, "It's fun."

"But is it useful? The drop shot to the line, sure, but how often are you going to hit a backhand facing away from the court? That's happened a few times, sure, but is it worth practicing?"

"Doesn't it make you feel better—" I stopped. "It makes me feel better to know I can do it. It's not my preferred shot, but it's a fun one. Like Tempest with his between-the-legs shots he likes to make."

"Those are just clowning." Braden frowned. "They make him seem…"

"Less imposing? Like someone you don't have to take as seriously?"

"No." But he was thinking about it.

"Trick shots can rattle the opponent," I said. "But it's not even about that. It's about being loose and being, I don't know, playing the game for yourself and not for your opponent."

"But you have to play the opponent," the fox argued. "If I'm playing Xu, I don't come up to the net because he has that passing shot. It doesn't matter if it's more fun for me, or whatever. It's not the best strategy."

"Course not. But you can do other things. If you just turn tennis into 'what's the best thing to do here' and you play the percentages the whole time, it's…it's just work. And plus," I said because I could sense his objection, "it makes you predictable. When people study your tendencies, they can figure out what you're going to do."

We passed the beaver and Braden signed an autograph for him, then we walked out into the muggy summer evening. "Listen," the fox said. "I don't want to go all the way back to the hotel. You want to just get a room here?"

I hadn't thought I was ready for sex so soon, but yeah, the thought of it got me warm almost right away. "Sure. There?"

I pointed to a run-down place called the "Pine Woods Motel," and Braden flicked his ears back. "I was thinking more like over there."

A block beyond the motel, a large Marriott rose. "Oh, well, okay."

"I can afford it." He set off. "We don't have to slum."

"I wasn't thinking slum," I said. "I don't even know what that means. I just meant it was closer."

"Slumming means going to cheap places intentionally to experience what they're like." Braden shot a look at the motel. "I don't need to come back to the tour with fleas."

"I'm sure they don't have fleas. I slept in cheap motels my first two years on the tour and we never got fleas."

He kept walking past the motel's driveway. "I can afford the Marriott, I want the Marriott. If you can wait one more block."

"All right." I kept pace with him. "I'll try to keep from grabbing you right here in the street."

His ears flicked again, and he didn't say anything in response, but he did hurry his steps.

On the way up to our room, I said, "Hey, can I ask you something?"

"You just did."

"Har har. Why'd you call when you have a match tomorrow? I was expecting you'd wait until you were out."

"Yeah, well. I didn't want to make this, like, a reward for losing. There's no reason we can't do this and still play well tomorrow. People do it all the time. So I wanted to mix it up."

I nodded. "Okay. Just wondering."

He was as eager as I was; it almost took us longer to get undressed than to get off. Afterwards, it felt as though the sun should've set and I should be hungrier for dinner. Well, I was hungry because I'd just worked out, but the sun was in pretty much the same place as it had been.

When we'd both cleaned up, Braden didn't move to put his clothes on, so I didn't either. We lay on the same bed, tails and legs touching but just relaxing there. I half-dozed off, mind wandering around to nothing at all and back to Braden. After a bit, I heard his stomach growl, and a moment later he asked, "What do you feel like eating?"

It was a nice evening, all in all, and when we parted back near the tournament site, we wished each other good luck in the matches the next day. I got back to my room with a smile still on my muzzle to find Ori and Aliq going over our schedule for the following day.

They didn't ask where I'd been as I sat on the bed next to Ori. I asked Aliq how things with Teresa were going and he said, "Fine," but it didn't feel fine. I would have asked him more, but he changed the subject right away to our practice time.

He played pretty well the next day, but it almost didn't matter because I was *on*. I was getting to everything and all my shots dropped right where I wanted them to. We blasted our way through to the semifinals in straight sets so quickly that at match point, our opponents looked dazed, like they expected there to be more tennis to play.

Braden, too, did well, winning his semifinal match with only one small hiccup, a service break that he got right back. Aliq and I won our semifinal the next day (our schedule had been disrupted due to thunderstorms), and then we got to watch Braden win the tournament on our day off. He looked fantastic, but to be fair, Bielovic wasn't at his best.

The next day, Aliq and I played the #12 ranked doubles team in the country and won the first set with a service break we got when I hit a perfect drop volley into the doubles alley. The second set they made few mistakes, and Aliq and I lost in the tiebreak. We played a tough third set during which Aliq and I got an edge in a few more points. That was enough to get us a 6-5 edge going into the last game, where I served out the set and the match, and Aliq jumped into my arms when our opponents netted their last shot.

We shook paws—we knew them a little, though not as well as Lowry and Tasman, whom they'd beaten in the semis—and then faced the cheers of the crowd. This was the largest audience we'd won in front of, and the first time on the Champions tour. Aliq couldn't stop grinning and neither could I.

When we went back into the locker room, a bunch of the guys were there to congratulate us, Braden among them. He clasped my paw while Aliq was talking to Lowry. "Nice job," he said.

"I guess it wasn't a reward for losing." I smiled.

His eyes widened, but his expression didn't change. "Glad it worked out."

"And congrats to you too. That was a pretty good match you played."

"Yeah, it was." He nodded and squeezed my paw. "It was a little bit fun. In spots."

"Good."

He glanced to one side, and only then did I remember that we were in the middle of a locker room. We released our paws at the same time and gave each other smiles and nods, and I moved on to talk to Aliq and Lowry.

Later, Ori showed me some of the posts she'd made, including of me and Aliq accepting the trophy and holding it aloft together. "Nice picture," I said.

"This guy Marro showed me some tricks with the phone camera," she said. "He's the one who takes pictures for Colluvic, remember? He knows about you."

"Lots of people know about me," I said.

"Yes yes, you're very famous." She swatted at me. "I'm trying to make you more famous."

Chapter Nineteen

We had two more tournaments before the States. Though Braden called even earlier in the next one than he had in the Hilltown one, he didn't call at all for the rest of the tournament. I thought about maybe calling him, because one night every couple weeks didn't seem like enough to me, but I refrained.

I got to the quarterfinals there, which was exciting even though I lost to Ljubo Colluvic, who gripped my paw afterwards and said, "Ha, great match, Rock." As we walked back to shake paws with the chair umpire, I looked for Ori in my box and saw her talking to a short fennec fox, both of them aiming their phones at us.

"Good luck in the semis," I told Colluvic.

"I play Braden," he said. "Got any tips for me?"

I shook my head. "You know him as well as I do."

The big wolf grinned and waved as he turned to face the cheering crowd, and I walked back to the locker room. A few of the other players hanging around came over to tell me, "Good match," including one I'd beaten on the way there.

And then a young, but still older than me, dingo walked up as I was getting dressed and just stood there, looking kind of at me but also not right at me. It was a little unnerving, especially because I didn't think I'd met him before. "Hi," I said finally. "What can I do for you?"

"Oh, nothing," he said, still with that strange slightly-averted glance. "I just wanted to see the flavor of the month."

I pulled my shirt over my head and smoothed it down. "I don't know what that means."

"Obviously you're Braden's friend now. I heard you practiced together at Hilltown and I saw the pictures from Londinium."

"Uh huh." I tilted my head, wondering how he knew about Hilltown but not wanting to ask. "That's allowed, right?"

"It's a free country." He leaned back against the locker two down from mine and thumped his tail against it, not waggingly, but aggressively.

I grabbed my bag and stuffed everything into it. "All right then."

"Tell him Rascal says hi."

"Is he not talking to you?" I hefted the bag over my shoulder and turned to look the dingo full in the face.

He studied his paw, clicking the claws against each other. "I dunno. You tell me."

"All right," I said. "See ya."

"Hah."

Ori and Aliq distracted me after that, but later that evening I remembered. I didn't want to bother Braden, but his semifinal was two days away, so it was either now or in a few days, and I didn't know if I'd remember in a few days. Plus, honestly, I was pretty curious to see what he'd say.

Hey

> *Hey.*

I ran into Rascal in the locker room.

> *Hope he didn't talk.*

A little. He said to say hi.

> *K.*

I waited for more, but nothing came. So I texted, *He seemed annoyed.*

> *Probably.*

At you?

Another pause. I'd just typed out the first word of a followup when Braden's reply came back.

> *Just avoid him.*

That was probably all I'd get out of Braden. He wasn't chatty on text even at the best of times, and if his limit was four-word messages then it wasn't going to be worth continuing. But while I was chatting… *Busy tonight?*

The reply came back much more quickly this time.

Hilton 389 10p.

After dinner?

Yeah, sorry.

So I went over to the Hilton at quarter to ten, knocked on the door of 389, and Braden let me into his room. He led me to the bed with hardly a word and got right down to business.

Afterwards, with both of us lying in our post-climax glows (his more recent than mine), I said, "So, Rascal?"

"Ah, fuck." He sat up. "That asshole."

"Why is he pissed at you?"

"Oh, you know." He waved his paw.

I frowned and sat up next to him. "I really don't."

He drew in a deep breath and let it out. "I dunno, I used to hang out with him last year, and then he got boring and I stopped. End of story."

"I never ran into him on the tour."

"He was on Champions for a while, and then he skipped a bunch of tournaments. I'm sure you and he have been at some of the same ones, but there's a lot of players."

It was probably because I could still taste Braden's shaft and come in my mouth that my mind made its next jump of logic. "Were you sleeping with him?"

"No." He said it matter-of-factly, not in a yes-but-I-don't-want-to-tell-you way. "I don't even think he's gay, though he's acting really bitchy this whole year. I just practiced with him and went out to dinner a lot."

"So what's his problem with me?"

Braden turned his muzzle. "What would his problem with you be if I had been sleeping with him?"

He'd be jealous, I started to say, and then realized that meant that he would have to know that Braden and I were sleeping together, which nobody did. "I—don't know."

The cross fox nodded. "He wanted to be best friends, but… sometimes it just doesn't work that way."

"You must have liked him at first."

"Yeah, he was great at first. Top hundred in the world, really exciting. But he didn't have any drive, and he didn't understand why I didn't want to 'hang out and chill.'" Here he made air quotes with his fingers.

That sounded like a familiar story. I still wasn't sure I believed that Braden wasn't sleeping with him, but I had to take him at his word. "So you stopped practicing with him."

"Yeah, he was getting sloppy."

I rubbed my chin. "If I get sloppy, will you stop practicing with me?"

He didn't bat an eye, keeping that same neutral expression turned on me. "You planning on getting sloppy?"

"Nobody plans to get sloppy."

"All right." He flicked his ears back, then upright. "Yeah, if you let yourself go like he did, I'll probably stop practicing with you."

"Will you stop sleeping with me?"

He made a show of examining his sheath. "You're not getting sloppy there."

"Braden."

"I don't know, jeez. Probably not? I wasn't sleeping with him, I told you that. I haven't slept with anyone on the tour before." He dropped his head between his knees. "But he might've known."

"Known? That you're gay?"

"Yeah, he—I went out to a club once and I wouldn't take him, but I think he followed me." I stayed quiet, thinking of all the times I worried about Aliq or any of my other friends discovering that I'd gone out to clubs, that time Danver almost found me at the gay club near Silver. "He didn't say anything, but I feel like he was acting different after that. He didn't ask to go out to clubs with me anymore. So it got uncomfortable."

"Sorry."

"Eh. It happens." He lay back on the bed and closed his eyes. "All right. I oughta get some sleep."

"You know," I said, "I know a pretty good ice cream place a couple blocks away."

One hazel eye cracked open and peered at me. "I like cookies."

"They have huge chocolate chip cookies."

He sighed and then levered himself off the bed in one smooth motion. "All right, you talked me into it."

* * *

I didn't see Rascal again that tournament. Braden beat Colluvic but lost in the final to Philippe Dubois the marten, and we all decamped for Plainville the next week.

There, when I walked into the locker room for the first time, one player nudged another and said, loudly enough for me to hear, "Hey, it's Braden's little friend."

I turned, but they were snickering together and not paying attention to me. Maybe something on their phones, I thought.

I won my opening match, and it happened again in the locker room afterwards. "Getting lots of help from Longacre?" one of the other players, ranked ten spots or so below me, asked.

"We practice together sometimes," I said.

"Uh huh." He walked away without saying anything more.

It wasn't a big deal, but it got my fur up. I asked Aliq if anyone was saying anything around him and he said he hadn't heard. So I tried to ignore it, but then a couple days later I ran into Rascal again, waiting by the practice court.

"You ask Braden about me?" he said as I was packing up, Aliq doing the same nearby.

"Yeah." I kept my tone neutral. "He said you used to practice together and then drifted apart."

"Ha ha ha!" The boisterous laugh took me by surprise. "Ha ha! Drifted apart!"

"Is there a problem here?" Aliq came over, bag in one paw, ready to drop it if he needed to.

"I need to get going," I said, turning to leave the practice court.

We'd gotten about five feet away when Rascal called, "It's all fine now, but just wait until you're not good enough for him anymore."

Aliq didn't say anything until we were in the hallway leading to the locker room, and then he murmured, "He talking about Braden?"

"Yeah."

The fox scratched his muzzle. "Was he…friends…with Braden before?"

I heard the insinuation in his voice, but he didn't know Braden was gay, so maybe I was imagining it. "I think they were practice partners, and he let his tennis go, and Braden kinda dropped him."

Aliq nodded. "Seems like Braden wouldn't be too nice about dropping someone, if I had to guess."

"That's what I'm thinking too."

We walked into the locker room and as we approached our lockers, Aliq said, "Take care of yourself, okay?"

I nodded. "I will. Thanks."

I worried that Aliq would want to talk more about my relationship with Braden, but if he suspected anything, he kept it to himself. To minimize the chance that he'd ask, I avoided the subject of relationships altogether, so I didn't ask how things were going with him and Teresa. He didn't volunteer much information, but he saw her at least twice during each of the tournaments, so I assumed it was going well.

We didn't win again, but in general Nashan was pleased with our progress. He spent a lot of time with me in my singles practices talking about specific matchups with the top 20 or so players in addition to working on my mechanics. We didn't spend as much time working on doubles, and when Aliq made a joking comment about it, Nashan said that my singles career had more potential. Aliq got a little sulky about that, and then Ori pointed out that we'd already won a Champions tournament as a doubles team, while I hadn't yet won singles, so probably all Nashan meant was that I had farther to go. That seemed to help, and it was so much like something Ma would have said that I remembered again that Ma had never met Aliq, and emotion overtook me for a moment.

By the time we traveled to the States Open, Ori had enough experience with tournaments that I was looking forward to her reaction to the enormous spectacle that was a Grand Slam. I wasn't disappointed, as she walked into the massive sports complex with wide eyes. "This is incredible," she breathed. "Did you ever imagine in our dirty little rec center that you'd one day play in a place like this?"

"Of course," I said. "What do you think I saw when I stepped onto those courts? Cracks and weeds and frayed nets?"

"That's what I saw." She smiled, tail wagging. "You had the imagination and the drive."

As nice as that conversation was, it reminded me of home in a way I hadn't thought about in a while. "Do you think we could build a better rec center in Lundara?"

"You mean you and me?" She gestured to include Aliq. "Us?"

"I mean my money. I don't know how much I have to spare, but it feels like we could at least make a start."

She nodded. "That'd be nice. Let's talk to Lochen about it next time."

We got to our two hotel rooms and I took her over to see some of the qualifying matches going on. This would be the first time I didn't have to play a qualifying match in a major; a top 60 ranking was enough to get me into the main draw. The prospect excited me, but at the same time I'd placed into enough main draws that it didn't feel as special as I might've thought it did a while ago.

I did notice a difference when I walked into the locker room. More of the guys above me recognized me and waved, and even Tempest, whom I'd seen a few times but who always remained aloof in the locker room, gave a nod when I passed him.

"Did you see that?" I hissed to Aliq, who grinned and elbowed me.

Along with the recognition were more murmurs of "Braden's friend," never to my face but within earshot, making me wonder how many times it was said where I couldn't hear. I wouldn't have minded the words except that there was often a malicious undertone to them. If it wasn't public knowledge that Braden was gay, and that I was gay, then what did people think was happening? When I was practicing, and later, playing, I could put it out of my mind, but every time it happened I spent time wondering. I didn't want to ask Aliq about it; I was already afraid I'd given up Braden's secret to him.

Fortunately, these issues didn't affect my tennis very much. The first and second rounds, I was paired up against players around my same ranking and played well enough to beat them. In the third round, I came up against Braden.

He was seeded fifth at this tournament and hadn't lost a set yet. I was determined that I'd be the first one to take a set off him, and I thought I could do it, knowing his tendencies. We'd practiced together a fair amount over the previous months and I'd watched more of his game than of any other player's, so it seemed like a reasonable proposition.

What I'd forgotten was that he knew my game just as well. I'd never thought that he'd be studying me the way I studied him, but he was a professional. He kept pushing me to my backhand, knowing that was one of my weaknesses, and although I knew that he tended to be predictable, it didn't matter. I could feel where the next shot was going, be correct, and still not be able to do much with the ball when I got to it. He blew through the first set, breaking my serve twice, and almost before I knew it I was sitting on my bench gulping down a BoltAde and trying to figure out how I could get back into the match.

I hadn't expected Braden to give any sign that we knew each other, let alone were sleeping together, and he did not. We shook at the beginning of the match and he didn't even smile. I did, but then felt ashamed of it afterwards, and I don't think that's what had me a little off in the first set, but it might have been.

In the second set, I got my serve going a little better and at least stayed competitive, but Braden kept playing at the same high level. I took control of many of the points on my serve, but the shots that had won points for me in the first couple rounds weren't enough to beat Braden. He broke my serve late in the set and won 6-4.

But this was a major tournament, so I had one more chance to win a set from him. I decided what the hell. Nashan had prepared me to play Braden, but I'd need a little more practice to be able to stay with him. Nashan had also told me to play my game, and I realized that for the first two sets I'd been playing Braden's game; even when I was controlling the points, I was trying to force my shots in a certain direction to attack his weaknesses, trying to keep it low so he couldn't unleash his powerful groundstrokes. If I were more polished at that kind of game—which I could work on—it might work better, but it wasn't entirely the game I liked to play.

So in the third set I mixed up my game. If I had a chance to hit a good low ball, I did, but if my instincts pulled me in another direction, I'd hit an inside-out forehand, and even though my backhand wasn't great, it had improved a lot, so I went to that. I even played a couple drop shots.

Whether it was my different playing style or just the malaise of a third set in the best of five—something I would become familiar with—Braden slowed down in that third set. His shots didn't have the same juice behind them, and for a few of the games he seemed flat-footed. One of those games was his third service game, and going up 0-30 gave me a lot of energy, so even though he came back to level it at 30-all, I won the next two points to get a break of his serve and go up 4-2.

That lit a fire under his tail, but I matched his energy. The next three games we played were the best of the whole match, with some great rallies, fantastic shotmaking, and amazing defense on both sides, both of us sprinting to one side of the court or the other to track down shots. In the end, I won the set 6-3 to a round of applause like nothing I'd ever heard. I glanced up at the box and smiled to see Ori and Aliq on their feet, not even taking pictures, just applauding.

In the fourth set, Braden recovered his poise and his energy and dispatched me 6-3, but I felt pleased I'd at least cost him a set. When we came to the net after my final shot landed long, he grabbed my paw and squeezed briefly. "Good match," he said.

"Good match," I echoed. I wanted to ask if I'd see him later, but everywhere I looked, the glinting glass eyes of cameras watched us, so I held my tongue. We shook paws with the chair umpire and retreated back to our separate benches to pack up and go back to the locker room.

Chapter Twenty

Both of us had to go face the media for a while, Braden more than me, of course, so we didn't get a chance to talk after the match either. That was fine, I thought; we could text later.

One of the interviewers was a familiar muzzle: the magenta and orange Cape fox who'd been writing an article about my homeland. After the media session was officially over, he stuck around and walked up to me. I waved to show I recognized him. "Uh…Streaks, right?"

"Yeah!" He perked up at that. "Hope you liked the article. It got a little bit of press. Listen, I heard your sister joined you so I wanted to talk to you both for a followup if you have a chance."

"Sure," I said. "She'll arrange a time." I didn't want to admit that I hadn't read his article, especially after he was so happy that I'd remembered his name. Mental note: ask Lochen if he read the article.

"Oh, uh." His ears went back. "Could you introduce me to her?"

"Sure." I pointed across the room to where Ori was sitting on her phone, ears perked toward me but not, I thought, listening closely. Just as I thought that, though, she looked up at me and smiled, so I waved her over.

"This is Streaks," I said. "He wrote an article about Lunda that was pretty good." I hoped it was. He seemed like a smart guy from the questions he asked, and he was still coming around with press credentials, so I assumed he was at least somewhat competent.

"Oh, of course." Ori smiled. "I read your article. It was lovely. You wanted to write more?"

He beamed and nodded. "Follow up with a little of your experience, I thought."

"You know, Rocky is starting a foundation to benefit Lundaran youth. Would that be of interest?"

"Oh, heck yeah! I'd love to help promote that. I haven't heard anything about it. Is it new?"

Ori flashed me a look and her smile widened. "Very new. You'd be the first to write about it."

The fox's tail wagged eagerly. "That'd be fantastic. Thank you so much!"

"You know," Ori said as she led him away, "I'd been thinking of calling you anyway..."

(Later I asked Ori if she'd really been thinking about calling Streaks, and she said, "No, but it made him feel better, didn't it?")

"Is that the first time you've played him in a while?" Aliq asked as we walked away, back on the topic of Braden.

I nodded. "He's gotten better."

"Yeah, but so have you." Aliq punched my arm. "You took a set off him."

"But lost three." I grinned. "Glad we're still playing. Gives me something to do."

We did in fact keep playing until just before the quarterfinals. I know very few people watch doubles even at the majors, at least compared to the singles, but our fourth round match was really exciting. We were playing this Oceanian team, a dingo and a tazzie, and had some fantastic rallies, shots that when we were in the middle of it I didn't realize were as impressive as they were—on both sides. Aliq was better than I'd ever seen him, energized and focused, and we took the match to a third set. We went to 6-6 in that set, so we played a tiebreaker, which at first favored them as they jumped out to a 3-1 lead when they pounced on a serve I didn't quite place right and Aliq was a step out of position. But we came back on some fantastic net play from Aliq, going shot for shot with the dingo, and when the dingo finally got one past him, I was there and had been keeping track of the tazzie, so I was able to hit the uncovered corner of the opposite doubles alley to break back and go to 3-3. And from there we played solid tennis, neither side breaking until we were at 10-10 and the crowd so hyped that the umpire had to call "Quiet, please," twice, and finally say, more sharply, "Please be quiet," before they would settle down.

And on Aliq's serve, the tazzie came back with a scorcher that Aliq barely got back over the net. The dingo tried to volley it cross-court past me, but I was already in position and split him and the tazzie—that was the theory, anyway, and it would have worked. But the tazzie sprinted, just barely caught the ball on the edge of his racket, and swatted it back over the net. Aliq ran for it, but the ball clipped the sideline and he missed it by inches.

They won the next point on their serve, and with it the match. We shook paws and traded compliments, and though Aliq and I were disappointed, we couldn't forget that we were one or two good shots from getting to the quarterfinals of a major. That was huge.

I hadn't been spending a lot of time in the players' lounge because the comments about being Braden's "little friend" were wearing on me, but Aliq wanted to chill there before we left, so I went in with him.

It was pleasant, I have to say. I didn't hear any of those comments behind my back, and maybe that's because it wasn't very crowded, but there were more than a few guys there. I ended up chatting with Colluvic for a bit, who'd just won his match to get into the quarterfinals, and when I looked over, Aliq was talking to a tall, athletic lioness, only she wasn't quite a lioness. She had the body of one, but her arms and legs were covered with light stripes, as though she'd gone to a costume party as a tiger and hadn't been able to wash out the paint completely.

She'd been around on the tour, I thought, because I vaguely remembered someone talking about a ligress and wondering if I'd seen her. Now I knew I hadn't before, because I for sure would have remembered.

Aliq caught me looking at them and waved me over. "Hi," he said when I joined them. "This is Shona."

I extended my paw and she took it with a strong, confident grip. "You played great too," she said. "You guys should be in the quarterfinals."

Her accent made me perk my ears. "Are you from Anglia?"

She laughed. "Londinium born and raised. And you're Statesan?"

"From Lundara originally." I nodded at my friend. "How do you know Aliq?"

"Oh, we ran into each other at Wimbledon. He was hanging about with my friend Teresa and we got to talking."

"Oh." I looked around the locker room. "Where is Teresa? I don't think I've met her."

"She's playing a doubles match later so she's out practicing. I've already been eliminated." The ligress laughed. "It's my first year on the Champions tour. Very exciting but also intimidating. And I feel like I don't quite belong with all the ladies who are so good at singles."

"You're not bad at singles," Aliq said.

"I'm crap at singles. Well, not crap, but only good enough to get here, not much farther. But doubles, maybe, we'll see."

"Shona and I were talking about maybe doing some mixed doubles," Aliq said. "Seems like our styles would work, and you've got singles. I mean, if you don't mind."

Shona put her paws on her hips. "Why should he mind?"

"I'm just asking because we're friends and partners." Aliq wagged his tail. "Rocky'd ask me if he had to do anything that might change our schedule."

"It's okay," I said. "I don't. I think it's a great idea."

I didn't miss the look they gave each other when I said that, but it took me a few minutes to think about how to ask Aliq about it when we went back to the hotel. "So," I said finally, "why didn't you think of playing mixed doubles with Teresa?"

He paused and flicked his ears back. "Well, you know, she already has a partner. I think."

"Uh huh." I elbowed him. "So how long have you been seeing Shona?"

Aliq made a huffy noise. "I'm not *seeing* her," he said.

"Are you still seeing Teresa? You haven't talked about her at all this tournament."

We walked a few more steps along the sidewalk and got to the hotel lobby before he answered. "I just haven't thought about it much," he said. "And I guess she hasn't thought about me either. So there's your answer." His ears perked up a little. "I mean, it feels like we were both just forcing it because we're arctic foxes. She's nice and all, but when Shona and I started talking, we had so much to talk about. We both like the same movies and she gave me a link to this band, they're great, you really need to hear them."

He fumbled with his phone as we got into the elevator. "That's okay," I laughed. "I mean, I'll listen, but I'm just happy you like her. And I think playing mixed doubles is a great idea. As long as Nashan is okay with it."

Nashan was okay with it. We'd sat down with him for our usual review session of what we'd done well and what we needed to work on for the next tournament, but instead of diving right into it, he took a breath and said, "There's something I've been putting off talking to you about, but now with all the majors behind us, it's the right time."

Aliq and I kept our eyes on him but flicked our ears toward each other. The red fox turned to me. "Rocky, you're doing great in singles. After this tournament you'll be in the top 50. If you want to break through next year and get to the top thirty or even twenty, there's a big decision you have to make."

I nodded. "Sure. Whatever it takes."

He took a breath and looked at Aliq. "You need to drop doubles and focus on singles."

Looking back, I should've anticipated that moment. I mean, I knew that not many of the top singles players played doubles. A couple of the other players had said things to me like, "Oh, you're still playing doubles?" as if I were still using a wooden racket or still into grunge. Aliq and I were doing well, though, so I was proud of it.

"Hey," Aliq said. "If Rocky needs to quit doubles, I'm—I'm fine with that. I can find another partner. There's other guys on the tour and there's always some shakeup around the end of the year."

"Hold up." I turned to Aliq, next to me on the couch. "I know doubles is taking some of my focus away, but it also gives me a lot of energy and a lot of excitement. Don't you think that balances out?"

This was also an appeal to Nashan. The red fox shook his head, then stopped. "It's taking preparation time away from your singles."

"Right, I know. But it's also good practice."

"Not for singles. Doubles is a really different skill set."

"I know." I leaned forward. "I mean just in being on the court in pressure situations, decision-making…"

"Sure, of course."

Aliq flicked his tail. "Rocky, it's okay. We can still travel together and be friends. I'll find another partner."

"If you want to find another partner," I said, "then I won't stop you. But," again back to Nashan, "are you doing this because you've seen my game suffer? Or because it's what all singles players do?"

He opened his mouth, then shut it again. "All right. All right, that's a fair point. But there's a reason all singles players—"

"Nearly all."

"Nearly all singles players give up doubles. Right now the only top twenty—heck, the only top thirty singles players playing doubles as well are on the ladies' side."

I shrugged. "So why not give me a shot at being the first guy?"

The fox leaned back and considered that. "Rocky, you guys hired me to give you the best shot at becoming a champion. I'm telling you that if you keep playing doubles, it's going to make it much harder for that to happen."

"But it's still my decision."

Here Aliq broke in again. "Look, I'd rather see you hoisting a Grand Slam trophy in singles than in doubles. I don't know if we'll ever win a doubles trophy. Maybe a fluky one once or even twice. But if you can be great in singles, I don't want to hold you back."

Both of them, if I was reading them right, regretted the necessity of me dropping doubles. I was the only one in the room who felt that it wasn't a necessity. And it was my career which meant that ultimately it was my decision. So I had to think about what playing doubles meant to me. Was it just Aliq's friendship? I was pretty sure we could still be friends even if we weren't doubles partners. Was it the chance of winning a title while I was waiting for my singles game to mature? Or was it the variety, the ability to take a break from singles? Or was it…

I straightened and composed myself, reviewing what I was going to say to make sure it made sense before I said it. "Okay, so…I want to be the best in the world. That's what I'm in this for. And if nobody else is doing doubles and singles…why can't I be the first? Or the first in a while, anyway."

"I don't want to slow down your career," Aliq said, and I stopped him.

"I know there was a time when I was freaking out about missing one major, how I thought I'd never get that opportunity back. But I did something worthwhile with that time. Looking back, I'd make the same decision again. So I'd like to keep trying doubles, but," I held up a paw to stop their objections, which was unnecessary as neither of them was going to interrupt me, but it felt like a movie-thing to do, "I'll give it one more year. If I'm not in the top ten in singles by the end of next year, I'll drop the doubles. Okay?"

Nashan and Aliq looked at each other. Neither one said anything. So I pressed. "Nashan, you think if I dropped doubles I could be top ten at the end of next year?"

"If you work hard," the fox said cautiously "It's a good stretch goal."

"Okay. If that's what you'd expect from me without doubles, give me a chance to do it with doubles."

He nodded slowly. "Fair enough. You're gonna work hard."

"I know."

"I'm still not sure," Aliq said. "I mean, you could be wasting a whole year."

"First of all, I won't be wasting it. I'll be advancing, just maybe not as fast as I could be. Second, I'm not even old enough to drink yet. Braden's four years ahead of me and only has one major under his belt. Tempest is probably past his peak and he's nine years older than me. I've got a lot of time, and this is how I want to spend it."

The arctic fox got a big smile on his face, and I knew that I'd made the right choice. "All right," he said. "Let's go win a major in doubles."

* * *

Braden went to the finals of the States and lost, and didn't text me the whole time. After his loss, I saw him briefly in the locker room, but we just said a quick hi to each other. There were other people around, and I got why he might've felt a little uncomfortable, what with the comments he must've heard too. Plus Braden is often pissy right after a loss.

I wanted to tell him that I thought it had been a good loss, that he was loosening up and playing a lot less mechanically. He really looked like he was having fun out there, as much as Braden can. Like, not smiling or anything, not so the announcers noticed, but to someone who knew him, he looked much less tense than I was used to seeing him in matches. His tail flowed easily and he held his arms more loosely. More importantly, his shot variety was great. It was just that the guy on the other side of the net, Geoffrey Bowson the caribou, was having one of those unreal days. He got to every shot and his serve-and-volley game was almost flawless. He had a few lapses, enough for Braden to make it a tight match, but not that many.

And still, Braden took him to a fifth set. But you know how sometimes the announcers say, "It was just his day"? That's what it was for Bowson. Like, I was rooting hard for Braden to get his second major, and I still knew that it probably wasn't going to happen. Bowson was in control from the first game and never let up. To Braden's credit, even when he was down a break, he didn't stop fighting. I've seen players—Braden, even, in other matches, and myself for sure—mentally check out when a match seems to be over. But Braden kept fighting, all the way to match point.

Then he had to endure the trophy ceremony, and I always thought that would be the hardest thing, to sit by and watch the guy who'd just beaten you get a trophy while everyone cheers him, and then they turn to you and say, "Good try," and everyone claps like they do in that Internet video of the six year old fox cub swinging the full size golf club. Isn't he cute, he almost did a grown-up thing. I know it's not that, that if you're the runner-up then you still beat a hundred-some people out to be standing there, but still.

So anyway, he endured the ceremony and I saw him in the locker room and then that night I texted him: *It was a pretty good match.*

He texted back about fifteen minutes later. *Thanks.* And then, right away: *Gonna be busy the rest of the time here.*

I wasn't really surprised, but I was a little hurt. *Okay. See you in Chester City?*

I'm going overseas for the end of the year.

I stared at those words for a while, and then typed out, *Is this a conversation we should have in person?* But I didn't send it right away. I waited, and read it over again, and when I was convinced I wasn't overreacting, I did send it.

He didn't answer for several minutes, and then wrote, *I'm back over the holidays. We can talk then or at the Ocie.*

I wanted to say a lot of things, to ask if this had anything to do with him losing, or if it was about the guys in the locker room calling me his "little friend." I wanted to ask if we were going to break up the next time we talked in person, but that was dumb because we weren't even dating. I wanted to ask if he was tossing me on the same trash heap as Rascal, which was also dumb, because they weren't dating either. In the end I just said, *Good luck, see you then,* and put my phone back into my pocket. Then I went to go spend a very nice evening with Aliq and Ori, and if they noticed my mood, neither of them said a word about it.

Interlude (2015)

September 2015

Strange thing: after nearly two hours of high-pressure tennis, you'd think I'd be at least a little tired. But after a brief break between sets, I jog out to receive Braden's serve in the fifth set feeling fresh.

The feeling doesn't last. I know Braden's going to come out determined to regain the momentum, because he's talked about that a lot. "When you lose a set, you have to regain the momentum," he's told me a bunch of times. He might've lost the tiebreaker, but he's going to have put that all behind him. And I know that his serve will be as sharp as ever, because it always is, even in the fifth set of the last match of a two-week tournament.

I believe that I'm feeling good enough to play him the way I have the last four sets, which would make this fifth set a toss-up. But a couple exchanges into that first point, I process that I'm not moving quite as well as I normally do, and that makes sense because I've been playing every other day for two weeks, intense matches, and it's about eighty outside (twenty-five in the system I grew up with, but I'm thinking in Fahrenheit now). Even with the bottle of water I've been drinking, I'm still panting, and even though I feel okay, my legs are a little fatigued.

Braden's panting too, for what that's worth. Like me, he has an icy wristband on and goes to it between points. We both play hard still, but we're playing smart as well. Maybe one shot in ten I don't run for the way I would have in the first or second set, and maybe I take a few more chances trying to hit a winner and end the point sooner. But Braden's doing the same thing, so in the end it evens out.

We're on serve at 3-2, my serve, when I hit a nice cross-court winner that is close enough that Braden does lunge for it. He goes down to one knee, and I think he just slipped, but as I walk to the ad court to serve, he takes a while to get up, and when he does, he tests his ankle.

The crowd gasps. The last thing they want is a default, and I sure don't want that either. I watch the cross fox hurry back to his receiving spot to get ready for serve, favoring the ankle as he does. He sets and looks across at me.

I lower my racket and gesture for him to walk around. He flattens his ears and glares at me, but I don't bring the racket up. The crowd sort of gets what's going on and gets vocal, but I can't tell the difference between "good for you" and "get on with it," so I just assume they're on my side.

After a good long Braden glare, he shifts his weight back and forth and walks around on the ankle. And right then, the chair umpire, a field mouse, says, "Mr. N'Guwe, please serve."

He has to warn me because I'm taking too much time, and Braden hasn't asked for a medical timeout (if the ankle is an acute injury, he can). I judge that I have another few seconds before he threatens to dock me a point, and Braden knows the timing as well as I do.

So the cross fox watches me, and as I prepare to serve, he gets ready to receive. He looks better now; at least, he's putting more weight on the ankle. Warning or no, I feel good about myself as I loft the ball and serve.

* * *

"Excellent display of sportsmanship there from N'Guwe, and he wins the point as Longacre is still favoring that left ankle."

"That's what we like to see in our young players, Daren. No question that Longacre turned the ankle, but it doesn't look more serious than that. Hopefully he can continue to compete, because for this final to end in a retirement, well, it's only happened twice before in a Major final in the Open era."

"Potter at '82 Wimbledon, wasn't it? Sprained his knee on the court and couldn't finish."

"Right, and then Farrier in '74 at the States. She suffered from migraines and had an attack half an hour after the match started."

"They've got better medication for that now. N'Guwe serving at 30-love and a beautiful ace down the middle."

"Longacre would normally at least have tried for that, but the ankle still seems to be bothering him."

"And N'Guwe closes it out with another ace."

"Longacre walking around his side of the court, testing the ankle again. He's definitely going to continue, but in a match this tight, any advantage could tip the scales."

"That's the foot he plants on to serve, so it's even more important."

"He's not asking for a timeout, so he's going to try to play through it. Longacre getting ready now, and N'Guwe sets to receive his serve."

* * *

I'm excited as Braden gets set to serve, but a mix of both happy and tense excited. The way he serves is going to determine how the rest of the match goes. Even if the ankle only bothers him for this one game, if that's a game where I break his serve, I'd be up 4-3, needing only to hold two service games for the championship.

But I'd also have won on an injury. Braden would forever think that at full strength, he could've beaten me. And to get three titles and two sets toward the Grand Slam and lose it on an injury—that'd kill him. Of course, it's Braden; win or lose, he's going to come back next year determined to win it again. "I'm gonna hoard those trophies like a dragon," he told me, "and anyone who wants one is gonna have to fuckin' earn it." (And then I laughed at him and asked if he learned that language from Two-Fingers Vinnie.)

We both know the breaks of the game, of course. If I turn my ankle and he beats me, I'll feel bad too. But I still let things go better than Braden does, despite all the help I've tried to give him on that front.

None of which means anything, really. We can only play the game in front of us, so I set to receive his serve.

He bounces a few times, taking his time, and then tests his ankle again. With his usual quick motion, he tosses the ball, plants, jumps, and serves—

—right into the net.

I move up a few steps to wait for the second serve. Braden's clearly thinking about the ankle and testing it out again, and now he has to give me an easier ball to return. But he knows how to field second serve returns too. He'll be ready for whatever I send him.

His ankle also looks like it's getting better. I've had turned ankles like that, and they hurt for a few minutes, they're weak for a bit, and then adrenaline takes over. Tonight it's probably going to hurt, but for the next half hour—maybe hour—he'll be fine.

The second serve comes in situated perfectly, and my response is automatic. Braden's moving to the ad side, anticipating that I'll send it down the line, but I see the cross-court angle and I take it. He can't switch directions as easily, so he just stops and watches it go by. Love-15.

Braden thinks again before the next serve, and this time gets the first serve in. It's returnable, and we settle into a rally. He's already moving better, I think, but not so well that he can catch up to a drop shot that isn't even one of my best. Love-30.

His first serve keeps improving: the next one is an ace, and the one after that is good enough to keep me off-balance, allowing him to win a quick, easy point. At 30-30, he gets a good serve in, but my return is good (I do go down the ad court sideline this time) and though he gets to it, he's off balance. I slice the ball back to the deuce court and run to the net, because he's sprinting for the ball and he won't be able to do very much with it if he gets there.

The lob is the right play in that case and he makes a pretty one, sending me halfway back down the court, but the lob is also an automatic play, and Braden often forgets that I'm taller than a lot of other players (when he's playing me, I mean). So the lob isn't quite high enough, and when I get back to midcourt I put a racket on it and smack it back down to him, trying to put enough force on it that it'll bounce up and out of his reach quickly. I don't quite make it, but his return goes wide, so effectively it worked.

And there it is. I've got break point.

As I walk back to the baseline, I think again about how it would feel to win this way. It's part of the game, I tell myself, and if it were anyone else on the other side, or even Braden in any other situation, that might be enough. But I can't shake a bad feeling in my stomach about it.

Braden tries for too much on the first serve, sending it long. He knows as well as I do that this could be the game that decides the match, the championship, and the Grand Slam. Nerves never get to him, but they are getting to him here. I move up, and he tosses, then delivers a second serve.

I get a good return in—not great, but good, and he's ready for it, smashing a strong forehand back. It puts me on my heels, and for the next few shots I'm acting out of reflex, getting the ball back as much as I can. Then I get an opening, I think, with a deep baseline shot, the perfect opportunity to move to the net. I take a step forward and then stop—instinct, but I can't say why. He sees it and pounces, a gorgeous passing shot that lands outside my reach and spins away. Deuce. I clap my racket to show appreciation for that shot, thinking as I do that if I'd gone up to the net, I might have been able to hit that. Did I hesitate because I'd been burned at the net a few times? I'd also won a few points.

Regardless, Braden's had a chance to recover and we're all even. If I break his serve now, he can't blame it on the ankle. And what's more, though he gives me a glare, he can't blame it on me.

Honestly, I don't think I hesitated to go easy on him. That passing shot he hit wasn't a gimme, even with me not moving. But I know I was thinking about the outcome of the game, and that'll mess up your tennis no matter what. And maybe a little part of me hit him an easier-than-normal return; maybe part of me made a bad decision not to go to the net, wanting to settle this game on equal footing. Either way, we're even, and I settle in for the end of the game and the match.

Part Nine: Tiebreak (2015)

Chapter Twenty-One
(2014-2015)

I didn't think Braden blowing me off would be such a big deal, but with only one minor tournament to distract me in November and one in December, and no Braden at either, I got more and more obsessed with figuring out exactly what he'd meant. He'd said he'd be back over the holidays, but I couldn't imagine breaking in on his family during their Christmas celebration. By this time I'd seen all kinds of posh Christmases on TV and in the movies, and the Longacre Family Christmas became in my mind a huge affair with extended family coming in, a house full of foxes singing carols and going to Mass down at their church and exchanging extravagant presents.

So when Aliq invited me and Ori to his house for Christmas again, I'd accepted before he even finished saying to Ori, "We don't celebrate religiously, but—"

"Ma and I never went to church," I reminded him, "not here in the States. But Ori, if you want to, we can find a church."

"I'd like to try," she said. "It's not terribly important, but I'd love to see what Christmas Mass is like here."

"There are plenty of churches around our house," Aliq said. "And Mom has been asking about you and she wants to see Ori again."

"I'd love that," Ori said, and so it was settled.

Braden's family was somewhere a few hours drive from Aliq's. I sent him a quick text telling him where I was going to be and offering to get together if he could get free. He wrote back a little later saying his Christmas was pretty packed, he'd try to get away but he'd see me in Oceania if not. Since I didn't have a car, I figured that

Oceania would be the next time I'd see him and I tried to put it out of my mind until then.

That worked well when there were other things to distract me, less well when I was alone. So I practiced with Aliq as much as I could and had a lot of fun afternoons and evenings talking to his parents. Ori and I told them about our Lundan Christmas (I had told them my recollections, but Ori had been there more recently and remembered more details) and they showed Ori their menorah and Mrs. Loize made "latkes," which are like little pancakes of shredded potato, and everything was delicious. Sitting around with the arctic foxes and celebrating a holiday, even if it wasn't ours, gave me and Ori a sense of family that we loved.

(Ori, more confused than I'd been by the Hanukah celebrations, read quite a lot of it on the Internet, and by the end of our stay she knew more than I did. I hadn't really thought about it much other than it was a different way to celebrate a holiday, but she told me it was really quite different from Christmas.)

And since Ori was more nostalgic for our Christmases than I was, they were nice enough to go shopping with us to get a few Christmas decorations as well. "It's so secular," Mrs. Loize explained as we walked through a department store with aisles and aisles of red shelving covered in snowy figures, angelic figures, all kinds of species in Santa suits, "that we're quite happy to celebrate a season of goodwill."

She didn't tell us not to buy manger scenes or even angels, but Ori and I had picked up enough of the differences in our religions that we stayed away from those and just bought Santas, elves, and one gingerbread house, which Mrs. Loize said they had never tried but were excited to. Ori and I hadn't tried one either, and that evening all of us sat down and put it together, nibbling corners of roofs and walls as we did so, and then decorated it with horrible sugary frosting that got all over our paws and in our fur, and it was the best time.

On Christmas, Ori and I, staying in the room Danver and I had shared the last time I'd stayed here (I told Ori about taking her call about Ma in the bathroom and she hugged me there, to make up, she said, for not being there in person), celebrated a quiet Christmas. She sang one of the songs from the Christmas pageant, and Aliq overheard and asked her to sing it for the whole family.

We had a roast chicken, because Mrs. Loize said she didn't know how to prepare a whole goose, and we had stuffing like at Thanksgiving and fresh bread and corn and peas and sparkling apple juice, because I had a few more months to go before I was old enough to drink. Aliq was old enough but didn't want to have alcohol, he said because he wasn't playing and therefore wasn't burning calories, but I think he didn't want to drink in front of his parents.

As I'd expected, I didn't hear from Braden during the holiday. The celebrations kept me busy enough that I didn't really think about it until the 27th, when Mrs. Loize took Ori out to shop for new clothes, and Aliq and I went to practice for the first time in a few days. It wasn't long; we were going to see a movie with his father later, but we both itched to get back onto the court.

We had a fun time and were happy to find that our reflexes and training were still sharp. Nashan had promised to give us a week off but said he'd be calling around the 28th or 29th to give us some drills to run. I enjoyed the time off, and it was important to reconnect with family (the Loizes were starting to feel more and more like family), but the practice with Aliq reminded me of what I really ached to do.

So it was a little weird when Aliq came up to me after the practice with his ears back and said, "Hey, I need a big favor from you."

"Sure," I said. "Anything."

He fidgeted, his tail curling. "I'm gonna take off tomorrow to spend New Year's with Shona. But I haven't told my parents about her, and I don't really want to until I know how things are gonna go, you know?"

"Your parents seem pretty chill."

He nodded. "They're great with you and Ori. But Shona isn't Jewish, or a fox, but..." His eyes went far away. "We have so much fun. We both want to see where it's going."

"Okay. So you want me to make up something?"

"Oh, no. I'm going to tell them I'm going to practice with my mixed doubles partner. I just need you to not tell them anything about…you know, us."

"Oh yeah, sure." I laughed. "Is that all?"

"I wasn't sure how you'd feel about—you know, about hanging out with my family without me, and not telling them the whole truth."

"I'm not going to be lying," I said, "so that makes me feel a lot better. No, it's totally fine."

"A little bit lying." Aliq grinned. "I don't know how much tennis we'll be playing."

I flicked my tail. "Just play some and that'll be enough," I said.

I was a little envious of Aliq going off to spend romantic time with someone, even though my time with Braden wasn't really romantic in that sense. I was probably just edgy because I hadn't had sex for a while—I'd gone out to a club twice since the States Open but only went home with someone once. I thought about that club where the ringtail had picked me up, but the memory wasn't a great one. I could hold out with my own paw for a while longer. If Braden didn't want to sleep together anymore, I'd worry about that in 2015.

The next day, we saw Aliq off and then went out with his parents on a boat owned by a work friend of Mr. Loize. Neither of us had ever been out on a boat before, and it was cold, but the boat had a little cabin we could all huddle into, and Mrs. Loize brought lots of thermoses of hot chocolate. The view out the windows was fantastic, and once Ori and I got over our light unease at the motion and the idea of being on the water, we loved it. I took a bunch of pictures, and Ori posted some to my social media accounts.

For the next few days I texted Aliq to hear about what a good time he was having. When I said something about missing my practice partner, Ori offered to hit the ball around with me, and though she wasn't as good a partner as Aliq, it did me good to get onto the court and hit some serves, and she helped me do Nashan's drills, too.

In between tennis and hanging out with the Loizes I tried not to check my phone too often, nor to wonder what Braden would say come January. Those problem belonged to the new year, and I wasn't quite done with the old.

The night of December 31, Ori and I sat in the Loizes' living room as midnight approached. Mr. and Mrs. Loize had gone to bed early saying they'd seen plenty of years turn over, so it was just the two of us. Aliq texted me to say *Happy New Year*, and I wished him the same back. Kim and Danver and Sean texted too, and I texted them back. Then I thought, what the heck, and I texted Braden: *Happy New Year and best of luck in 2015!*

We were counting down to the ball dropping on TV when my phone buzzed, right at twelve seconds. So it was just around the time 2014 was becoming 2015 that I read Braden's reply.

You too.

It was better than not replying at all, and that was what I was used to with Braden. So my tail wagged a bit and I hugged Ori and we talked about what we wanted to do in 2015 until about one in the morning. Ori was looking forward to going overseas with me in January, and I had the goal of course of getting into the top ten.

It wasn't until the next morning that I found another message from Braden on my phone, sent at about 2 am.

I think it's gonna be a good year.

* * *

Nashan wanted us to head down to Oceania the first week after New Year's so we could acclimatize and be ready for the Open three weeks later. So I met Aliq at our hotel near the Port City airport, where he and Ori and I had dinner with Nashan at a steak place. Nashan started off by telling us that he was talking to Lochen about hiring a trainer to travel with us, an expense that we were on the fringe of being able to afford. They were talking to other players on the circuit to see whether anyone who was going to match our schedule wanted to share someone, but also they thought it might be better to wait and see if we made enough in the first half of the year to hire someone dedicated to us, which both of them thought we would. Nashan asked if we had any preference, but honestly I just wanted to hear about Aliq's time with Shona, so I said I didn't, and Aliq said the same. Ori was the one who spoke up and asked whether we'd be able to use the help in the first half of the year or if it would hurt us to wait, and she and Nashan talked about that for a little while.

They decided to wait, I think; the arrival of our steaks distracted me and Aliq both, although he had fish. "Mmm," he said, digging in. "The preparation is better, but there's nothing like really fresh fish."

The grin as he said that made me ask, "Like you've been having for the past week?"

"We went to Lauder Beach down in Pensa. Nothing but sand and sun. Well, rain for a lot of the time, and clouds. But there's an indoor tennis center."

I laughed. "You actually practiced?"

His ears folded back. "Well, yeah. What? We're both tennis players."

"I know, but I thought you were going be just..." I waved my paws. "Dating."

His grin came back. "We did that too. But you can't do that all day."

"Couldn't you go..." I realized that I didn't know what people did when they weren't having meals or practicing or playing. Aliq and I watched movies sometimes, but surely other people did more than that. In the movies they were always going to galas, or office parties, or barbecues. They went shopping at fancy stores and thrift stores, planned parties and cleaned their houses or apartments. They took vacations to sunny tropical destinations where they lay on the beach and got into romantic troubles with other guests or the local staff (who rarely had their own stories). They played video games and miniature golf and regular golf and sometimes tennis, although then very casually and in a manner that suggested they had seen people play on TV but never picked up a racket before.

But the only dates I'd been on so far were with Shawna, back in Palm Gables, when we went to movies and dinner because evening was the only time we had, and Marquize, who'd been with me on the tour so we had to practice together.

Aliq had cocked his head as I trailed off, and then shoved me. "What did you do this past week?"

"We ran errands with your parents," Ori said, "and practiced when we had free time."

The arctic fox's ears perked up triumphantly. "There you go, then. If you and Braden were hanging around all day, you'd be playing tennis."

"Who's hanging around with Braden?" Nashan, like Ori, had perked big ears our way.

"Rocky's friends with him," Aliq said. "They hang out at tournaments and stuff."

Nashan shook his head at me. "That guy's only out for himself," he said. "Be careful with him. I know he's useful to you now, but trust me, he wouldn't be spending time with you if he wasn't getting something out of it."

Aliq shot me a sideways glance that confirmed that he suspected what Braden was getting out of our time together, and Ori looked thoughtful, but Nashan was earnestly worried for me. I reminded myself of that and didn't snap back at him. "It's fine," I said. "I mean, thanks. But it's some Palm Gables stuff we had in common, and we started talking, and I don't think he has a lot of people to talk to."

"Not surprised," Nashan grumbled. "You know, talent alone doesn't make it on this tour. You've got to be nice to people, too. Make friends and your life is a whole lot easier."

"I know," I said. "I'm friends with Ljubo and with Philippe, sort of, and Tempest nodded at me the other day."

"And Tempest doesn't talk to anyone," Aliq chimed in.

"That's more because he's been taken advantage of." Nashan picked up his wine glass. "At least, that's what some of the guys on the tour tell me. Plus, when you're number one for a while, the media pressure is huge." He took a drink. "And that's why you need friends on the tour."

After dinner, we were supposed to get to bed early because we had an early flight to the West Coast and then a layover before the long flight to Oceania. But Aliq and I kept talking after we'd gotten ready for bed.

"She's really nice," he told me, lying on his bed. "And we were gonna take it slow, but…"

"But nobody goes on a week-long vacation to Pensa to 'take it slow,'" I said.

He grinned and his fluffy tail flicked. "Yeah. So we did go a little quick, but it wasn't all just that. We talked a lot, too. We have a lot of things in common, like stuff we want to do after tennis."

"After tennis?" The thought had only occurred to me briefly, in flashes. It was years away, I hoped, barring a serious injury.

"Yeah, I want to be a commentator, talk about the matches and stuff like that, and she does too, but we both know there aren't that many spots, so we talked about working for the broadcast team, like doing editing or writing for the on-air people or things like that, if they'd have us."

"That's cool. I didn't know you wanted to do that."

He rolled over on his back and stared at the ceiling. "I mean, I never really thought that much about it. We're playing, right? So we look to the next match, the next tournament. But when I'm watching matches, I'm calling them in my head, and I dunno, I think I might be good at it."

"All right. Hey, if I can help, let me know."

He twisted his head around. "When you get into the top ten and you're being interviewed by all the major networks, tell 'em you have a friend who wants to work for them."

"Absolutely," I said.

We talked a little more about Shona until there was a knock at our door. We exchanged looks, and I got up and padded over.

"Ro, it's me," Ori said as I got near the door.

So I let her in. "Couldn't you sleep?"

"I can hear you two talking through the wall and I'm not sleepy either," she said. Aliq sat up as Ori came around to sit at the foot of my bed, and I climbed up to sit near the head. "What were you talking about?"

We recapped the conversation and then she asked Aliq whether Shona was going to Oceania (she was) and whether he was going out with her there (he was). Then she turned to me. "And what's this about Braden? Isn't he that player you told me was so terrible?"

"That was a long time ago." I hadn't told Ori much about my work with the TIU because Altamont had impressed upon me the need for secrecy. "I've gotten to know him a little better."

She flashed Aliq a smile. "Did you pull a thorn from his paw?"

"It's complicated."

That got a raised eyebrow. "Complicated like sleeping with him?" When my eyes went all big, she waved toward Aliq. "I saw the way you looked at each other at dinner. He knows, doesn't he?"

The moment hung there. I didn't want to lie to her, but it was hard to talk about my private life like this. Then I remembered telling Ori about Marquize, telling Aliq that I was gay. They looked back at me with patience and understanding and love. I drew in a breath. "We're not, like...boyfriends." I glared at Ori. "And I hadn't told Aliq. I mean, not out loud."

"Dude," Aliq said. "I figured it out."

"It's not really my secret to tell." I curled my tail around my leg.

"We won't tell anyone." Ori looked at Aliq, who nodded. "I'm glad you're seeing someone, though—why not boyfriends?"

"He doesn't want that. It's just...you know, going out to bars is risky for a lot of reasons, and we're both...so why not just do stuff together?"

They looked at each other. Aliq flicked his ears. "Makes sense to me, I guess."

"Do you like him, Ro?"

My sister's muzzle remained open and caring, but with a set to her jaw now. "Yeah," I said. "I mean, I wouldn't...you know...with just anyone."

"Not like you have a lot of options. Not in the life," Aliq said.

"No," I said. "But I do like him. There's...more to him than being an asshole. I think he's, like, like Tempest, like Nashan was talking about. He's had a lot of people be terrible to him, so he keeps them away."

"And you pulled a thorn from his paw."

"Sort of." I leaned back against the headboard, remembering. "But he reached out first. Palm Gables stuff. I don't really want to talk about it." I'd talked about Frio to Ma, and I would not have minded sharing that part of my life, but it was over and done with and I didn't want him to have any more power over me.

Ori and Aliq glanced at each other, and then Ori said, "As long as you're happy."

They asked me more about him, but not a lot, and then we talked about the trip to Oceania and stayed up for another forty-five minutes until we were all yawning. But after Ori had left and we'd turned out the light, I lay there asking myself: Am I happy?

Chapter Twenty-Two

In the morning I texted Braden on the way to the airport to ask when he was going to Oceania. He texted back as we were boarding.

> *Heading down tomorrow.*
> *You playing Ganbra?*

Yep. And Redcliffe too.

> *Dinner at Tea Club*
> *again?*

Sure.

I'd just entered the cabin of the plane.

> *Boarding plane, got to go.*

> *See you there.*

So at least I felt good for the first leg of the flight. Rather than watching movies, I pulled out my tablet and looked at film of the top ten players from the States Open and the end of year tournaments. I put Braden off 'til last because I knew his game already, so by the time I finally pulled up his footage, I'd been studying tennis for three hours.

As I'd thought, I already knew the way Braden played pretty well, and the match at the States was the one I'd played. Still, it was interesting to watch the footage without the urgency of having to respond to it. Nashan had also loaded footage from the year-end tournament, which I watched more closely.

After going through all the matches, I wanted to compare his play to Braden of a year ago, so I called up the previous year's States

Open. Then I nudged Aliq, who was watching movies, to look at the different footage.

"What am I looking for?" he asked, leaning over the armrest to get a better view.

"Here." I played one of the points from the 2013 States Open.

He watched Braden return a serve cleanly, rally, play good defense on a couple good shots, and hit a winner. "Nice. He's good, we know that."

"That's how a lot of his points went in 2013. Okay, here's a couple months ago." I pulled up one from the year-end tournament. Braden again received a serve, but this time the rally looked different.

"He's moving better," Aliq said. "Is this how his matches went last year?"

This point only lasted six shots; the other had been ten. "More or less. I don't know if the numbers bear this out, but it feels like his points aren't lasting as long. He's being less predictable, but only a little."

"Yeah, in 2013 you can see him settling in and then pouncing on an opportunity. That one," he jabbed a claw at the screen, "he hits a couple groundstrokes, but it looks more like he's probing for a weakness. He puts a little more spin on the forehand here." He rolled it forward and then stopped. "And he's jumping around more."

"That's what I saw, too."

The arctic fox leaned back. "You want to try to get more dynamic like him? I don't think that's a weakness in your game, to be honest."

"I can always get more dynamic," I said. My tail was curled to the opposite side of my seat from Aliq, so he couldn't see the flicking of the end of it. I didn't want to say that Braden was picking up some tips from me, but while Aliq was looking at the cross fox's movement—definitely a little more dynamic—I'd been looking at his muzzle. The intensity was different: in 2013 his focus narrowed his gaze until it felt like his entire being was poured into it. In 2014 he was no less intense, but his tail swung more freely, he rocked and shifted, and after the winning shot, he smiled. He wasn't just more dynamic. He was having fun.

I'd done that. I'd helped a top ten player get even better. That pride saw me through our four-hour layover in Crystal City, all the way until getting on the plane to Townshend, when the plane's cabin lights dimmed and Aliq, next to me, settled into his neck pillow and closed his eyes. I closed mine too, but my mind wasn't ready to sleep yet; it chose to dwell on Braden's aloofness during the holidays. What if Rascal was right? What if Braden had gotten what he wanted from me: an extra dimension to his game? He'd clearly learned something from me and now he didn't need me anymore.

So what? It wasn't like we were boyfriends. I had other friends on the tour, friends who didn't worry about what the locker room said about us. Colluvic had invited me to hang out again, and I was sure if I asked Dubois to grab dinner sometime, he'd say yes. As for the sex, well, the bars were still there, and if anything the atmosphere was more accepting every year.

(It felt weird to me that the tour was pretty chill, apart from a few people whispering about me and Braden. Doubles teams spent a lot of time together and nobody whispered about them being gay; lots of guys kept to themselves and the attitude on the tour was mostly a shrug. And yet the perception was that if there was anything different about you that wouldn't play well in the media, you should keep it to yourself. One of the guys on the tour was Muslim—probably more, but one that I knew—and he'd asked me not to mention it to anyone because he didn't want it to get out.)

My rational mind knew all those things, and yet there was something else there. I'd enjoyed having a secret, sure; I'd enjoyed being close to one of the best players in the game, yes; I kept going back and replaying his game footage, both on the tablet and in my head, of course, why wouldn't I? I thought about his body under my paws, and not just his muzzle on me but the times we lay together quietly. The best times with Marquize had had that quality, and maybe that's why I was putting Braden in that same category.

Clearly he didn't feel the same way about me, and that was fair, because he'd laid out from the start that we weren't going to be boyfriends. So I shouldn't even be letting myself feel these things.

Am I happy?

* * *

I didn't know, not then, nor when I woke up to the flight attendant asking what breakfast I wanted, nor when we landed in Townshend. But in the summer heat of Townshend there was a schedule to keep, a flight to Ganbra, tennis to be played. I had opponents to study both in singles and doubles and travel to coordinate, and I had a sister to show around Oceania.

We'd asked Lochen and Nashan if we could have a day to acclimate and sightsee around Townshend. So I took Ori to the harbor, we gawked at the bridge, went out to dinner yawning, and got back to the hotel at nine in the evening barely able to keep our eyes open.

"Winter was strange enough," Ori said. "But here it's summer now. It's amazing. The world is so big. And everyone's so nice."

"I like Oceania," I said. "I like how everything is different, but not all that different. It's fun to remember that there are lots of ways to do things. You can put meat in pastry, for example."

"I'm still getting used to the States," Ori said, "so this feels like a States city where everyone talks with an accent, like in Taysha."

That disappointed me a little. Aliq jumped in. "What freaks me out is the big bats. And the birds are all different, so the background noises here are weird."

"That's true." Ori stifled a yawn. "I'm glad that my paperwork went through so I could come along."

"Me too. Hope I can win here one day. Everyone seems great."

"Hope *we* can win here." Aliq threw a small pillow at me.

"That too."

"All right, all right." Ori laughed and waved. "Goodnight, you two."

She retired to her room, leaving me and Aliq to doze off on our beds. "Hey," Aliq said, "Shona wants to practice in Ganbra and I thought it'd be nice to have her to dinner with us one night."

"Sure," I said. "I like her."

I hadn't expected her to meet us at the airport in Ganbra, though that was fine. She'd been in Oceania for most of a week so the jet lag wasn't affecting her anymore, and she wanted to whisk Aliq off to practice right away. He and I had planned to grab food and then practice, but I said we could reschedule for the afternoon, that Ori and I would get settled and walk around a bit. Nashan stepped in and said that he'd use the morning to go over film with me.

The main hotels near the tennis center in Ganbra were all along the same street, and that's how it was that Nashan, Ori, and I were supervising the unloading of our luggage when I happened to glance next door and see a familiar dark-furred vulpine muzzle walk out, dressed in a red polo shirt and khaki slacks. In the split-second where I thought I should say hi, he turned and held the door, and a red fox in a white blouse and pastel-yellow skirt stepped through. Braden said something to her, she took his paw in hers and smiled, and he led her to a waiting taxi.

"Rocky?"

Nashan tugged at my sleeve. "Come on, let's get inside. It's stifling out here."

"Yeah." I tore my eyes from the taxi and tried to think of alternate explanations that weren't "Braden has a girlfriend" as I followed my coach into the cool air of our hotel.

I came up with a couple explanations—she was his publicist, she was a cousin or a distant relative who lived in Oceania—but I didn't really believe any of them. After tossing my bag on one of the beds I went to the window and stared down at the street even though Braden and the vixen were long gone.

Why was it bothering me so much? We'd said we weren't boyfriends, and even if we had been we hadn't promised not to date other people. So he was probably dating that vixen, and that was fine. He didn't owe me any loyalty or fidelity or anything like that.

And he'd still said he wanted to see me at the Tea Room. Maybe that's where this explanation was going to come. He hadn't expected me to see him at the hotel; maybe he wanted to tell me in person.

(Again, though—why would that be important? The only answer I had was that it was important even though maybe it wasn't supposed to be.)

Ori knocked on the door, pulling me out of those thoughts. "I was talking to Marro," she said when I opened the door. "He says the Tea Room has good lunches. Want to go there?"

"Um." I didn't want to run into Braden and his date. "I went there last time I was here. I was thinking about trying something new?"

"It's new to me," Ori said. She tilted her head. "You know a better place?"

"Doesn't this hotel have a restaurant?"

Ori's ears went back a little and she looked at her phone again. "Marro says the king tiger prawns there are fantastic."

I sighed and came up with an excuse closer to the truth, if still not dead center. "Braden and I are meeting there later."

"Oh, well." She paused, and then said. "So you can try something different later. Come on, Ro, I'd like to go."

Her tone pulled me all the way out of my self-reflection. "Marro is the fennec who works with Colluvic, right? Is he going with us?"

She smiled. "If that's okay."

"Of course. All right, all right." I took a breath. Braden liked to sit back in private anyway, so if he had taken his date there, they'd be tucked away in the back and likely I wouldn't even see them. "Let's go to the Tea Room, then."

Marro stood nearly a foot shorter than both me and Ori except for his ears, whose tips came up to the top of my head when they were perked straight up, as they were when he met us. "Hey, hey," he said in a high voice when we met him outside the Tea Room, "I'm Marro. It's really a pleasure to meet you. Watched you play a lot, of course, and your sister is great."

"I know she is." I shook his paw: warm, firm grip. He smelled of some floral perfume, but under that his warm scent reminded me a little of a desert. Not in an inhospitable way, but the part where there was an oasis maybe, sunny and dry but with vibrant life at its core.

True to his scent and maybe his species, he fairly bounced on his heels as he opened the door for us. I'd just breathed in the fragrant air of the Tea Room, full of lovely food smells and of course about thirty different teas, when I glanced to my left. A small crowd of four people stood around a table talking apparently to a red fox. I knew even before I spotted the dark fur on the back of the head of the fox sitting across from her that it was Braden and his date, right there in the front of the shop.

Ori and Marro came in behind me and almost bumped into me, so I stepped to the right as a koala hostess came up to the stand and asked how many people were in our party.

"Could we have something near the back?" I asked.

"I'll see what we have," the koala said, and then Marro stepped up to her stand and put his paws down.

"We'd really appreciate it," he said.

When he lifted his paws, there was a hundred-dollar bill there. The hostess pocketed it and smiled. "Right this way, please."

"Money changes everything," Marro whispered back to us as we followed the koala back. I nodded but I wasn't really paying attention, my mind on the foxes on display up at the front of the Tea Room.

Lunch was pleasant enough; thankfully Ori and Marro did most of the talking. I answered questions when asked and even talked with Marro about a few of my upcoming singles opponents. Worrying about tennis helped distract me from thinking about people Braden was willing to be seen in public with, and when I was able to shake off those thoughts, I enjoyed Marro's company. He had a sense of humor about the tour and all the players, but you could tell that he also respected them. "It's funny," I remember him saying. "Put me on a court and I can't do a tenth of what Ljubo can. But he's hopeless online. He doesn't look at any social media except when I make him. His whole world is so small." And then he turned to me and said, "I don't mean that in a bad way—that's what works for him. If it works for you, great."

"I look at social media," I said. "Sometimes. I'm just not interested most of the time. I'm interested in tennis." But then I wondered if Braden had mentioned his date on social media. If he was willing to sit with her in a front restaurant window...

It made sense, of course it did. Tennis players went out with dates all the time, were written up in blogs and gossip sites, especially when you were top 100 in the world at something. Maybe top 50. I hadn't been bothered very much, but I'd only been top 50 for a few months, and not at any big tournaments. None of the journalists or bloggers who were bothering Braden had even batted an eye at me and Ori entering the restaurant, and I was sure there weren't a lot of six-foot-plus jackals out there, especially in Oceania.

Nor were we bothered on our way back to the hotel. Marro walked with us, and then when we were out front, Ori said, "You're going to practice, right?"

"Supposed to." I checked my phone. "If Aliq is done with his date."

I said it jokingly, but Ori and Marro looked at each other and then away, and then I realized what I'd missed over lunch, wrapped up in my own thoughts as I'd been. "I mean, he's practicing mixed doubles," I said, and indeed there was a message from Aliq confirming he'd meet me over on the practice courts in about forty-five minutes. "And he's done, or just about, so I'll go grab my stuff and head over to warm up. Hey, Marro, thanks for joining us. It was really nice to meet you." I shook his paw, and he said it was nice to meet me too, and then I smiled at Ori and headed up to my room.

Ha, I thought as I checked my gear bag and closed it up. So Ori'd met a cute fennec. Well, good for her. Maybe I couldn't have a relationship, but I'd be happy if she and Aliq could have theirs.

The afternoon practice went very well. Tennis took over, so I was able to forget about Braden and worry about improving my backhand. Nashan met me and Aliq at the courts and worked us out in preparation for our first opponent, and after an hour he dismissed Aliq and worked with me for another hour and a half. By the time I got through that, fatigue and jet lag were combining to kick my tail, so I staggered back to the hotel and fell into bed to nap before dinner.

I woke to a dark room and light snoring—Aliq's snoring—from the other bed. Bleary, I grabbed my phone. One in the morning, it said, and my empty stomach testified to the fact that it had been half a day since lunch, and seven hours since even the couple protein bars I'd eaten post-practice. But I also had three messages from Braden on my phone.

Hey. Dinner tonight?

yt?

Okay guess not.

And that was it. Damn. I sent him a quick text back: *Sorry, crashed hard after flight, tomorrow?*

I lay back in bed cursing myself, but as I reflected, a little satisfaction crept in as well. Braden hadn't told me about this vixen, and then he'd come looking for me and I wasn't available. Maybe he shouldn't take me for granted.

Ugh, I was thinking about him like he was Marquize. I covered my eyes, and then my phone buzzed.

I reached up. Braden wouldn't still be up, would he?

He would. *How about now? Q Inn 224*

I didn't have to ask whether this was a late dinner. *omw*, I sent, and jumped out of bed. Aliq stirred as I was leaving, but I hurried out the door before he could come all the way awake and ask me where I was going in a t-shirt and workout shorts at one in the morning. Fortunately, not many other people were awake either. The clerk at the hotel reception didn't blink an eye as I hurried through the lobby, which I suppose is the result of having a lot of tennis players staying in your hotel.

Outside, warm humid air enveloped me, giving each of the streetlights a haze as I walked quickly under them, consulting my phone for walking directions to the Q Inn, a small building a couple blocks away from the tennis center. I passed several tall, glamorous hotels, and then spotted the large yellow 'Q' across a street that appeared to divide the wealthy part of town from the less wealthy.

The Q Inn rose above its neighbors on the block, a towering three stories over the one-story outdoor shopping center beside it on one side and the gas station on the other. I double-checked the message, because this did not look like a place Braden Longacre would have his rooms, but there it was, so I crossed the street and went up to the door.

The front door didn't open. I rattled it, then saw the sign that said, "Please use key for entry after 11 pm." That stumped me for a moment, but fortunately the lemur at the desk saw me and came over.

"Forget your key?" he asked through the crack in the door, his Ocie accent thick, expression bland.

"No, I, uh, I'm meeting someone here."

That didn't surprise him. "Room number?"

"Uh." I checked my phone again. "224."

"Just a second." He ambled back to the desk and picked up the phone. I probably shouldn't have done that, because now he'd talk to Braden and Braden would have to say that yes, the jackal should be let in, and the clerk would remember that the fox in 224 had let in a jackal at one in the morning. One-fifteen now.

But the clerk just held the phone the way you do when you're waiting for someone to pick up, and after a few minutes he put it down again. In the ten seconds it took him to amble back to the door, I'd already run through options in my head: Braden had fallen asleep. Maybe this was a prank. No, he'd just fallen asleep; it was late. So I had my phone out and was texting him again when the clerk said, "No answer there."

"Hang on," a voice said behind me, and a black-furred paw slid a key into the slot next to the door. The green light lit up and the door clicked, and Braden pushed the door open. "I know this guy," he told the clerk.

"Are you room 224?" the lemur asked.

Braden looked at me, then back at the lemur. "Yeah."

"Okay." The guy stepped aside for us to come in, then retreated back behind his desk, ignoring us as Braden led me to the stairs.

The room reminded me of the rooms I'd stayed in with Marquize back on the Futures tour. One bed, a king, with bedsheets frayed around the edges and their flower patterns faded. The wood veneer of the dresser chipped in several places, a quarter-sized patch ripped away at the top right corner. None of those things bothered me; the room smelled fresh and everything was tidy. It just didn't look like a place Braden would willingly set foot in.

He wasn't staying here, I told myself. He'd arrived after I had. Still, I asked the question because I wanted to know the answers to the ones that would come after it. "You're not staying here."

"Pff, no." He tossed the key onto the dresser, then went to the window to pull the heavy curtains shut. "My manager rented it and got me the key. He thinks it's for me to get away from journalists and pressure and my entourage. Which it is."

While he talked, he peeled his shirt off in one smooth motion and then unsnapped his pants. One leg came off, his sheath exposed (and half hard) as he worked his underwear down, and then he looked at me and noticed I wasn't making any move to undress. "You want to do me with your clothes on?"

"No," I said, and then, "I mean, sure, maybe. But it's not that."

He gave me a look, a very Braden look that said that he wasn't really interested in anything that would delay the sex, but to his credit he just flipped his tail back and sat naked on the bed, one paw between his legs. "What?"

"That vixen."

His ears perked. "You saw her?"

I nodded. I'd expected him to act angry, or guilty maybe at being found out, but his paw kept moving and he smiled. "I was gonna tell you about her, but after."

"How about before?"

"Sure." He'd gotten himself fully aroused and now played with himself while talking. "She's a friend of mine—well, of my parents really—and she agreed to go out with me."

I swallowed disappointment. "Okay. I mean, we're not boy-friends, and we didn't say we wouldn't date other people, so…"

Now his paw did stop, and he barked a short laugh. "Not 'go out,' just go out. In public. The press takes pictures, people think I have a girlfriend, they stop asking questions about my private life." He removed the paw from his sheath and gestured to me. "We can keep doing this."

"So you were blowing me off. Going away, over the holidays."

He exhaled and leaned back with both arms, his erection promi-nent and visible, and honestly more than a little tempting. It had been a while, as I think I've mentioned. "People noticed we were hanging out together. I've never had a girlfriend on the tour. They put two and two together."

"You hung out with Rascal and you weren't sleeping with him."

"But people thought I was. Hell, they still think he's gay, or at least bi."

I wanted to sit down, but the only other place was the chair by the desk, and I didn't want to sit there because it felt too formal. Sitting on the floor meant I would be looking up at Braden, and though that position had its appeal, I wasn't quite ready for it. So I sat beside him on the bed and he turned to face me. "I don't want people finding out either," I said. "But…this feels…like we're ashamed of what we're doing."

"Ugh." He exhaled. "It's not shame. We have to be aware of the world we live in. If we were accountants, we could probably fuck in the office after hours and nobody would care. Hell, if we were football players even. But some of the guys on the tour can be really shitty and they're always looking for an edge. You think if we came out they wouldn't find some way to use that against us?"

"I guess so." I hadn't really thought of how it would affect my tennis career.

"And it shouldn't bother you to see me with Ellen. Think of how it is for me, all the time I'm spending keeping up appearances."

"And the time she's spending."

"Yeah, well." He rolled his eyes. "She gets to travel around the world, watch awesome tennis matches, and do her environmental videos."

"What videos?"

"She goes around the States filming endangered animals and habitats and raising money to save them, so she's doing some of that here, too. It's a good cause."

"That's pretty cool."

"Yeah." He looked down his chest at his flagging sheath. "So are we okay?"

It still felt weird to me, the whole arrangement, but the part that didn't feel weird was pushing Braden to lie back on the bed and taking his length into my muzzle. So I concentrated on doing that until I got him to shudder and clutch at my shoulder, until I felt that warmth and taste on my tongue that I'd missed.

"Now you," he said. "Get those clothes off."

I started to and then lay back on the bed. "Get them off me yourself."

He stared a moment, then grinned and crawled across the bed on all fours to come up next to me. He slid a paw under my shirt and pushed it up my chest, feeling the lines against the grain of my fur along the way, and then helped me ease it over my head, ears, and muzzle. The shirt flew to land atop the pile of his clothes, and then he grabbed the waistband of my shorts and pulled, catching my sheath and wiggling the fabric so it rubbed against my protruding erection and pulled it down.

I yipped and squirmed until my shaft popped free and Braden got my shorts down over my legs. Then he bent, cupped my sac in one paw, and licked up to my tip.

A moment later I was inside his muzzle, and several warm slurps later I was gasping. Braden liked to tease me to the edge and then stop, wait a moment, and start again, but tonight he was as eager as I'd been. He got me to the edge, hesitated, and then kept going, and I grabbed his shoulders, every nerve in my body tingling and then exploding and I shot into his muzzle, bright hot surges of pleasure that crested and then died down.

"Mmmf," he said, lifting his muzzle slowly. "Feels like you need-ed that as much as I did."

"Ah-hah," I panted, my body still singing. And maybe it was just the orgasm, but it occurred to me that Braden could have gone back to hooking up in bars. We'd started fucking because it was "easier." But he was going to a lot of trouble now just to be able to keep seeing me, and I couldn't believe that it was still "easier."

So I grabbed him impulsively and pulled him up to lie on top of me and I wrapped my arms around him and hugged him tightly.

He struggled for a moment. "Hey," he said. "What—"

"Shut up," I told him. "I just want to hug you."

"Your sheath's all messy," he grumbled, but relaxed into the hug.

"Yeah, so's yours." I rubbed paws down his back to his tail and then over his butt. It was a really nice butt and I hadn't properly appreciated it before.

He sighed dramatically into the pillow next to my head. "Fine." But after a moment, he slid one arm under my shoulders and hugged me back.

A little while later, his breathing evened out and his head rested against my shoulder. I wasn't all that sleepy, or so I thought. I lay there thinking about how it wasn't all that bad, this arrangement, and now that I knew what was going on with him and Ellen, it wouldn't bother me to see him with her in public. The argument, sound though it seemed, still felt like I was talking myself into something.

I woke to Braden rolling away from me and off the bed. The lights in the room, still on, showed his dark brown and orange fur as he got to his feet and then bent to pick up his clothes.

"You leaving?" I said.

"Yeah, I didn't mean to fall asleep. People will be getting up in an hour and wondering where I am." He pulled his pants on. "You can stay here if you want."

"I should get back too."

"Well, don't leave at the same time." His head disappeared inside his shirt and then reappeared. He smoothed it down. "Weird enough I'm walking around at four in the morning."

"Maybe I'll shower."

"Sure, good idea." Dressed, he fished in his pants pocket and then placed a plastic key card on the dresser. "Uh, I got you a key too. Maybe do this again in a week?"

"Yeah," I said. "Sure."

"Okay. Cool. I'll text you." His tail flicked. "Uh. Bye."

"Good luck," I said.

He looked quizzical. "In your matches," I clarified.

"Oh. Yeah, you too." He grinned. "If you make it to the quarterfinals, I'll see you there."

I snorted. "Maaaybe here. Not the Ocie. That's a year away probably."

Braden's smile grew. "You never know," he said, and left.

Chapter Twenty-Three

Whatever I thought of it, Braden's deception worked. We said hi in the locker room but didn't go practice together or anything, and I didn't hear any murmurs of "Braden's little friend" around. Maybe he felt very pleased with himself, or maybe his tennis had just continued to improve; Braden lost in the final in Ganbra and then won the next tune-up. Aliq and I got to the semifinal in Ganbra and the quarterfinals in the next one, and while I didn't do quite as well in singles, I did better than I had last year, and Nashan made sure to remind me of that often as we traveled down to Bourkeville for the Ocie Open.

This was my first showing at a major tournament where, despite my modest words to Braden, I thought I might be able to do well. Aliq and I were playing better than ever, and while I hadn't made it to the quarters in either of the tune-ups, I hadn't expected to. I'd done better than my ranking would predict, and partly I thought that was thanks to Braden.

We'd had one more night in Ganbra after I lost my match but before he won his semifinal. After getting each other off, we lay together on the bed quietly for a minute, and then he said, "Don't get discouraged."

I turned. "I thought I did pretty well."

"Not about that. I mean about losing. You're good, you're just still putting things together. But you're close. You'll be out there and something your coach said will make sense one day when it didn't every day before that. I see you adding to your game every tournament."

"Oh." The warmth I felt from that had nothing to do with my fading climax.

"But don't lose that feeling of fun." Braden almost never smiled, and he didn't now, but he rested a paw on my chest.

That bit of advice, generic though it was, really helped. Nashan was working with me on taking advantage of my left-handed play by putting better spin on the ball. I got good topspin on my forehand, and Nashan kept telling me that if I wanted to make it at the higher levels, I'd have to add some complexity to my spin. As a lefty, my spin went the opposite direction from right-handers' groundstrokes, but, as Nashan said, over the course of a match my opponents would get used to it if I didn't add some variety to my shots. I'd need to hit a loopier ball with greater depth once in a while, or a flatter shot with less spin and more penetration, something different that would keep my opponent off balance.

I was reluctant to play with new strokes because whenever I did, my mishits and misses went way up. I knew there would be things I couldn't do, and so I was sort of fighting Nashan on this. Stubbornly, like a good coach, he insisted on pushing me to try again and again at each practice.

Warming up for the Ocie Open, I thought about Braden's words. Maybe if I gave myself a little credit and used some patience, I could get to where Nashan wanted me to be. I didn't know why just thinking it was possible made a difference, but I took to practice energetically enough that Nashan commented that I seemed more motivated than normal. He specifically praised my progress in putting spin on the ball even though five out of the six shots had gone out.

I took that confidence into the locker room. A lot of the guys on tour greeted me, asked me how my holidays were, and offered to go out, and I carried myself like I belonged there. I'd talked to several of them before, and some had been friendly at the States, but the combination of my ranking climbing and being in a foreign country seemed to make everyone more sociable. Intense, too, because this was the first major of the new year and everyone wanted to get a jump on points.

There were still a few of the top ten players who didn't socialize with me, but they didn't socialize with anyone. Tempest, down to #7 at this tournament with everyone saying his best days were behind him, kept earphones clipped to his small ears and did meditation exercises. Geoffrey Bowson, who'd risen to #1 after beating Braden in the States, didn't socialize, and Phillippe Dubois, a marten currently at #4, stuck to his circle of close friends, though he had gone out of his way to chat with me last year and remained friendly. But Li Xu, the tiger who at #6 was hoping for a resurgent year, took an interest in me, and Manny Luongo, a Cape dog who'd finished the year strong to end at #9, did too. Braden was #2 after his strong finish at the States Open last year, and the #3 player was Milos Daryavic, that maned wolf who'd beaten Braden in a match I watched a couple years ago. Daryavic hadn't had much time for me then, but now he knew me and actually came over unsolicited to give me a little bit of advice about patience in games. When I told him I was grateful for his interest and advice, he beamed.

"Qanif did the same for me years ago," he said. "I have always appreciated it and promised to do the same when I can." Qanif was a fennec, so I presume our common caninity had something to do with it too.

The other consequence of people relaxing about me and Braden was that Braden felt comfortable inviting me, along with Colluvic, to stay with him at the house of Desmond Robin, a past Ocie champion who had a big mansion with three tennis courts out back. Desmond was a tazzie, a small but jovial guy, and of course I'd seen his two Ocie wins back in the day. He and Braden had gotten friendly the year Braden won, and this year Desmond had asked Braden to come stay, and because he'd seen our pictures from Londinium, he said, "Bring that black wolf and the black-backed jackal too."

"That wolf" was always Colluvic, even when his fur color wasn't specified, even though there were half a dozen other wolves in the top 50. None of the others was as brash or loud or well-known outside the fanatical tennis world. Me, for instance, the guys all knew, but I hadn't made much of a name for myself outside yet; my endorsement deals, though not small, weren't high-profile commercials. Colluvic did TV ads for outdoorsy hiking gear and wore their logo on his shirts; no other tennis player wore their stuff. There were about a dozen companies we all knew and recognized, from my own up-and-coming player One Two Three to the giant in the athletic gear world, Kinetic.

Anyway, there weren't any other jackals at the Ocie, black-backed or otherwise (there was a golden jackal who played in the lower-tier Champions tournaments but I'd only met him once), so clearly he meant me. I asked whether Ori and Aliq could come stay as well and before Braden could answer, Colluvic slapped me on the back and said, "Of course, bring your whole team! Robin's house is bigger than this arena!"

That wasn't quite right, but it was impressively large. It was twenty minutes from the arena, but Desmond had a driver and a minivan to take us to and from the tournament, and they had our schedule so they knew when to pick us up (not Aliq's mixed doubles but they added that) and all in all it was very much like staying in a low-key luxury hotel where we didn't have to worry about photographers—and by "we" I mean of course Braden and Colluvic, because nobody wanted pics of me at that time.

The four of us practiced together once or twice, but more often Aliq and I practiced while Colluvic and Braden worked with their coaches and trainers. "They're so different," Aliq said to me after the first two days, drinking water after our workout. "I can't believe they're friends."

"Well, Braden isn't outgoing, but…" I thought about it. "If someone reaches out to him in the right way, he's receptive. And Colluvic reaches out to everyone."

"I guess that makes sense." Aliq shook his head. "Colluvic is so easy to talk to I forget he's the number four player in the world sometimes. But I still can't find anything to say to Braden." He gulped the rest of his plastic bottle and crushed it in a paw. "I'm afraid I'm going to say something about you two without meaning to."

"That doesn't seem like the kind of thing you'd do."

"I know, but I still worry about it." He sighed and got up. "All right, I'm gonna go work out in Robin's gym. Have you been there yet?"

"Not yet."

"Come with. It's amazing."

Aliq wasn't selling it short. Desmond's personal fitness room rivaled any hotel I'd stayed in, and the equipment was better than in most gyms. He clearly used it often, too; the well-tended machines showed wear on the edges of the plates and the seams of the benches.

I had a good workout with Aliq, and that night before the tournament started officially, he and Ori wanted to go out with their respective paramours. They invited me along, but I said, "there's no room for a fifth in doubles," and said I wanted to get a good night's sleep.

Once they were gone, I settled into the big bed in my room and called up some film of my and Aliq's doubles opponents. I'd watched it a bunch of times already, but I couldn't keep my attention on it now, so I swapped it out for a movie. Which I'd only seen one or two times, but it was nice to turn my mind off.

A knock interrupted me. Thinking it might be Nashan, I stopped the movie, but a moment later my imagination told me it might be Braden and then I smelled the cross fox. I said, "Come in," putting my tablet away, and a moment later the fox was closing the door behind him.

"You able to take a break from studying?" he asked.

I grinned and patted the bed next to me, letting my tongue loll out. "Sure."

Blow jobs don't leave much scent other than arousal, and Aliq was as familiar with my scent as I was with his; that was something roommates got used to pretty darn quick. Braden's arousal scent was another matter, but the weather was nice enough that I could open a window and air out the room after he left, both of us content and smiling.

By the time Aliq got back, I'd fallen asleep with the smile still on my muzzle and a paw on my warm sheath. I woke before him in the morning and slipped out to get some breakfast in the guest kitchen (Desmond had told us to help ourselves). Voices perked my ears as I went down the back stair to the kitchen, first Braden's, and then a female voice.

I stopped there. The female voice wasn't one I recognized, not one of Desmond's friends nor any of Braden's staff that I remembered. And then I knew in a moment who it was, even though I'd never heard her talk.

She was here? Had she been here last night when Braden came to my room? Sleeping in his room, waiting for him to come back, not knowing where he was? My stomach's hunger soured, and I no longer wanted anything to eat.

It wasn't serious between them, of course it wasn't; Braden had said so. But if it wasn't serious then why was she here in the kitchen first thing in the morning, eating breakfast with him (eggs and toast, from the smell of it, plus some of that Oceanic sausage), laughing at his stories and telling him about some rare thing she'd managed to film?

As quietly as I could, I turned around, and ran immediately into Ori coming down the stairs. "Morning," she said with a broad smile. "Going to get breakfast?"

My tail curled down, but I don't think she noticed. "I, uh—I'm not sure I'm hungry."

"Don't be silly. You've got to play today, right? Get something to eat."

"Come on in," Braden's voice sounded from around the corner. "There's plenty."

"I made double," the vixen said.

Ori grabbed my paw and there wasn't any excuse I could make to get out of it. So I had to sit and have pretty good eggs and toast and slightly weird-tasting sausage and be introduced to Ellen (I think Braden gave me some sort of look that might have been warning me not to admit I already knew her name, but it wasn't necessary because I'd forgotten it), and then listen to her talk about flying down to Tasmania where there were some flowers that didn't exist anywhere else in the world and a type of hummingbird that fed on them and how she'd caught it on film. And all the while I was watching Braden feign interest.

He'd watch her, but his eyes kept flicking away to something else—a couple times, to me. I never met his eyes for more than a second or two, but looked down at my plate and focused on eating. And when Ellen asked about where Ori and I were from, I let Ori do most of the talking.

"The boys are focused on their matches," Ellen said as we were finishing up the meal. "Staying all quiet."

"Yeah," I said. "Sorry."

"I'm getting used to it from this one. So intense!" She rested a paw on Braden's shoulder and he flashed her a smile.

There were no cameras here, no reporters, no bloggers. So what was going on?

I didn't get a chance to ask him. We all rode together to the tournament, where Aliq and I had a doubles match in the morning before my singles match in the evening.

The team we were facing, a kangaroo and a tazzie, hadn't played much overseas and we didn't know them. The crowd was behind them, though—local favorites—and from the start things didn't go well for us. I think—I know—that I was still frustrated from that morning, because I wasn't placing shots well and my communication with Aliq, now usually one of our strong points, broke down a few times—my fault every time.

Normally, we could've afforded a few errors against guys at this level, but with the crowd pumping them up, they played terrific. We won one set but lost the rest and the match, and by the last set I was so dispirited that I didn't even think to challenge a call that might have saved us a service break (Aliq could have challenged, but he didn't have as good a look at the ball, so he deferred to me). The loss felt inevitable at that point, and I'd shifted from feeling frustrated about Braden and Ellen to feeling terrible about letting Aliq down.

He knew as well as I did who was most responsible for the loss, and after we'd shaken the paws of the other team ("you guys are fantastic," they said, "we were lucky to catch you on an off day") and returned to our bench to pack up our gear, he said, "Everyone has a bad day."

"Sorry," I said. "I don't know what happened."

"You were distracted," he said. "Thinking too much about your match this evening?"

"That must be it." Then I felt bad because I was lying, and I corrected myself. "I'm thinking about you-know-who."

We were still in hearing range of some of the nearer members of the audience, so Aliq just flicked his ears. "Tell me about it later?"

"Yeah."

"And," he added with a punch on my arm, "forget about it for tonight. Let it go—you and I both have more matches to play."

Nashan, to his credit, didn't say anything about my doubles and singles conflicting. He sat me down and said, "Sorry I didn't prepare you well enough for that match," and then overrode my protest with, "Let's focus on tonight. You shouldn't have much trouble with Dallawon, but after this morning I'm not taking any chances."

We didn't practice, instead focusing on stretching, hydrating, and eating to recover from the morning's match. Doubles wasn't as strenuous as a singles match would've been, but it still took a lot out of me; I didn't stop panting for half an hour even after drinking a liter of electrolyte-heavy Frost (some local drink). But I had a good five hours between the end of my doubles match and the beginning of my singles one, so by the time that rolled around, I was fine.

This time, I put aside my worries about Braden and my guilt about letting down Aliq and I focused on the match. Dallawon, a rabbit ranked #120 in the world, must have flown here directly from the States without doing the tuneups, because he sure seemed jet-lagged during the match and when I talked to him afterwards: a step slow, reactions not quite there, all the symptoms I'd learned to recognize in myself.

I beat him handily, 6-0 6-1, and after that match Aliq grabbed me for a just-the-two-of-us dinner. His mixed doubles didn't start until the next day, but he wasn't worried about it. "We're getting better and it's really fun being out there with Shona," he told me when I asked him about it as we sat down in a back corner of a small burger place across the park from the Tennis Centre. "But this isn't about me. Go on, kvetch." And he perked his ears and shut his muzzle.

I took a breath and found that I didn't know how to express what I was feeling. "It's this vixen," I said, and felt stupid.

"The one at Robin's place."

LOVE MATCH BOOK 3

"Yeah."

"Who's hangin' all over your guy?"

I half-laughed. "He's not my guy, that's the thing. He can hang with her, she can hang with him. She seems nice and all."

"But."

I rested my muzzle in my paws. "Yeah. But."

He let me sort through my thoughts until I was ready to go on. "The thing is, he said it wasn't anything with her. They'd be seen together in public and that was it. But she's up at the house this morning, and he was...you know, with me last night, and..."

Aliq held up a paw. "In our room?"

My ears flattened. "Um."

He shook his head. "All right, as long as it wasn't in my bed." I didn't answer right away, and he leaned forward. "It wasn't, was it?"

"No! No."

"Good." He relaxed. "Okay, so...he said it was nothing serious and it looks serious."

"Uh huh."

"And he said it wasn't serious with you, but you feel like it is?" I nodded. "At least more than with her?"

"Yeah."

"So what are you gonna do?"

I exhaled. "That's the problem. I don't know. I should talk to him about it. But he doesn't want to be closer, so what if I scare him off? And he already told me about her and we've, y'know, a couple times since then so how can I bring it up now?"

"I dunno," Aliq said. "I mean, I'm not exactly super experienced, you know? You gotta talk about it, though. Or else just walk away. Look what it did to your game."

"Not singles." I regretted that as soon as I said it. "Sorry. I mean, because I'd learned from the doubles game."

"It's cool." He laughed. "Won't lie, I thought this was our best chance to do well in a tournament. I'd like to win one with you before Nashan makes you quit."

"He can't make me quit."

The arctic fox perked his ears and grinned. "He can quit, though."

302

I hadn't thought about that. "I'm gonna make it work."
Aliq's amber eyes sparkled at mine. "With who?" he asked.
"I guess…both?" I nodded more firmly. "Yeah. With both."

* * *

Make it work. I had no idea how I was going to do that in either
Nashan or Braden's case. Nashan continued to keep quiet about my
doubles loss but worked with me extra hard to prep for each succes-
sive match.

The farther along I got, the more people crowded the stands. I'd
reached the point at the States where I was playing in front of pretty
big crowds, and even though this was in a smaller country, the tennis fervor felt as great or greater. When I came up against the #11
player, a nimble dhole named Prasad Balakrishnan, we played on the
second largest court even though it was a second-round match, and
the stands were full.

Warming up, I reminded myself of all the things Nashan had
said: that this was just another match, that I'd played Prasad last year
and taken him to three sets before losing. At the States, the pressure
of playing in front of such a large crowd gnawed at the edges of my
mind, but that was my adopted country. It was in a small way like
playing in front of Ma, worried about making her proud. Here, the
only person I had to make proud was myself.

Well, and Ori and Aliq, sitting in the players' box with Nashan.
But I knew they'd be proud of me no matter what. Most of the pressure on me came from inside. I knew that despite the forty-spot difference in our rankings, Prasad wasn't that much better a player than
I was. If we played ten times, I would probably win three of them.

(That was what I thought at the time. In hindsight, probably my
chances were more like one in ten, maybe two.)

So my mission was to make this one of those times. It didn't
look good early on; he obviously knew me and did a good job mixing up his shots to keep me off balance so I couldn't set up anything
on my side. But I hung in, returning his shots, and at the very least
I protected my serve. He had studied how to play a lefty, but the
thing I remembered from the last time we'd played was that he was

vulnerable to the wide serve from the ad court, which I could do well. So we stayed on serve in the first set and went to a tiebreak, and there I got my first lucky break when I returned his serve solidly and his answering groundstroke landed two inches beyond the baseline.

Then it was just a matter of protecting my serve until I was serving at 6-4 for the set. It was from the deuce court, so Prasad was shading toward the middle because I'd had a lot of luck going down the T on deuce serves and now he was expecting it. So I served it right into his body. He had a moment to step aside, but his return didn't have much on it, and I was already charging the net to put it away and take the first set.

He got the better of me in the second, playing sharp and aggressive and breaking my serve. I couldn't get him back and ended up losing 6-3. I resolved to do better in the third, and that was right when the heat of the day crested. Neither of us should have gained an advantage from that; we were both well accustomed to heat. But today it affected him a little, just enough to slow him down in the third set. I picked up on that and caught him off guard with some well-placed drop shots, working on the backhand and missing it once but hitting it well enough four more times, one of which got me a break point that I converted, and that held up for me to win the third set.

Good, good, I told myself on the break between sets. I only had to win one of the next two sets and I'd have beaten an almost top-ten player in a major. I'd already beaten a top ten, so I knew I could do it. This didn't feel like Prasad's day, but I knew how easily a match could turn.

I needn't have worried. Prasad also must have felt like it wasn't his day, maybe depressed by the crowd being firmly in my corner (not because they knew me, but because they like an upset). He battled on my serve, getting me to deuce before I held, but then his service game fell apart. He double-faulted, hit a weak second serve for an easy return winner, and if I hadn't missed the sideline by an inch on one of my shots, I would've broken him at love. He barely put up a fight the rest of the set, giving it to me 6-1, and at the net when we clasped paws, he said, "Good match," and that was all.

It was a significant enough upset that I rated an interview on the court after the match, and I tossed out all the usual banalities about how tough an opponent Prasad was, how happy I was to be moving on at this great tournament, and I threw in an easy lob about how great the fans were—which wasn't a lie. They'd been cheering for me since about midway through the first set, I think when they realized this wasn't going to be a walkover for Prasad.

That opened up the draw for me a little, as did some upsets in other games, and I won my next match, and my next. People were starting to buzz about me—the lowest ranked player in the quarterfinals, one of only two unseeded entrants—but also some people said I'd only played one really good match so far, the one against Prasad. Nobody gave me much of a chance against world #1 Geoffrey Bowson.

And they were right. I kept it close but lost 6-4, 7-5, 6-4, broken once in every set and twice in the second, the only time I managed to break him back. My serve just never got going—looking back on the match with Nashan, I think what happened was that I couldn't get anything past him the first few games, and rather than being steady and plugging away, I tried to get closer to the lines, so I missed a lot more first serves than I normally do.

I felt better when Bowson made it to the final ("he is the number one in the world, remember," Nashan said), where he faced Braden, number one against number two. Bowson was favored slightly but Braden came out ferocious and aggressive, slamming his forehand into the court and pressing the caribou on every point. Watching from the stands, Aliq and I spent most of the match making appreciative noises, though once after Braden pumped his fist and yelled encouragement at himself after an easy putaway, Aliq murmured so low that I barely heard it, "I wonder if he's *always* like that."

I elbowed him, ears flat, caught between laughter and embarrassment. At the same time, I loved that he knew my secret and felt comfortable enough to joke with me about it.

Braden won the match and the Open, his second Ocie and his second major overall. He took the mike and thanked all the usual people, and of course he didn't mention me; why would he? But he looked right at me in the stands during a pause in his speech, and he was smiling.

(And in case you think maybe he was just looking around at the stands, Aliq nudged me and hissed, "*Dude*," so it wasn't just me.)

I'd planned to spend that evening watching the doubles final and then relaxing, but in the middle of the final I got a text from Braden that simply had an address and a time and the note "bring whoever."

"That's the party," Aliq said excitedly when I showed him the text.

"What party?"

"The champion sometimes—maybe always, I dunno—throws a party, and sometimes they invite a bunch of people, sometimes not so many. So…who you gonna bring?"

"It says 'whoever,' so…" He was staring at me with big wide eyes. "You wanna come?"

"Can I bring Shona?"

I laughed and showed him the text again. "I'm going to bring Ori, too, so yeah. Whoever."

We didn't know what we'd be expected to wear, so we went shopping in Bourkeville and got a couple shirts that could be buttoned up to be nice or hang open to be casual, whichever way things went. We started formal with Shona and Ori, who both complained that they couldn't just take off their dresses the way we could unbutton our shirts, so we promised to stay formal even if the rest of the party was casual.

The party was in a hotel, I think the one Braden was staying in (we'd only hooked up once this tournament, at his side hotel), in one of the suites on the top floor—actually, it turned out, two of the suites with the connecting doors open. There were probably over a hundred people packed into those spaces (in a mix of formal and casual wear), so any guilt I had about bringing extra people evaporated pretty quickly. So, unfortunately, did any idea I had about maybe getting to talk to Braden for more than five seconds. Here, unedited, is the entirety of the words we exchanged that night:

"Hi!"

"Hey, Rocky! You made it!" A quick hug, a friend-hug.

"Yeah, thanks so much for inviting me. I brought—"

"Help yourself to champagne or whatever, relax, just have fun, okay?"

"Yeah, sure! Thanks."

"I'll see you in a few."

And then, hours later:

"Hey, I think we're gonna take off."

"Okay, sure. You have a good time?"

"I did, yeah. Talked to Colluvic a while, and Luongo a little. That guy is—"

"Ah, don't worry about him."

"No, he's cool, I mean."

"Hey, I'll see you back in the States, yeah?"

"Sure. Okay, good night. And good night, Ellen."

Chapter Twenty-Four

The whole flight back to the States I sat with all my memories of wandering around Braden's party talking to tennis greats and watching Braden circulate with Ellen on his arm. Of course that couldn't be me, even though anywhere but a professional sports league it would hardly raise interest anymore.

If I quit tennis, if I hung it up and got a regular job, I could meet someone and we could be together. Somewhere in one of the big cities, somewhere where a gay couple could just blend in, I could have a house or an apartment; I'd made enough money. But…hang up tennis? I might as well fantasize about becoming female so I could be with Braden. It was possible, but it wasn't me, and so following that path wasn't going to make me happy. What I had now was better than nothing, so until something better came along, I should get used to it.

When I could wrench my mind away from the party, I kept going back to the shabby hotel room that he thought was fitting for our relationship. That was his solution to our problem. On the one side, it did allow us to meet privately and have some time to spend with each other, and it had reduced the whispers around us. But on the other side…it felt bad to me. I didn't want to associate those feelings with Braden, but there they were. Could I keep doing that for the rest of the year? For more years?

* * *

Waiting for me back in the States were more requests for interviews than I'd ever had and a shiny new ranking at #31, highest of my career. Lochen had already booked me at the States-side Champions tournaments for the spring, but in a call after we landed he told me excitedly that I was going to be going to some of the high-profile international ones in the summer.

And so I lost myself in the world of tennis for a week or so. Braden and I would be at the same tournament once in the spring and then not again until we went to Europe for the lead up to the Gallic Open, so I could put him out of my mind. Theoretically.

Going to the local tournaments had the benefit that some of the top players were off playing other ones, and I had a better chance of getting to a final or even winning. At one of the locals that had a draw of 32 singles players (and 16 doubles teams), I would be ranked sixteenth in singles, and Aliq and I were ranked tenth in doubles. For the longest time, Aliq and I had been ranked the same in doubles because we only played with each other. But now that he'd started playing mixed doubles with Shona, he was accumulating more doubles points and edged ahead of me in the rankings, which he teased me a lot about.

Ori tried to insulate me from articles about me and about Braden's romance, being my social media representative. She couldn't stop me from searching for articles about myself on my phone, especially when the interviews started coming up online. I wanted to see whether I'd been portrayed well and quoted accurately so that I knew which interviewers to avoid in the future. There weren't many, but there were a couple.

When I did that, I would inevitably get to pages of tennis news with sidebars and linked articles, and because Braden was coming off a big win, there was a lot about him. I was in a good mood coming off the ranking move and the flush of making it to the quarterfinals at a major, but as the week went on, more and more the images of Braden's party came back, and not the fun ones where I built friendships with the other top players on tour. I remembered him and Ellen moving easily through the party, laughing with each other, talking to players and trainers and family, Braden with his characteristic withdrawn air but ears perked attentively as Ellen charmed the people they were talking to. Every time I was in good spirits, it seemed, I'd catch sight of the two of them and sink into my own thoughts again.

I kept reminding myself it was stupid, and that made me feel worse because I was feeling bad about something stupid. Then it would take me a few minutes to pull myself out of that, but I managed every time to remind myself that I was at a party, I was meeting people I should be friendly toward, and that moping wasn't going to do me any good right now. It was like hearing Ma behind me saying, "What can you do *now*, Rochi? Go do that."

So I met some interesting people at the party, people I wanted to keep in touch with, and on the occasions when I did go online, I looked them up so I remembered them and could talk about things that were happening with them. It was during one of those sessions that I saw a link from TMZ labeled "Tennis Romance Spotted Down Under." It couldn't be about me and Braden, could it? And it didn't seem like it would be about Braden and Ellen, not with how up front and in everyone's face they were about their fake dating. But my hackles raised as I stared at the headline. If I didn't check, I'd wonder forever, so with a little trepidation, I clicked.

The first picture in the article was a generic picture of Bourkeville and the arena where the Ocie Open took place. "The first order of business in Bourkeville was tennis," the article began, "but where there are male and female players together, there's always the chance of more."

As annoying as that line was to read—what about males and other males?—it relieved me. The article wasn't about me and Braden. I scrolled down and there was a picture of Aliq and Shona.

"The only ligress in professional sports appears to have found a mate in her mixed doubles partner. The two of them have just started matching shots on the court and now, it seems, off the court as well!"

I had no idea why this would even be worth an article, but as I read more, it became clear: hybrid people, what few there were, were a curiosity, and people wanted to know who they'd hook up with, especially when they were public figures. Would Shona, whose mother was a tiger and father was a lion, select a mate that took after her mother or her father? The chances of her finding another liger were vanishingly small; the article said that there were only a few hundred in the entire world, and rarely did they pair up.

The problem wasn't Shona, though. Aliq hadn't told his parents that he was dating a ligress, much less a non-Jewish one (there was a word for that but he told me it sometimes had bad connotations and I shouldn't use it). At the time I saw this article, we were eating lunch after an early morning practice, so Aliq was right across the table from me talking to Ori about something. I passed the phone over to him, and he grabbed it with a questioning look at me. "What?" he asked, but I didn't have a chance to answer before he saw the picture.

His ears flattened and his eyes widened. "Oh shit," he said, and scrolled through the article. "God damn it, are they allowed to do this?"

Ori leaned over. "Do what?"

"It was a private party!" Aliq gave her the phone. "They said 'no pictures'!"

"It's a cameraphone," Ori said. "They can't take people's phones away. Someone probably sold this to TMZ. Liger pics always sell."

Aliq dropped his head into his paws. "Fuck, if my parents see that I'm…"

I didn't know how to comfort him. "Do your parents read TMZ?"

"Maybe some of their friends do." His voice came muffled through his paws. "Shit, Rocky."

"Hey, uh." I looked to Ori for help.

"You can't do anything about it now," she said. "So be ready for what you're going to say to your parents."

"And tell Shona about it." That popped into my head because I had gone back to thinking about what if it had been me and Braden there.

"Right, I should do that." Aliq sighed and grabbed his phone. "Text me that article link?"

I did, and he sent a text message while Ori and I exchanged frustrated, helpless looks. When Aliq put his phone down, I said, "You knew this was going to happen eventually."

"Sure. I just thought it'd be farther down the road." He grabbed his cup of water and gulped down several swallows.

Ori gave me a look and put her paw on Aliq's. "We're here to support you," she said. "No matter what."

"Oh yeah, of course." I felt bad that I hadn't thought to say that first.

"Thanks." He smiled at both of us.

Ori went on. "And if you want us to talk to your parents at all, or help you come up with what to say…"

"Maybe." He sighed. "The thing is, I don't even know where this is going. But we're playing together so I can't just break things off."

"You'd break it off with someone if your parents didn't approve?" Ori's ears swept back.

"Well, yeah." He looked like she'd asked him if he was going to keep breathing. "They're my parents. I can't—what am I going to do? Never talk to them anymore? Go home for holidays alone?"

Ori and I exchanged another look. If Ma were still alive and had disapproved of someone I'd been dating—well, she had disapproved of Shawna, and of Marquize at some points in our relationship, but she'd never threatened to disown me if I kept dating them. If she had, though, what would I have chosen? I couldn't have abandoned Ma for either one of them. I saw the same thoughts in Ori's eyes.

Later, when Aliq had gone off by himself to take a call with Shona, Ori and I talked quietly by the side of a tennis court while I bounced a ball in my paw. "I can't imagine Ma ever telling us not to date someone," she said.

I told her about Shawna and Marquize, and she nodded. "She didn't tell me to stop dating Raji either."

Respect kept my muzzle shut for a moment as we both remembered the lion. I bounced the ball off the concrete to her. "How are things going with Marro?"

She caught the ball and turned it over in her paw. "Well enough. We're enjoying hanging out together and not doing much more."

Colluvic was over in the same tournaments Braden was, so that meant that Ori and I would get to see our respective "going well enough" partners at the same tournament. "You miss him?"

"We text a lot, so…not really." She bounced the ball back to me. "Do you miss your guy?"

Discreet even though there wasn't anyone around. "Yeah. It's…" I bounced the ball, caught it again. "Aliq's my best friend on the tour, and he's great. But that fox…he pushes me, challenges me to be better. And I feel like I'm pushing him too. We're moving slowly, but together."

"Even though…?"

I rubbed my eyes. "I guess you saw them."

"They were hard to miss, especially at the party. And she was in his box for most of the tournament."

That I hadn't noticed. "Really?"

She nodded. "So what does he say about it? And why didn't you talk to me about it?"

"There was a whole major tournament going on," I said. "I didn't want to be super distracted or anything. And anyway, he says it's just for public appearances. He wants to keep seeing me." I turned the tennis ball over and stared at the logo, then bounced it again.

She nodded. "As long as you're taking care of yourself." She reached out and grabbed the ball mid-bounce, holding it up between us. "And as long as you come see me if you need help."

I took the ball from her and hugged her. "Thanks, Ori. I will. But I'm okay, really. We should worry more about Aliq."

Nothing happened with Aliq's parents by the time we made it to the next tournament, it turned out. He talked to Shona about his parents' inevitable disapproval, which conversation had led her to say they could cross that bridge when they got to it, and though I thought that was a dismissive answer, Aliq thought it was perfect, so maybe she was really right for him.

At the tournament, I pushed myself pretty hard. I didn't want to tell Nashan he'd been right, but as Aliq and I improved in doubles and I improved in singles, what had been a few days of intensive matches followed by a normal workload tournament became several days of intensive matches. We reached the quarterfinals in doubles and I reached them in singles, too, so I played my singles match in the early afternoon against Luongo. He was the second highest-ranked player at the tournament after Daryavic, still #9 after his Ocie Open showing, but he was struggling to get into a rhythm and I got a few lucky shots in. I mean, not to be humble, because I was also playing really well, but the lucky shots were the reason I won in straight sets (with a tiebreak) and not three.

Everyone after the match was wagging and patting me on the back, Ori and Aliq and even Nashan, who didn't often do that. I appreciated it, but honestly I wasn't all that excited, even about beating the #9 player in the world. I knew I could beat him if I played my game the best I could, and if he made a few mistakes, which is how it went. Luongo, too, didn't look all that surprised; mad at himself, if anything, but he was really nice as we wrapped up the match. I reminded myself to be that polite when I was in the top ten and an up-and-comer beat me.

I didn't have time to get too excited about that match because I had to go play my doubles quarterfinal with Aliq a few hours later. That was a tough match against a very active team we had beaten three times and lost to three times. This time we beat them 7-6, 7-6 to set us up for a semifinal match against our old friends Lowry and Tasman. They were on a tear, coming off a semifinal appearance at the Ocie and a victory in one of the previous tuneups, and were the top seed at this tournament.

I had a day off in between my matches, but both semifinals would fall on the same day, just like the quarters, and so Nashan cut short my practice time on the day off, focusing on reviewing film of my singles opponent, Daryavic. We got in an hour of film on the doubles match, too, and by the end of it I felt as exhausted as if I'd played both my matches already. But a good night's sleep and a good breakfast got me energized and ready to go the next day.

Everyone on my team, me included, was optimistic about my match against Daryavic because of my success against Luongo, but things went wrong in the second game. Lunging to return his serve, I turned my ankle, and though it wasn't serious, it disrupted my timing on my next service game enough to give him an easy break. Disheartened, I lost the first set 6-3, and though I played better in the second set, I never managed to press him back far enough to get an advantage on his serve. We went to a tiebreak, where a net cord clipped one of his shots on my serve, turning a powerful baseline forehand into a drop shot, one I raced to come up six inches short of reaching. That mini-break gave him the tiebreak and the match.

"I see you taking my advice," the maned wolf said at the net.

"Trying," I said. "You had it working today."

"Thanks. Good luck in doubles." He clasped my paw, and we went to thank the chair umpire before retiring.

The doubles match didn't go a whole lot better. My ankle wasn't bothering me; Tasman and Lowry just had their game on. Aliq and I kept it close throughout, but a point here and a point there cost us a break in each set and thereby the match.

Ori went to take pictures of the tennis complex and post my reaction to the match. Aliq's answer to the frustration of the day was to go do a cooldown workout at the gym, which was kind of like aggressive stretching. I, like him, had spent the post-match hours listening to consolations and silently replaying points in my head, growing unusually discouraged. Sure, a year ago we would've lost a match like this, but we were better now, and it had been really close, and we could've been playing in a final. Winning one tournament gave us a taste for more and made the losses even more bitter.

Thoughts of Braden, which intruded on a daily basis now, didn't help my mood either. All I really wanted was to ice my ankle and hopefully dull my thoughts along with the pain.

My coach had other ideas. "I think you could have won either of those matches," he told me that evening, after we'd been sitting in the training room together in lovely silence for five minutes or so.

"I think so too," I said. My ankle had reached the point where the cold had soaked through the fur and my whole foot was numb verging on aching. But it felt good, even though my ankle hadn't really hurt by the end of the day.

"But not both."

I didn't say anything, stubbornly quiet though I did stare pointedly at my ankle. Nashan went on. "I saw you miss at least three shots you should've made in the doubles match. The singles—well, you turn your ankle, that's a little bit luck and a little bit foot placement. We can take care of it."

"I told you to give me a year," I said.

He paused, sizing me up. I wasn't a 75th-ranked jackal with potential anymore; I was a player in the thirties—maybe high twenties after this match—who'd beaten the #9 player in the world and was being mentioned in conversations about the next generation of States tennis players. I had made enough money to fire him and get almost my pick of coaches out there. I was as aware of this as he was and it definitely made a difference in our dynamic.

"Sure," he said finally. "And I mean it. I just want you to be fully informed so you can make a good decision at the end of that year."

"Right." I leaned back and closed my eyes. Between two losses and not seeing Braden, not to mention the whole weirdness of his "girlfriend," I wasn't in a great mood. The issue of Braden had come up for two reasons: one, I was pretty sure that after posting to my InstaPic, Ori had Skyped with Marro, who was currently overseas with Colluvic, and two, it had been a few weeks since my last night with Braden, and I was starting to look at Nashan and remember what he looked like naked and wonder if he'd maybe want to blow me.

My mind was still in firm control; there wasn't any danger I was even going to do anything like adjust my sheath in front of him. But I was irritated because I wanted a blow job and the only guy currently offering them to me was an ocean away accompanied by a fake girlfriend, unless I wanted to go out to bars, and with my new status and media coverage I didn't want to risk that.

So I said, "In the meantime, let's worry about who I'm playing on the court and not what might happen if I let down my best friend."

Nashan was quiet, and then he got up. "You've had a tough day," he said. "I've been there. I'll catch up with you tomorrow." And he left me alone with my foot in an ice bath.

For a little while, I lay there with my eyes closed. My sheath still felt the need for release as a pulsing warmth, so I thought with a little humor that if I put some ice on it maybe that'd stop me thinking about Braden.

A little while of those thoughts, still undisturbed in the training room, led me to consider them more seriously. Why not? See if it did any good. Guys had ice packs near their groins all the time for injuries; it wouldn't look all that weird. So I got a cloth pack, scooped some ice into it, and dropped it on the front of my tennis shorts.

It sort of worked, in that my sheath got cold, but the pressure also felt uncomfortably good, and I started thinking about what Braden's shaft would feel like in my mouth if he iced it up first, and then I wondered what a cold shaft inside me would feel like, and then I thought about Marquize doing that and wondered when Braden was going to do it and dammit I was all the way hard and partly humping an ice pack.

The training room was still quiet. I trusted my ears to tell me if anyone was close as I slipped my paw into my shorts, found my (nicely cool) shaft, and gave it a few strokes. I jerked off not for pleasure but with determination and efficiency: get myself off in the shortest time and stop thinking about Nashan and Braden and even Marquize and, and, and …

I came into my paw with a soft, "Ah-ah," not as vocal as I was often with Braden. Keeping my shorts down, I got out of the ice bath and rinsed off, and still nobody came in. And with that, ankle and sheath both feeling better, I went to find myself some late dinner.

Chapter Twenty-Five

Feeling a little more sensible as I got back to my hotel room, I texted Braden. I couldn't say I missed him, because this was Braden. So I told him about my day, losing twice, and looked up what was happening in his tournament (he had won his semifinal match earlier that day—much earlier) so I could congratulate him.

When I woke up the next day, I had a text from him saying that he knew how tough days like that were and congratulating me on beating Luongo. He even sounded sorry that he hadn't checked to see that earlier. I hadn't expected him to, and I hadn't been following his progress either, so I wasn't upset about that at all.

Unsolicited, I also got a text from him a few weeks later on my twenty-first birthday, which was a bit of a surprise. I thanked him and said, half-jokingly, that I wasn't sure we were celebrating birthdays together. He replied with a very Braden message about thinking it was something he thought I'd like and that we didn't have to, but I told him it was fine. Then I looked up his birthday on his ITF webpage and put it in my calendar to remember.

Ori wasn't old enough to drink yet, so Aliq and Nashan took me out to a bar where I legally ordered a beer, drank half of it, and switched back to Coke. We had a nice night out, but I came back to my hotel room and I still had practice the next day and I didn't feel any older.

The Blue Springs Champions tournament Presented By Tamarin Global Investments in Hellentown was the only one Braden and I were both going to play before the Euro tuneups for the Gallic. I was looking forward to seeing him; we'd arranged to meet at his spare hotel, as he'd taken to calling it, on the first night of the tournament.

This was the last week of March and Braden had still lost only one match all year. He texted me an address and room number the day before the tournament started, and when I went there I found a Premier Suites with a room that still smelled of cheap cleanser, where the window looked out onto a construction site that seemed to double as a dump. Seagulls wheeled around it constantly and their screeches came through the window even though thankfully the smells did not.

Braden had smiled when he opened the door for me and now, as I looked out at the seagulls, sat on the bed taking his pants off. "You're killing it this year," I said, leaning back against the window to watch.

"Yeah." He lifted his t-shirt off in one smooth motion and tossed it aside, then swung his legs up to lie on the bed. "Hey, you wanna try something different?"

I flicked my ears. "Like, standing up?"

"Ah-heh. No, I mean, like…" He had a small white plastic bag on the nightstand; I hadn't paid much attention to it, but now he took out a package of condoms and a small bottle of personal lubricant. "Like this. You ever done this?"

"Once." I eyed the condoms.

He watched me and then dropped the things back in the bag. "We don't have to. It's not a big deal or anything."

"Sometime, maybe," I said. His erection had gone down a bit, and I felt bad about that, so I crawled onto the bed and took care of things. And once I had him in my muzzle, felt him squirming below me, had that warm fur and tight muscle under my paws, I lost the initial reaction I'd had to the room. After all, I liked being with him, and wherever we were was okay, right?

"Take your clothes off," he ordered when I was done, and I complied with a smile. He bent to my sheath and got down to the blow job with surprising enthusiasm and enjoyment, or maybe I just enjoyed it more because it had been so long.

When I came, I groaned and grabbed at his shoulders, and he lifted his head with a satisfied smile. "Been a while for you, too?"

"Yeah," I said, lying back and panting. "Yeah."

After a little while of lying on the bed together, Braden shifted. I don't know if he was really going to leave or if he was just getting comfortable, but at the time I didn't want him to go. So I said, "I'm working on beating Daryavic. Remember when you told me to focus on certain players?"

He settled in next to me. I rested a paw on his stomach; he draped his fingers over my wrist. "Sounds like something I'd say."

"You've beaten him a couple times. Any insights?"

"Don't roll your ankle, for one." He grinned, looking sideways at my surprise.

"You watched the match?"

"Highlights. You looked good. Ankle and all, I mean. I don't know what I can tell you that your coach can't."

Warmth grew in my chest. "You've been on the court with him. Nashan hasn't."

"So have you. You're smart. What would you do?"

I lay back and sighed. "Play to his backhand. Use the slice to keep him from getting a good forehand on it. Bait him to the net and be ready with the pass."

"That's risky. He's good at the net. If you're not precise with your passes, he'll make you pay for it."

I tried to remember how I'd seen Braden play him at the Ocie. "Wear him down?"

"That's my game, not yours. What's your game?"

"Angles," I said promptly. "Pulling him off the court and finishing with my forehand. Or maybe the first volley."

"Okay. Just play your game. But play it the best you've ever played it, and maybe you have a chance. He's really good."

I curled my fingers, rubbing his stomach through his fur. He made a little noise and slid his fingers up my arm, against the grain of the fur, then smoothed the fur back down. "I know he's good," I said. "I think I'm close to that too."

"You're close," Braden said. "One out of five times maybe you beat him. You could get that up to two out of five pretty soon, to be honest."

"Thanks."

He turned his head, one hazel eye fixing me. "Just calling 'em like I see 'em."

I moved my fingers from his stomach up his chest to his shoulders. "Can I say you have a fantastic body?"

"Sure." His lips twitched.

"I know we don't talk like that often, but…you really do. And I appreciate you making these arrangements to see me."

"Yeah." He exhaled. "I think it's working out pretty good."

We lay for a moment while I worked up the nerve to say the next thing I wanted to, and then finally did. "Do you think sometime you'd want to get away outside of tennis? Like after the end of year tournament, maybe just before the holidays or something."

"Maybe. Depends on what I have to do with Ellen."

I flinched, but he didn't react, so I kept going. "It'd be nice to have more time. Maybe daylight."

"Yeah, I'll see." He stared up at the ceiling. "Right now I just want to worry about tennis."

"Right, sure."

He didn't stay the whole night, so I didn't either, and on the way home at two in the morning I repeated that to myself. *Right now I just want to worry about tennis.* Fine, that was good advice. That's what he was going to do, so I could do that too.

* * *

This wasn't a major tournament, but most everyone on the Champions circuit competed in it because the money and prestige were comparable, so except for the three-set matches (rather than five), it was pretty close. In the locker room and on the practice courts, I saw most of the guys I'd known from the Ocie: Dubois asked when I was going to come on the international tour, and Colluvic hugged me and told me I would've loved the courts in Guanabara. "It wasn't Carnival time—that's crazy, I want to get down there sometime—but it was so colorful anyway, and all the buildings near us were this pretty old style like the ones you liked in Londinium. Next year." He poked my shoulder.

"Next year," I agreed. I'd be good enough next year to warrant flights down to Papaga and out to Dibei to compete in those major tournaments, the ones with prize money in the millions rather than the hundred thousands.

"Fantastic. Hey." He elbowed me. "Marro says he really likes your sister. This is okay with you, right?"

"She's not mine to give away. And yeah, I know, I went out with them back in Bourkeville or something."

"Okay. You never know!" He spread his paws. "Marro's a good guy. He and I been friends for years now. You can trust him."

"Thanks." I smiled. "I'll tell Ori."

It was good to see him again, and everyone else; it made me feel like a real part of the world again. We joked about local restaurants and reporters, talked about the tournament rules and the weather, and recommended movies and sometimes e-books to each other. Braden, Bowson, and Tempest remained aloof as always, but I was happy to socialize with the other guys.

I also spent time with Aliq and Ori, but each of them had a partner to spend time with. At one of my practices, Ori sat next to Marro in the stands, and he had his paw twined with hers. I didn't ask how things were going, but she smiled a lot around me and all of the posts she made on my behalf had a little extra bounce and positivity to them, which made my tail wag.

Aliq's romance existed in a strangely suspended state, he told me in the first week of that tournament. He still wanted to be with Shona and she with him, but he knew now that the countdown to when his parents would confront him had started. I had the chance to talk to Shona about it and she remained very practical. "If he wants to be with me," she told me over a quick lunch while Aliq had run off to get his racket looked at, "then he'll stand up to his parents. And if he doesn't, then I guess it was nice."

"Just like that?"

She stretched out, tracing the faint stripes on her arm with a claw. "I'm not gonna sit around for years and wait for a momma's boy to get the balls to stand up to his parents. He knows the choice he has to make, and if he doesn't want to be with me, then he's not the right guy for me and I'm better off moving on. I'll be sad, sure, but…" She leaned back and looked up at the bright clouds drifting over us. "Better to be sad for a short time than for a long one, huh?"

"What if he wants to try to keep both sides happy? Like—what if he asks you to stay with him but tries to work it out with his parents in the meantime?"

"Tricky," the ligress said. "I'd respect that, but also I'm not gonna be pushed to one side, you know? Like, I don't see rings in our future right now, but if it gets to that point…the decision can't be put off forever. Know what I mean?"

"Yeah," I said. "I do."

Early in the tournament, I hit on a mindset that worked pretty well for me. If I got to the point where I could beat Braden in a match, I told myself, he'd have to reconsider things with me. It didn't make any sense and probably wasn't true, but it made me feel better. After all, he was the best player in the game, so beating him would have more significance than just me beating my—

Friend? Boyfriend? None of those seemed right. Friend-with-benefits? Not quite.

My fox. That's how I started thinking of him there at the Blue Springs tournament. If I could get good enough to beat my fox, then things would change. It would force a decision. Like I said, Braden had never said anything about that, and I knew it wasn't necessarily true. But I loved tennis and I wanted to be better at it, and I—I liked Braden a lot and I wanted to keep seeing him, so in my head, combining those two goals made a lot of sense.

Besides which, something Nashan told me a bunch of times was that it didn't matter what I used to motivate myself as long as it worked, and this was working. I blew through the first two rounds, and in the third got my first win over Li Xu, which was pretty exciting. It took three sets, and frankly Li was not on his game, but he still played pretty well. I got into a zone with him by the third set where I felt like I knew his patterns even better than I did by studying film. I got a few lucky shots in, but as Nashan told me afterwards, I earned that win.

"That cross-court you hit for break point in the third," he said, "that was better than any shot I've hit in my life. If you can do that whenever you want, you're going to be winning majors within a year."

Extra nice for me was that Aliq and I also won three doubles matches, including upsetting the top seed. That put us into the semifinals again, the day after I won my quarterfinal match to get to the singles semifinals as well.

My next opponent: Braden Longacre.

* * *

In a way, there wasn't a lot I could do to study for Braden. I already knew his game well; I'd watched most of his matches that Nashan had film for. But I went through the videos with him anyway, watching and rewatching Braden's brilliance over the last year. "You beat Luongo and Li, and you played Daryavic close," Nashan said. "And at these smaller tournaments, sometimes the better players aren't as dialed in. I think if you're really focused you'll be able to give him a good match."

Maybe, I thought, but that's my best-case scenario. I just couldn't see a weakness in Braden's game. Forehand, backhand, serve, return, net play: everything was solid. His forehand had, if anything, gotten better, blistering strokes that he could unleash in a crazy small window. The problem of him being too predictable was gone, maybe in part with my help, and the problem of inattention and distraction that plagues so many top players at smaller tournaments, that Nashan was counting on, had never been an issue for Braden. He was driven in a way I hadn't encountered before.

But I dutifully studied and practiced and I found a few places where Xu and Dubois had had success against him that I thought I could replicate. The cross fox was quick, very quick, but he could be pulled out wide, and as a lefty I would have a few chances to do that especially on my serve. His backhand wasn't as flexible or dangerous as his forehand, and most of the service breaks Dubois especially had gotten against him had come when the marten played extensively to Braden's backhand and the fox had made a mistake.

So there was my game plan: wide serves from the ad court, play to his backhand. Braden, for his part, would likely be playing to my backhand as well, which he did often when we practiced together. I couldn't get as much power behind my backhand, so it was harder for me to hit a good approach shot; I either had to passively send it back to the baseline or take a risk and come to the net. I enjoyed net play and was good at it, but against Braden it wasn't a smart play unless I managed to push him beyond the baseline and get him off balance.

And this was the first match we'd played in a tournament since we'd been sleeping together. Would that factor into it at all?

On the morning of the match, Braden and I got dressed in the locker room together and were as cordial as two friends normally were before a match. "Good luck," I said.

"You too." He shook my paw and we headed out to the court to warm up, escorted through the grounds by a couple security people.

The small stands had filled more than for any other match, but I didn't have any illusion that it was about me. The cheers when we came out happened when Braden's brown and russet head cleared the sunlight in front of me, and they didn't get stronger when I followed. The announcer listed my achievements first, mentioning my doubles title as well as my placement at the Ocie and my current ranking of twenty-seven, and then my education at Palm Gables. I got some polite applause for that. Then he introduced Braden Longacre, the number two player in the world, two-time Ocie Open champion, and the applause exploded.

We rallied for a bit, practiced our serves in the 90-degree sun, and got used to breathing in the soupy humidity. Braden, of course, had also spent a couple years at Palm Gables (which the announcer hadn't bothered to mention as the fox's other achievements crowded out that little factoid) and was just as used to this weather as I was.

In the end, Braden's experience and skill was the biggest factor. I broke his serve early in the first set with some very sharp returns; he broke mine right back and won the set in a tiebreak. I got the second set to a tiebreak as well and went up 3-1 after an ace and another good return down the line on his serve. *Here it is*, I thought, *I'm taking you to a third set*. But Braden smoked an ace out wide, and then on my serve mimicked my return with a crosscourt laser blast of his own which I could only watch go by.

On my next serve, we settled into a rally, and in trying to find an angle that could get past him, I dumped the ball into the net. He won the next two points on his serve to go up 6-3, and even though I held him off with an ace and a forehand winner on my serve, the match wasn't really in doubt.

Sure enough, serving at 6-5 in the tiebreak, he pushed me to my backhand side over and over, and then hit a soft drop shot to the opposite side of the court. I sprinted across the court and actually got my racket on it, but hit it into the net, and the match was over.

We shook at the net, and this time, in a space that was unusually private despite thousands of people watching us, he clasped my paw a little longer and said, "You did great."

"You're amazing," I replied. "That was a great match."

And then we were thanking the chair umpire and I went to my bench while Braden raised his paws to the crowd. The PA announcer gave the score again, told the crowd who Braden's opponent in the final would be, and then said, "Rocky N'Guwe will be appearing later this afternoon in his doubles match. Don't miss it!"

There, to my surprise, I got applause again, louder and more sustained than before. I raised a paw and the applause responded, and that made me smile. I walked off the court and met a bobcat in a red shirt emblazoned with "SECURITY" who escorted me across the grounds to the locker room.

Aliq and Ori met me for lunch and acted almost as though I'd won the match. "You broke his serve," Aliq said. "That's fantastic."

"True fact," Ori said. She'd picked up that expression lately. "You played really well. He's just...out of this world right now."

I nodded. I knew all that, but I couldn't help thinking that with a little more practice, a little more preparation, I could've taken at least one of those tiebreakers. I'd been cautious for the most part because I knew he'd pounce on any mistake, but the problem with being cautious is that I'd ended up allowing him to dictate the points. I'd played at his tempo for most of the match, and Braden doesn't lose very often when you play at his tempo. The thing is that it's really hard to get him off track.

In the afternoon, Aliq and I went out for our doubles match. I thought I'd be tired, but when I came out, even though the crowd was a third the size of the singles audience, I got a huge ovation, and that gave me a big boost to start the match. Aliq and I dominated the first set and then survived a dip in our energy in the second set to win that one too, putting us in the final.

Ori and Marro watched together from the stands—Colluvic had been knocked out in the quarterfinals—and once when I looked over I saw their paws clasped together. Their quiet happiness together relaxed me and gave me a warm feeling in my chest, but I still made time after the match to take Marro aside.

The fennec's ears went back a little, not flattened all the way, but clearly he was on the defensive. "Is this going to be a 'protective older brother' chat or a friendly chat or what? Just want to be sure I'm prepared."

I smiled. "Friendly. Ori's an adult and she can make her own choices. I just wanted to say it's nice to see you two getting closer. She doesn't tell me a lot."

"Oh yeah. Okay." His ears came back up. "She's great. We're having a good time together. But respectful!"

"It's cool," I said. "I just want to say that as long as you guys are dating, you're welcome to hang out with us. Time permitting. No pressure or anything."

He nodded. "Okay, thanks. Usually, I mean, I'm with Ljubo's team and we go out together, so I've been inviting Ori there. I guess if you guys wanted to hang out too…"

"We'll work things out." I extended a paw. "I'm glad you're making Ori happy."

"Aw, shucks." He grasped my paw. "She's making me happy."

That brought another smile to my muzzle. "Well, she's great. Of course she is. Hey, we're going out for a little celebration dinner. Want to join us?"

The fennec took his phone out. "Technically if Ljubo asks me to do anything I need to do it, but if he's cool, I'm happy to join."

"All right," I said. "Let me know. I hope you can make it."

"Me too," he said.

Marro did join me, Ori, Aliq, and Shona that evening out at a burger place, and I appreciated the chance to get to know him better. He'd grown up in a small town in the southwestern States—"you wouldn't even have heard of a place that's heard of it," he said with a laugh—and gone to college in the northeast for a change of pace. He and Aliq had gone to some of the same local tennis tournaments, but Marro had been there to write about them rather than play.

"I wanted to be a sports journalist," he told us, "and decided to get into it right at the time all the jobs were drying up. Perfect timing. So I studied social media, posted some blogs about tennis, and started going to tournaments on my own dime, meeting players, doing social media stuff. I worked for Linean Martell for a year and then he decided he wasn't going to keep throwing money at his career, but I'd gotten to know his coach, who knew Ljubo's coach and knew they were looking for a social media person."

"I've never heard of Linean Martell," I said.

"No reason you should, unless you keep track of players in the thousands." Marro shook his head. "Another rich kid who liked tennis enough to travel to tournaments for a couple years and score a win here and there. Imagine Longacre but with about a thousandth of the talent."

"I don't know how rich Braden is." By the time I'd gotten to know him, he'd already been highly ranked enough that he could afford things like an entourage, a second hotel room, and first class travel just from his tennis earnings.

Marro nodded at me. "His parents are loaded. Northeastern real estate, but also old money probably dating back to robber barons."

"Like…in Europe?"

Aliq elbowed me. "Early 1900s industrialists, bought up factories, abused workers, raked in millions."

"Anyway, yeah, Longacre's loaded." Marro drank a little more of his margarita and grimaced. It can't have been that good, not that I was much judge of those things.

"Hold on, though." Aliq bristled a bit. "You went to school across the country, and even U Plymouth is pricey."

Marro's big ears swept back. "I got a partial scholarship and I worked my ass off in work-study to pay for school. I rode the bus to tennis tournaments and slept on the floors of friends from the Internet. Sometimes I slept in locker rooms."

"Our family didn't have a lot of money either." Ori glanced at me.

"Oh, Mom and Dad have money." Marro looked back at Ori. "Their salvage business does pretty well. They just didn't want me going so far away for college, so they said I'd have to pay for it myself." Into the silence, he said, "It's okay, I've got a little brother who's going to Sand State. Wouldn't even go to Bianca for school in case the 'big city' corrupted him."

"They didn't help you at all?" Ori asked softly.

"You notice how I don't mention my folks much?" One side of the fennec's mouth twisted into a grin. "That's why. We don't exactly talk."

"I'm sorry," I said.

"Don't be." He lifted his head. "We mutually decided we didn't have a lot to contribute to each other's lives, and so we don't. No rule says parents and kids always have to get along, right?"

Aliq didn't say anything, but I caught his paw stealing over to Shona's. The ligress nodded at this point. "I haven't seen my mom in years. She took off when I was ten and it's just been my dad and me since then."

"And Ori and I—" I caught my sister's eye and realized that she might not have wanted to talk about our dad with Marro yet; at least I should leave it to her. "Ma was great. Just the best." Aliq leaned against me.

"Our dad, not so much," Ori said with a smile.

"What happened to your ma?" Marro asked.

My sister met my eyes again. "I'll tell you another time. Let's talk about tennis for a bit."

So we did, going over Aliq's and my opponents in the doubles final as well as talking a bit about Braden and his finals opponent, the #15 ranked maned wolf Kiman Montes. "Montes isn't as good as you most days," Aliq said. "I don't think Braden will have a problem with him."

"He's ranked higher," I said.

Marro agreed with Aliq, and to my surprise, Shona did too. I didn't know she'd been watching my matches. It was nice, though, having them all agree. I hoped my play the rest of the year would prove them right.

Aliq and I played our doubles final in the morning, three hours before the start of Braden's final. We knew our opponents well, a white-tailed deer and red panda against whom our record was 3-3. But, as Aliq pointed out, two of those losses had been a year and a half ago in two consecutive tournaments, and we were much better now.

They came out very sharp, challenging me on my service game (which I held) and then breaking Aliq's. I held my game and then conferred briefly with Aliq about the red panda's serve, which had been their weak point the last time we'd played. I told him that I was going to try to return it down the doubles alley so he'd have an idea of where to be prepared with his net play. On his returns, he liked to go cross-court, which carried a greater risk of the deer getting a good net volley back, so I was prepared for that.

We broke the panda's serve and then I held, and when the deer came up to serve we broke his serve too. Aliq held in another close one, and then we broke the panda again to take the first set.

After that, they fought harder, trying to cover for the panda's serve. It wasn't bad per se; it was good enough to get them to the finals of a small tournament. But it was just predictable enough that Aliq could get a good jump on it, which he couldn't do with the elite servers, and that gave us enough of an edge to win the second set in similar fashion, and with it the match and the tournament.

We beamed our way through the trophy presentation, Aliq muttering to me, "Not a bad consolation for losing to Braden, huh," and got some pretty nice checks for winning, a few hundred thousand dollars each. Just a bit more than my prize money for being a semifinalist, so all in all I picked up my best take from a tournament yet.

The money from this tournament would be enough to keep us going for most of the year even without my endorsement deals, which had only grown since my showing at the Ocie. A few hundred thousand sounds like a lot of money, but I was always surprised how much of it disappeared into travel and paying Nashan and other fees and things—and "keeping us going" didn't count hiring on all those other staff that Nashan and Lochen were talking about.

With that win behind us, Aliq and I went to see Braden's finals match. We didn't expect a lot of suspense and didn't get any, as Braden won 6-3, 6-2, and hoisted the trophy after what seemed like a very brief hour and ten minute match.

Afterwards, Aliq went off with Shona and Ori and Marro, and I went to the locker room to congratulate Braden. There were a bunch of other guys there, all telling him what a great year he was having, so I limited myself to a quick hi and shake of his paw, and got a smile in return. And then, just as I was turning away, Braden announced to the room, "Thanks, guys, but I got to get dressed and meet up with my girl."

My mood soured. I didn't turn back toward him, but I knew the words had been meant for me, in case I was thinking about asking him to meet up that night. I curled my tail down and stalked out of the locker room to return to the hotel.

I didn't go back right away. I was sure Aliq would be out and Ori too, celebrating, and I didn't feel like joining them or returning to an empty room. Our conversation with Marro had made me think about Ma, and plus here I was back in Pensa, so I walked out of the tennis center and a few blocks down to the beach, amid a press of people largely unaware of tennis or of the fact that I'd just won a tournament. It was nice.

At the beach, I found a health drink place and got some kind of vaguely nutritious smoothie that perhaps a personal nutrition consultant would approve of, or not, and I found a spot on a bench to sit and look out at the blue-purple sky over the ocean, listening to the crash of waves and the excited burbling of the crowd, smelling the fur conditioner and the salt water and the dead sea creatures washed up on the beach. I missed Ma and her steadying presence, and I felt bad that I hadn't thought about her last year when things were going well as much as I did now when I was having a harder time.

I wanted to ask her if this was normal, to be wanting more than someone was prepared to give you; if it was just watching Ori and Marro, Aliq and Shona, that made me want something from Braden at least in the same vicinity as those relationships. I wanted to lean on her and be young again, feel her solidity next to me and the confidence that she could handle anything. She couldn't make Braden be different any more than she'd been able to make Marquize be different, but she'd always been there for me. She'd helped me sort through feelings to come to a realization about what was reasonable.

Rochi, she would say, you have to take care of yourself.

My breathing eased, and I closed my eyes against the breeze. I knew that. The question was how. I didn't want to give up Braden, but I couldn't keep getting my heart slapped every tournament.

If I could talk to him—

My phone buzzed. Maybe it was him. Maybe he wanted to—no, it was Aliq. *Where r u*

I almost didn't answer. But Aliq was my best friend and the text felt oddly desperate, more so than if he just wanted to make sure I was celebrating properly. *Beach*, I texted back. *Home in a bit.*

Need to talk, he wrote back, and then, *Parents.*

Really? I was sitting here aching for Ma and he wanted to talk about his parents? But of course he couldn't know that, couldn't know what Braden had said to me. Which meant that something had gone wrong with his parents, and there wasn't much doubt what that was.

Chapter Twenty-Six

We were supposed to leave in two days for the tournaments in Etrusca that began the warmups for the Gallic Open, and Nashan wanted me—us—to play as many of them as possible, because we didn't have a lot of experience on clay. So when I got back to the room and Aliq said, "I have to go home, Rocky, please come with me," I told him I would, and the first thing I did was text Nashan and Lochen.

Need to see Aliq's parents ASAP, I wrote, and then put the phone away to listen to my friend.

"They saw something that referenced the TMZ article, this piece about me that said that I've been 'romantically linked' to Shona, and they called because they've been following my matches and asked if it was true and I didn't know what to say."

"What did you say?"

"Ugh!" He clutched his head. "I told them that not all the stuff in articles is true, and they said, 'is this true?' and I just said I was going to come home before we went to Europe and we'd talk about it then."

I sat down on my bed while he paced back and forth and waved his paws. I had never seen cool, composed Aliq this agitated, his tail all fluffed out and his hackles up. "All right," I said. "I told Nashan and Lochen to get us tickets back to your parents. I'm sure we'll be able to go tomorrow."

He exhaled. "Thanks, Rocky. You're coming too?"

"Of course. I don't know what I can do, but I'll be glad to help."

"They like you. And Ori, can Ori come too?"

"Okay, but…" I reached back to imagine what Ma might have said. "What do you want to tell them?"

He stopped. "I can't tell them about me and Shona. I mean, that we're dating, that we're serious."

"Are you serious?"

He waved his paws over his head. "Oy, Rocky, I'm thinking of telling my parents about her! Of course we're serious!"

"But if you're not serious, then you don't have to tell your parents."

Aliq squinted at me. "They've already seen."

"She's your doubles partner. Rumors go around all the time. Just tell them it's not true."

He sat down heavily on his bed, tail settling down. "Can I do that?"

"I don't know. Can you?"

For a moment, Aliq stared past my shoulder as though Shona were standing behind my bed, and then he buried his amber eyes in his paws. I couldn't pick up what he mumbled after that. "What?"

"I said, I feel like either I lose her or I lose them. I can't choose. I don't want to lose either."

"Won't your parents understand? What if they meet her?"

He sat up, ears straight up, eyes wide. "Oh, no. They can't meet her, not yet. Mom will be so—well, you don't know, she's always been nice to you. But she can be really mean if she thinks someone's threatening the family. I can't—I need to settle things with them first."

"So they won't understand if you're in love?"

I didn't know whether he was in love or not. He didn't protest the word. "That doesn't matter as much as our faith."

"You don't go to church," I said. "Or synagogue, I mean."

"But they do. And they might cut me off if I try to marry a shiksa. Sorry—a non-Jewish girl. That's not a nice word." He ran claws through the fur between his ears.

I wanted to do more to help him, and honestly it was a relief to focus on someone else's problem, but I couldn't see a way out of this one. Aliq knew his family and knew his faith far better than I did, and he was going to have to confront this head on. "This must have come up in the past, right? People fall in love outside their faith. What did they do?"

He exhaled. "They gave up one or the other."

When I didn't say anything, he went on. "I mean yeah, there are more progressive communities. But you have to understand that our faith is our culture, and it's endured for thousands of years. And the way it endures—people say—it's because we marry our own." He twined his fingers together. "Bringing in outsiders—I don't think Shona would convert, honestly. She's not all that religious."

My phone buzzed. I ignored it. "Have you asked?"

He gave a short, unhappy laugh. "Would you change your religion for someone you love? That's a huge thing to ask."

"If she's not that religious..."

Aliq shook his head. "You can't just...say you're Jewish, or Christian, or whatever. You have to really believe it. If she's not that religious, she's not going to suddenly become religious just for me."

I tried to puzzle this out. "But you're not that religious either."

"But I have my family, and they are."

I lay back on the bed. "Sorry, Rocky," Aliq said. "I don't mean to dump this all on you."

"Hey." I sat up quickly. "You're my best friend. Don't worry about it. I just wish I could help you more."

"You're helping by coming along." His tail tapped the bed, wagging gently.

"All right, then. Let's get some sleep and we'll see how it goes in the morning." I checked the phone and saw questions from both Nashan and Lochen, but Lochen had also booked a flight and put it on hold for us.

Ori ended up coming along. "Because what am I going to do, stay here?" she asked archly the next morning when we told her. Lochen procured another ticket for her—sitting nearby but not next to us—and so we all three stood on Aliq's stoop the following morning at 11 am waiting for him to ring the doorbell.

On the flight and in the car, Ori and I—mostly Ori—had come up with an approach that we hoped would work and which Aliq, bereft of other options, now clung to. "The thing is," Ori had said, "your parents don't want to push you out. So make them part of the solution. Tell them that you love Shona, but you're conflicted between her and your faith, and ask them to help you figure it out. If you ask them for help rather than pushing them to accept Shona, you have a better chance of figuring out an answer. Get them on your side."

Right away it was clear to me that that was the best answer, but it took another half hour of arguing to get Aliq to accept it. He kept talking about how strict his parents were about the faith, but in the end, with no other options, he finally agreed.

His tail flicked back and forth and then finally, as I was about to ask if he was ever going to knock, he reached out and opened the door. "Hi," he said, "I'm, uh, I'm home. Rocky and Ori are here, too."

His mother came out and greeted us all warmly; by the time she'd hugged everyone, his father had descended the stairs. More hugs all around, questions about the tour, congratulations for our wins. They wanted to show us the photo they'd put on the wall of the living room of Aliq and I accepting our trophy for the latest tournament, and in general seemed so cheery that at one point I sought out Ori's eyes and widened my own, with a sweep back of my ears to indicate, *what's going on?* She replied with equally wide eyes and a shake of her head: *don't know.*

It wasn't until after we'd eaten lunch and were all sitting in the living room that Aliq swallowed and said, "Mom, Dad, can I talk to you?"

Then his parents' ears went back and their smiles stiffened. "Of course," his father said. "Let's go to the den?"

"Sure." Aliq glanced at me and Ori.

"Rocky, Ori, if you'd like to watch Netflix, it's on the TV there. Will you be okay?"

"Of course," we chorused, just like we used to answer Ma together back in Lundara.

So the three arctic foxes disappeared back into the den. Once the door had closed behind them, Ori and I turned on the TV but only to cover our conversation.

"It's going to work out," she said with a confident smile. "It has to. They love him, clearly."

"I hope so. I've heard him talk about his parents and their faith before. They're pretty deep into it. More than Ma or Kamina, and remember you didn't want to tell them about Raji?"

She opened her mouth to object and then nodded. "Maybe you're right."

I didn't think about it then, but it was nice that we were able to talk about Ma—and Raji—without overwhelming sadness. There was sadness, of course, but both Ori and I were able to remember Ma for all the positives she'd given us. "But Ma knew about Raji and was okay with him," I remembered.

Ori nodded. "She told me—one of the last things she said was 'it doesn't matter who you find, as long as that person makes you happy.' And I suppose you should make them happy, too, but she was talking about Bompaka at the time. Making him happy was mostly a matter of staying out of his way and sewing and possibly producing lots of little jackals."

"I wonder if that's a part of it too." I looked toward the den. "They want grand-cubs, right?"

"They can adopt." She waved a paw. "Marro's sister adopted three cubs, all different species, with her husband. I think he's a bear or a sloth or something."

"I don't know how their faith feels about adopting." I'd had a Jewish friend in Palm Gables who had talked about that. I thought he'd said that faith was the most important part, that adoption was all right as long as both parents were Jewish, but I wasn't sure.

I leaned back on the couch and thought about adopting a cub myself. There were so many complications that went along with that—I was never home, I didn't have anyone in my life even remotely close to wanting to be another parent, just to name the top two—that I figured I'd much rather be the fun uncle to Ori's cubs, whenever they came along. If she stayed with Marro, possibly she'd adopt, or they'd find a jackal to be the father. Or a fennec to be the mother.

Ori, meanwhile, had flipped through Netflix and landed on a movie, a romantic comedy I didn't know much about. "This looks good," she said. "Want to watch it?"

"Sure," I said, and so we watched and waited. All the while, I thought about how interesting it was that Aliq's relationship was okay with the world at large but not with his family, while my family was fine with me dating Braden, but the rest of the world—maybe not all, but many in the tennis sphere—would look down on us. I wasn't sure whose situation I would have chosen, given the choice, but here we were both stuck with the situations life had thrown at us.

We hadn't quite finished the movie before Aliq and his parents reappeared, his mother with her ears determinedly up, Aliq and his father with theirs to the side and tails drooping. At least they all looked moderately unhappy, and Aliq didn't look devastated, so I hoped things had gone better than he'd anticipated.

"I hope you'll all stay for dinner," Mrs. Loize said brightly.

"We'd love to," Ori said.

"I'm going to go practice with Rocky, if that's okay." Aliq's tone wasn't hostile; he sounded more weary.

"Of course." His mother smiled, but tightly, a little forced. "Be back by six, please."

So we gathered our things and hiked the half hour walk to the tennis court. As soon as we were out of earshot of the house, though, Ori put a paw on Aliq's shoulder. "So? How did it go?"

He heaved a sigh. "They said I can keep seeing her. But they want to meet her—of course—and they're going to want to talk to her about converting—of course—and they want us to adopt arctic fox cubs and raise them Jewish."

"Adopt cubs?" I said. "You're not even married."

"We're not going to be if she doesn't agree to all this." Aliq sighed again. "Ori, your suggestion really helped. They were angry at first and I told them that I wanted to figure out how I could keep the person I'm in love with and also my family, and Mom was softer after that. Dad stayed angry for a little longer but once I got Mom on my side, she helped."

"So...that sounds good?" I had my racket out and bounced a tennis ball on it, a little ritual to keep me steady.

Aliq nodded. "It's better than it could have been, but I don't know what she's going to say. This makes things so much more complicated and we don't even know if we want a long-term thing."

"It sounds like you do," Ori said gently.

"I do, but I don't know if she does."

"Well," I said, "if she's willing to talk about all this, then I guess she is."

I thought that was perfectly logical, but it didn't seem to cheer Aliq up much. On reflection, maybe Ma's straightforwardness wasn't for everyone. It made me think again about my situation with Braden. I had a pretty good idea that Braden wanted to continue our relationship, and I did too, but not the way it was going. So why hadn't I talked to him the way I was telling Aliq to talk to Shona?

I was afraid. If I talked to him, if I made him choose between me and Ellen, of course he would choose Ellen. She was the one he could be seen with in public, the one he could take home to his parents, and even if there was nothing real between them (which I was beginning to doubt), the relationship would provide enough cover for him to go have his hookups in bars.

I was afraid that he only wanted to see me because it was easier than going out to a bar and finding a new person every time he wanted to get laid.

But if that's the case, I seemed to hear Ma say, you should find out and end it right away. Don't be in that relationship if it's not the relationship you want.

But. But Braden had changed. He'd become more open with me, he'd tried new things. I'd gotten to him, and we had a connection. Didn't we? Did I want to throw all that away just because... just because—

(*he didn't feel it too*)

—I wasn't comfortable with the way things had to be, with our lives being under a public microscope? Look what happened with Aliq. What if Braden and I were at a party and happened to, I don't know, hold paws for too long, or brush our muzzles against each other? And someone took a picture of it and in a moment our relationship became public?

Braden dealt with more media attention than any of us except maybe Tempest, at least this year with his run of wins. I was getting more this year than I'd ever had. Braden Longacre was a name known outside of devoted tennis followers now, and if there were rumors that he was gay, things would just explode.

"Rocky."

I turned around. Aliq and Ori stood twenty feet behind me, at the entrance to the tennis courts. "Where you going?" Aliq asked, a smile on his muzzle.

I shook my head. "Sorry. Just thinking about stuff."

"Let's get on the court," the fox said, and so we did.

Practice wasn't as good at distracting me as a live match, because I was simply going through rote motions that my body knew very well by now, leaving my mind free to wander. Thoughts of Braden weren't conducive to a good practice, though, so I forced myself back to working on my shots. And by the end of practice, Aliq and I were both panting pleasantly and I, at least, was not thinking about the pitfalls of my relationship.

* * *

The rest of the visit with his parents went well in that all three arctic foxes studiously ignored the conversation they'd had. We had to leave very soon to get over to Etrusca, where the clay court season began, and Aliq's and my excitement for our first real professional visit over there took over once we'd let the relationship worries go. None of us had been to Etrusca, and Ori hadn't been to that continent even, so we pestered Nashan with questions the first couple hours of the airplane ride over, until he pointedly put his headphones in and watched a movie. Without him to pester, we talked excitedly among ourselves for a bit, which still left us plenty of time to watch a movie or two.

We disembarked in Ruma and stood in line to be admitted to the country. Aliq and I went through first and waited on the other side of the line while Nashan went through and then Ori. Only Ori didn't go through as easily as we did. She stood at the window for a minute, then five, then ten, her smile fading as she shot us increasingly worried glances.

Nashan told us to wait and walked up to one of the security guards. "I'm with her," he said. "May I go back and see what the problem is?"

The guard, a tall wolf, shook her head, but told him to wait while she went to Ori's window and talked to the official behind it. After a moment, they beckoned Nashan over, and the red fox stood next to Ori for five more minutes talking to the official. Finally Ori said something to Nashan and the fox waved me and Aliq over.

Unsure because of the guard, we came over slowly. Nashan turned to us while Ori kept talking to the guard, and now I could hear something about "accommodations."

"What's going on?" I asked.

"Ori's paperwork." Nashan sighed. "We were supposed to get her a different kind of visa because she has a green card. Lochen should have filed it and he told me he did, but it might have gotten delayed or lost, or something. I'll check with him. In the meantime, they want Ori to fly back to the States right away, but I've convinced them to wait 24 hours and we'll hope it comes through by then."

"I, uh," I lowered my voice. "I know a guy who knows…Oh, that was Lochen's friend, wasn't it."

Nashan nodded. "I'm confident Lochen can take care of it. Let's just say 'see you tomorrow' to Ori and get to our tournament. We need to check in."

"Sorry," Aliq said. "If we hadn't had to go home…"

"It's fine." I put a paw on his shoulder. "Lochen's going to take care of it."

Calming him down helped me calm down as well. I had visions of the Lundaran authorities waiting for their bribes, of our father trying to get Ori back. Nothing like that is going to happen to her, I told myself.

So I said, "See you tomorrow," as I hugged her, and Aliq did the same, and then we made sure Ori had cell service so she could call us, and then we—reluctantly—walked away.

"I hate this," I grumbled to Aliq after we'd rounded the corner and left Ori out of sight.

"She'll be fine," he said. "Send her a text now."

So I got out my phone and sent Ori a text that said, *Miss you already*, but of course she was still arranging things with the officials and didn't answer me all through the time we waited for our bags.

Aliq's and mine and one of Nashan's were in the pickup area, but Nashan's other bag, the one with all his clothes in it, wasn't there. He went to talk to an airline representative when it was clear that all the bags had been unloaded, and the uniformed weasel helpfully explained to Nashan that he had no idea where the bag could be, but if Nashan called the airline's customer service number, they would look for it. So he called, standing there, and talked for fifteen minutes trying to sort out where the bag could be.

"Come on," the fox said to us finally. "They say if they find it here, they'll send it to our hotel, and if they find it in the States they'll send it over on the next flight, so there's no point in waiting around. You guys need your rest."

We'd been warned that the hotel rooms here would be even smaller than in Oceania, but I didn't think the room was that bad. Anyway, it wasn't like we were going to be in it for very long. We only stayed long enough to use the bathroom and then hurried back downstairs to get dinner with Nashan, because we were all starving.

"The good thing is," Nashan said over dinner, "we've gotten all the bad stuff out of the way on this trip, right? It'll be smooth sailing from now on."

We'd all gotten wine—one glass for me and Aliq was our limit— and so we toasted to that.

I didn't think much of the sniffles I had going to bed; after all, when I was tired, especially after a long flight, my nose got a little congested like happened with a lot of canids. Long noses have some common problems. But when I got up the next morning, one side of my nose was completely blocked and my throat was scratchy. I didn't get colds often, but I knew the signs, so I went to Nashan and told him, and he dug into his bag and came out with some caplets. "Take two of these every six hours," he said. "Let's hope it's not a bad cold."

By the end of the first day, I'd smashed that hope to pieces. I was running a mild temperature—not a fever—and even with Nashan's medications I felt lightheaded and off my game. Practice went fine, because I can play tennis in a lot of different states. My body remembers how to play it even when my mind doesn't; it's just that when my body isn't a hundred percent, it can't always do the things it remembers how to do.

"You'll be fine," everyone told me, but Nashan cut out one of my practice sessions so I could get rest, telling me that sleep was going to be the best medicine in the long run. That didn't do me any good when I had to get up and play a match in 48 hours.

Two days and two boxes of tissues later, Nashan was out of medicine and had to get something at a local pharmacy that would work the same as the States version, and that he hoped didn't contain any banned substances. He checked the ingredient list and called someone at the main ATP office in the States, who told him to check the ingredient list against the latest list of banned substances, and as Nashan related it to us, the conversation wasn't very productive. "But you've got to play," the fox said, "and I'm 99% sure there's nothing bad in here. I talked to a couple other coaches here and they said they've used it with their players, so…"

"If I don't take it, I won't make it through a match," I said, and grabbed the small bottle.

The medication helped—I won my first singles match—but it wasn't enough to give me the typical energy level I needed. Aliq and I had to play that afternoon in doubles and I was exhausted halfway through the first set. Losing that much energy ended up being too much for us to overcome, and we lost the match.

I felt terrible as we headed back to the locker room and sat by our benches. "Sorry," I said to Aliq, and I was going to say more, but I had to blow my nose. Thanks to the medicine, there wasn't a lot of stuff in my nose, but there was a seemingly ever-present tickle that I couldn't get rid of. I couldn't blow my nose much during the match, so by now it was a blessed relief.

"It happens." He picked at his shirt, not taking it off. "You're sick."

"I just want to lie down on the floor." I meant it as a joke, but as I thought of it and looked at the floor, it felt really tempting.

"We'll be back at the hotel soon." Aliq acted like how I felt, lethargic and uninterested in getting dressed to go back.

"Sorry," I said again. "I'll be better next tournament."

"It's fine." He flicked his tail.

"Hey." I punched his arm. "Don't think about Shona."

He groaned and leaned his head back. "I wasn't, but now I am."

"Then what was it?"

"Ah…" He shook his head. "It's dumb, but…this is a different country, the surface is different. The ball feels different here."

"It's clay. We've played on clay before."

"Yeah, but this feels different. I dunno. The language is different, my serve doesn't feel like it's landing." He shook his head. "What if this whole trip was a mistake? I should've stayed home."

"See, you are thinking about Shona. Or your parents, anyway." Shona hadn't made this trip over; she said clay was her worst surface so she was playing on grass to prepare for Wimbledon.

"We spent a ton of money to come over here and we didn't even make back our hotel money."

I went to grab his shoulder, but had to blow my nose first. "The money's not a problem. We're in a new place. Give us time to adjust."

"I guess." He didn't look happier.

"You know what Ma used to say? She said, 'storms come through all the time, but you don't have to go outside in them.'"

He gave me a sideways look. "So, like, just hide away from your troubles?"

I grinned. "No, she was telling me and Ori not to go out and play in a rainstorm."

The arctic fox frowned at me. "What?"

"There was this big dirt lot across the street from us, and it got really muddy in the rain. We wanted to go splash around in it and Ma hated that because she had to clean the mud out of our fur. So she told us we didn't have to go out in the storm."

Aliq shook his head. "You need to get some sleep."

I stood, a little wobbly, and took my shirt off. "No argument. But hey, instead of being worried about this new country, why not go work out at the gym? I bet that's the same. Then go find a place for us to have dinner."

He stared up at me. Then he sighed and pulled his shirt off.

* * *

Ori's visa took two days to clear up, and in the meantime I tried to take my own advice and not worry about her or a certain cross fox who was also at this tournament. It was hard enough getting through a tennis tournament with a cold; even though I rested up and won my next singles match, I was drained almost all the time. When Braden did finally text me, after that match, I responded with "*Sick, maybe later,*" and he said "*k.*"

The next morning I saw that he'd added, "Get better," which at least showed a little bit of thought, and though it wasn't due to those words, I did feel better that morning. I'd made it to the third round of this clay-court tournament and my opponent was currently ranked twenty spots below me, so I felt pretty good about my chances.

Of course I went out and lost in straight sets. "You're still weak from the cold," Nashan said, which was kind of him and also maybe true. Regardless, I didn't feel as uncomfortable on clay as Aliq seemed to, and I felt good about the next tournament. Ori kept taking me around to local sights, museums and old churches, and taking tons of pictures of me with them.

I insisted that Aliq use some of our free time there to practice more on clay, and though the argument with his parents stuck with him, he got used to the surface. Ori took pictures of him and me with red dust coating our fur; on me it looked dirty, but on Aliq's white fur it looked like he'd stepped out of a grisly crime scene. He hated it and took three showers a day sometimes.

Braden didn't text me again, but I saw him once out around the complex, with a few of his team talking to him, and he excused himself to come over.

"Hey," he said. "Feeling better?"

"Mostly." I tapped my muzzle. "Still gunked up a bit but at least I'm not falling asleep on my feet anymore. You're looking great."

"Yeah, it's going really well. We'll see about Dubois; he's great on clay."

"You can beat him."

"Thanks. You going to Ursaria?"

"Yep."

"Good luck."

"You too."

He paused. "Maybe we can grab dinner there?"

"Sure. I should be all better by then." I smiled. "And I'd like to."

"Great," he said, and left.

I didn't think about it at the time, but I guess he'd somehow figured out that he shouldn't mention Ellen around me. She was there too, going around with her camera and her team and working on some charitable thing to do with saving something or other. I didn't know the specifics.

Braden did beat Dubois to win that tournament, a feat that sounds more impressive than it looked. The marten fought in the first set and then when he lost it, seemed to decide that it wasn't worth tiring himself out with a major coming up and basically mailed in the second set. We watched from our hotel, and I didn't see Braden until the next day.

We'd all booked flights to Ursaria around the same time, so a bunch of us States players clustered in the airport to check in, chatting and gossiping and pretending not to notice the paparazzi around us taking pictures and leaning in to eavesdrop. It was a little stressful, but it helped that all the players were going through the same thing.

My cold was 98% gone, and Aliq had found his clay-court footing, so we did much better in Ursaria than we had in Ruma. I got to the quarterfinals, and in doubles we got to the semifinals, and Aliq didn't worry about money anymore. He was still thinking about Shona, whom he talked to almost every night, but as far as I knew they hadn't discussed what his parents had said. Aliq talked to his parents too, but only to tell them how interesting the trip was and the sights he was seeing. I wanted to tell him that you can't just let a situation go and hope it'll resolve itself, but it had only been a couple weeks. After the Gallic Open, I resolved, I'd talk to him. Wimbledon at the latest.

Meanwhile, Braden had booked a room at a cheap hotel in Ursaria, and I met him there for a night. The night was fine, even though we didn't go out to dinner ("too many cameras on me now," he growled, "even here"). After the glow of sex had faded, though, and we were lying pressed together in the small bed, from which I could reach out and touch two of the walls and almost a third if I stretched my feet out, I felt again the annoyance of being kept to one side. The sneaking around I could understand, but Braden could easily get another room in the same very nice hotel where he was staying. Heck, I could afford another room, and with pretty much everyone on my team knowing my situation, it wouldn't be a big deal for Braden to come visit. But I suggested that and he said that this way was working fine and why change it? I made a remark about the smell of mildew in the walls and he said it was only for one night and he liked the smells we were making enough that the room didn't bother him.

If he'd talked about Ellen then, like he did a little later that tournament when I saw him in the hotel lobby, we might've had a longer and less amiable conversation. Regardless, that conversation was coming. I knew it the next morning. The question was when I was going to have the balls to start it.

Chapter Twenty-Seven

B raden, to everyone's surprise, lost in the quarterfinals, the same round as I did in singles. When I talked to him, he shrugged it off. "Bad day," he said. "On to the next one."

Aliq and I generally enjoyed our time in Ispania more than we had in Etrusca, and our doubles success was part of that, but not all. Aliq had taken Spanish in school, enough to get around, and Ori was with us for the entire trip, and I was over my cold. Also, if I'm being completely honest, it helped that I'd hooked up with Braden. If I forgot where we'd hooked up, the rest of the feelings around it made me feel good.

Rested and winning put Ori and I in a better mood to talk to Aliq about Shona. I wanted to anyway because it took my mind off my own problems. He'd been calling her and texting her, and they'd had two talks about where things were going to go between them and neither of them had really resolved anything except that his parents' demands were a lot, and that they both cared about each other.

We sat in a cool evening on an outside patio at a small restaurant near the tennis center, and Aliq, just having finished the second of those two talks, told us where they stood. "That's a good place to start from," Ori said. "It sounds like maybe she needs to decide whether she's willing to change her life to be with you, and then if she's not, you need to decide if you're willing to change your life to be with her."

"That's a good summary of it." Aliq nodded.

"The thing is," I said, "if she isn't willing to change her life, it doesn't mean she doesn't love you. She's got family, too, and she has other things going on. So she might love you, but maybe she can't commit to raising cubs because it would interfere with her career."

Aliq nodded. "We talked a little about that, too. She's okay with cubs if my parents can wait. And she doesn't need them to be lion or tiger cubs. She said if she loves me, she'll love my cubs even if a surrogate has them. I don't think that's the issue. It's more the religion. She doesn't want to convert just for the sake of converting, to 'have another label by her name,' as she put it."

Ori leaned forward. "Do you feel like, when all's said and done, you and she both want to be together?"

The fox gave a short laugh. "I don't know, I mean, how do you ever know these things?"

Ori and I exchanged a look, and then I saw that maybe she was a little more serious about Marro than I'd suspected. I returned her smile and said, "I know this isn't the kind of stuff we usually talk about, like serious feelings and whatever, but…go with your gut. Yes or no?"

He sat back and shook his head. "Yes. I think we both want it."

"Then," Ori said with a smile, "it's just a matter of finding the path that gets you there."

I had my doubts that it could be that easy, but her words encouraged Aliq, so I let them lie.

We took a train to Lutèce because Nashan said it was easier and more scenic than a plane. I'll allow that the mountains between Ispania and Gallia are breathtaking, and that the farmland between cities in Gallia is a beautiful, peculiar shade of green. However, the trip took half a day, and though we got to relax, we had to change trains once, and the whole process seemed to me overly complicated. Had we flown, we could've been in Lutèce in an hour.

Ori loved the train and took numerous pictures. I suppose it was worth it in that respect. And I got several hours to watch video of my clay court play, both on my own and with Nashan, to identify areas where I could improve. Ruma and Ursaria had been smaller tournaments; the Gallic Open was a major tournament, so everyone would be there. Five-set matches, more rounds, a more grueling test.

I'd done well at the Ocie, though. The idea of playing longer matches in front of immense crowds no longer intimidated me. Clay courts didn't frighten me. As long as I kept going, I'd reach the goal I'd set out for so many years ago.

* * *

Braden texted me our second day in Lutèce, not with a hotel name and room number, but with a question: *Want to see a cool bar?*

I said that I would, so he texted me an address. *Don't be followed,* he added, which sounded amusingly like he thought we were in a spy movie. Of course he meant the Euro press, who had followed him all over Ruma and Ursaria. They had not yet sniffed out our friendship (though it had been mentioned spottily in States blogs), so apart from me being a top twenty-five player, there wasn't much to attract them to me. Top twenty-five was good, very good, but really you had to be top ten and ideally top five to really catch the attention of the press. If their readers know your name, you're on their list. N'Guwe was not yet a household name, though I promised myself it would soon be.

So I found a back door out of the hotel onto a fragrant alley, cut down it and around a closed bakery, and let my phone guide me from there. After two blocks, I hurried around a corner and then peered around to see if I recognized anyone who'd been behind me at the hotel, or if anyone was hurrying to catch up to me. Nobody was, although a badger did stare at me and then shake her head, moving on. My ears flushed warm and I walked the rest of the way without acting like an idiot who thinks he's in a spy movie.

The address Braden had sent me brought me to a tall, elegant hotel. At first I thought I'd gotten the address wrong, but then I saw a sign for the bar: Arge-en-Ciel, flowing script in rainbow colors. In the hotel lobby, I waited a moment where I could do it casually, looking around for the entrance to the bar and also watching the doors I'd come in. Still nobody was following me.

The door marked "Arge-en-Ciel" did not lead to the bar, but to an elevator with a perfumed fennec fox in a smart navy blue uniform. He said something to me in Gallic, and then at the puzzled cant of my ears, repeated (I assume) in slightly accented English. "To the roof, sir?"

"Yes, please."

The elevator sped up twenty stories, both of us keeping silent, and then the doors opened onto lights and music, but not the stuffy scents of the usual bar scene. As I stepped out of the elevator, the only roof over my head were the clouds far above me, and the river and city smell of Lutèce hovered over the brightly lit crowd.

Now, having ensured I hadn't been followed, I had to find Braden: spy movie subplot number two. I could've just texted, but I set myself a sort of test: what would he like about this place? The anonymity, probably. Possibly the view: the Koechlin Tower rose glittering off to the east, and beyond it the rest of Lutèce, but that side of the bar attracted everyone, stacked three deep at the railing. So I turned toward the other sides of the roof, and soon noticed the other thing that might have attracted Braden to this place.

Right in front of me, a muscular boar in a leather jacket held a plump hedgehog, topless in shiny red leather pants, and as I watched they kissed, rather passionately. I turned away, slightly embarrassed even though nobody else seemed to care, and my eyes lit on a female dingo in a flannel collared shirt and jeans holding the paw of a female red squirrel in a pale blue dress, her long fur elegantly styled, silver glittering around her ears.

At least this was a public place, and it explained why Braden didn't want to be followed. Forget being together; if we were just seen in this gay bar, the press would have a field day with it.

But the crowd was large enough and the night dark enough that despite the rainbow lights shimmering through the crowd, there wasn't much chance we'd be recognized. Braden's distinctive coloration wouldn't be nearly as obvious, and there were more jackals in Europe than in the States, so I wasn't worried about being spotted either.

I found him leaning against a potted tree of some sort, looking out over the dark mass of the suburban park where the tennis center stood. "Hey," I said.

He turned and gave me a smile. "Hey. I thought it'd be nice to get out of a hotel room for once. I told my team I was turning in early and snuck out the back."

"It's cool." I looked around and reached out to take his paw. He let me. "Good drinks here?"

"I guess so. I just got soda here in the past, and tonight I didn't want to talk to anyone. The less someone sees me..." He shrugged.

"That's why I came and looked for you in the darkest corner." I said it a little teasingly, but he nodded, serious.

"Yeah, I mean, the view of Lutèce is pretty nice, but it's nice and quiet over here too." He pointed. "There's the tennis center."

"I see it."

"You ready for the tourney?"

I nodded. "About as much as ever. You?"

"Ursaria was disappointing, but I'm ready to go. Got to show Dubois that he doesn't own the clay."

His smile showed his teeth, gleaming white. I grinned back. "If I were allowed to bet, I'd put money on you."

"Damn right." He looked back out over the tennis stadium. "Seems so small from up here, but when you're in it, it's huge."

I leaned on the railing, my paw still in his. I wondered if we were going to do anything more than hold paws. "So this is the main reason you like this bar?"

"Pretty much."

I waited a moment to see if he'd turn and offer to kiss me, but he didn't. "You want a club soda or something? I'll go order it."

"Sure, I guess."

Club sodas in paw, I returned to the railing where Braden stood alone. He said "thanks" as he took the glass I held out to him and sipped the drink.

"You have family coming out?" I asked.

He nodded. "Parents are flying in next week. Assuming I don't flame out in the first few rounds."

"You won't."

The fox flashed me another smile. "How about you?"

"All my family's here except my father, and I don't give a shit where he is. Hope he stays far away."

Braden nodded. "I remember. He's not doing anything else?"

"No, seems to have settled down." I liked that he remembered. "You don't talk about your folks much. Get along with them?"

He shrugged. "We talk on the phone a bit, I guess. Why?"

"Oh, one of my friends is having parent problems right now. It's on my mind."

"What kind of problems?"

I hesitated and then forged ahead. "They don't approve of his romantic partner."

"Mmm." Braden sipped his drink.

The view didn't change much, but he seemed to keep enjoying it. After a moment, I asked, "You have a hotel room for us here?"

He gave me a sideways look. "Yeah. Little nicer than usual. But I thought we could enjoy the bar here for a little. I really liked this place a couple years ago."

"It's nice." Though if we weren't going to take advantage of being anonymous in a gay bar, I wasn't sure I saw the point. So I leaned in to kiss him.

Braden met my muzzle with a brief kiss and then set down his drink. "But look, if you just want to go back to the room, that's fine too."

"We can stay up here," I said, leaning back a little.

So we talked about Gallia and politics, on which we fortunately agreed, and then on the hassles of travel, and a little about the food in Ursaria, which we both liked. Then our drinks were done, and Braden said, "All right, let's head downstairs."

I felt like I'd let him down by not appreciating the bar enough, but I still felt annoyed that he'd misconstrued the kiss. Still, it had been a pretty nice evening, and sex was always a good way to end things.

Even though I'd gotten used to the hotel rooms over here being small, I was surprised when Braden opened the door and had to stand to one side to allow me to get in. When I did slide my way into the room, I had to step half into the bathroom so he could close the door.

The bed took up a third of the room space, and for some reason a giant wardrobe took up a quarter of what was left. But the carpet was silky soft under my feet and the curtains framed a view from the window that looked like a painting, glittering lights and elegant buildings. For a moment, I felt as though I'd stepped back a century in time, between the carved wooden furnishings and the decorative bedspread and the slightly musty smell I associated with old pre-served houses.

"Beautiful," I said.

"Yeah." Braden smiled a satisfied smile. "Better than an old Qual Inn, huh?"

"Much." I walked to the window and looked out at the city. "It's my first time in Lutèce."

"Like it?" Braden came up behind me and rested a paw just above the base of my tail.

"I like it a lot."

The bed was not the softest I'd ever been on, but it was extremely adequate for our purposes. It was even almost big enough for us to lie in afterwards side by side, as long as we pressed close together, which neither of us objected much to.

"Gonna do better here?" Braden asked me, his paw resting on my hip. He always felt softer, closer, after sex.

Mine ruffled his chest fur. "I bet I can get at least to the semifinal. I'd meet the hottest cross fox on the tour if I got there and I don't think I could get past him."

"Heh." He whuffed warm breath onto my whiskers. "He's tough to get past, for sure. Not perfect, though."

"You've lost, what, twice? Did you really think you weren't going to lose another match all year?"

His fingers curled through my fur. "Until I lost one, I did."

"Huh." He'd taken that more seriously than I'd thought he would. "Well, if anyone could do it, you could."

That got me a pleased smile. "I feel so good out there this year. Everything's going right. I'm seeing the ball well, I haven't had any health issues…sometimes luck knocks on your door and you've got to be ready."

"Uh huh. Maybe in a few years I'll have my year."

"You will." He patted me. "You've got the talent and the drive. But this year…this year's mine."

"I believe it." I pressed my paw against his chest.

Eyes half-lidded, he smiled. Then he stretched and half-rolled away from me. "I should get back," he said.

I bit back the first thing I wanted to say, staying quiet until he'd gotten out of bed and picked up his underwear. Then I said, "Why can't we stay here all night? It's nice."

He gave me a look, the one that said I hadn't annoyed him yet but was heading down that road. "The bed's small."

"We've been lying on it for half an hour. And before that we were being pretty active."

He scanned the floor for his shirt, found it, picked it up. "I need space to sleep."

"We could try it. Neither of us has a match tomorrow."

I propped myself up on one elbow to look at him, leaving his space on the bed. He held the shirt in one paw as though weighing it, and then he sighed. "I guess…"

That sigh annoyed me. I knew he had a lot going on, I knew that he was probably right about the bed being too small, I knew all of that. But I also knew that this was the only time I'd get with him probably for another couple weeks. It had been nice and I didn't want it to end, but clearly he didn't care as much.

So I swung my legs over the side of the bed. "You know what, it's fine. Go ahead back. I should get back to my room, too."

"The bed's really small," he said. "I don't see why you're getting annoyed about that. It's just a fact."

"Right." I found my underwear and yanked them on. "It's a fact. It's fine. There's always a fact, always a reason."

He shook his head and pulled his shirt on. "Don't be a jerk about this."

That stopped me for a moment. Me? *I* was being the jerk? And then I worried about it, remembering what Marquize had said. *Was* I being a jerk?

While I thought about that, Braden got his pants on. "Good luck," he said, gathering the rest of his things. "I won't have this room the whole tournament but I can book something if you want to get together again."

It was a nice offer, all things considered, but the thought that ran through my head was, *what, so you can blow me and walk out again?* I managed to not say that, but I did say, "Ok. Say hi to Ellen."

That brought a puzzled frown to his muzzle. He shook his head again and waved to me as he walked out.

I sank back onto the bed and slammed the pillow with a fist. Again the conflicting emotions: I was sure I had reason to be upset, but I hadn't articulated my feelings well, and I'd ended a nice evening on a sour note. The bed still smelled like us, like sex, like him, and so I rolled onto my side and stared out at the window until my eyes got heavy, and I opened them into sunlight.

Aliq had texted me, *Bfst?* I texted back in the affirmative and collected my things.

A day with my sister, my best friend, and my coach pretty quickly drove Braden from my mind. I had a major tournament to prepare for, and I was higher ranked than I'd ever been going into a major, which meant more press, more photographers coming around my practice, and because it was a foreign country, interpreters for some of the reporters whose English wasn't great. All of this took away from my free time, but not my practice time thanks to UTP rules.

Ori and Nashan, but increasingly only Ori as Nashan trusted her even in this environment, coached me before and after media sessions, reminding me what not to mention, telling me what I could do better next time. Nothing blew up as far as they let me know, so I guess I was doing okay. The stress of being a public figure, new and unfamiliar, was a distraction from thinking about my relationship with Braden, but like that stress, I put it aside once I got on the court.

There I did very well. Playing those two tuneups had helped my confidence on clay immensely, and I dispatched my first two opponents with ease. Aliq and I similarly did well, getting through one tough match and one easy one. The schedule meant I was playing two matches a day, but I got a day off in between, and when we had rainouts early on, I got two days off. "How you holding up?" Nashan asked.

I grinned at him. "I'm young," I said. "I'm fine."

Braden, meanwhile, had taken new motivation from his defeat in Ursaria. He didn't lose a set in the first few rounds, and twice won sets at love. More than the scores, though, he played every game in a determined mood and never even had a brief lapse like he'd had in our match, a few games that gave me hope that I could beat him sometime. We watched one of his matches with Nashan, who said four games into it, "I can't believe someone from the States is this good on clay. He's adjusted his play so much, not just staying back from net, but look at his groundstrokes. On hard court he goes for the corners with flat penetrating groundstrokes; here he's hitting with a lot of topspin so the ball kicks up more. It gives him more margin for error and pulls his opponent off the court. Like there!" Braden had just forced an error on a sharply angled forehand. "He almost never tries that shot on hard courts."

I squinted, imagining how to replicate that shot. "I'm trying to use more topspin."

"If you can do that," Nashan said, indicating the court with his head, "then you'll win some clay court tournaments before too long. But it's a matter of retraining your instincts. Longacre's in complete control of his game."

I played a lot of my game by feel, I knew. Besides which, if winning on clay was simply as easy as "hit more topspin forehands," everyone would do it. There was a rhythm to clay: serves felt slower and so returns of serve were also slower and less effective, and that was a big part of my game.

What Ruma and Ursaria had taught me was patience, to get beyond the serve and return where I expected to control things, to look for later openings to assert myself. Once I adjusted to the slower pace, I had more success, although I'd lost at Ursaria to a lower-ranked player who'd played on clay all his life. Nashan said that I'd done well up to that point because I'd mostly played hard court players who were struggling on clay, and I wasn't sure how to take that, but I thought it was a positive that I was adjusting more quickly than some of these other players.

When I stopped thinking about my game, it was a joy to watch Braden play, like a clinic on tennis. Only a little bit of sadness crept in when I thought about him off the court.

* * *

The second week of a major starts with the fourth round, more or less, so if you make it to there, you're halfway through and that's considered an accomplishment. When I won my third round match, another tough one against a hard court player who, like me, was making good adjustments to the clay, Nashan, Aliq, Ori, and I all went out to celebrate. Earlier in the day, Aliq and I had won our third-round doubles match, so he was also into the second week.

"If you get to the quarterfinals in the first two majors of the year," Nashan said, "people will take notice. Especially here."

"I'm playing Devreaux," I reminded him, "so that's probably not going to happen."

"Pfff." Aliq lifted the one glass of wine we were allowed in our diet. "He's fifty-one."

"He grew up playing on clay," I said. "They say in the locker room that he used to be a white deer but he spent so much time on clay it turned him red."

Everyone laughed, and Ori chimed in. "I think you can beat him. You've been playing really well."

"He's Gallic, so he's going to have the crowd behind him. And if I beat him then I get Tempest playing fantastic in his last year, maybe, and he'll have the crowd behind him too."

"Tempest won't retire," Nashan said.

"So you play against the crowd a couple times." Aliq waved a paw. "Remember when they had no idea who you were?"

"Sure." I hadn't gotten wine, myself, preferring to stick with Coke even though the rabbit waiter had given me a disapproving look when I'd ordered it. I liked the reassuring familiarity of it in a foreign country even though the taste was subtly different here. "But not knowing me is better than rooting against me because I'm playing their favorite player."

Ori lay a paw on my arm. "You can do it."

"I know I can do it," I said. "I just don't think I will."

"Maybe we will." Aliq grinned. Winning had relieved him of thinking about his girlfriend-parents dilemma for most of the time. Also he liked the gym at the hotel we were staying at, which he was forced to use since his gym chain didn't have any branches over here. I found that joining him for workouts also helped me keep my mind off of my problems.

Ori showed me how my following on social media was growing and told me I wouldn't have crowds against me often. People liked me and were rooting for me, especially when she linked me to stories about Lunda. We donated money to help people in need there, and once Ori decided to run a matching campaign where she (on my behalf) pledged to match every donation sent to war victims. We raised twelve thousand from my followers and matched it from my private funds, and Ori posted pictures of the supplies our relief aid had brought.

So I had a good following, but it wouldn't compare to Gallia rooting for a Gallic deer who was the last of his countryfolk left in the tournament. Nowhere at the other majors had I been playing someone who was such a crowd favorite. They roared for him when he came out in his white shirt and shorts with red and blue piping. They roared for him when he hit a good warmup serve. They roared when the chair umpire introduced him. They roared when he served first. And though they quieted down during the match, he got applause for every point he won.

It didn't rattle me. He was just playing lights-out that day. My baseline game was good, but he jumped around the court and got to everything. I tried putting more topspin on my strokes, but he played deep enough that I couldn't keep the ball out of his strike zone. I had a little success with drop shots, but I missed one early on and it made me wary of trying them.

I played a tough second set but lost in straight sets, 6-4, 7-6, 6-3. The third set was dispiriting to play. I knew that I was going to lose, and though I really wanted to win at least one set, I felt in my fur that it wasn't going to happen. He broke my serve in my second service game when I was pushing too hard to make something happen, and as soon as the game was over, I knew what I'd done wrong.

There at the end of the match I got a nice round of applause, and a bunch of cubs ran up to where I walked out of the stadium, holding out balls for me to sign. As I'd been told and always tried to do, I stopped and signed every one of them. Here, one was a little jackal cub with his mother, holding out an oversized tennis ball. When I signed it, he said something to me in Gallic, and I smiled and looked questioningly at his mother.

She said, "No English," and shrugged.

Her accent reminded me of Ma's when she spoke English, so I took a chance. "From Lunda?" I asked in Kikongo.

She brightened and nodded. "He says he wants to be a tennis star like you one day." The cub looked confused and she rested a paw between his ears. "His Kikongo is not very good. We make him speak Gallic so he fits in better."

"I understand. I've spoken mostly English since I came to the States. Tell him he has to work hard and practice every day, but he can make it like I did."

She spoke to him in Gallic, and he clapped his paws as I moved on to the next outstretched ball. But I thought about him as I changed in the locker room. He was probably seven or eight. At that age I'd already gotten familiar with a tennis racket. If he started now, maybe he could still catch up to the boys his age who'd been playing for a couple years. If he had the talent. If he had the work ethic. If he had the right coach, the right environment. I thought about how lucky I'd been over the course of my life, and I thought about Ma, and the loss didn't sting so much after that.

Nor did our doubles loss later that day, where at least we took one of the sets. Afterwards the other team (native clay court players from Etrusca) talked to us a bunch and offered to show us around Lutèce, so we exchanged contact info.

They lost in the semifinals, and after that we went out with them to a couple fun bars. There was dancing, which Ori and Marro engaged in, but the rest of us just enjoyed the music and the drinks. We talked mostly about Braden's semifinal match, which we'd all watched (Aliq and I live, the others on TV in the locker room). He'd played Devreaux, who had made it through, and had made very short work of him. The deer's main advantage was that he was comfortable on clay and very proficient at extending points until his opponent made a mistake. That didn't work against Braden, who just played solid, crafty points until he saw an opening and then rifled a topspin forehand down the line, or sliced a perfect drop shot across the net, the kind of thing I'd tried to do and failed.

The other team wanted to know about Devreaux; I'd played him and neither of them had, and he had a reputation on the Euro tour for being kind of stuck up. I said he'd been fine, very polite, and he just had a really good day playing me. "But he didn't take you out to bars like we did," one of the others said. "And he grew up here. That's not true hospitality."

"Maybe not," I said. "But it's okay. Not everyone needs to be friends."

They wanted to know who we liked in the final, and I said that I would never bet against Braden, not this year.

In the final, Braden met Robino, an Etruscan who'd upset Dubois in the quarterfinals, and the rabbit couldn't get anything going. His usually sure groundstrokes fell flat, easy prey for the fox's swift racket. Braden's game looked even better than it had when he'd won in Ruma; he might've been one of those native clay players. He won in four sets and that was only because Robino clawed his way through a tiebreak.

After he won, Braden ran up to his box to greet his team. This win meant a lot to him; his first non-Ocie major, his second consecutive, and I could see the enthusiasm in the arch of his tail and in his energy even after those four sets. The first person he embraced was his coach, and then he turned and Ellen was there, the red fox wrapping him in a warm hug and pressing a kiss to his muzzle.

I looked down, squeezing my paws together in my lap, and didn't look up again until they had assembled the stage. Braden thanked the crowd in clumsy Gallic, but they loved him for the effort, and in his interview after the match he said he'd never felt as much at home as he did here, and he thanked his whole team, "and Ellen Jacobs, who's been with me much of this year and she's just been really great."

I didn't say anything, but Ori knew. She reached over and took my paw and held it until we got up to leave.

We arranged to go out again with the Etruscan guys that night, which I hoped would take my mind off Braden, but that only partly worked. I did have a fun time and was more relaxed the next day, which we spent seeing all the sights around Lutèce. Ori took a bunch of pictures of me and Aliq for half the day, with Marro along, and then she abandoned us to go with Marro to do the same for Colluvic.

"They seem to be getting along well," Aliq said. "Marro's a nice guy."

"Yeah. I like him. If they stay together…"

His ears perked. "Why wouldn't they?"

"Oh, no reason. Things happen." I shrugged.

That reminded him of his own problems, but he didn't go all quiet like I was worried he might. "Hey, in a few days I'll see Shona again," he said, and his tail wagged.

"You guys been talking?"

"A bit. I think we might be able to work something out."

"Ah, that's awesome." I patted his shoulder. "I hope so."

"Me too. Mom and Dad will maybe have to compromise a little bit too, but I think they will."

Here, thousands of miles away, that optimism seemed entirely reasonable. So I felt good about relationships in general, until that evening when Braden texted to invite me out to that hotel again.

Chapter Twenty-Eight

I stared at the text message for a long time, it seemed, but according to my phone it was only three minutes later when I texted back that I'd meet him. I'd been relaxing, not thinking about Braden, but even not thinking about him took a conscious effort and when it came down to it, I wanted to see him again. It wasn't just physical, either. I wanted to congratulate him, wanted to share his excitement in his victory.

The room he sent me was the same as the one we'd met in a couple weeks ago. Had he kept the room for the entire two weeks of the tournament, despite saying he wouldn't, or just requested the same one? I didn't ask. Either way it showed at least a little bit of affection for me, so I clung to that.

He greeted me with a huge grin. "So," he said once the door was closed, "want to blow the Gallic Open champion?"

I grinned back and hugged him. "You looked great," I said. "And heck yeah."

With that invitation, I reached for his pants and undid the clasp. His tail wagged as he stepped back to the bed and pushed his pants down, and I wrapped my paw around his hard cock and went to work, remembering how well that body under my paws had moved just a few days ago.

With the pleasant taste of fox in my muzzle, I stripped down myself and took my turn. Lying back on the bed with Braden's tongue washing over me, it was easy to let everything else fall away.

Or so I thought. Without warning, my images of him dominating the competition on the red clay courts gave way to the memory of him kissing Ellen with that same tongue. I squirmed, which got him to put his paws on my hips to hold me still. I banished those thoughts as best I could, but they didn't go completely away until Braden had me entirely in his muzzle, his tongue bringing me to the edge and past it.

"Take your shirt off," I murmured, patting the bed beside me.

Braden obliged, giving me a good view of that dark-furred body with the russet trim around the chest and muzzle. He sat on the bed and I put a paw to his stomach as he reclined at my side. My tail wagged against the bed and his did too, with an almost identical motion at first. Braden rested a paw at the base of my sheath, touching the warmth there as well as the sac below, his fingertips teasing lightly.

"Looking forward to Londinium," Braden said next to my ear after a few moments. "Already got a hotel lined up there."

I didn't say anything, and after a moment, he went on. "It's nice like this one but it's a bit out of the way, so we might only have one night during the tournament, but maybe I could stay the whole night if you want."

I felt so good physically, nicely worn out, my nose and tongue full of his scent, and I didn't want to ruin the mood. We were at the top of the riverbank, where just a slight push would send us sliding down the mud. I didn't want to give that push, but I knew I couldn't keep balancing forever. So I asked, "You sure you can get away from Ellen?"

His paw stopped and rested where it was. "Sure I can." His tone remained casual, but had cooled.

"Can you stay tonight?" I asked.

After a long silent moment he said, "What is this about? I got a nice hotel like you wanted, we met up twice."

"It's…" His warmth, the closeness of his fur next to mine, wouldn't let me shade the truth at all. "You said it was just for show."

"Yeah?"

"It seemed like a really good show," I said. "You kissed her, you thanked her. So like…what's the deal?"

"There's no 'deal.'" He shifted on the bed to lie on his back like I was. "I mean, what's the 'deal' with you and me? We get together here, we have sex, we talk a little tennis."

"Yeah. Don't you want...I dunno, more?"

"Like what?" He stared at the ceiling, his tail not moving now. "We can't date. Things would get crazy on the tour and we don't need the distraction."

"I don't want to be public or anything."

"Then what?"

This was the problem. I didn't know how to articulate what I wanted, even though I'd been thinking about it for a while. "I don't know, just...I'd like to feel like I'm important. Like maybe we could get together when it wasn't just about sex, and spend time."

"Like practicing, which we can do more of. We'll spend a couple days in Londinium again after Wimbledon."

"I know," I sighed, "but like...there's stuff going on I want to talk to you about."

"We can talk." When I didn't say anything, he went on. "Okay, since you bring it up, I had something I wanted to talk about too. The thing with Ellen—you keep bringing it up all the time, like it's something bad."

"Uh—"

"She's a friend. She's doing me a favor. And you keep making me feel guilty about it. I don't like that feeling."

"Sorry," I said automatically, and then caught myself. "Wait, why do you feel guilty?"

"I don't know! You keep..." He waved a paw in the air and brought it down on his own hip. "Talking about her like I'm seeing her to hurt you. I'm seeing her so I can keep seeing you, so people don't get suspicious."

"If you're doing it for me," I said, "then you can stop."

"I'm not doing it just for you." He lay back and sighed. "My parents really like her."

"See?" I propped myself up on one elbow. "I don't know anything about your parents."

"What's to know? Dad sells real estate, Mom's an EVP at some huge publishing company."

"I don't mean what they do. I mean—what's your relationship with them? How did they get you started in tennis?"

"Ugh." He put a paw over his eyes. "I don't know, it was something to do and it kept me out of their fur, and I got good at it so they let me keep doing it. We didn't have a long heart to heart about it. And what does this have to do with Ellen anyway?"

"Why does it matter that they like her?" I countered.

"My parents have to like my girlfriend."

"Fake girlfriend."

"Yeah."

There was a pause before the "yeah," and I jumped on it. "What, you love her now?"

"No." No pause before the answer, but a pause afterwards.

I filled in the word that clearly wanted to be there, set up as neatly as a mishit drop shot. "But?"

He kept the paw over his eyes. "My mom wants to know when we're getting married."

"And?" I hated having to drag the answers out of him, but he wasn't offering them up on his own, so what alternative did I have?

"Ellen…likes the idea."

"Of course she does. She runs around the world spending your money."

"Hey." He lifted his paw and turned to glare at me. "You don't know her."

"Are you going to get married?"

"No." He looked away from me. "Probably not."

"Probably not." I lay back on the bed. "You were going to tell me?"

"Of course I was going to tell you. I was actually…I mean, they're all here, it just came up last night. I wanted to ask you about it."

"Ask me what?"

Braden breathed in and then exhaled. "You know what, it doesn't matter. I know what you'll say."

"That you shouldn't marry someone you're not in love with? That I don't want to be the guy you'll cheat on your wife with?"

He shook his head. "Something like that, yeah."

"You're right. I'm saying it. So?"

"So I don't know. How is being married different from just having a girlfriend?"

Even though we were side by side, it felt like we were in different countries. "Are you seriously asking me that?"

"Functionally, it's…" He shook his head. "So what else can I do? Okay? You want me to break up with Ellen?"

"Yes."

"Just like that."

"It's not really breaking up," I pointed out. "If you're not dating."

"To the press, it will be. I'll have to deal with that on top of everything else."

"'Everything else'?"

"Mom and Dad." He sighed again. "Ellen."

I sat up and looked down at him, the gorgeous body hiding the spirit I wanted to know better. "What about you?"

"Huh?"

"What do you want?"

"Grow up," he said. "It doesn't matter what I want. I mean…I want the same thing you do. I want to be the best. And if I'm going to do it then I have to live with these rules and shit. I don't have to like it. But my other option is to walk away from the game. You think that's how this ends? You think we walk off paw in paw and live happily ever after?"

"No," I said. "I don't think so."

"So we're doing the best we can. Just…deal with it."

I thought about that. I could deal with it, for nights like this one. Even the fight was giving me more of a window into Braden than I'd seen before. Eventually I'd get to know him, eventually he'd get to know me. So what if he got married? We'd always have the tour. And when it was over…

That would be years away. I didn't think I could do that to myself, be quiet and appreciate the scraps of his life. I knew with my mind that his charade with Ellen was a screen so he could be with me, but what I didn't know was whether if I walked out, he'd replace me with random bar hookups again. I didn't know whether he'd miss me. I hoped so. I might have even thought so. But he'd never come out and said he would. He'd never asked me to stay.

So I got out of bed. The weird thing about this fight was that it didn't feel like a fight. If we were sliding down a muddy riverbank, we were doing it slowly and together. As much as we might try to prolong the slide, the river still waited at the bottom.

Braden watched me get dressed, propped up on his elbows, without a word. When I'd gotten my shirt on, I said, "I don't think we should see each other in Londinium. If you want to practice or something, I guess, but…I can't keep doing this. I can't keep dealing with it. It wouldn't be so bad if it was just sex. I just, I keep getting glimpses of something more. Like looking through a fence at a place I can't ever get to. And if I can't get to it, that's fine. But then I have to stop looking."

He didn't say anything, just stared at me with those hazel eyes, his ears not perked, not back, just listening. I went on. "It hurts too much. And maybe it doesn't hurt you, and I get that. You can do the things you need to do for your career, and I'll do the things I need to do, and maybe we'll keep being friends, or maybe that doesn't fit into your image or something, I don't know. But, uh. Good luck at Wimbledon."

The cross fox watched, and when I took a step toward the door, he said in a tired voice, "If you're going to go, then go."

So I went.

Chapter Twenty-Nine

Leaving that hotel was sad, sure, but also freeing in a way. I wondered if this was how Marquize had felt after our last breakup. I kept seeing Braden's naked body in my mind, the brown fur darkening his face, orange highlights framing his muzzle and curling around his chest, continuing enticingly down his leg.

I shook my head to clear my thoughts. Braden was attractive, sure, the most attractive guy I knew, but there'd be other guys. There'd be guys in Londinium, there'd be guys in Port City, and guys in Bournemouth, and everywhere in between. And they wouldn't have some kind of attitude like they could do no goddamn wrong, and they wouldn't be fitting me into convenient places in their schedule. And they wouldn't know anything about tennis. They wouldn't have little bits of advice that would make me a better player. They wouldn't be the number one player in the world (which he was, even if the rankings didn't officially say so yet).

They wouldn't do little kindnesses that revealed the heart they tried to hide, and they wouldn't try so hard to hide that heart when anyone came looking for it.

I walked out the door of the hotel into the warm, humid Lutèce night. This, of course, was the city of romance, and the scent of it surrounded me. My steps carried me to the river and along its bank, and though I could have gotten a taxi at any time, I wanted to keep walking. Many other people walked around the quais, so I wasn't alone by any means, unless you counted the fact that I was several inches taller than most people in the crowd.

Briefly, I considered the question of whether I was in love with Braden Longacre. I didn't linger long on it, because that wasn't the important question just at the moment. The question was whether

Braden was in love with me. That wasn't one I could answer nor do anything about. As Ma would've told me, spend your energy on the things you can control. Was I in love with Braden? Didn't matter; it was over.

All that said, the amount of regret that was mixed in with my relief led me to the very strong suspicion that I knew the answer.

* * *

I slept fitfully back in my own hotel room, and when I got up in the morning I didn't say anything to Aliq or Ori about what had happened. They assumed I'd had a good night with Braden and in general we didn't talk about my relationship unless I initiated it, so I didn't.

We walked around Lutèce being tourists for the next day and a half, seeing museums that were as famous as the paintings inside them, cathedrals a thousand years old that still felt majestic and unique, and little bakeries and cafes that made me finally see what several places in the States were trying to imitate. The weather held, a mostly blue sky with tinges of clouds at the edges, and Aliq and Ori were lovely company, Marro having already gone with Colluvic to Anglia for the next round of tournaments.

I wasn't the only one with relationship problems going on, of course, and Aliq had told me that he was going to call his parents with the proposal he and Shona had worked out once we got to Anglia. He told me that a lot, actually. In the hotel room before we left on our tourist walk, during a quiet moment on the Métro, that night as we were lying in our beds, and again at the airport.

"I think it'll go okay," he said on the plane to Cobauch, the city north of Londinium where the first tuneup tournament was held. "They said they really want something to work out."

"I'm sure it'll be fine."

"I'm sorry I keep bothering you." He flexed his paws.

"It's fine." It really was. Thinking about his relationship made mine feel more distant. Here was a relationship where both of them wanted badly for it to work and were making compromises to help.

"She says she's willing to have fox cubs raised Jewish. She doesn't want to convert, but she doesn't mind if the cubs are. That's reasonable, right?"

"I think so, but I'm not Jewish."

"Right, right."

"I mean, it's not like she's telling you she doesn't want to get married at all."

He nodded. "Yeah. She's happy to have a Jewish wedding or whatever. It's not what's important." Aliq clasped his white paws together. "I can't wait to see her. It's been forever."

I grinned and shook my head. "You've Facetimed with her like every other day."

He gave me a look. "It's not the same and you know it. Anyway, you got to see, you know." He gestured. "Twice."

"True enough," I said, keeping my tone neutral.

"How's that going?"

"Fine." I flipped through my tablet, looking for a movie. "Want to go through what you were going to say to your parents again?"

He did, and I gave him what helpful advice I could think of, and then it turned out the flight was too short to watch movies so we talked tennis until we landed. On grass we were more comfortable, so we looked forward to getting back to playing our game.

Especially in doubles, I found that our practices were going better. "It's just the grass," I said, because I really liked the feel of the light carpet of slender grass blades over hard dirt. It felt natural to me, and even though I'd played more than half my matches on hard courts, maybe three quarters if I counted them up, I liked the grass courts from the moment I stepped onto them.

Aliq didn't think it was just grass that was responsible. "You're playing looser," he said as we were cleaning up after practice. "The last month or two you've been really tight, and I thought it was the clay, but maybe not."

"Maybe not," I agreed.

"I think you feel more confident because of how you did in Lutèce."

"That might be it," I said.

I was spared from further conversation by Aliq's phone buzzing with the news that Shona had arrived. "She's here!" he said, and hurried to throw his rackets into his bag. "Come on!"

I hurried to keep up as he half-jogged out of the courts and two blocks over, still lugging all our bags, to our hotel. The ligress jumped up from the couch where she'd been sitting and put her phone away, running over to hug the arctic fox.

They were a fun couple to watch. She stood almost my height, still a few inches taller than Aliq, and yet they fit together perfectly, him leaning his head on her shoulder as they wrapped their arms around each other. When they kissed, their smiles bubbled over into little contented murmurs that brought a wag to my tail.

"Hey, Rocky," Shona said when she and Aliq were done. We shook paws and she pulled me into a hug, and then I let them go off together to have a late lunch because I had to meet with Nashan that afternoon anyway.

We went through a rigorous practice on grass and then he showed me a lot of the little adjustments I'd have to make to play on grass, which could be nearly as fast as the hard court. Unlike the run of clay court tournaments, I'd already played a bunch of matches on grass and I knew the surface well. With my skill at returning, Nashan thought I might do well at following my return to the net, "but only if you get a good deep return and you see they're off balance," he said. "Someone like Braden Longacre is likely to take your best return and whip a forehand past you before you know what happened."

You don't know the half of it, I thought, but I nodded and went on with the lesson, pushing away thoughts of Braden.

He still hadn't texted me by that night, late, and I tried my best to stop hoping he would. He didn't have to, after all, and the whole point of me walking out on him was acknowledging that I was okay with that.

Fortunately, Aliq's situation sufficed to distract me. That evening around ten-thirty, he told me he was going to call his parents at eleven, which would be just before their dinnertime. Shona, keeping a tight grip on his paw, told him she'd wait up until the conversation was done.

"I can keep you company if you like," I said. "Aliq makes a lot of noise when he comes in so I won't be going to sleep anyway."

He didn't even laugh at that, just paced back and forth staring at his phone. Shona shook her head and then gave me a smile. "I'd like that."

We spent the next twenty minutes trying to calm Aliq down to little avail. He offered to leave the room to make the call, but Shona and I both insisted he stay in this familiar environment and that we'd go down to the lobby.

"Can we go to your sister's room?" she asked as we padded down the hallway.

"She's out with Marro tonight. I don't expect she'll be back."

"So her room's empty?"

I pushed the elevator button. "Probably, but I don't have a key."

"Ah well. Might've been more comfortable than the lobby."

"There's a VIP lounge or something on one of the top floors." The elevator arrived, going down, but as we traveled to the lobby, I checked my phone and found the lounge on the eighth floor, so I asked if Shona minded, and she didn't.

The lounge had some free soft drinks and a nice view of the big church and modest downtown of Cobauch. During certain hours they'd have appetizers and an open bar, but clearly not after eleven at night. So we got a couple bottles of water and sat by a window.

"Aliq told me about your compromise," I said. "I think it's great."

Shona nodded, looking out over the city. "Thanks. I really want this to work."

"I'm curious, though." She tilted her head toward me. "If religion doesn't matter that much to you, then why not just convert?"

She nodded and folded her paws together. Her arms really were striking, what I could see below her short sleeves: shadows of dark tan tiger stripes over tawny fur. The same stripes patterned her muzzle and down her shoulders. "I thought about it. That seems easy, doesn't it? But they take their religion very seriously. I don't think I would feel right pretending to do the same. If I'm not religious then I shouldn't be religious. It's not like wearing a dress once a month for photo ops where I can put it on and it doesn't matter how I feel about it."

"Okay." I rubbed my whiskers. "I guess I see that. If you convert without believing then it's almost like you're making fun of their religion."

"Kind of. I don't think it would be appropriate. Just because it doesn't mean anything to me doesn't mean that it's wrong that it means something to them." She snorted. "I think it's kind of fucked up that it means more than a loving, stable relationship."

"Right." I perked my ears forward. "But Aliq means something to you."

"Of course he does. I really think we could make something happen together." She paused and laughed nervously. "I haven't even told him this yet—I mean, I told him I want cubs, but the truth is I never really thought about it much. Until him. Does that make sense?"

"Sure." I smiled.

"I didn't want cubs just to have cubs, but...I want cubs with him. I feel like between the two of us we can get it right where our parents messed up."

"Makes sense." I thought about it a moment. "Don't be too hard on him with the religious stuff. People get locked into parts of their lives and they feel like they can only act a certain way or else they're...doomed, I guess."

"It depends where your priorities are," Shona said. "I get the faith and everything, but to say that your partner needs to be the same religion as you implies that yours is somehow better."

"Don't you have to believe that to follow it?"

"I guess, but you could acknowledge that in terms of dictating morality, they're all pretty much the same. One tells you to pray with these words in this way, one tells you to pray with some other words in some other way, but they all say, basically, be nice to people."

"I think every religion has to have some measure of not trusting other religions," I pointed out. "Otherwise their people could go join other religions without penalty."

"And that's the fucked up part." Shona leaned forward. "Because it makes the other religions seem bad and then it's a small step to thinking of them as less than people. That's what's going on with his parents, you know. They don't think of me as a real person unless I'm of their faith."

"Oh, I don't think—"

She cut me off with a wave. "Christianity isn't that bad. I don't think they ever said you can't marry non-Christians. I mean, don't get me wrong, they do some other bullshit stuff, but like if I wanted to marry you, I don't think your family would object."

"My Ma's dead," I said.

"Right, sorry." She folded her ears down. "But Ori would be fine with it."

"Of course. Ori's a sweetheart."

"And if Marro isn't Christian, you wouldn't care."

"I've no idea what he is," I admitted. "My best friend for a while was a Muslim. But a non-practicing one, or lapsed, or whatever."

She nodded. "Friendships are one thing. Families are another." She looked through her reflection out at the glass again. "Sorry. I'm just nervous they're going to turn down the compromise."

"They're good people," I said. "I'm sure it'll be fine."

But when Aliq texted us and we returned to the room, we could tell from the downcast muzzle and flattened ears that it was not fine, not at all. Shona went to hug him, and I stood. "If you want to be alone," I said, "I can go."

"No, no." He sat heavily on the bed. "You should hear this too, I guess. Then I won't have to tell it twice."

I could already guess how it had gone, but I let him tell it. "They, ah, they didn't like it." Shona put an arm around him. "They said...they said that if my wife wouldn't be part of the faith then she wouldn't be part of the family, and they couldn't live with that."

We waited, both of us looking at him. "I tried," he pleaded, grasping Shona's paw. "I told them how much you wanted to be part of the family, how we agreed on cubs and you said you loved me and I loved you and how important this was to me, and they said they understood but our faith and culture were more important than any one relationship or person."

When he said "loved," Shona's arm around him tightened. I was a little surprised, because I hadn't heard him use that word before. But I didn't say anything because it was so clearly true in that moment that I would have known anyway.

"So where are we?" Shona asked finally.

Aliq took in a breath and let it out. "They said that if I insist on continuing this relationship, I shouldn't come home again."

"What?" I yelped. "Seriously?"

He nodded. Shona lifted her arm from his shoulder. "We knew they might do that: make you choose between them and me. I understand you don't want this outcome, but you have to take it. You can't turn your back on your family."

"Well," Aliq said. "I don't know." He took Shona's paw. "They turned their back on me."

She widened her eyes and even I caught my breath. "Are you serious?" She searched his eyes. "You'd leave them for me?"

He swallowed. "I look at it like this. If I leave you, I'll never see you again. But if I stay with you...they're my family. They'll come around. Maybe not this year, or the next few years, but...they'll realize they made a mistake." She still didn't say anything, and he choked out a little laugh. "Besides, I like mixed doubles. What am I gonna do? Find another partner? Rocky here's gonna leave doubles behind in a year or two anyway."

Again, it wasn't the time to argue with him. In fact, I was starting to feel like it was not the time for me to be in the room with them at all.

"Take some time," Shona said. "You don't have to decide right away."

"Do you want this?" Aliq gripped her paw.

She squeezed back. "I want you to take some time. Because if you're going to resent me for taking you away from your family, then no, I don't want it."

"I'm making the choice," he said. "They're taking themselves away from us."

"Take a few days." She smiled and kissed his nose. "Let's play this tournament. After that you can make a decision."

"I know what I'm going to decide."

I stood up. "Hey," I said. "I'm gonna go because…I feel like it's time for me to go. But Aliq, you should listen to Shona. It's a big decision and you don't want to rush into it."

He nodded, and Shona smiled at me. "Thanks, Rocky," she said.

"Text me when I can come back," I said with a grin.

"Maybe you can spend the night with someone else," Aliq called as I left.

Maybe. Not likely, though. That bridge was maybe not burned, but certainly smoldering and unsafe to step onto. I took a walk through the town with a lot on my mind, both the intransigence of Aliq's parents and the similar inflexibility of Braden. And then the understanding of Shona and the love of Aliq. All of those things existed in my life, I thought, but in the wrong combination, like I'd tried to put one of those square wooden blocks into the wrong hole in the wooden board because the colors were supposed to match. Maybe some people were given better boards, where the colors and shapes matched up, and some people got defective ones.

That was a depressing thought, and I tried to leave it behind, looking instead at the buildings around me. This wasn't Londinium, but it didn't matter where you went in Anglia; the area was steeped in history. Our hotel was two blocks from the tennis center, and along those two blocks was a house that a plaque marked as the birthplace of Lord Alger Holdersham, the first badger to be appointed Prime Minister. I had no idea who that was, but he seemed to have had a nice house.

There were a fair number of badgers about, so maybe some of his descendants still lived here. Even though the residents of Cobauch probably weren't used to seeing a jackal, they barely gave me a second glance. With the tournament in town, international people flooded it for these two weeks. After that, they would all move south to Londinium for the Queens tournament and then Wimbledon.

I wasn't sure where I was headed. I wasn't dressed to practice, but I didn't want to drink and I didn't want to look for a gay bar. I

thought about it—for a year it had been a large part of my tournament life—but after the breakup with Braden and tonight watching
Aliq and Shona, I didn't want a night of anonymous sex. The physical pleasure would only have been followed by a night of remembering that that was my only option.

That only left the tennis center. I figured I could at least grab one
of the rackets in my locker and hit balls against a wall or practice my
serve, any kind of repetitive low-impact exercise. It wouldn't necessarily be useful in an "improve my tennis" way, but it might calm me
down and wear me out and it would take up some time.

As I entered the locker room, my ears picked up a repetitive
thunk, thunk, thunk, the sound of a tennis ball hitting a wall over
and over. Someone else had had my idea.

I padded out to the practice area and poked my nose around a
corner. There, standing in white shirt and shorts, a basket of tennis
balls beside him, Braden Longacre methodically hit ball after ball
directly into the same spot on the wall.

Chapter Thirty

I didn't go up to Braden, much as I wondered what had driven him to the tennis center. I walked quietly back through the locker room and then out into the street, where I followed the sounds of conversation to a pub that was still open. It seemed half filled with badgers, and even the non-badgers all knew each other, but I sat at the bar and asked for a club soda and nobody bothered me for the hour until Aliq texted that I could come back to the room.

That tournament was weird. I did well in singles, but Aliq's personal problems clearly affected his doubles play, and we lost our first match in an upset. "Sorry," he said after, as we were changing.

"It's been a tough year," I said. "This is just a tuneup."

"Go kill 'em in singles."

I promised to try, and indeed went out and won my next match. Nashan picked up on a few problems I was having and worked with me on them over the next two days. Only once did he remark that it felt like these problems stemmed from distraction. "Anything going on off the court?"

"Aliq's having some problems," I said. "I guess that's on my mind." I didn't tell him that I kept seeing the image of Braden hitting the ball against the wall.

That bothered me more than our breakup. Everything he'd done that night had been very much according to the Braden I knew. The brooding fox mechanically repeating an exercise was, too, but in a strange way. It meant that something was bothering him, something that had driven him out of his room to seek relief in physical exercise. Was it that he missed me? He knew where I was; he could find me to talk. If it wasn't me, then what else could it be?

Whatever it was, I reminded myself, it wasn't my problem anymore. Armed with that resolve, I promptly went out and lost my next match to a polecat who, to be fair to me, had his serve going much better than the film I had of him. I didn't seem to be able to get a racket on anything. There was a three-game stretch in the second set where I broke him twice, but he came back strong in the third and won.

After the match, after the press conference where I gave bland answers I was starting to know by heart, Nashan said, "Sure there isn't anything bothering you?"

"He was just playing over his rank," I said. "He's going to lose to Colluvic next round."

"There were a couple points where you looked like you lost focus. Down 30-15 at 2-1 in the first? Down 15-40 at 3-5?"

"30-15, he hit a great serve that pushed me back behind the baseline and then put it away crosscourt. What was I supposed to do with that?"

"You hesitated after your return. You should have come up a couple feet; that would've changed his decision. He might still have made that crosscourt but you'd have made it more difficult for him."

I remembered that point well and I knew I hadn't been thinking about Braden or Aliq. But if I were being honest, I'm not sure I was a hundred percent focused either. I should've moved up after that shot, knowing my opponent's tendencies and abilities. I didn't want to fight with Nashan, so I told him he was right and promised to bring 100% effort at Queens.

In the interest of avoiding Braden, I stayed away from the public areas for the rest of the tournament until Ori told me she needed pictures of me for my social media. So I dressed in my tennis whites and walked out and around the tennis center, one posing next to the club, one shaking paws with one of the security people, a badger who proved to be local to the town. We ran across another player I didn't know well and got a picture with him, and then Ori gave him my social media info and he gave her his.

"How is my social media doing?" I asked Ori.

"Oh, fine, fine." She scanned through the pictures she'd taken. "This is a nice one. I like your smile in it."

I changed tacks. "How's Marro?"

"He's great." She slid me a smile. "We're great. Just enjoying being together, and…" She flipped through her phone to find a picture of her and Marro in a rose garden. "There's this lovely garden not too far from here where…"

I checked her paw. "He proposed?"

"No, no." She laughed. "Marriage is far off for both of us. But we talked about staying together, and not dating other people, and seeing where this takes us. We're both traveling with our teams so we don't control our own schedules and until that happens we don't want to commit to anything big."

"That's nice," I said, although I thought that if you found someone you wanted to be exclusive with, you wouldn't mind making a commitment and trusting your relationship to see through the times you couldn't control. But maybe that was just my ache over what I'd lost.

Braden won that tuneup, though many of the top players were over at another tuneup in Deutscherbund. I saw the scores go up online but didn't go to the final or show up after for the ceremony. As much as I was trying not to let the situation bother me, I didn't want to see him embrace Ellen again.

For the Queens tournament we took a train back down to Londinium, which was a fun experience. Almost all the top players were entered in this tournament (Tempest was nursing an injury and still hoped to play Wimbledon, but withdrew from Queens), so the suburb of Londinium was much more crowded with tennis players than Cobauch had been.

The press, too, in this run-up to Wimbledon, buzzed around like flies, and we could hardly go around the tennis complex without phones being held up and pointed at us. I'd been to majors before, so it must have been my higher ranking that attracted so much attention.

"Plus," Aliq pointed out, "you're a jackal. Like, I can go out in street clothes and people don't automatically think, there's that arctic fox doubles player. There's half a dozen arctics on the tour and a bunch that just live here. Emigrating from Kanata is easy."

"Aren't there jackals here?"

"Not a lot of six-foot-tall ones hanging around the tennis complex."

"Fair enough." And of course, there weren't many six-foot-tall cross foxes, either.

Where Cobauch had been sleepy and full of badgers, Londinium bustled with all different species and never seemed to rest, night or day. I couldn't escape photographers in the tennis complex, but when I slipped outside, I was only bothered once or twice. I liked the city for a day or two, but I think living there all the time would exhaust me.

Three weeks on, I had not had a word from Braden. This, of course, was what I would expect whatever his state of mind. He wasn't the kind to make a snap decision and come back; he wanted time to think it over, to figure out what the best course was, and maybe he'd decided he wanted Wimbledon behind him before he made a decision. That hope, faint though it was, remained constantly under fire from the rest of my mind telling me that if Braden wanted me back, he would have told me so a long time ago.

Aliq and I had spent the last week in Cobauch practicing as hard as we ever had, working on our communication and on shutting out "outside distractions," which meant one thing for him and two things for me, but we both managed. And in Queens, it felt like our practice paid off. Granted, we were matched up against the number 58 team in the world, so we were expected to win, but we won in convincing fashion. And then I went out and won the singles match I was supposed to win, so we seemed to be on track again.

Marro had recommended a pub to Ori so the four of us went out there that night to relax, because we only had practice the following day. It was nice to see Marro and Ori being a little more physical together, leaning their shoulders against each other, playing with each other's fingers. I can't speak for Aliq, but I enjoyed their closeness without thinking of what was missing from my own life.

We had a good day of practice and went into our next match optimistic. But we were matched against the twelfth ranked doubles team in the world, and though we played well, they were better and beat us in three sets.

Nashan made sure to cheer us up after the match. "This wasn't a loss like in Cobauch," he said. "You guys played great, focused and communicated well. There are a lot of things we can work on but we won't be covering old ground again."

So we felt good about that, at least. I went out and won my singles match, getting one away from the round of sixteen. I avoided a lot of the places the players went so that I wouldn't run into Braden and make things awkward, but that also meant I wasn't seeing a lot of my other friends on the tour.

A few people commented on it but I passed it off. Then after my win, just after I talked to reporters, I saw Colluvic, who'd also just played. Impulsively, I went over to him and said hi.

"Ho," he said. "So Marro says things are good with your sister."

"They seem very happy."

He hadn't put his shirt on yet and now he stretched, showing off the muscles in his shoulders and upper arms. "And what about you? I thought we'd hang out in Londinium again but I've barely seen you."

"I didn't do well in Cobauch," I said. "I'm practicing a lot."

"Uh huh. Early in the morning, out on the farthest court where the qualifiers practice?"

"I practiced on the main practice courts too."

He grinned. "All right, all right. Let me know when you're not feeling so antisocial."

I hefted my bag over my shoulder. "How about tonight?"

The big wolf's grin got bigger. "Sounds great."

We settled on a pub called The Bleating Ram. Because it was me and Colluvic, two distinctive players, we had a small cluster of reporters with phones follow us to the pub. Two or three boldly followed us in, whereupon a large otter hurried over from a table and stood with paws on hips in front of them. "Good folk," he boomed, "you're welcome to eat at the Ram, but the phones stay in your pockets. This is a place for folk to enjoy an ale and a bite in peace without worrying about having their photo snapped."

He glared at them, and the whole little pack shrank back and then hurried out onto the sidewalk. The otter turned to us and shook his head. "There's always two or three, ey?"

Colluvic laughed. "Always. Thanks, sir."

The otter touched one ear in acknowledgment, as if tipping a cap. "Ay, hope you'll remember the Ram as a good quiet place. Sit wherever you like."

We chose a place out of sight of the front windows anyway, more out of habit than because we were specifically worried about that group of reporters. For a while we talked about the tour and the Queens tournament, and it was nice to just talk tennis without any personal drama involved and without always wondering what lesson I'd have to take from it.

He asked about Ori and I asked about Marro (that didn't count as personal drama because everything was going well) and then, as we were finishing up our meal, I couldn't help myself. "Hey," I asked, "you hear much from Braden these days?"

The big wolf's ears perked up. "Not very much. Less than you. I invited him to the townhouse again after Wimbledon but he has not even answered." His whiskers lifted in a smile. "I would think you would hear more from him."

"Oh, I mean, we hang out, but…no, he's been quiet with me too, that's why I asked."

"I know you practice together. I thought you had become great friends and I even gave myself credit for this. I brought you together last year!" The smile became a laugh as he brought his two large paws together softly. "But some problems I suppose one must address alone."

I nodded. "I guess so."

All in all, it was a very pleasant dinner, and when we parted, Colluvic said, "We should do this more than once a year," so I guess he thought so too. I agreed, shook his paw, and went back to my hotel.

I don't know what I'd been hoping for, asking him about Braden. Maybe Braden would have said something to him about being stressed. Really I wanted any news about him, and the fact that I had to go around asking people who weren't even necessarily his friends depressed me.

So I threw myself into practice the next day, and the day after that I won my match, and I won one more time, getting to the quarterfinals. There I met Dubois, who dispatched me in four sets. The one I won from him, though, was really valuable. Nashan and I dissected it on film over the next few days, looking at where I'd actually managed to upset his game, get him off balance. "You couldn't keep it going in the fourth," he said, "but your instincts were good. Next time you meet him, you've got a good chance, I'd say."

I kept up my practice and film study for the rest of the tournament, and I hadn't intended to go to the final, where Braden was meeting Colluvic. But Marro had to go, so Ori went, and still I wasn't going to go until I ran into Colluvic on the practice court and he said, "Hey, Rocky! You're coming to the final, right?"

"Oh, Ori's going, I know, but…"

He slapped a paw to my shoulder. "Come on! Your two favorite players fighting for the title! You must come."

The joke startled a laugh out of me. "Two favorite? Where do you get that from?"

"Your doubles partner does not play singles, you practice with Braden, you practice with me. Who else on the tour?"

"That's fair."

"Besides, I have many seats in my box. You can sit with Ori and Marro."

"All right, all right, I'll go."

He pointed a finger at me like a gun. "It will be worth it to see Braden lose for the third time this year."

Braden did nothing of the sort, of course. Colluvic took him to three, but that was only because halfway through the second set Braden seemed to lose focus and drive for about two games. He recovered quickly and then there was no doubt who the better player was.

We were seated not too far from Braden's box. I tried not to look over there, but at the end of the match Ori elbowed me and pointed that way. "I'm fine," I mouthed at her, but she elbowed me again and shook her head insistently, so I glanced at the box. Red foxes, Braden's coach, and some of his team. I leaned back.

Ori turned to say something to Marro and then elbowed me again. "What?" I hissed.

"Look who's not there," she said softly.

I sighed and leaned forward again to check out the box. For a moment I didn't understand what she meant, and then... "Oh," I said.

Ellen wasn't in the box. But that didn't mean anything. She could have gone to the bathroom. She could be out on one of her trips. This was a tuneup, after all, not a major. There wasn't a big ceremony when Braden won, but he did make a speech, and he didn't mention Ellen at all in it.

All right, I thought, but maybe he'd only mention her if she were in the stadium? Strange, but could be a Braden thing. Or maybe he'd decided to dump her and me both and just go on himself. Honestly, that might be the most Braden thing of all.

So when people started getting up, I walked over toward his box to see if I could spot Ellen. Maybe I'd just missed her. I didn't think I had, though. There were a lot of red foxes in that box, but I hadn't recognized any of them as Ellen.

I was about to turn back to Ori when an older vixen took a step toward me. "Excuse me," she said. "You're not Rocky N'Guwe by chance?"

"I am." I took her proffered paw and put on my celebrity smile. "It's a pleasure to meet you."

"I'm Alicia Longacre. Braden's mother. I watched him play you once or twice and I have a good memory for fur patterns." She touched her muzzle and laughed. "And there aren't many jackals wandering around here in the boxes. You're here with Ljubo?"

"Yes." I pointed back to Ori. "My sister is dating his social media person, so he invited me...anyway, it's quite impressive, what your son is doing."

"Isn't it?" She beamed. "We never thought, when he took up tennis, you know, that he'd be this good at it."

I thought that was odd; Ma had always said she knew I had the potential to be great. Wasn't that a parent's job? But I said, "Anyone who watched his game knew it was possible. He's got such focus and athletic ability."

"He's mentioned you, you know." She favored me with a bright smile. "He says you helped his game."

This startled me. "When, a year ago?"

"A few months ago. We asked him about his winning streak and he said that his coach has been helping him break down his opponents, but you helped him play with more energy and, oh, how did he say it? Bertrand."

An older male fox who'd been standing behind her talking to someone else turned. Alicia said, "What did Braden say about how that jackal helped him?"

"Made the game more fun." Bertrand Longacre looked as though he hadn't had fun in a very long time and in fact probably thought it should be strictly regulated. "Is this that jackal?"

"Yes, this is Rocky N'Guwe."

I started to hold my paw out, but Bertrand made no move to extend his, so I pulled mine back. "Well," the older fox said, "'fun' didn't get you to the finals here, did it?"

"I made it to the quarterfinals," I said.

"I believe we saw a bit of your match." Alicia's lie of politeness was obvious even to me. "Well, good luck at Wimbledon. After Braden, of course."

"Of course," I said, and then, heart pounding, had to leap at the chance to ask the question I'd been kicking around in my head the entire conversation. "Say, I hoped to say hello to Ellen. Do you know where she is?"

Alicia looked from side to side and then leaned in, so close her whiskers almost brushed mine. "I shouldn't say anything," she whispered, "but she's out shopping. She and Braden are going to announce their engagement next week."

Chapter Thirty-One

That's great," I said. "Congratulations to them."

And then I made my excuses and I walked back to Ori and Marro. Ori asked who I'd talked to and I said, "Just a couple people at Braden's box. I checked to see if Ellen was there."

"Was she?"

"No."

Ori smiled and patted my paw. "So that's good, right?"

"Yeah."

I didn't say a whole lot as we left the tennis arena. Ori and Marro were very involved in each other and I'm not sure they noticed me being quiet. I was thinking through stuff, though, and trying to talk myself into the fact that in a way, it was better that Braden was getting engaged. He'd made his choice and I could stop thinking about it, stop asking his friends and family about him, and move on with my own life.

And all that was left for me to move on to right now was tennis. So I would go down to Wimbledon, and play my singles, and play my doubles with Aliq, and we'd do the best we could. And who knew? Maybe I'd meet another gay tennis player while I was there.

* * *

Last time we'd stayed in a cheap Londinium hotel that was a 40-minute ride to the Tennis Centre. But this time, Lochen surprised us. He'd rented out a little bungalow for me and my team: three bedrooms, only one bath, but our own kitchen. Ori, delighted, immediately went out to get groceries and planned out our meals, and Nashan went with her to make sure they conformed to his dietary regimen for us.

The rooms were smaller and not as luxurious as the hotel rooms we'd grown used to, but Aliq and I liked the little house the moment we stepped inside. Paintings of landscapes filled the walls, and the owners had placed little vases all around with flowers that filled the air with their fragrance. Wooden beams of the cottage's roof showed through the plaster, and the hardwood floor had enough fuzzy rugs for us to walk comfortably around the place, except in the kitchen, where we walked over polished white tile with blue designs of flowers and teapots.

The flowers didn't quite cover the scent of the foxes who owned the place, but that scent reassured me: the upholstery was claw-guarded and scent-guarded, and I didn't worry about leaving scent in someone else's bed.

The inside was only part of the appeal. From the windows we could see rows of similar cottages, and though some glass towers rose in the distance, they were faint enough to be nicely remote. I could see why someone would want to live here; the whole area had the feel of a small village, so much so that it was hard to believe we were so close to Londinium proper. Our bedroom window looked out over the Tennis Centre and it felt right to me to be living so close to it. This felt different from a hotel; it felt like Aliq's house, only right over there was the world where I belonged. I was sorry to think that I would have to leave it in two weeks.

"Is this cheaper than a hotel?" I asked Nashan.

"No," he said, "but Lochen and I both thought that being closer to the Centre would benefit you. No long commute in the morning like we had in Lutèce."

"Sounds better. And this is more relaxing."

"Right." He clapped me on the shoulder. "So go one more round and earn a bit more money."

Whether it was the new setting or the reduced commute to the matches, I had little trouble setting aside my troubles with Braden and devoting those couple weeks to tennis. Aliq seemed similarly focused, though we didn't talk about it until after our first-round doubles match, which we won.

He'd already won a mixed doubles match with Shona, and I asked him how things were going. "It's tough," he admitted. "I miss my parents. We used to talk and I still get the urge to call them when something happens. But Shona makes it easier and we're communicating really well on the court too."

"Good. You seem a lot..." I considered. "Less stressed."

He nodded. "It's not the way I would've wanted it resolved, but you know...at least it is resolved."

"Yeah," I said. "I know what you mean."

Wimbledon for me has always had a lot more media around it than the other tournaments. I know Anglia is famous for its tabloid papers, but it wasn't just them. Everyone, it seemed, wanted an excuse to come to Wimbledon, so we had bloggers from all over the world camped out—some literally—around the tennis area. I recognized Streaks, the Cape Fox, and went over to say hi.

He perked up when he saw me and asked how I'd been. "Now you're in the twenties, I didn't think I'd get to talk to you," he said. "I really appreciate you coming over."

"You wrote some nice things a year or so ago," I said, hoping that was the right time frame. "Anytime you want an interview, you're always welcome to it."

"That's so nice." He beamed at me, and a couple other bloggers behind him sidled up, trying to get in on the exclusive it looked like I was about to give.

"Not much going on right now," I said. "I'm excited to be back at Wimbledon and to show people what I can do here."

"Of course," he said. "You're still playing both singles and doubles?"

"Still. Aliq and I have a good rapport and while we're doing well, I don't see any reason to quit."

"Makes sense, makes sense." He jotted down some notes. "How about your charity back in Lunda?"

I talked a little about the charity and then about the situation in Lunda: much the same as ever. The war raged on with little help for the refugees, who fled to Lundara and crowded it there. Ori and

I donated to hospitals and to the resettlement foundations, but both were woefully understaffed anyway.

With my States citizenship, I felt like I belonged to two families, and more and more often, my Lundan heritage was the family that got left behind. So it was nice to talk about them again and I felt as I did that I was reconnecting with that part of me.

And then as we were parting, Streaks put his notebook away and said casually, "You're friends with Braden Longacre, right?"

"Oh, uh, yeah, we practice together sometimes." Just like that, I was back in my current life.

"Any chance you can confirm a rumor for me?"

"Maybe, though I haven't actually seen him in a while."

He nodded. "You haven't looked at the papers, I guess?" When I shook my head, he went on. "I guess his girlfriend wasn't at the Queens final, but she is here in Londinium, and Prasad Gupta wrote that they're getting engaged. You know anything about that?"

"Yeah," I said. "I heard the same thing."

I extracted myself from that conversation and went back to my afternoon practice. It looked like I wasn't going to be able to leave Braden behind no matter what, not as long as he and I were going to be playing tennis. I'd just have to get good enough to play him on the court.

At Wimbledon, if we were going to meet it would be in the semifinals. All right, then, I thought, I'll get to the semifinals.

First I had to win my second-round match, which was against a young okapi who wasn't much of a challenge, to be honest. I was a step faster than him everywhere on the court, and afterwards I said something nice to him about being at the beginning of his career and he thanked me for it and we both knew he wasn't going to get much farther than he already had. You can work out and improve your reaction time and quickness, but he'd been a pro longer than I had and if he wasn't improving his conditioning and athleticism by now, he probably wouldn't be.

We won our next doubles match as well; it seemed that whatever had improved between Aliq and Shona was helping him across the board. And despite that little hiccup with Streaks bringing up

Braden, I managed to keep my mind wholly on tennis through to the fourth round of singles.

Before I played that match, though, Aliq and I had to play Tasman and Lowry. They were five spots ahead of us in the rankings and had been playing really well of late, so we spent a lot of time prepping with Nashan. He told us we could beat them, and going out for the match, we believed we could too.

But that first set they played lights out. We both had our serves broken and though we broke back once, it wasn't enough. We sat there after the first set with our heads down and then Aliq said, "You know, I'll shade farther over to the sideline on your serve to Tasman. He's been going for that passing shot a lot more and I just wasn't ready. And if we play back on Lowry's serve, we should be able to handle it better if whoever's at the net is ready to jump on their return."

"That's all?" I asked with a grin. "Just those couple things?"

He matched my grin. "And play our best."

"Oh, okay. That too."

And the funny thing was, maybe it was his confidence or maybe it was his tactics, but damned if we didn't break Lowry's serve and Tasman's that second set and then again in the third. They fought hard in the fourth and won in a tiebreak, but in the fifth set we regrouped and it looked like Lowry was getting tired, and we won 6-3.

Aliq hugged me hard after we won, and then we went and shook paws with the wolf and fennec. "Good job, guys," they said. "Go get 'em."

* * *

My fourth round singles match was against Daryavic, and the maned wolf was playing terrific thus far in the tournament—but so was I. If I beat him, I'd only have to win a quarterfinal against someone worse (probably a squirrel named Lancaster, an Anglian who was having a great home tournament run, but their match was after mine so I wouldn't be sure) and then I'd have a shot at Braden in the semifinals.

But Daryavic was first. He played great defense, long and rangy and able to cover the court well, so Nashan had me practice net play, pushing him far back or to the side where I could negate his defense. It wasn't easy because his length and speed meant he recovered quickly; I watched film of someone coming to net against him in the second round and he demolished them with passing shots. So I'd have to hit better establishing shots and come to net later and quicker, give him less time to react.

Easier planned than executed, but Nashan and I felt confident that I could give him a good run, if not beat him outright. "Let's face it," Nashan said. "At this point there's only one player in the world I'd say you don't have a chance at beating, and we all know who that is. The chance may not be over fifty percent here, but look what happened last time. Maybe this time he turns his ankle and you take advantage of that."

"I'd rather beat him outright."

"Of course, but lucky breaks are part of the game." He'd taped off alleys at the edges of the court to force me to think about placing shots there, and now he pointed at them. "Your skill puts balls here. That's what you can control. The things that happen that are out of your control, you've got to use them when they help you and ignore them when they can't."

Good advice in general, I thought, seeing a cross fox rather than a red across from me. I went back to firing topspin forehands at the corners and working on my net approach timing.

The evening before the match, I did an interview with a hedgehog from a Londinium paper that took over an hour. They asked me about my childhood in more depth than anyone had, and about my time at Palm Gables. It was only a few questions into that that I realized they were talking about Coach Murphy and Frio and the betting scandal. I guess Coach Murphy ended up retiring when Frio was arrested, which I vaguely remembered, but the whole thing was so long ago—not just my time at the school but also the scandal—that I didn't have anything to tell them about it. I was pretty sure I wasn't supposed to talk about my work with the TIU, but they'd sniffed out something about it; they kept asking whether I'd done anything with

Coach Frio or if there were any connection to bringing my sister over from Lunda.

I gave them the abbreviated version of my story, how Ori was promised to a village chief but I wanted a better life for her. Usually that sent them off on a tangent about the opportunities in the West and so on, but this time they went in an unexpected direction. "What about you?" the hedgehog asked, leaning forward. "Anyone special in your life?"

I was used to this question, too. "I'm just focusing on tennis right now."

He met my eyes with what looked like a bit of a smile. "Really."

"Really."

"Because there are rumors linking you to someone on the tour."

My ears flicked back despite all my practice at media interviews. I did my best to keep my voice calm. "And who would that be?"

The hedgehog sat back in his chair. "You've been seen out to eat with him, you've practiced with him, even stayed at his place. People are wondering what your relationship is, you two confirmed bachelors."

Two confirmed...wait. I tilted my head slightly, relaxing. "Me and...?"

The hedgehog smirked as though I were playing dumb. "Ljubo Colluvic."

Here my media training did me good. I didn't laugh, just shook my head. "Ljubo and I are friends, that's all. And neither of us is gay."

"That's not what my sources say." The hedgehog consulted his notes. "Your sister is dating his social media director."

"Yes. That doesn't mean he and I are dating."

Logic didn't rattle him. "You and he were seen going into a hotel together in Lutèce."

"I'm sure we were. We were staying in the same group of hotels." Honestly, I didn't even remember a time when I'd seen Colluvic outside the locker room at the Gallic, though I knew he'd been around. "Is that all you wanted to ask me?"

"Uh...look, if you do end up sleeping with him, you'll let me know, won't you?"

I rolled my eyes and got up. "Of course."

The interview rattled me a little bit. I knew people were watching me, but I'd always thought that Braden's level of paranoia was unnecessary. Now I realized how critical it was. People were taking pictures of who I went into hotel rooms with? Noting when I went out to dinner? It was impressive that Braden and I hadn't been spotted together before now.

I made sure to leave that worry behind for my fourth-round match. After all, on the court, I knew people were watching me.

From the beginning, I knew this wouldn't be a repeat of our previous match. I didn't turn my ankle, for one thing, and for another, my film study and experience had paid off. I remembered his tendencies and anticipated his movement better this time. My net approaches didn't always work, but they worked often enough that he started taking more chances with his shots, hitting deeper to keep me pinned to the baseline. After ten games we were at 5-5 and neither of us had earned a break point yet.

Daryavic served at 0-15 after I'd won a rally, a good serve that took me out wide, but perhaps not as far as he'd hoped; being a lefty let me get a good angle on the return. He got to it, but he was clearly off balance and so I ran to the net. He tried a passing shot but went too low and hit the net, and I had a love-30 advantage.

He got back one of those points with an ace, but on the ad court he again had problems with his serve, and I smacked a clean return back to draw an error for 15-40. He was worried, or at least he took an extra bounce or two to think about his next serve before delivering a great one down the T. I got a racket on it but he controlled the point and put it away two exchanges later.

On my last break point, though, his first serve went into the net, and when the second one came, I aimed for one of the corners away from him. He anticipated that shot, long legs getting him in position, so I changed my mind about going to net and stayed back to get a better look at his return. He hit it cross-court and re-established himself quickly in the court, so I settled in for a baseline rally and waited for an opening.

We traded shots, me with a little more control of the point, and though Daryavic tried to run me around the court, my defense was up to the challenge. I moved him toward the deuce court sideline, and he saw that I was doing it and tried to creep back toward the center with some strong forehands that didn't give me a lot to work with.

And then I caught him off balance, and his return had a little less zip on it, and I saw my chance. He was already racing toward the opposite corner, knowing he'd hit a weak shot, and in that split second I saw that he'd get to any approach shot I tried. So I went to the drop. I sliced it cleanly back to the deuce court he'd just run away from, lifting it centimeters over the net and down onto his side.

To his credit, he spun and raced back for it, giving me a tense moment, but his racket came up just short. I had the break and went on to win the first set 7-5 after an easy service hold.

Confidence filled me during the break, and Nashan pumped his fist encouragingly from his coach's box. The crowd had woken to the possibility of an upset and cheered heartily. I could do this.

In the second set, I kept up my momentum, and the maned wolf matched me. He broke my serve when I tried to hit a corner and missed; I broke back when he double-faulted trying for too much on a second serve. We went to a tiebreak, where he played excellently and got a point on my serve first, enough to give him the 7-6 (7-5) win in the second set.

I didn't go into the break daunted. I knew I could play with him; it felt like this match was going to go all five sets. The crowd knew it too: they cheered and roared during every break in play.

In fact, maybe the tiebreak affected me a little in the third set. I hit a slump in the third game and spent a few minutes doubting myself, enough to lose a service break and, later, the set. But I came back in the fourth, determined to make a good showing, and my net play won me the set. Daryavic looked tired by the end of it, and I thought the fifth would be easy.

We had a great point that later went viral when Ori posted the clip to my Instagram: I painted the corner and came to net, he had the presence of mind to lob it over me, I jumped for a smash but he was in position and got it somehow back with a good enough shot that I had to scramble to flick it back down the line and he barely got to it, returned it to the net where I was waiting to smash it, but he was deep enough and my smash weak enough that he got to it and returned it, dropping a lob on my baseline, and then it was his turn to come to net but I rifled a passing shot out of desperation and it just caught the sideline for my point.

I won the spectacular point but came up short on several of the ordinary ones. The maned wolf was #3 in the world for a reason. He didn't give up on a single point during that set, and now that we'd gotten to five sets, much of the crowd seemed to be back on his side. I tried everything, but he'd learned my play a little better than I'd learned his, and I ended up losing the set 6-3 and with it the match.

At net, he embraced me. "Wow," he said. "That was great."

I hated losing, but I couldn't deny it had been great tennis. "Can we just play every tournament?" I asked. "That was fun."

"Yeah." He laughed and patted my shoulder. "Hey, if you've got any tips for Braden, let me know."

"Oh," I said as we walked toward the chair umpire, "If you get there, I think I can come up with a couple."

Losing always sucks, but a loss like that to a good guy like Daryavic stung less than usual. I'd have loved to make the quarter-finals, but the draw and upsets hadn't worked in my favor this time. Still, I'd played well enough that I felt like I'd be hanging around the quarterfinals of majors for a while to come.

Also helping was winning our fourth-round doubles match, and then our quarterfinal match to put Aliq and I in the semifinals. He and Shona had made it to the fourth round in mixed doubles and then lost, so he was having a great tournament all in all. I never brought up his parents, and most of the time he didn't talk about them either, but every now and then when he was sitting quietly I'd see his ears go back and I figured I knew what he was thinking.

For as much as Nashan hadn't been excited about my continuing with doubles, he threw himself into coaching me and Aliq through our run. Especially when I didn't have any more singles to play, he ran us through film of our opponents, watched our communication, and even made Ori come and play alongside him against us for our practices.

The semifinals did not feel as loud or crowded as my fourth-round singles match; doubles is less popular and most people couldn't name the top doubles team in the world at any given time. We could: Echo and Sirber, an Ozzie grey fox and a Brazilian zorro. They'd won two of the last five majors and been to four of the last five finals, and intended to beat us in the semis here to make it five of six. They played a fast, sure game, but most of their success was because they rarely made bad decisions on their shots. Both of them had a fantastic sense of when to go for a shot, and they almost always won the point when they did.

Nashan thought that we could play with them if we adopted the same philosophy. They'd lost matches to opponents who'd been patient; they didn't get frustrated easily but sometimes they did, and a crack here and there could make the difference in a match. So we tried to rein in our instinct to go for the winner, only taking it when it was certain. This was easier for Aliq than for me, especially coming off my match with Daryavic, but we had to try and see if it would work.

In the first set our strategy seemed to be paying off. We played conservatively and so did they, and a couple times we thought we had an advantage. Certainly we were playing right there with the best doubles team in the world, but at the end of it they came away with a 6-4 win.

Aliq and I sat on the sidelines gulping down the drinks Nashan had mixed for us. "What do you think?" he asked. "Keep going like this?"

"Nashan would say to stay the course. Maybe in the next set the breaks will go our way." But of course, the fact that he'd asked meant that he was thinking the same thing I was.

"I feel like we'd be doing better if we played our game. I defend, you attack. Play more like your singles game."

"You want to go back to that this set? See how it goes?"

He looked up at the stands. Even though this wasn't as popular as singles, banners flew (some Ozzie flags for Echo, Brazilian for Sirber, and States flags for us) and cheers rose every few minutes, and the noise only died away when the chair umpire said, "Quiet, please."

"I dunno," he said finally. "We're doing well. Maybe next set we'll get to them, like you said."

I finished my drink. "We've got five sets," I said. "Why not try for one? If it doesn't work, we can switch it up."

"It's the semis."

"Yeah." I flashed him a grin. "So let's play our game."

We did. To our delight, the change in our style caught them off guard. They'd adjusted to our play, so when I started forcing shots and taking more chances, trusting Aliq to cover the court when I had to lunge a bit far afield, our opponents seemed rattled. We took a break early on and then held on through the set to win the second.

In the third, though, they came back strong. Clearly they'd scouted us and were prepared for that style of play; they more often took chances when I was trying to poach. It didn't help that more of my shots seemed to miss in the third, whether because I was more excited or because they were covering the net better or just random chance. Sometimes that happens.

So there we sat, Aliq and I, on the sidelines between the third and fourth sets. "What now?" he asked. "No more room to mess up."

"What feels right?" I asked.

"Honestly? I really enjoyed the last two sets. I know they play fast and we maybe can't match their energy but that first set was draining."

"Yeah. I think we should play our game. They want to play conservative? Let's let them."

He grinned. "Nashan's gonna be pissed. 'Why did you hire a coach if you won't listen to me?'"

"He's already pissed. Look at him."

We both looked up toward our coach, who when he saw us made a gesture with his paw that we knew meant "tone it down." We smiled back at him without acknowledging it, because we could get in trouble for that (coaching from the stands is illegal), and he rolled his eyes and went back to talking to Ori.

So we went out in the fourth and relaxed, and I went for passing shots and cross-court shots that aren't as effective in doubles as they are in singles, and we had a lot of fun playing. What's more, we held our serve and went to a tiebreak, and in the tiebreak I hit a crazy backhand that somehow dropped into the corner just out of reach of Echo's racket, and we won the tiebreak and the fourth set.

And now the crowd was into it, cheering us on as we took our break between sets. We looked at Nashan briefly, but he'd given up any pretense of telling us what we should be doing and looked like any other spectator in the stands. So we went back out in the fifth and played our game.

Echo's backhand wasn't strong, and they knew they could hide that in a doubles match, but over four sets I'd figured out a few ways to poke at it. In the fifth, whenever I had a chance, I made him hit that backhand, and more often than not that ended in something good for us. It gave us a break point in the fourth game, and another one in the eighth game, both of which we converted. Their steady play wore us down somewhat, and they broke Aliq once, but it didn't matter when I served for the match in the ninth game and won.

Aliq jumped into my arms and almost knocked me over, both of us laughing, and we hugged again after I set him down, then we had to hurry to the net to shake the paws of the foxes. Both of them smiled—restrained, sure, because they'd just lost a semifinal, but sincere—and told us how great the match had been. "Can't play five sets anywhere else anymore," Sirber said.

"In three, we'da had ya for sure," Echo said.

We laughed. "More chances for us to get lucky," I told them.

"Nah," the Ozzie fox said. "You guys play great. Good luck on Saturday."

As it turned out, Nashan greeted us after the match outside the locker room with proud hugs while also saying, "You guys are paying me to coach, so why don't you listen to me?"

"We won the match," I reminded him.

"I know." His ears were up and he was clearly excited but trying to look serious. "If you'd stuck to our strategy, maybe you'd have won in four."

"We lost the first set," Aliq said. "We talked about it and we decided to try playing our game. It worked."

"It did." Nashan shook his head.

Ori, standing next to him, hugged me. "You should listen to him," she said, "but also, you played great."

"I know," I told her.

"All right, all right." Nashan herded us toward the media room. "Interviews, then back home, unwind, and film for Saturday."

So we did the interviews, which also weren't as numerous as when I'd lost my fourth-round singles match. People really cared more about singles than doubles. If I'd gotten to the singles final, I'd be bombarded with media requests and hounded by reporters—at least, that happened to Braden. Maybe it was only when you'd been there for a while.

That evening, Daryavic texted me, which was a bit of a surprise. He wanted to meet at a practice court, but at night so people would be less likely to see us together. This seemed a little strange until he said he wanted to ask me about Braden.

What did I still owe Braden from our friendship? Could I tell another player anything that would help, and if I could, should I? Daryavic was a nice guy and had given me advice, and I wanted to keep this friendship going, but on the other paw, would I be betraying Braden? Were we still friends, if not lovers?

The situation had me confused, but I went anyway, deciding that I'd give Daryavic only a few nebulous hints, things anyone could find out from scouting Braden: that he was very good and your best shot was to be aggressive and give him something unexpected to throw him off balance. "Great," he said. "How do I do that?"

I laughed. "If I knew that, I'd be ranked higher than twenty."

He grinned. "Fair enough. You feel like hitting the ball some?"

I wasn't in tennis gear specifically, but I was in shorts because the days were hot and the nights warm, so I agreed to run around a court hitting with him for a bit. It was fun and relaxing, and he didn't bug me about Braden anymore.

Of course, none of that did any good. He lost in the semifinals and Braden looked to be on a mission. I checked the cross fox's box during the match, and though his parents were there the whole time, Ellen didn't show up at all.

* * *

I was a little worried that Daryavic would be mad at me for not giving him good advice about Braden, but he actually texted me that evening to ask if I'd seen the match and if I wanted to join him and a bunch of guys for drinks. I told him I had a match to play the next day and he took a little while to answer and then said, *Oh right! gl,* with a four-leaf clover emoji. I asked if Saturday night would be okay and he said sure.

"If I give you advice," Nashan asked Saturday morning before our match—Wimbledon final!—"will you actually listen to it or just do your own thing?"

"That depends," Aliq said with a grin at me. "Is the advice to do our own thing?"

The red fox rolled his eyes. "Keep communicating."

"We know that," I put in.

"These guys aren't as fast but they're great at defense and at extending points. Anytime you can hit to Gupta's forehand, do it, but watch out for his backhand. Moravian is more balanced but attack his serve."

"Right, got it."

"And most of all." He smiled down at us. "Go out there and have fun. It's just another match."

But of course it wasn't. It was a final at Wimbledon, and even though everyone was waiting for Braden's singles final the next day, the arena was still packed and people were excited. Gupta and Moravian weren't strangers to this place; they'd won a doubles title here two years ago. For me and Aliq, as much as we'd thought we were okay with the pressure, cracks showed in our game from the first set. We miscommunicated on one shot, both going for it so that we were out of position for their next shot and lost the point. Both of us netted what should have been easy forehand volleys, and after that we second-guessed ourselves too much. We fought well after losing the first set, and with the best of five format we had a slightly better chance—we won the third set but dropped the fourth and lost the match.

We still made a tidy pile of money (amusingly, only a bit more than I made for my fourth-round exit in singles) and felt much more confident about playing in major finals after we'd exited. We did a lot of press afterwards, where I had to answer questions about my singles vs. doubles career, and was it hard to switch between the two, and was I going to keep playing both, and so on. I didn't worry about interviews, as long as they weren't going to ask me about whether I was sleeping with Colluvic, and all the people at the press conference, though they were eager to have their questions heard and answered, were still very polite when asking them.

When they delved into the strategy questions, some of them asked what the difference had been between this match and our semi-final win, and I didn't want to say that in the last game we hadn't listened to our coach and in this one we had, because honestly it wasn't Nashan's fault. Sometimes the best advice isn't enough, and sometimes it's not the only way to win. On average, though, it's usually best to follow your coach's advice. Except, I guess, when you're in the moment and you feel the match going a certain way. Or maybe that's when you most need to follow it. I don't know.

I was still puzzling over that one when we had time to sit down with Nashan after the match. We sat around the small table in our hotel room, ears perked, as he called up his notes on his tablet. "First of all," he said, "obviously this is a fantastic result and we should be very pleased with how well you played. I'm learning about you two just as you're learning about me, and one thing I'm learning—again—is that you both have pretty good instincts, and you're not afraid to follow them. So let's go over the semifinal win and the final and we'll keep trying to find that balance between what I tell you to do and what you feel you should do. Sound good?"

It sounded good to us, particularly because he had stopped hinting that I should drop doubles. So we had a good discussion about using his advice, about changing our style to suit our opponents, and about finding ourselves in a major final again. We left it all feeling better about working together.

That night I went out with Daryavic and I dragged Aliq along. He protested that he hadn't been invited and I told him that he'd just been to a Wimbledon final and he could come out drinking if he wanted. "I feel like a tag-along," he complained as we walked out.

"I don't know what that is," I said, though I had a pretty good idea.

He started to explain, and I cut him off. "First of all," I said, "Like we talked about, you just played in a Wimbledon final."

"Doubles. These guys are all singles players."

"They respect the game," I told him. "Second, you're my friend and I want you to come."

"That's what a tag-along is."

"Then it's not a bad thing."

Still, Aliq was a little withdrawn when we got to the pub. Daryavic waved us over and when I tried to introduce Aliq, he said, "Oh, I know, I watched the final. Good job! Your backhand was a little tight, it looked like."

"A little maybe," Aliq looked like one of the kids in a high school movie who's been pushed into a group of more popular kids. "Uh thanks."

"Was that your first major final?"

He nodded, and the maned wolf clapped him on the shoulder. "I got jitters in my first final too. Don't worry, you'll get back and you'll be amazed how much calmer you are."

"Thanks," Aliq said.

"You know the rest of the guys, right?"

Phillippe Dubois was there, unusually, and Li Xu the tiger, and Manny Luongo the Cape Dog, and Colluvic, and five or six others from the top 20. Tempest wasn't there, nor was Braden, of course, who would be playing tomorrow against Bowson again, with the #1 ranking on the line. Braden was heavily favored because Bowson had injured his back during the semifinal. He'd held on to win, but we all knew how those injuries tightened up with rest.

For a lot of the time we were there, the players stayed in smaller groups. Manny and Ljubo were friends; Dubois and Daryavic similarly (which explained why Dubois had gone out to socialize). I sat with the latter two at the beginning, Aliq and I between the marten and maned wolf discussing not tennis but movies and popular songs. Dubois loved States country music, which none of the rest of us did, but he pulled up a couple songs on his phone and we admitted they were catchy. "It's about the lyrics," he grumbled good-naturedly. "You can't hear in this place."

What unified all the tennis people was when someone, I think it was Ljubo, said, "Ha! Three sets, and Bowson doesn't win more than ten games."

Then everyone got into the debate. "Four sets," Dubois said.

"Three, but one tiebreak," Daryavic suggested.

"Ha!" Ljubo slammed down his mug. "Bowson won't win even eight games."

Aliq and I grinned at each other, enjoying the spectacle, until Ljubo yelled across two tables at me. "Hey! Rock! You know Braden, what you think?"

It wasn't exactly that movie moment where everyone goes quiet and stares at me, but people sure did focus their attention my way— Aliq included, damn him. "Um," I said intelligently.

"Ha, don't put him on the spot, poor guy." Daryavic—Milos, he told me to call him Milos—knocked the table with a fist. "Don't worry about it, Rocky."

"No, it's okay. I think…I just can't imagine Braden losing a set, but Bowson is good and I think he'll hold serve pretty well. I think he'll win…" I added up games in my head. "Ten games."

"Rocky's got ten." Someone, another maned wolf with Milos, was keeping a tally. "Who else is in?"

"Four sets, Bowson wins fifteen."

"Five sets, Bowson wins twenty."

This suggestion was mocked and laughed at, and a few others trickled in. Nobody would bet that Braden would lose. When everyone had made their prediction, Milos said, "Hundred each?"

Everyone reached for their wallet and pulled out bills. I hadn't changed out my States currency because I was mostly using credit cards, so I said, "Dollars or pounds?"

"Doesn't matter," the maned wolf grinned. "It's all for fun anyway."

For fun, though there was well over a thousand in the pot by the time everyone had tossed in. But it broke the ice and set me and even Aliq more at ease with the group. We talked some tennis that evening; when you get a bunch of tennis players together, it's hard not to. But we didn't talk about matches so much as rule changes, how Wimbledon handled the rain, which were the best tournaments, where the best food was, and so on.

When we left at the end of the night, Aliq said, "Thanks for making me come along."

I grinned at him. "You belong there, with these guys."

"Ha." He shook his head. "But you do. I'm happy to be your plus-one. You'll get to a major final one day. I—"

"We already did," I said.

Chapter Thirty-Two

I didn't go to the final, not out in the stands. Ori went because Colluvic's team had tickets and Marro invited her. Aliq and I watched from the players' lounge with a few of the players, Daryavic—Milos—and Dubois chief among them. We talked shop during the final: "great shot there," "he misjudged it," "Bowson's back is hurting him, you can tell," and had a fun time watching Braden cruise to a straight set win and the number one ranking in the world. To give Bowson credit, he did force a tiebreak in the second, which turned out to win the betting pool for Milos.

He strutted around the players' lounge saying, "If I can't be in the final, this is the next best thing," and everyone laughed because he'd won maybe fifteen hundred dollars in the pool and had earned nearly a million for his placement in the tournament. I came in third because I'd said Bowson would win ten games and he won eleven total (someone else had picked eleven exactly but not the tiebreak).

We watched the finals ceremony, where Braden made a nice speech about his team and did not mention Ellen at all. As far as I could tell, she wasn't in his box, and it looked like his parents left right after the ceremony.

The get-together in the players' lounge broke up not too long after that and we wandered out into the area past the main locker room. There I spotted two foxes and I thought they were Braden's parents, so I asked Aliq to hold on for a moment and I walked over.

They were, in fact, Braden's parents, both staring down at their phones and typing messages. "Hi," I said.

Braden's father didn't even glance up. His mother did, but her ears didn't come up and I wasn't sure she recognized me. "Rocky," I said. "From Queens?"

"Queens?" Alicia said.

"The tournament."

"Yes, of course. I'm sorry, Rocky, it's not a good time right now."

"Oh." I didn't know what to say to that. She had none of the ebullience she'd had just a few weeks ago. Some family drama, no doubt. Maybe, I thought, Ellen had left Braden, and I got excited about that and then felt guilty about being excited. "Sorry. I'll, ah, I'll leave you to it."

She gave a curt nod and returned her attention to her phone.

"It was them," I told Aliq, "but they're in the middle of something."

"At least they're here," he said, and I felt bad all over again. I'd thought that turning 21 and becoming a so-called adult would make life easier, but here I was in the middle of a number of different personal dramas. It was like high school all over again, but bigger and more important somehow, as though high school had just been practice.

I was glad that at least Ori's life had settled down. She was dating someone she wanted to, had a job, and seemed more self-possessed every time I talked to her. She and Marro met us after the match that evening in our hotel room, and Ori was bouncing and smiling.

"Look," she said, thrusting her phone at me. "Marro spotted it while we were watching the match."

The fennec had his ears partly back and a kind of abashed smile. "I just found the piece," he said. "I didn't know...I mean, hey, it's cool. I'm cool, I mean. With—you know."

That slightly puzzling confession was made clearer when I saw that Ori's phone showed an interview with Braden. I'd figured Ori had told Marro about Braden and I, but we'd never talked about it, so that explained his awkwardness.

The interview was in the middle, so I scrolled to the top, and Ori snatched her phone back. "No, no. The part on the screen. Here." She gave me the phone back and stabbed her finger at the top. I read:

But conquering the world of tennis has not been all big cheques and universal acclaim. Braden has faced criticism for his aloof nature, and confesses himself that the stress has taken a toll on his personal life. "Sure, there have been people I've driven away," he says, and after a moment, delivers an understatement worthy of any Brit: *"I'd have preferred not to."*

One can only assume he is referring to Ellen Jacobs, a fixture at his matches during the first half of the year who has yet to make an appearance in Londinium. The two were rumoured to be on the path to matrimony until the grass-court season, and now the silence out of the Longacre camp is deafening.

If true, it's hardly a crack in his armour. Braden Longacre would join a long list of tennis greats whose personal lives crumbled around them even as they went on to win title after title. And Braden has the discipline and the team around him to make the Grand Slam not just a possibility, but a likelihood. His personal trainer, Jeff Langhorne, has a background in…

It went on to talk about Braden's team and returned to non-personal issues, which I assumed was not what Ori had thought I would be interested in. I gave her phone back. "So?"

She rolled her eyes. "So!"

"His fiancée left him. I saw his parents, they were upset. That'd explain it."

She turned to Marro and shook her head; he gave her a smile and a shrug in that way you do when your girlfriend expects you to react in a certain way. Ori leaned toward me and used the tone Ma used to use when we were slow to understand something. "He's not talking about Ellen, is he? The 'people he's driven away'?"

I clamped my jaw shut. Aliq perked his ears up and took Ori's phone, scanning the text. "Wait, is something wrong with you guys?"

"Ever since Lutèce, you've been moody and quiet. You had a fight." Ori pointed accusingly at me. "You kept it to yourself, but you had a fight and you haven't seen him since, have you? You haven't gone out on your own at all in Anglia."

Marro looked as uncomfortable as I felt under Aliq and Ori's scrutiny. "Seriously?" Aliq said. "You did?"

"I can go," Marro offered.

"It's fine," I said. "You're practically family now." His ears went back but he looked pleased, and Ori did too. "It wasn't really a fight."

"Then what's been bothering you?" Aliq asked.

I sighed. "It was more like…we broke up."

Ori's ears went back. "I knew it. He dumped you."

"No. I dumped him."

They took that in, not really understanding, so I went on. "I didn't want to. But I couldn't keep going the way we were, with him insisting that Ellen didn't mean anything and then thanking her at the tournaments and she's sitting in his box and we were sneaking around to crummy hotels and, uh." I stopped and sat down on the bed, paws clasping each other in my lap.

"Really," Marro said, turning toward the door, "I'll, uh, I'll go get a drink in the bar."

"Really," I said, "it's fine. You don't have to. We're a sharing family."

"I thought we were." Ori glared at me.

"You were all dealing with stuff. You," I gestured to Aliq, "with you know, your stuff, and you," to Ori, "you were so happy that I didn't want to ruin things."

"We care about you," she retorted. "It wouldn't 'ruin' my happiness for you to tell me what's going on in your life."

"There wasn't anything anyone could do. It's up to him to make the next move."

"We could talk it out with you." Aliq sat next to me on the bed. "There wasn't anything you could do about my parents, either, but it felt good to talk to you about it. You helped me get a lot of my thoughts out; when I wasn't talking to anyone I would go around in these crazy circles and get more and more anxious."

"Sometimes, ah," Marro cleared his throat. "Sometimes it's helpful after a breakup just to have other people call your ex a…" He paused. "A jerk."

"He is a jerk," I said. "Everyone knows that." It felt weird to hear him called my 'ex,' though, because it implied that there'd been something for him to be the ex of. That Ori and Aliq had both thought of us as boyfriends, even though Braden had resisted that label and I hadn't insisted on it.

"Or," Aliq said, "just friends to tell you what you're feeling is okay. It's okay to be sad after you dump someone even though it was your call. Maybe you wanted it to work out but you realized it couldn't and you're still sad about it. That's okay."

"All right," I said, "I get it. I'm sorry I kept it from you, and I would've told you eventually."

"Hey," Marro said, ears lifting. "Is it partly because you're gay?" Everyone turned to him and he raised a paw, slightly defensively. "Sorry, I mean—hear me out. Like, you couldn't be open about the relationship so you felt like you had to hide it, and you just accept that as the way things have to be. But then when it's over you still feel like you have to hide things, like you can't be open because of the nature of the relationship, so you end up with all this shit bottled up inside you."

"Duh," Aliq said.

"Sorry." The fennec's ears went back down. "I read about it but it's all been theoretical for me until now."

"Seriously?" Ori said. "It's 2015 and you've never met a gay person?"

"Well, come on, I mostly hung out with macho pro athletes my whole career. I mean, there was a snow leopard I knew in college who was gay but we never talked about relationships or anything."

The exchange made me smile. "I don't know if I'm a typical gay person," I said. "They all seem to be living their lives normally and I'm trapped in this weird place where I can't be myself."

"That's how it used to be all over," Aliq said. "Things are getting better. They'll get better for you, too."

"So." Ori sat on the other side of me on the bed, "are you still in love with him?"

"Ugh." I buried my muzzle in my paws. "What the hell."

"I think it's a valid question," she said.

"I know. I've been asking myself that for weeks."

Everyone was quiet. Then Ori said, "And?"

"This is a really weird conversation," I said. "I think you should know that."

Marro backed up a step. "Seriously, I can go."

"She'll just tell you later anyway." I glared at Ori. "I don't know. What's being in love mean? How do you know you're in love with him?" I nodded toward Marro.

"Oh, that's easy." She smiled brightly. "Because he makes me feel better when I'm around him. Because he does little things for me and I want to do little things for him. Because he encourages me to be the person I want to be, and I think the person he is is pretty great."

The fennec had his ears back but a big grin on his muzzle, and when Ori finished he went over to her and put his head against hers, and the two of them just stayed sweetly like that.

"I hate you," I said.

Marro stepped back and Ori grinned at me. "Your turn."

"Okay." I sighed. "He's not sweet. As a person he's not that great. He doesn't really do little things for me—well, he does, kind of, but they're like 'get a crummy hotel room we can meet up in.' And I want to do things for him but I don't think he'd like that. And usually I feel better when I'm with him but then sometimes I feel worse.

"But he's trying. It's like there's a good person in there buried under layers of 'how to behave' and 'worry about reporters' and 'macho athlete crap.' I don't like his parents and I don't think he does either. I mean, I don't think he hates them or anything, but they're definitely not like Ma was with us. And I think, how sad for someone who didn't have a parent like that in their life. Maybe they're trying to be better and I can help them."

The room fell silent. Aliq coughed after a moment. "I don't know, but all the movies say that you shouldn't be in a relationship with someone if you're trying to make them someone different."

"But what if they want to be someone different and they need help?"

Ori put a paw on my shoulder. "You're still thinking about him after a month. If he was talking about you in that interview, would you want to talk to him, to see if he wants to try again?"

If. If if if. "Yeah."

She tapped the pocket where my phone was. "So text him." She stood and took Marro's paw. "Come on. Now I think we should go."

After Ori and Marro had gone, Aliq stood and walked to the door, but paused there. "So, uh, Shona and I argue a lot, but it's fun arguing. And we're on the same page about the big things. We don't do sweet little things for each other. I think she'd hate that. But she challenges me and she says I challenge her too, I dunno."

"Okay," I said.

"The point is, I guess, we trust each other. And love doesn't have to be the same for everyone. In fact, it's probably not. And what the hell do any of us know about it? I mean, I thought my parents—" He stopped and his muzzle dipped.

"It's okay," I said.

"The point, though." He raised his head to meet my eyes. "The point is, whatever it is for you, that's great. And if it is, then…then I hope it works out."

"Thanks." And then, because he put his paw on the door handle, "You know, you don't all have to go. It's not like he's going to text me back this minute. He's out celebrating. He's probably drunk right now."

Aliq grinned at me. "So much the better," he said, and walked out of the room.

What would I even say to Braden? I took out my phone and stared at it, composed a message in my head, discarded it, composed another, discarded that one, and finally just called up his number.

The last text he'd sent me had been the address of that hotel in Lutèce, the one where I'd walked out on him. That would be what he saw when my message went through. But I couldn't help that.

Congrats, I typed. *Great win. Number one.*

I sent that, and then before I could tell myself not to, I typed, *I miss you*, and sent that too.

Despite what I'd said, I stared at the phone for a minute, then another minute, and then I called up Aliq's number and typed, *Hey, where'd you*

I didn't get to type "guys go" because my phone buzzed, showing a message from Braden. *At Colluvic's, come over.*

It made me laugh out loud because it was so improbable, because a whole bunch of tension drained out of me in that moment. I lay back on the bed and stared at the ceiling and laughed, the clean warmth of the message washing through me and leaving giddy joy in its wake. And it wasn't all because I hadn't gotten laid in a month. I was pretty sure of that.

So I changed my message to Aliq to: *going out :)*, which I was sure he'd understand and convey to Ori. I did that in the elevator on the way to the lobby, and then I shoved my phone into my pocket and grabbed a taxi to Colluvic's condo.

Braden himself greeted me at the door. "Hey," he said, as though we'd just seen each other the day before, as though the last time we'd talked hadn't ended whatever our relationship was. "C'mon in. There's beer and Coke in the fridge if you want it."

I followed him to the kitchen, grabbed a Coke, and then we went upstairs to the guest rooms. "What are you doing here? Why aren't you out celebrating?" I asked, following his swinging tail up the staircase.

"I was." His words echoed in the stair. "But my parents were there and everyone on the team wanted to talk about the Grand Slam and I got tired of it. We have to go start the hardcourt season in a week."

"Okay, but you have to take time to stop and enjoy the win. I mean, you won fucking Wimbledon," I said. "I grew up watching this tournament. I can't imagine what it was like. What did the Duke and Duchess of Kent smell like?"

He paused. "Strawberries."

"That's cool." I followed him into the bedroom he'd had last time, a small room with one queen bed and his suitcase atop the dresser. He sat on the bed, and after a moment, I sat beside him. "What did they say to you?"

"The usual stuff, I guess. How impressive I was on the court. The Duchess said I looked 'exotic,' which I guess she meant as a compliment."

I snorted. "You've won three majors this year, you're number one in the world, but your fur is the thing she picked to talk about."

"Her husband said the tennis stuff." He stared straight ahead.

"How did you feel? Winning, I mean." I watched him closely.

He shifted his eyes from the door to me, and beyond. "I dunno. I mean, Bowson's limited with that back injury, but you never know, he might tough it out, just be fuckin' on and there's nothing you can do. I knew after the first game that wasn't going to happen, so after that it was just playing it out."

"Even the tiebreak?"

He flicked his ears back. "If I'd lost that, I'd have beaten him in four. I wasn't worried."

"So when you realized you were going to win," I persisted. "You felt...?"

That got a slight grin out of him. "Like the best player in the world."

"Which you are."

"For now."

"Yeah." I didn't want to touch him, but this was the point where I would have, if other things hadn't been the way they were. "Everything is only for the moment, right? You're not going to be number one forever, but you know how many people get to be there? I probably never will."

"Don't sell yourself short."

"Not while you're playing."

He inclined his head and the grin got wider. "You'll have a few years after I turn 30."

I nodded and wanted to go on to ask about us, where we'd be when he turned thirty and I turned twenty-six, but I couldn't find the words, so I just stared down at my paws.

"You're a pain in the ass, you know that?"

My head snapped up and my ears folded back, but he didn't look angry, just thoughtful. "I had this plan, you know. I had a training regimen and I had practice partners, and I had an attitude, and I had a plan for the non-tennis parts of my life. And you came along and fucked it up."

"I didn't mess with your training regimen." Confusion gave my words a bit more heat than I'd intended, so I tried to dial it back. "And I'm sorry about the rest. Why'd you even invite me over?"

"Because I didn't think I needed more than to fuck some guys I picked up in bars. I sure didn't think I wanted to fuck the same guy over and over again, and if I did, I sure as hell didn't want some kind of," he waved his paw, "emotional baggage to go along with it."

"Dog Christ, you're an asshole," I said.

"No argument." He held out a paw, hesitated over one of mine, then lowered it. I didn't move. "And you're the first guy I haven't managed to scare off or drive away. Well, hadn't managed. After Lutèce I told myself you weren't anything special, you were just like my friends, my parents, everyone I was better off separated from."

I bit back my retort because I was getting where he was going with this now. He went on, now dropping his eyes so he didn't have to look at me. "I thought I'd marry Ellen and it would be fine and whatever, I didn't have to care about it. But things hadn't been good between us either, me and her, I mean, not since before Lutèce. I kept telling her this was all for show, and she would go, 'Sure, sure,' but then she'd talk about me coming to one of her charity things, and when I said I was too busy, she said she guessed she was just a prop, and what should I say to that? I wanted to say, 'Yeah, exactly, did you not get it?' But even I wouldn't do that.

"So then my mom got involved. She loves Ellen. She asked when we were going to get married, and I got suckered into it for a bit. I figured I could sleep with her a couple times, have some kits, and then she'd have a family to occupy her and she'd leave me alone."

"That doesn't sound healthy," I said.

He shook his head. "We had a fight sometime after Lutèce, like the week or two after. She was talking about the engagement announcement and I was looking at film and she asked me some question about flowers and I said I didn't care, and she said, 'Do you care about any of this?' I was distracted and I said, 'Not really, it's for you and Mom.' Then she went all quiet and when I looked up she had her arms folded and she said, 'I don't think we should do this,' and I said, 'Fine with me,' and she walked out and I haven't seen her since then."

"Your mom told me at Queens that the engagement was still on."

His eyes widened. "Why were you talking to my mom?"

"I went over to your box. I, uh, I didn't see Ellen there, and your mom recognized me, I guess."

He shook his head. "Well, shit. Yeah, I didn't tell her until last week when she finally figured out there was something weird about Ellen being gone for two weeks without any word."

"Ugh." I thumped my tail on the bed, wagging but also a little frustrated. "I thought you guys were getting engaged."

"That's not my fault," he said, and then he paused and said, "Or maybe it is. Sorry."

This apology caught me off guard. He'd said it off-handedly but in earnest, and I believed it. "All right," I said. "So...where are we?"

"What do you think?" he parried.

I shook my head. "Uh uh. I'm not bailing you out. You have to say the words."

"God dammit." He glared. "You really are a pain in the ass." I grinned at him, and he exhaled. "Fine. Here goes."

I waited. "Obviously," Braden said after a moment, "you miss me. You're here, and also you told me so."

He waited, but I wasn't going to give him any confirmation, so he went on. "And I miss you. Which I told you, and also, I invited you over here, so you know that."

I flicked my tail against the bed and smiled. He tapped his fingers together and stared down at them. "So we miss each other and we should keep seeing each other. But I need to do some things better. I'm done with Ellen and I'm not going to start seeing someone else as a diversion. I still don't want to come out to the public or anything."

He challenged me with a look, and I shook my head. "I don't think we should either."

"I don't even want to come out to the guys on the tour."

"Okay," I said. "But are you out to anyone but me?"

"Not including the random hookups?"

"No." I put a paw to my muzzle to stifle a giggle.

He gave a quirky smile. "All right. My personal trainer knows. He covers for me when I go out some nights. But nobody else knows."

"Wow."

He tilted his head, ears perked. "Why, how many people know about you?"

I counted off on fingers. "My ex-boyfriend, probably his current boyfriend, my doubles partner, my sister, her boyfriend, now."

"Jesus Fox."

"What? They're people who share my life."

He nodded. "You don't think one of them will spill the secret sometime?"

"Maybe. I haven't really thought about it. But if it happens then I'll deal with it. It's so much work to hide things from them, and I'd rather put that energy into other things."

His muzzle turned down into a scowl. "It didn't take a lot of energy for me until you came along. I had a routine and it was easy to follow."

I reminded myself that he wasn't actually mad at me. "You seemed pretty worried when I saw you at the gay club that time. What if some other player runs into you there? You're a cross fox; you don't exactly blend."

"Pot; kettle," he said.

That was an expression I'd heard: the pot calling the kettle black. "I'm not pretending to blend in to keep a secret, though."

"Right. Fine. Anyway, so we both agree we don't want to come out and shock the world or anything like that."

"Agreed."

"Okay." He leaned back on his elbows and looked at me. "So then what?"

I shook my head. "Where do you see us going in the future? What do you want to say to me, what do you want to hear from me?"

"I won't take you to shitty hotels anymore?"

"Good, but I mean…" I sighed. "Fine, I mean, like this. I don't know why this thing between us works, but it does. It's not just the sex, but that's good too. It's that I like being around you. I get a kind of charge from it that I don't get from anyone else. It's exciting and it's," I waved a paw, "I don't know, energizing maybe. And also though, when I thought you were going to marry Ellen, I was mostly upset because I wasn't going to get to see you again, but if you'd said that was going to make you happy, that'd be okay. I just didn't think that's what was going to make you happy. You know?"

"It wasn't going to make me happy. I told you."

"I know. And if you'd told me about that a month ago, maybe—" I raised a paw, stopping myself. "You know what, that's in the past and we're here now. Your turn."

"Okay, I think I get it." Braden flicked his ears forward and back. "Stuff like feelings. You know I'm not good at that like you are, right?"

"You don't have to be me. Just be you."

"Be careful what you're asking for." He grinned so I could see the tips of his canine teeth over his lips. "All right, here it is. You made my life interesting for the first time in a while. Tennis is interesting but predictable. My family is—my family. I had this whole routine. And you messed it up, but." He held up a finger. "I liked that you messed it up. It was worth it."

"Thanks."

"No, listen. It's like—hah. You know Vulparel?"

"Sure." They made athletic clothing for foxes and "honorary foxes," a group I was included in. Lochen had talked to them but they wanted actual foxes for their endorsement so nothing ever happened. The shirt I tried on was comfortable, though. They seemed small for Braden to have been endorsing, unless this was five or six years ago.

"You know how I ended up with them?" I shook my head. "My agent had me this endorsement deal with another company, um, Cooper Caldwell or something like that, their logo was CC, anyway. They sent me these shorts and shirts, and the sleeves on the shirts were like an inch too long. I tried them, they messed up my rhythm, my routine. My coach said, you can adapt. I said, I'm not going to adapt. My agent said, for two million dollars, you adapt. I said, find me another deal. Vulparel paid me one million for that deal. I lost a million dollars because I didn't want to adapt to a shirt whose sleeves were an inch different from what I was used to."

"Wow." It was a story that I was surprised I hadn't heard before, the story of a fantastically picky, stubborn, asshole who would rather have things just the way he was used to. It was also the story of someone with enough privilege to be able to make million-dollar decisions like that, but that probably wasn't the immediate takeaway.

"People make shirts to my specifications now, but that's not the point." He stared down at his fingers again. "When you messed up my routine, I thought about those shirts. There were other things too, but nothing that cost me a million dollars. I thought, my routine is what got me here, and if I start changing it around, taking focus away from my game...well, you know. But I did it anyway. I kept in touch with you. I started reserving new hotel rooms."

"It probably didn't hurt that you were winning championships."

"Yeah." He grinned. "If I'd started losing, you'd have been gone."

I thought that was a joke but also maybe it wasn't. "I wouldn't have let you keep losing."

"That's part of why you're worth it." He put a paw over mine. "I've never met anyone like you, who wasn't easy to get rid of, who didn't expect anything from me, who helped me out without wanting something back." He paused. "All that and you're good in bed too."

I snorted and flattened my ears back. "You too."

"I know. I've practiced. I have a routine for that too." He smiled a sly smile at me. "So I dunno. I like you a lot."

"I like you too. So what do we do moving forward?"

"Moving forward..." His ears came up and he rubbed his fingers over my paw. "I guess I'd like you to be part of my routine."

The words surprised me even though he'd been building to them. I started to respond, couldn't get the right words in the right order, and then said, "I'd like that too. And uh, I don't have a routine, but I want you to be part of my life too."

"All right." He squeezed my paw. "So, we good?"

"I mean...we should keep talking about stuff, I guess, but I mean, that's, you know, as long as we're in the same, you know, mindset about where we are and what we want..." His paw had moved from my paw to my pants, his muzzle coming closer to mine. "Then uh yeah, we can move on."

"Good." He moved his muzzle down my shirt, but I touched my paw under his chin. He turned his muzzle up, hazel eyes meeting mine. "What?"

"My other boyfriend and I kissed. You want to try it?"

"We've kissed."

"I mean like a real kiss."

He hesitated. "Is this part of the new thing? We get each other to try stuff?"

"Sure."

"Well. All right, then."

So he touched his lips to mine, whiskers brushing. I pushed my tongue through my lips and against his, and his were soft and warm and tasted like some kind of alcohol, very faintly. He made a surprised noise and then parted his lips and we were kissing more deeply. We did that for a little bit and then he, being Braden, pushed his tongue against mine and into my mouth, and I let him.

By the time we broke the kiss, I was pretty hard. Braden was too, to judge by his, "Huh, that worked better than I thought it would."

"It takes practice," I said. "Mar and I kissed a lot before we got really good at it."

"Something to add to my routine," he said, "but for now let's stick to the basics." His paw undid the front of my pants and I helped get them off, and then he lowered his muzzle, took me in, and I leaned back and closed my eyes.

I finished pretty fast, with a strong overpowering climax that left me panting as Braden worked my pants all the way off. While I recovered a little, Braden undressed, and by the time he sat naked on the bed next to me, I had my wind back, enough to take my shirt off. I ran my paws over that lovely orange and brown-furred body, working my way down to where he waited, hard and ready. I took him in my muzzle and he didn't take much longer than I had.

"Ooof," he panted, lying back on the bed. "Maybe we should take a month off more often."

"I don't think I'm okay with that." I lay next to him and rested a paw on his stomach.

"No, me neither." He wiggled to free his tail, which had been trapped below his legs.

I closed my eyes. His warmth against me and the post-orgasmic glow set my tail to wagging. I kept hearing those words in my head: I want you to be part of my routine. They weren't a lot, but from Braden, they meant the world to me.

I'd half-dozed until Braden's paw pressing on my chest shook me awake. The sky outside had darkened, and the fox next to me now lay on his side, muzzle next to mine, his knee resting on my thigh. "Hey."

"Oh, uh." I blinked up at him. "You, uh, should I head out now?"

He frowned. "I was gonna ask if you want to get under the covers. It's a warm night but I always have to sleep under a sheet or something at least."

"Oh." My tail tip flicked against the bed. "Yeah, sure. I'll have to go grab my stuff at some point but I can…" I met his eyes. "I can stay."

"Okay, good." We got up and he pulled the covers of the bed back and we climbed in together. There was enough room for both of us, and at first we just lay there, kind of apart, waiting, and then at about the same time we rolled toward each other. "I haven't really slept with other people in the bed before," he said. "Sorry if I kick you."

"It's okay." I smiled, because my muzzle was next to his. "Do you want to try kissing again?"

By way of answer, he pushed his lips against mine and slid his arm around my chest.

* * *

I hadn't woken up next to someone in a long time, and waking with Braden's scent in the room was definitely a new experience, but not a bad one. I'd rolled onto my side facing away from him and he was on the other side of the bed, so I rolled over and found him lying on his back looking at his phone.

"Hey," he said, and put the phone down.

"Morning." We slid together and stayed there for several minutes, remembering the curves of each other's bodies with our paws. Both of us were pretty hard just from waking up, and soon enough our fingers found those hardnesses and played with them.

Then he pushed his muzzle at mine and we found that kissing was more fun when we were sliding paws up and down our cocks, each of the two activities amplifying the other, until I had to break the kiss with a giggle. "Okay, okay, I'm gonna come all over your paw like that."

He panted, grinning at me. "That's okay. I'm not going to be around anyone who's smelling my paws today. And even if I were, what would they say? I fucking won Wimbledon."

"Oh yeah." I squeezed his cock, which got him to widen his eyes. "I mean, I will if you want, like, if you keep going I won't be able to stop, but I was just thinking there might be other things we want to do."

"We've got time." He turned his ears back and then forward again without losing his smile. "Hey, if we're still asking each other to try stuff…?"

I nodded, and he disengaged from me and slid out of bed, over to his suitcase. After rummaging around (while I watched his tail wag and thought, *that's a super attractive butt*, and then, *that's my boyfriend's butt*, and that thought took my paw down to my cock), he turned around with a small bottle and a condom in his paw and held them up. "So?"

I relaxed back into the bed. My rear felt fine, pretty clean. And the time was right for it. It had been a long time since Marquize, and even though I still felt an echo of the bad feelings from then, I thought that if anything was going to erase those associations, this would. So yeah, I'd let Braden fuck me. "Sure," I said.

He smiled and tossed me the condom. "Get ready, then."

"Wait." I picked up the little packet. "Me? Sorry, you want me to…"

While I talked, he squeezed some liquid out into his paw and reached around under his tail. "Hm? What did you think I wanted?"

"My last boyfriend…he wanted to go inside me. I thought that's what you wanted."

Braden raised his eyebrows. "We can try that too. But right now I want to bottom. I haven't in a long time and I miss it."

I opened the condom packet. "I've never been inside someone."

"Topping," he said, squeezing out more. "It's called topping when you stick your dick in. It's bottoming when someone sticks their dick in you."

"Okay, I've never topped." I turned the condom over, found the right way and rolled it down over my shaft.

"It's easy. You put your cock here." He lifted his tail and pointed under it. "And push. Repeat until done."

"But what if I don't do it right? How will I know if you're enjoying it?"

He climbed onto the bed on all fours and stuck his muzzle right up at mine. "Like kissing. We'll get better with practice. I mean, if you're okay practicing a few more times."

"I, uh." He grabbed my wrapped cock and slid his slick paw up and down it, making me squirm. "I'm willing to put work into this relationship."

"All right." He grinned toothily. "Then get back there and let's start practicing."

So I crawled up behind him and he flicked his tail out of the way. I ran my paws down his rear, smoothing down the fur and stroking the muscles, following them down the backs of his legs. Between his legs hung his sac, which drew my fingers to it, and he made a contented noise and spread his legs wider as I played with it and then slid my fingers forward up his sheath and along his length.

But the smell of the lube reminded me what I was there for, and so I pulled my fingers back and, wondering all the while if I was supposed to be doing it this way, I traced up between his legs, up into the crack of his rear until I found the patch of slickness and warmth that allowed my finger to push into it.

Braden made a soft huffing sound and I took that to mean approval, so I slid my finger in and out, remembering vaguely that Marquize had done something like this to relax me. Braden felt very tight around my finger, so I worked a little more until I could fit a second finger in, and that brought a long exhalation from him.

When I moved to add the third finger, he growled, "Put it in already."

I was glad to hear that because I was getting pretty impatient myself. So I situated my tip at his entrance, rested my paws on his hips, and I pushed.

His rear was warm and tight around me, and the low moan he let out as I buried myself in him made me even more excited. I let go of the worries and rocked back and forth, finding a rhythm that worked for me.

Partway through I noticed that he had one paw on his own cock and I reached under him to take it; he let me without comment, but his ears flicked around and his tail brushed back against me. I meant to get him off around the same time I finished, but I didn't judge it very well and my own excitement took over. I stopped stroking, holding onto his cock as my thrusts got faster and faster, my climax building until I gasped and moaned, folding forward over his back and burying my nose in his neck ruff.

I stayed like that, panting, and then went back to stroking him as I was recovering from my climax. Braden squirmed under me and around my cock, bucking as I got him close to where I'd just been.

It didn't take him much longer. Within a minute he moaned through clenched teeth and his ears flattened back. Breath rasped harshly through his throat in long, ragged pants, building into, "Rrrh…rrh…aaaahh," until his whole body jerked under me and his rear clenched around me and he threw his head back. I tried to keep my strokes to the rhythm of his panting as my paw got warm and sticky and then I stopped as he seemed to.

His body wobbled below me and listed to one side, so I pulled my weight to that side too and gently eased us over to lie spooned against each other, my cock still inside him. "Ah-huh," Braden gasped, reaching to clasp my paw in his. "Stay."

"I'm not going anywhere," I murmured, and he relaxed back against me.

We must have fallen asleep again, because I woke up a bit later to a bright room and I wasn't even hard anymore, much less still inside Braden. I could smell his come strongly and mine a little; the condom had fallen off when my cock slid back into its sheath, so it was lying in the bed between us.

My paw was still resting on his side, and when I moved my fingers, he stirred. "Mmf."

"We fell asleep."

"Uh huh." He rolled onto his back and turned his head toward me. "Good morning again."

"Morning." I rested my paw on his stomach. "So. What should we do today?"

He yawned and his nostrils flared. "First thing, we should clean the sheets."

We got up and showered and threw the sheets in the laundry. I worried about what to tell Ljubo if he asked, but Braden said he had people who did his laundry and he would never even know we'd changed the sheets.

I had to go back and get my stuff, so I invited him to come with me, but he declined, saying that he wanted to relax and didn't want people swarming him if he went out in public. "You're going to meet my friends and my sister eventually," I told him.

"Yeah, yeah." He waved. "Just not right now."

I leaned in to kiss him goodbye, and he rolled his eyes but then gave me a pretty good kiss that left my tail wagging as I walked out the door.

On the way back I checked with Ljubo to make sure I was invited ("of course you are! you want to leave me alone with Braden Longface?"). When I got back to my room, Aliq grabbed his phone as soon as I came in, before even saying hi.

"Hey," I said, and he held up a paw.

"Ori told me to text her as soon as you got back and you're not supposed to tell me anything until she's here, but it went well, didn't it? You're smiling. And wagging."

"Yeah." I stopped my tail and then thought, screw it, and let it go on wagging. "I'm going to stay with him at Ljubo's for the next couple days. You guys'll be okay, right?"

"We'll be fine." He wagged his own tail and grinned real big at me. "You're happy?"

"I'm happy."

"That's all I need to know."

Ori knocked on the door a few seconds later, loud and fast, and when I let her in she asked me basically the same questions but with more detail, like, "what did he say? what did you say? did you forgive him?" and so on. So I recounted for them the PG portions of the night and I did tell them that I kissed him, even though I wasn't sure how Aliq would react to that. I mean, dating a guy in the abstract is one thing, but hearing about the physical intimacy is another.

It did seem that a faint shadow passed over his muzzle when I said that, but he banished it quickly. Ori hugged me, told me how happy she was that I was happy, and asked when she was going to get to meet him.

"Soon," I told her. "He's on notice."

"Good." She stepped back and folded her arms. "I'll chase him down if I have to. If he's going to be family then I have to meet him."

"Agreed." I laughed to hide the weirdness I felt at Braden being considered family. But family, I thought, is loving bonds. Ma had taught me that. So when you make loving bonds with someone, doesn't it make sense to consider them family? In the end, isn't that what matters?

Chapter Thirty-Three

The few days at Colluvic's condo were nice because Braden and I got away from our respective teams and spent time relaxing, practicing, and having a fair amount of sex. Colluvic had invited an Anglic player, a spindly mouse ranked in the fifties, so we practiced doubles sometimes for fun, and other times paired off in various configurations for singles. The mouse, whose name was Todd, had a very grass-court serve-and-volley game, but he tended to rely on his serve too much. For lower-ranked players, that worked well, but when he ran into a top-20 player who didn't have as much trouble returning his serve, he got stranded at the net and at the very least ceded control of the point immediately. "My coach tells me to be more cautious," he told me after I'd won three straight points on his serve and his ears and whiskers were drooping, "but I won so many tournaments just firing the ball and running up after it that I always think this time I'll get it."

"I know how that feels," I said. "You've got a good serve. Just got to retrain yourself."

"This is brilliant." He looked over at the next court, where Braden and Colluvic were going at it, and smiled. "The chaps on tour, they're nice, but it's not often you get to, you know, really dig in with other players. Everyone's so protective, don't want to give you an advantage in case you end up playing them, but really, there's so much else that affects your matches."

"Also some people on the tour are jerks," I said, and he laughed and agreed.

In the evenings, of course, Braden and I often retired as soon as we thought it wouldn't raise eyebrows. We'd gotten adjacent rooms so it was easy to sneak from one to the other and then back when we got up in the morning. One morning we daringly left my room together to go down to breakfast, because we couldn't hear anyone else moving around.

At the end of our stay, Ljubo took me aside. "Winning agrees with Braden."

"I guess so."

"Maybe it is also that you are a good friend to him. I do not think he's had that before."

"Oh yeah." I shifted, tail flicking back against my legs. "I mean, I think winning Wimbledon loosened him up. He's got a lot of confidence. The States Open is his second-best tournament after Ozzie."

Ljubo smiled a big wolf smile and put a paw on my shoulder. "Confidence has never lacked in Braden."

"There's a difference between arrogance and confidence," I said. "I think he uses the one to hide his lack of the other. But you're right, he does seem more relaxed now."

"Take the credit for it." The wolf shook his head. "If I were cruel, I would tell you to stop being his friend. Maybe after he wins the Slam."

"I don't think he'll want to slow down. But I'll fight you for second place."

Ljubo laughed, big and boisterous. "You have a fight, Rocky. See you on the court."

Braden and I had a longer good-bye, but also it wasn't quite a good-bye. "This has been nice," he said as we waited for cars to take us to separate airports.

"It's not over," I told him.

"I'll see you at Cuyahoga, at least, and then Port City. Good luck at Parsons and Littlefield."

"Good luck at Potomac and Boliat."

We had a moment where I thought he was going to lean in and kiss me even though we were on the sidewalk and anyone might have seen. He didn't, but he did something almost as startling: he reached out and took my paw in his. "Call me."

I looked back into those hazel eyes and squeezed. "I will. And you call me, too."

"Will do." We held the grip a moment longer and then released it.

* * *

I'd chosen to play Parsons and Littlefield, two lower-rung tournaments (still on the Champions circuit, though), specifically because Braden wasn't. Not that I didn't want to see him—well, partly that, because I'd booked these with Lochen before Wimbledon—but I thought those gave me a better chance to win. There are enough tournaments going around to divide up the field pretty well, and half the top 20 goes to one tournament over here, and some go to this other one, and then there's this third one. The highest seed at the Parsons tournament was Tempest, now at #9 in the world, while I'd moved up to number 20, which still felt surreal to me.

Tempest got knocked out in the semifinal, which left me to face #15 Ilanu, a gazelle, in the final. He had a tricky serve and a good return, but my return was better and my baseline game held up to his groundstrokes. It took me three sets but I won the final 6-2, 6-7, 6-4 for my second tournament win on the Champions circuit.

We celebrated, me and Ori and Aliq and Nashan. Aliq and I had gotten to the semifinals in doubles, and though this tournament didn't pay as well in dollars or points as some of the larger ones, it still felt like an accomplishment. I got interviewed by a couple tennis bloggers, and Ori got some traction on one of the articles, titled, "Rising Stars of States Tennis."

Lochen landed me another endorsement deal ahead of the States Open, which helped secure our financial status and allowed us to add a couple more people to my team, something Nashan had been wanting to do for a while: a personal trainer and a day-to-day coach who could manage our practice sessions so Nashan could focus on the larger picture. They were paid what I thought was a small salary, but Lochen explained that they would get a bonus in the form of a percent of whatever prize money I won. That seemed fair to me.

I also called Braden that night, because he'd won the tournament at Potomac, but the first thing he said when he picked up was, "Hey, congrats!"

"We won on the same day." I laughed. "How likely is that to happen again?"

"I hope not often," he said, "because you better start coming to the top events with me. You're too good to be shitting around in those second-rate tournaments just to get a win under your belt."

"A win is a win." I was getting pretty good at interpreting Braden's words and putting the positive spin on them that I knew he meant.

"Oh, I get why you have to do it. I did it too, for a while. Next year though, you gotta keep getting those points up or you'll slip."

"I'm letting my manager worry about that." I wagged my tail. "It's good to hear your voice."

"Same here," he said. "Wish I could feel your cock."

I laughed and looked through the doorway to the rest of the suite where my team was still partying. "How do you know I wasn't in the middle of a bunch of people?"

"If you call me from the middle of a party, that's on you." He sounded smug and I could see the smile on his face as clearly as if he were in front of me.

"Noted," I said, and then lowered my voice. "Wish I could feel yours too."

"Cuyahoga," he said.

"Cuyahoga," I replied.

But first I had to play in Littlefield, where I didn't do quite as well. Aliq and I won in doubles this time, but I got knocked out in the quarterfinals of the singles side by Tempest, proving he wasn't quite on the way out. I think I was a bit in awe of him at first, and by the time I got over that, I managed to win the second set, but he was too good that day. Afterwards, he complimented me on my play and talked to me about how the tour had been for him as a younger player, and even though the scene had been very different ten years ago, I enjoyed hearing the stories. More, I appreciated him opening up to me when he hadn't before, which made me feel like this panther, winner of six major titles, regarded me as a peer. When I called Braden to congratulate him on his win at Boliat, I told him about that and he said Tempest had never talked to him that way. I said that maybe that was because he probably didn't seem like he needed life lessons from Tempest, and he said that was probably true.

Nashan took some lessons away from the loss for me, and we worked with my day-to-day coach on getting some of my technique sharper for Cuyahoga and the States. I liked having this extra coach to work with; the rat was a former tennis player, recently retired like Nashan, but he was a better returner, so he worked with me on both my serve and my return.

That was just singles; though Aliq and I were doing well, we practiced together either with Nashan or without a coach. Aliq shared my trainer and his winnings helped pay him, but not the day-to-day coach, whom Nashan wanted to concentrate on me. The message was clear, and still I clung to my friend and our doubles career. After all, we were winning titles.

(Meanwhile, Aliq and Shona were also doing well at mixed doubles, if not quite as well as we were. But they hadn't been playing together as long, and every tournament they got better.)

Aliq and my trainer talked workouts and techniques just about all the way through every workout we had, with my trainer talking about articles he'd read, new techniques, making minor corrections to Aliq's form. It was cute, and I liked that it meant that both of them left me mostly alone to do my workout.

And then August was halfway over and it was time to go to Cuyahoga, the last hardcourt tournament before the States Open, where I'd see Braden again.

* * *

Cuyahoga in August is not somewhere I'd want to spend a lot of time. It's hot, it's muggy so my fur feels sticky all the time, and there's not a lot to do around the tennis pavilion. Fortunately, all the indoor facilities are air-conditioned, so the only time you have to be outside is when you're actually on the court. We brought extra bottles of water and BoltAde out even for practices.

It was fantastic to see Braden again, and to judge from the speed with which he shed his clothes when we got together, he felt the same way. After some passionate reunion sex, we lay together panting and naked and grinning, paws sliding over each others' fur.

"Hey," Braden said when we'd both gotten our wind back. "Couple things. First off, the last week in August, right before the tournament starts. I have access to a condo an hour or so outside of Port City. Would you want to hang out there for a few days, just the two of us?"

"Fuck yes," I said without a moment's hesitation. "But can you spare the time?"

His smile widened. "I'm going to need it. That's the other thing. My parents are here, they're going to be in Port City."

"Uh." I searched his eyes. "You, uh…you want me to meet them?"

"Oh hell no. That might kill Dad. On second thought…" He pretended to consider it. "No. But I'm going to have to deal with them, and they're not happy about Ellen, so you know, if I'm even more pissy than usual, that's why."

"You've got tennis," I reminded him.

"I've got tennis." He put a paw on my chest. "Tennis helps me focus on what's important. Really important. I know people say family is, and maybe it is for some people, but for me it's mostly a distraction."

"Family's important if they make themselves important. They can also make themselves be…not important."

"Hm."

"But also." I laid my paw over his. "Family isn't just blood relatives. They're the people who care about you and put the work in. That's what I learned this last year. Family can reject you, they can leave you, they can betray you. But they can also choose you. Aliq, Lochen, you…you're all my family, one way or another."

He looked steadily at me. "Family is family. I think there should be another word for the people you choose to be around you."

"All right," I said. "We'll come up with one."

"I don't want to have to distinguish between the family I don't care about and the family I do."

"I get it." I rubbed his paw. "But…you don't really care about them at all? They still come to your matches."

He left his paw where it was but lay back on the bed staring at the ceiling. "I don't want to care about them. They raised me but always seemed more busy with their work or their hobbies, you know? I had a nanny and I loved her. She's the one who got me into tennis. And now I feel like I'm one of my father's prize boats or something, something he can say to all his friends, 'look, there's my genes in there.'"

I stayed quiet and let him talk. "I guess I'd like them to be proud of me, but I hate that I want that. You know what I mean?"

"Kind of. I mean, I understand it, but I always wanted Ma to be proud of me. I still want that."

Braden didn't say anything for a moment and then went on. "Most of my friends have what you had: good parents who cared for them and are still friends with them. I'm not friends with my parents. I guess it doesn't bother me that much that they come to the games and everything, not enough that I want to make a big scene with them. It's just…ugh. After Ellen left, my mom cried at me for an hour, never going to have grandcubs, Ellen was so nice, how could I do that to the two of them, all of that."

I curled my fingers around his. "She didn't ask how you felt about it?"

"I, uh…" He went silent for several seconds. "I guess not."

"That sucks."

"I didn't expect her to, to be honest."

"I don't know if that makes it better."

He grinned. "I appreciate that you asked, even though I know you already know."

"That's what boyfriends do."

"Heh. I have a lot to learn."

"Not so much," I told him, and rolled over to kiss him.

We both did well in that tournament, though of course Braden did better than I did. We chatted in the locker room about the matches we'd played and seen; we practiced with Ljubo and even Milos and several of the other players we knew; I spent time with Aliq and Ori, and Braden spent time with his team. I didn't hear anyone say anything about "Braden's little friend," but I didn't know whether that was because we were also socializing with other players or because I'd gotten my ranking up high enough that it made sense for me to hang out with him.

I lost in the quarterfinals, so I had time to see Braden win his quarterfinal match. He looked fantastic out there and I sat with Ori admiring his grace and power on the court. After he'd won, I waved to him and he gave me a smile before heading to the locker room.

"When do I get to meet him?" Ori asked, elbowing me.

"After the tournament," I said. "Or at least, not during the tournament. We're going away for a couple days but I'll see if I can drag him to dinner with us."

"Can Marro come too?"

"Of course," I said. "He's family."

I got up to leave and an older vixen blocked my way. Her pure white formal dress almost blinded me in the sun and her perfume made me feel like I was standing in a garbage dump full of roses. "Rocky, isn't it?" she said.

Ori gave a small squeak of surprise behind me. "Alicia Longacre," I said, "this is my sister Ori."

"I see the resemblance." She barely even looked at Ori. "I have a question for you. You know my son."

Behind me, Ori made a noise so faint that I was sure even Mrs. Longacre with her fox's ears couldn't hear it. "Yes," I said. "I—"

"I want to know if you know anything about what happened with his fiancée."

I had prepared for another question, my heart racing as I wondered if she'd smelled me on Braden one morning, and this one took me aback. "What?"

"Ellen. You came around asking about her. Do you know her? Did my son talk to you about her?"

"I, er…" I took a step back, my head swimming. "Hadn't you better ask him about that?"

"Oh." She flattened her ears and tossed her head, letting me see the diamond earrings she wore. "I have asked him and he just says he doesn't know. Of course he knows. How could he not? But Ellen

won't return my calls and my son won't talk to me and it's just such a frustrating position for a mother to be in."

Ori said, "Aw," behind me, but I wasn't moved. "I'm sorry I can't help you, Mrs. Longacre," I said. "Braden never talked to me about Ellen after they broke up."

She leaned closer to me, nostrils twitching. "But you know they broke up."

"Well, yes. I mean…" I fumbled for words. "They were together a lot, and then they weren't. I asked him and he just said it was over."

"So he did talk to you about her."

"Just that one time." The day was hot but I hadn't felt really warm until that moment.

"And that's all he said. 'It's over.'"

"That's all."

She examined me for another moment and then exhaled, said, "Typical," and turned and strolled off without saying another word.

It took me several breaths to relax, during which time Ori put her muzzle close to my ear and said, "That's his *mom*?"

We chuckled about it on the way out of the stadium, but afterwards I felt bad about it. Not really for his mom; she sounded more like someone who'd come home to find one of her china pieces broken than someone worried about her son's emotional well-being. But sorry that they couldn't find a way to repair their relationship. Maybe it wasn't worth it. Maybe there wasn't a relationship there to mend anymore.

I resolved not to mention it to Braden until we had time alone together, and I'd thought that would be after the tournament was over. The night before the final, though, he texted me asking where we could meet—he'd reserved a separate room but told me we didn't have to use it—and I asked Aliq if I could have our room for the night. He then had to go ask Shona if he could stay with her that night, so it ended up being twenty minutes later that I texted Braden back and told him to come over.

It was nice having him in my room, nice knowing that even if Aliq smelled something it wouldn't matter. We cuddled in bed, taking our time for once rather than diving on each others' cocks (as was our custom now, we saved dinner until after the sex, but neither of us was hungry enough to push us to go faster). Braden asked me to top him again, so I did, reflecting that I could get used to that.

We ordered room service and I put on a robe so that I could greet the server at the door. Braden took a quick shower to rinse the lube out from under his tail and then remained naked on the bed. I sat down next to him and decided this was as good a time as any. "Hey," I said, my paw on his tail, "would this be an okay time to say something that's not romantic and might annoy you?"

His eyes narrowed, and his tail curled under my paw. "Am I going to be annoyed at you?"

"No. I mean, I hope not, but it's mostly not about me."

He nodded and his tail relaxed. "All right. Go ahead, then."

So I told him about the encounter with his mother, remembering it as best I could. I expected him to grumble about it, but he laughed when I was done. "I'm sorry you had to deal with her," he said, "but you did exactly the right thing. Don't let her bother you, and don't think that it bothers me. If she's asking you then she must be desperate to understand what's going on, and I don't want to tell her."

I stroked his tail. "Do you think they'll ever leave you alone?"

"When I stop winning."

"I'm sorry." I said it without thinking.

His tail stopped twitching. I looked over into a thoughtful expression. "I never thought of it as something people would pity me for. It's just what it is. The way they are made me the way I am." When I didn't say anything to that, his ears canted and he leaned back. "Which is maybe not great. But I feel like at some point I bought into it, you know? I liked the fight. I like it when my mom's frustrated because it means I'm winning."

"It doesn't have to be a fight," I said, but I was thinking of Aliq's parents. He had confidence that they would mend their relationship, but what if they didn't?

"It doesn't," Braden agreed, "but if it's not, then what is it?"

I didn't have an answer for him.

* * *

Braden had his alarm set for a ridiculous time of the morning, something like 5:30 am. Aliq and I only ever got up at 6:30, even on a match day, and when we didn't have a match, we slept in. He didn't insist I get up, though he did kiss me good-bye before I fell back asleep.

He won the tournament—nothing in tennis is sure enough to say "of course," but I felt like at this point in the year he was playing well enough and everyone was intimidated enough by him that it was an "of course"—and the final was pretty good, though not his best match of the tournament. I watched from the locker room with Milos, worried about running into Braden's parents again, and as Braden wrapped up the title easily, the maned wolf stood up and strode around the locker room. "Not gonna be that easy for him at the States," he said, pointing. "If he gets the Slam, good for him, but he gonna earn it."

"Of course he will." I grinned. "Nobody's gonna let him walk over them."

"Everyone's gonna be gunning for him." One of the other players in the room joined in. His tone was tentative enough that it made me stop and wonder, am I one of the people other players are intimidated by now? I'd gotten to the quarterfinals here, and Milos had gotten to a semifinal before losing to Braden, but none of the other players in the room had made it to the final eight.

So I turned, smiled at the squirrel who'd talked, and said, "You're right. But they've been gunning for him all year, at least since the Ozzie. He's gotten to number one through all that."

He perked up at being included, and I felt good about that. I knew his name (Roa Lakuni, from Kanata) and that he was ranked in the forties, but not much more about him. He turned out to be a nice enough guy, although he talked too much about his own accomplishments and the one tournament he'd gotten to the finals of last year.

I didn't give him my contact info as we were leaving, but I did say I hoped I'd run into him at the States. I wanted to make sure that

I was nice to the up and coming players the way Ljubo and Milos and a few others had been nice to me.

Braden arranged for us to take a flight to the East Coast from Cuyahoga airport very late Monday night, to lessen the chance of running into anyone we knew. We talked about taking a chartered jet but both thought that would attract more attention. On a commercial flight we could sit separately and meet up outside the airport. So anyway, that gave us time to have a drink on Monday afternoon with Aliq and Ori and Marro.

Overall I think it went pretty well. Everyone was kind of on eggshells; my friends didn't want to offend my boyfriend and my boyfriend didn't want to offend my friends. Aliq said something about how amazing Braden had been playing, and Braden thanked him, and then he surprised us by telling Aliq that he thought he had a very good court sense.

"You've seen me play?" Aliq said, and then looked at me. "Oh, yeah, that makes sense, I guess."

"I don't think Rocky should be playing doubles," Braden said, "but when he plays with you I see why he's still doing it. You guys are good together. I never found anyone I had that kind of communication with." He glanced at me. "On the court, I mean."

Aliq got very flustered and stuck his nose in his glass while Ori said nice things about me. Later, Aliq would tell me he wasn't embarrassed by Braden acknowledging our relationship, but at the idea that "the number one fucking player in the world was critiquing and complimenting my game, fucking hell, Rocky, keep him and don't let him go."

Ori said the same thing, with less cursing, and even Marro said that anyone who could get Braden to be polite and even pleasant to be with for an entire meal had to be good for him and for the game. I think by the time we'd finished up, everyone was a little more at ease. I know at least I didn't feel like I was trying to defuse a bomb anymore.

Braden had things to take care of before our flight, so I didn't get to talk to him until we'd landed at the Stagford airport and gotten into our private car, where we put up the privacy screen. "Thanks for coming to meet my friends and my sister," I said. "It meant a lot to me."

"They're nice. Did they like me?"

He said it casually, but his ears flicked and I felt he was actually invested in the answer. "They did. Did you like them?"

"Of course."

"You don't like anyone."

He laughed. "Most people give me a reason not to like them, often in the first five minutes of meeting them. Your sister and your friends didn't do any of that."

I leaned against him. "It felt nice to acknowledge you in front of them, you know? That we were sitting there talking and they knew that we're..." I glanced at the privacy screen. "Anyway, it felt freeing, kind of."

"It was more weird for me, but yeah. I haven't sat down with—well, I never had a boyfriend before, so these are all firsts. But good firsts." He nosed my ear.

"Kinda for me too." I watched the suburban landscape go by. "So where is this place?"

"It's a surprise," he said. "Boyfriends do that, right?"

"As long as it's a good surprise."

"It is." He grinned.

We pulled up an hour later in front of a gate set into a big stone wall that disappeared on either side into darkness. A big brightly-lit sign proclaimed this to be Tranquility Cove. "A place to relax," flowery script wrote underneath it.

Braden dropped the privacy shield and said, "Give them the code 90969."

The driver did, and the gate opened. "Directly across that circle up there and then the second left."

When the driver's window opened the salt air of the sea rushed in, and with it the smell of so many different kinds of flowers that it was hard to sort them all out. Once the privacy screen was back up, I leaned back in the seat and turned to Braden. "You have a place here?" I asked. "Or is this just a rental?"

"It's my parents' place," he said, and then laughed when he saw my expression. "Don't worry, there isn't going to be one of those movie scenes where they walk in on us. They're in Pensa visiting my grandmother in between tournaments. I saw them off this morning."

"As long as they don't fly up unexpectedly."

"I told them I was going to be here. If they do decide to cut the Pensa trip short, they'll call."

"All right." I grinned. "Can't wait to see it."

I didn't have to wait long. The car stopped in front of an attractive little cottage with a spotlight on the number 20. The driver took our luggage up to the door and waited until Braden unlocked it, then said, "Good night, sir," and returned to his car.

The cottage had two bedrooms, a charming kitchen, and a living room that smelled of violet-scented cleaning products. The light blue flower pattern on the chair and couch matched the soft lavender carpet, and on the cream-colored walls hung seascape paintings, an odd touch considering I could hear the ocean outside the window and was certain that in the daylight it would be visible; that was the point of this cottage being here. Braden took his suitcase to one of the bedrooms and I followed him in.

"The bed should be big enough, right?" He gestured toward a double bed. "Because I don't want to sleep in my parents' room."

"It's fine." I grinned, stepped forward, and kissed him.

Braden's phone woke us up the first morning and didn't stop buzzing for an hour until he turned it off. He used my phone to send a message to his personal trainer telling him to call my number if a real emergency came up but otherwise he was off the grid. My phone buzzed too but less frequently, enough that it wasn't an issue for me to check. Ori called me once to make sure I was okay, Lochen once to talk about a meeting he was setting up at the States. The other calls I let go to voicemail.

It was a very nice two days overall. The cottage had a delivery service that provided meals for us, left outside the door. They could either be hot or ready-to-heat, and we enjoyed both. The sex was great, but we also had a lot of very relaxing times, walking down by the ocean (colder and angrier than the beaches in Pensa but also more starkly beautiful), watching movies on the house's streaming service, and talking.

We watched movies we'd both liked; we watched movies we both wanted to see. We watched movies Braden liked and I hadn't seen, and movies I liked and Braden hadn't seen. We listened to music and we talked about the movies and the music and everything.

And of course we talked about tennis, with a major tournament just a few days away. That was the only time Braden got intense. I'd seen his public comments about having won the first three majors of the year, how he just wanted to play his best and he wasn't thinking about winning the fourth to complete the Grand Slam. "It's just another tournament," he said, "and I'm going to do my best to win like I always do."

But in private, with me, he sounded different. "I want this," he told me. "I want it badly. You know how much this would set me apart?"

"I know."

"You know how I'd be able to rub it in my Dad's face?" His father had told him when he was ten that he could chase this "silly hobby" with their money for as long as he wanted, and the condescension had never left Braden's mind, even when his father openly admired his skill.

"Don't think about that part," I advised. "I know it's hard, but think about what an incredible feat it would be. Think about seven more matches. Who are you going to beat?"

He laughed. We were sitting out on the enclosed porch of the cottage in the warm late afternoon air, shirtless, and he reached over to pat my bare chest. "Honestly, there's only maybe four or five players who scare me."

"Dubois."

"Of course."

"Milos. Not Colluvic, I think. Li? Bowson?"

He wiggled his paw. I thought about it. "Tempest?"

"Yeah. Home crowd, plus he caught fire at Cuyahoga."

I guessed a few more players, and he shook his head to all of them. "All right," I said, "I give up. Unless it's me."

He grinned. "Bingo."

"What? Seriously?"

"Uh huh."

"What, are you afraid I'll kiss you on a changeover, or you'll think about my cock or something?"

His paw slid down to the front of my pants. "I'll probably do that, but not more than you'll think about mine. I think we're evenly matched there. But seriously, you're making big jumps. Just this year you've gone up, what, twenty spots, something like that? You're playing better and better and you're good enough to get hot and blaze through seven matches."

I flattened my warm ears and gave a nervous, "Heh heh," to cover how good that made me feel. "Thanks. But you saw the draw, right? We wouldn't play until the final. So I don't think you have to worry about that this time."

"Plus in the final I'll be really focused," he said. "In an earlier match there's a small chance you could catch me looking ahead. But not in the final."

"I'll remember that for future tournaments," I said, and leaned over to kiss him.

Chapter Thirty-Four

And here we are, less than a month later, both of us panting even though the sun's been down for half an hour. It's the fifth set of the States Open final and we are in a tiebreak, because of course we are. How else could this match end?

He starts off the tiebreak with an ace, I follow up with a good rally and passing shot and then an ace, and we're off and running. Both of us are tired; I know I am and Braden's dragging his tail, not moving with the same hops he usually does. So we're both going for safer shots, trying to wear the other out with long rallies, pouncing on openings when we see them.

At 2-3, on serve, I miss my first serve and Braden inches up. I get the second serve in and he jumps on it, sending it down the deuce court side with a scorching forehand that just clips the line. In, mini-break to Braden.

Then we have to change sides, and I probably spend too much time thinking about being down a mini-break. My attempt to get an ace down the T misses by inches, and then I'm worried about the second serve and I clip the net cord. It bounces and drops out. Double fault, and now I'm down two mini-breaks at 2-5. Braden just has to hold his two serves and the championship is his.

He doesn't look at me as he bounces the balls, preparing to serve. The crowd's roar is building, and even when the chair umpire reminds them to be quiet, there's background whispering that my ears pick up. I tune it out, focused on the ball and the cross fox bouncing it, tossing it into the air, and sweeping his racket around.

The serve is a good one, but I guess right and get a good return. He has to run to get there, but he gets to it and sends a forehand back. I stay at the baseline and try to hit it to his backhand, and he does the same to me. Just keep it in, I tell myself. Wait for him to make a mistake.

Never mind that that strategy almost never works with Braden. He's tired, I'm tired, maybe—

Nope. He switches up on me, sends a backhand slice to the deuce sideline, and when I run for it he comes to the net. I try a crosscourt pass but I don't quite get the angle, and I hit the net.

Match point. Slam point. The umpire has to tell the crowd to quiet down three times before they reduce their roar to an acceptable level. Braden waits, feeling the moment as much as I am, and then he lofts the ball, swings—

Bang, into the net.

He prepares for the second serve, and I'm weirdly calm. If this is it, then this is it. But another part of me is automatically thinking about Braden and where he'll go with a second serve that he absolutely needs, serving to left-handed me on a deuce court.

But wait; he doesn't absolutely need it. If he loses, it's still 3-6 and he has three match points left. No; I know Braden. He wants to end it right now. So he's not going to serve it wide, to my right side, trying to make me backhand it—that's what he's been doing all match. He'll serve into the body or down the T.

The last time we practiced, he caught me off guard with a serve to the body, aimed right at me. Braden would remember that, of course he would, so he's probably thinking that I'll expect him to serve into the body again, and that means he'll go down the T. Or will he? He knows me and knows that I know his thinking, so will he go one step farther and actually serve into the body? I think he will.

As soon as he lofts the ball, I jump to my left. If it's down the T, I'll have a forehand on it, but I'll also have a good backhand on it if he was going for the body. And sure enough, the ball zips right to where I'd been standing. My backhand, the shot I've worked on for the last couple years, comes through when I need it, scorching a passing shot down the line as Braden follows his serve to the net. Mini-break back to me, 3-6 to my serve, and I still have to break Braden once more or he'll be serving for the set again.

I get a good first serve in and control the point until I can work Braden into a favorable position and then I hit him with a crosscourt shot to the open court. On the second of my service points I get a good deep baseline shot that lets me come to net and end the point quickly.

So it's 5-6 and Braden is once again serving for the match. This time I read his body language and I can tell he's thinking that he overthought the last point. He's serving to the ad court this time, so out wide will go to my forehand, but he's thinking I'll be expecting it down the T, and I feel like he's going wide.

But I don't have to jump on this side of the court like I do on the deuce court. I wait, and here comes the serve, and oh shit, it's down the T. I send a backhand back to him, deep enough to keep him from coming to the net, but he has time to see where I am and send a topspin forehand to the other corner. I get there and I see him move out of the corner of my eye, thinking he must be coming to net, because I'm deep enough, so I hit a forehand down the line, desperate, a good passing shot—only he's not at the net. He's back at the baseline, and the ball is bouncing, lifting up into his strike zone.

My momentum carries me into the doubles alley on the ad court; I reverse as fast as I can, but Braden snaps his racket up, putting topspin on the ball but also killing its momentum. It curves back over the net on the deuce court; I see what's happening and I run, but my legs are lead and it takes only one step for me to realize I'm not going to get there. The ball lands in and spins away from me, hits the ground another time, and the match is over.

The crowd erupts. Braden stands still for a moment and then drops his racket, falls to his knees, and topples forward onto the court, arms outstretched. He lies there for a second and then rolls onto his back, and the grin that splits his muzzle is huge. Joy radiates off him like heat, and his tongue lolls to one side. I walk around the net—it's not protocol but fuck it—and get to him just as he sits up.

I reach a paw down and he grabs it. I help him up and pull him into a hug and he hugs me back, and I tell him, "You're the best, you're the fucking best," and he laughs into my ear.

After a moment in which he doesn't let go either, he says, "Hey, this hug's going on a little long."

"Yeah," I say. "So what?"

* * *

"Alastair, I think they're already cueing up this match to replay on the Tennis Channel's Classic Finals series."

"You could not be more right, Daren. We're going to talk a lot about Braden Longacre, but let's recognize Rocky N'Guwe, looking like a seasoned professional in his first major singles final. Braden is the best in the game, but on this day I'm not sure this young jackal isn't second best."

"They're still hugging, still talking, Rocky no doubt congratulating his friend on completing the Grand Slam—now they break apart to shake the chair umpire's paw. And whatever Longacre said to N'Guwe after that first set has been long forgotten, it seems. Rocky is almost as happy for Braden as Braden is himself."

"The jackal starts packing up his equipment, but Longacre, who has always had a dicey relationship with tennis crowds, turns and basks in their cheers. This crowd knows what they've just seen and they want to keep this moment going for him as long as they can."

"I don't know how he has the energy to walk around after that grueling final."

"Oh, to be young again."

"Indeed. Folks, we'll be right back with the trophy presentation, and you'll hear from Braden Longacre himself on the historic occasion of being the first male player in nearly fifty years to complete the calendar Grand Slam of tennis."

* * *

I am standing in the middle of the court where they've got two trophies and two checks and this is surreal. I mean, I've won tournaments before, obviously, many times. But they've never had this much fanfare, this many people clustered around to present the award. They have to have a guy from the ITF speaking and then a guy from Chufrolet motors, who's sponsoring the tournament, and then there's the head of the tournament who finally gets around to talking about the fantastic match we just saw. He leads, of course, with the fact that we've all witnessed history, one of the greatest individual achievements in tennis, and waxes nostalgic about the great players of the past and how Braden's going to be listed among them. "But of course, nobody can win a tennis match without beating someone, and this year's runner-up certainly didn't make it easy for Braden, ha ha. Let's have a warm round of applause for this year's States Open runner-up, Rocky N'Guwe."

The applause is more than I've ever heard for any tournament I've won; then again, there are probably three to four times as many people here as at any tournament I've won. I smile and wait for it to die down.

This is a weird speech. I've never been asked to speak as the loser of a match. But I know this is an important occasion and I've watched enough major final presentation ceremonies to know how to be a graceful loser. "Thanks everyone," I say, "for an amazing two weeks. Every tournament is special, but this is my adopted home country and I have to say that this is my absolute favorite tournament. Thank you to all you fans for making it so wonderful here." Pause to let them cheer for themselves. And then I thank my team, my coach, my sister, my trainer, all the people who made this possible. And lastly, of course, "I want to thank Braden Longacre for being such an inspiration all through this year. I never thought I'd get to play him in a major final, and if I did, I sure didn't think it would go five sets. He's kicked my tail pretty thoroughly every other time we played. But he's inspired me to elevate my game…while keeping himself head and shoulders above the rest of us. It's been the greatest honor of my career so far to play him in this final match, and my consolation in losing it is that I know I'll be back and I'm younger than he is."

I get a laugh for that, wrap up the speech, and then accept my check, which has "1.6 MILLION" written on it in huge letters. One of the tournament staffers holds it for me while I hold up the runner-up trophy, a nice plate. I'll get to keep a replica of the trophy, engraved with my name, but I want that winner trophy. I need to keep this momentum going.

That's a conversation for next week, with Lochen and Nashan. Right now I step back to let Braden have the spotlight.

He thanks his team, thanks the fans, and then turns to me. "This guy," he says, and laughs. "This guy. I've been watching him for a while, and I never thought he'd be the toughest match of the year. But he's getting better so fast, it's been a real pleasure to watch. I thought he had me a couple times there. He sure came closer than anybody else. But one of the things I've learned this year is that even when you're really tired, and you think you've lost your chance…you gotta keep trying. The match isn't over until it's over. Rocky, I tell you…you're great. You've got a great future ahead of you."

He goes on to talk about the year, his support, this tournament, and all that, every bit the smooth winner. My tail wags a little, but heck, so is everyone's on stage. It's a happy moment and I'm almost as happy as if I'd won. Maybe happier, because if I'd won I would've felt so bad for Braden that it would've tainted things.

After we pose with the trophies for photos, there are the interviews. Mine are shorter, mostly talking about the game where he turned his ankle in the fifth set and wanting to know about the tiebreak, specifically my double-fault. Was I tired? I talk politely about how Braden's game is so well constructed that there are almost no cracks in it; that my game is made to rattle people with well-constructed games, but you can only rattle Braden so far. Later, in retrospect, I will realize how cool it is that I'm being interviewed by the top tier tennis personalities, the ones I've been watching on TV for years. They're good; Jack Forte, the pine marten, watches me earnestly as he asks the questions, making me feel like he really cares about the answers. Of course, when the cameras are off, he's still nice, but a lot more casual. "Great tournament," he says. "Hope to see you at the Ozzie."

"I'm figuring things out," I say.

"It shows." He flashes a grin. "Welcome to the Golden Age of States tennis."

I think he comes up with that on the spot, or else he's been thinking about it for a while. Either way, later that night on the wrap-up broadcast he says it to the whole country. I don't hear it that night, for obvious reasons, but Ori records the whole thing, the match and the aftermath, and puts it in a file on my phone I can access anytime.

Of course there are a bunch of the guys in the locker room to greet me when I get back, Ljubo and Milos primarily grab me and slap my back and tell me what a good match I played. "Could've been just a little better," I say, but I feel great about it.

"Ah, a little better, always can be a little better." Ljubo laughs. "You will have to tell us the secret of playing Braden."

"No secret," I say. "Just play better. And, uh, wait for him to turn his ankle."

They laugh and keep buzzing about the match: even if it hadn't been for the Grand Slam, it would've been a great match, and so on. The warm feeling in me grows and grows, bigger than I've ever felt after a loss.

My phone is buzzing even more than the guys in the locker room. Texts from everyone in my contact list, pretty much: Bret, Dom, Kim, and a few other Palm Gables friends; Danver and Sean and my Challenger tournament friends; even Marquize. *That was fantastic*, he's written. *I knew you'd be great.*

That one my thumb hesitates over. The rest I'll reply to with one or two-word thank-yous, and everyone will understand that I'm busy now, busier than I've ever been. But I want to say more to Marquize, to tell him in a sentence about the journey I've been on and how I've come to a place where I still don't forgive him for what he did, but I understand it better and I hope that he's as happy as I am.

That's a heck of a sentence. I settle for writing, *Thanks, give my best to Craig*, and I add a heart emoji at the end of it. I think that's pretty close.

And then I come out of the locker room into the lounge and a flurry of hugs and squeals, mostly from Ori, but Aliq gets in a few good hugs too, and even Nashan's grinning hugely and gives me a big hug when everyone else is done. And it's the whole thing all over again, not that I was getting tired of it: how great I played, how close the match was, how that one point was completely lucky.

I hug back and laugh. "Come on," I say. "I'm starving. Let's get some dinner."

Dinner has already been arranged by Lochen at one of the fanciest steak houses in Port City, along with a limo to take us there—all of us, Ori and Aliq and Nashan and my trainers and even Marro squeezes in as Ori's date. There's champagne in the back, so we all get a little giggly on the way there, and for me there are protein bars, which I devour.

The maitre'd, a tuxedoed raccoon, knows my name from the reservation and knows who I am and what I've done, so on the way to the private room he tells me that some of the staff would like to know if they can get pictures with me, and that the restaurant would like a picture for their wall. "Of course," I tell him, "but after the meal if that's all right." He assures me it will be.

The meal is fantastic, both the food and the company, and we're there for three hours. In the middle of it my phone buzzes (it hasn't really stopped, but it's slowed down), and this time it's Braden. I excuse myself, saying, "Bathroom," but I stop in the hallway outside the bathroom to read the text.

Four Seasons Hotel 1020, it says. *Come when you can.*

Out at dinner, will be there soon, I type back. And then I add, *Can't wait to see you, Mister Grand Slam.*

I look up to see Aliq with a grin on his muzzle. "Bathroom, huh?"

I slip the phone into my pocket and flick my ears. "Some texts you gotta take. I didn't want to be rude."

"It was him, right?"

I wait as a bear shoulders by me to the restroom. He pauses and looks back, maybe because I'm a jackal, maybe because he recognizes me. When he's passed, I say, "Yeah."

Aliq slides up next to me, leaning against the wall. Across from us are pictures of famous musicians who've eaten here, females by their bathroom and males by theirs. "So," Aliq says quietly, "how weird was it? Playing him?"

"Not really. I mean, we're both about the game, you know? I didn't think about him in that other way at all, really."

"I wasn't sure, from the hug."

He smirks, and I elbow him. "That was just a fellow player and friend overjoyed that his friend won the Grand Slam."

"Sure, it plays like that," he says, and elbows back. "Is he being smug about it?"

"Not yet. He just texted me to come over. I told him I'm at dinner."

Aliq grins. "Playing hard to get?"

"He's already got," I point out. "I'm enjoying my celebratory dinner with my closest friends and family."

"All but one."

"He's got his own celebration. Even if he isn't there right now."

Aliq put an arm around my shoulder. "I'm glad you're here with us, but I'm also glad you've got someone else to go to tonight. Does that make sense?"

"Sure. I'm glad I'm here too."

"One more thing." He leaves his arm there. "Shona and I were talking. I think I'm gonna focus on mixed doubles for a bit."

My ears go down. "You're dropping our doubles?"

"Yeah. I mean, you've got so much potential in singles, I really want you to do every single little thing you can to make it."

"But I won my bet. I'm going to be top ten—or damn close—and I did it while playing doubles."

"Uh huh. And if you hadn't played doubles this tournament, maybe you'd have had that one little extra burst of energy when you needed it and you'd be the States Open champion right now."

"That's—"

He holds up a paw. "I know you'd never do it on your own and I appreciate that. Look, after the last month I've had a bunch of people say, 'when Rocky drops you for singles, give me a call.' Some pretty good players too. I'll be fine."

"We'll talk about it later," I say, although I know it's settled.

"Sure we will."

"And you don't get to stop being my friend."

"Oh," he laughs, "don't worry, I'm gonna mooch off you for as long as Lochen lets me. We can even still room together at tournaments where neither of us have a reason for a single room."

"Damn right." I stare him right in the eyes. "*Akhi.*"

He blinks. "Gesundheit?"

My ears fold back. "Didn't you call me that once? I looked it up on the Internet. It means 'brother.'"

"Oh. Oh!" He laughs. "*Achi.* That means—it's more like 'dude.' Or 'bro.'"

"Ugh. Stupid Internet." Now my ears are warm.

"I called you that a couple times, but not since…not since like you came out to me." He tilted his ears. "Were you calling me your brother?"

"That was the idea."

He hugs me. "All right, well, sentiment received, but you can stick to English, brother." He tilted his head. "What is it in your language?"

"I guess *mpangi*, if you're older," I say. "But 'brother' is just fine."

"All right," he says, and disengages. "I do really have to use the restroom. So answer that text and get back to dinner."

"I will. And thanks."

When he's in the restroom, I take out the phone to see Braden's answer. It's nothing but a heart.

* * *

Somewhat to my surprise, when I get to his hotel room, Braden's fully clothed. Tail swishing, he paces back to the window as the door closes behind me and then comes back to me. "Good match," he says.

"Yeah." I hug him again, and he hugs back, but in a way that I can tell something's on his mind. "You're great. Made history."

"Uh huh." He pulls back and looks in my eyes.

"What?"

He doesn't need more encouragement. "Break point in the fifth, after I turned my ankle."

"Yeah?"

His hazel eyes stay fixed on mine. "You could've come to the net and put it away, but you didn't. Did you stay back to give me more of a chance?"

I snort. "After that ultimatum you snapped before the second set?"

Now his focus wavers, a little uncertain. "I didn't give you an *ultimatum.*"

"You said, quote, 'if you're throwing this match, we're through.'"

His ears go back. "That's—that's—"

I raise my eyebrows. "What?"

"That's not an ultimatum."

"Ha." I go sit on the desk, tail flicking. "Okay, explain that. Do I just not know what the word means?"

"No, no." He sits on the bed facing me. "I mean, I wasn't saying, 'if you do this thing, I'm breaking up with you.' I was saying that if you had already made the decision to throw the match, then I misunderstood something about you and we shouldn't be dating."

"But," I argue, "if I were throwing the match in that first set—I wasn't—and then I decided to stop, we'd still be dating."

He considers that. "If you made the decision in the first place, I don't know that that's something I could respect."

"What if I wanted you to win more than I wanted to win? I know what it means to you."

"Sure," he says, "and that's sweet. But if you know me, you should also know that it would kill me to know that I got this given to me by my boyfriend, that I didn't earn it."

I nod. "Course I know that. So I'd never let you think that you didn't earn it."

He squints. "You mean, if you did throw it, you wouldn't tell me."

"You should trust me not to. I wouldn't. I didn't." He still looks worried, so I lean forward and try a different tack. "Break point in the fifth. You didn't get that first serve in. Did you do that on purpose?"

He scoffs. "That happened 31 percent of the time in that match."

"Right, but when it did, was there a part of you that thought, well, if I lose, I can blame it on the ankle, and I won't mind if Rocky wins, better him than, I dunno, Dubois or something?"

His ears flick. "No," he says. "I mean, I'd rather you win than Dubois or anyone else. But…"

I hop off the desk and go to sit on the bed next to him, and I take his paw. "I love you," I say, "and I want you to have this the way you'll feel best about it. So I tried my hardest to beat you because I know you'd rather lose fighting than get something you didn't earn. Even though honestly you've earned this the way you've been playing all year."

He shakes his head. "I don't get you. You're a pain in the ass, but you're the best thing that's ever happened to me."

"I'll take that." I lean forward to kiss his muzzle.

The kiss is nice and sweet and warm and leads to his paws on my sides and mine on his tail. After a nice little while of that he pulls back. "I, uh, you know I have this problem with certain words, right?"

"Okay."

"But, uh." He scratches his ear. "I don't want you to think that just because I'm not saying certain specific words that I'm not feeling the same kind of thing you are. It's just that—"

"Quiet," I say, and kiss him again. "I know. I haven't spent months—years—around you not to know that."

"The point is." He pushes me away, mock-annoyed. "The point is that I want to be able to say that."

"Oh, is that the point?" I grin at him. "It'll happen when it happens. It's fine. So what now? You hungry? Or…"

"Definitely 'or.'" He presses his paw to my pants. "I want to get that inside me. Then we can grab food." As he rubs my sheath, he says, "If you want, we can go back to my party. I'm sure it's still going on."

"You'd bring me there?"

"Bring your whole team. Sure."

I'm hard and it's difficult to focus. "Because it's less weird with the whole team, I guess?"

"Because they're important to you and it'd be good for them to be there."

"Ah, uh." I slide my pants off. "Won't that be a little weird?"

He strips his shirt off and pulls down my boxers. "Sure. But I'm the best tennis player in the fucking world. I can invite my runner-up to my party if I want. Nobody has to know we just fucked."

"Okay, yeah," I say. "Let me just text—" But my phone's in my pants on the floor and his muzzle is on my cock, and soon enough all of our clothes are off and I'm buried under his tail, and so the texts can wait.

When I do finally get around to texting, it takes a little while to convince Ori and Aliq that they're welcome at the party, but I say, hey, it'll be more suspicious if I'm just there without my team, which is maybe true but also I want them to be there. So they agree to show up, and Braden invites Ljubo and Marro and some of his team as well, and when we get to the party it's going strong.

We walk in, me and Braden, like we were just out having a smoke or a drink or something, and it takes people a while to notice Braden. As they cluster around him, he introduces me and says we were talking about the match, and then everyone recognizes me and says what a great match it was, and so on.

Ori and Marro show up later, and Aliq and Shona too, and it feels nice that we're all at a party. I meet a lot of people from the tennis world, but mostly they're people from Braden's team or people those people know, and later, a few other players show up and it becomes a nice little gathering.

It's a celebration of Braden, even though the year isn't technically over, and while I'm not at his side all night, I hear people tell him over and over how fantastic his year was. He basks in it, smiling more than I've seen him in public in a while.

Ori catches me watching him at one point and elbows me. "Things are good, yeah?"

"Things are good," I tell her.

"Good." She eyes Braden too. "Ma would be proud of you."

She's being mindful of the ears around us; I know she doesn't just mean about making the final. "There's a lot of work to do," I say, "but I think I'm on the right path."

"You never know until you're at the end, do you?" She smiles. "But I think so too. We both are."

I can't argue with that.

Later, Braden pulls me out onto the balcony of one of the hotel rooms the party spreads across and we slide to one side so we're not immediately visible from the room inside. "It's a good party," I say.

"Good." He covers my paw with his. "I wondered if you might be uncomfortable here."

"Nah. Everyone seems really happy that you invited me. Said it's a classy move. People are trying to console me and I finally figured out that the best move is not to tell them I don't need consoling but just to say 'thank you' and let them do it."

He chuckles. "I'm glad you can let things go like that."

"If it's a skill you want to have, you can learn it." I give him a smile.

"I think I'm doing okay." He pauses. "But you never know, I guess. Maybe it would help. Maybe it's worth a try."

"I think you're doing okay. Not to belabor a point, but you are the best tennis player in the world."

"Heh. For the moment." He stares out over the balcony, out toward the dazzling lights of Port City.

I imagine the feeling. You've gotten to number one, what next? Grand Slam feels great now but you can already look over the railing and see down to the pavement. The higher you've risen, the farther there is to fall. "Well," I say, "what's the record for most majors in a row?"

We both know the answer. "Six," he says.

"You can get two more. Heck, the way you're playing you can get four more. Who's gonna stop you?"

He gives me a meaningful look. "All right, all right," I say, "maybe Dubois."

Braden laughs and gives me a quick hug, a bro-hug in case anyone's peeking around the curtain. "Yeah, or you."

"For real, though," I say, leaning into the quick hug. "Enjoy the moment. I know you've been number one for like half the year almost, but still."

He perks his ears. "It doesn't get old."

"The thing is, though, I think where you are is more than just numbers. You know, we all get caught up in those numbers by our names every week—"

"Says number twenty to number one."

"Number twelve, probably."

His ears flick and he gives me a smug smile. "Not until the list comes out tomorrow."

"The point is, we get attached to these numbers and to our little tennis clubs, you know, who's won a major, who's been in the top ten—"

"Congrats in advance on cracking that one early next year, by the way."

I blow him an air kiss. "And all that stuff is important. But so is this." I gesture between him and me. "If you get all that stuff but you're alone, what fun is it?"

"But if you've got a boyfriend and you're stuck at number 90 or something, what fun is that?"

"Right. So the best is to have them both together." I nod my head back toward the party. "Aliq and Shona, though—they're never going to be number one in mixed doubles."

"Way to support your best friend."

"But they're going to do better together than they'd do apart. And they'll have each other for—well, you know, as long as they both want it."

He gives me a sideways glance. "Is that how long we'll have each other? As long as we both want it?"

"Unless you think we should keep dating when we don't want to anymore."

He shakes his head. "That doesn't sound like fun." Leaning over the balcony, he exhales. "Whoof. This whole year has been so…so…"

"I know." I put a paw on his shoulder, not caring if anyone's watching.

"But you know, I think the best part was winning the Grand Slam."

I laugh, and when he turns I see he's laughing too. "I would hope so," I say. "But I hope I'm at least a close second."

"I feel like you'll be around longer than my ranking."

"That's the plan," I say, leaning forward with him. In the lights of my adopted country, Braden at my side and Ori in the next room, I feel serenely content. I feel at home.

Patreon

Love Match was created with the help of Patreon, a web site that allows fans to support their favorite creators with monthly donations. Every week, another segment is posted on my Patreon site, with extra content available for those supporting at higher levels. If you'd like to read future stories before publication, you can find them at http://www.patreon.com/kyellgold. I'd greatly appreciate your support! Patreon helps my income be more predictable and allows me to do things like continue to commission interior illustrations for this book. There are many other excellent creators on Patreon, so browse around and see who else you might find there.

My deepest thanks to Patreon and to all these contributors from June 2017 to March 2019 who have supported this book in whole or in part:

a stray cat	belladann	Christian Lopez
Ace Saber	Benjamin	Clarke Macbeth
Adept Omega	Brandon	CloudedBlep
Aethial	BerryFox	(Wdz)
AJ	Bill Welsh	Cole Stryker
Alex Bauer	binaryfox	Crimson
Allister Damien	BlackMoon	ct030912
Gray	blargh	Curt Kihlmire
Anamosus	Blizzy Fox	Dale Farmer
AnubiTitus	Broadpaw Fox	Darwen
Arabian	buu38	Dave B.
Darkstone	Canis Rufus	del
Artur Silveira	Cassandra Mann	Devyn Scott
Fortes	caudamus	Diego P
Ashen Hugo	Charles Trelford	Dmitry P
Athelstan	Charlie Payne	Donovan Elk
Ayven	Chris	Doug Kelly
Barium45	Chris Beningo	Dunkelpfote
Baylei	Chris Paw	Dynaphus

Echo Foxx
Ed Haynes
Edward Haynes Jr
EgoSaber
Eliezer
Elizabeth Tseng
EmberFox
Erik Johansson
erisil_lightarrow
Evey
F'yacin
Fabi
Felrnn
Fentic
FireHellion
Flann Moriath
FlatFootFox
Foxon Silverfur
Furiia
Furtastic Voss
Futura
Geemo
Genisu Windpaw
Glassan
GoodBLeo
Grey
Gruffy
Ian Brandeberry
Injy
iqbunny
Ivy the Snivy
Jack Devries
Jakebe
Jared
Jasmine Smith
Jay1743

Jem
JL
JLeet
Jmuttler
Joe Brasen
Joey Watts
John Silver Fox
John Tomblin
Joshua Owens
JS
K H
Kairan Otter
Karmakat
Kato Okami
Kayode Lycaon
Kevin Borge
Kevin Frane
Kieran Gallagher
Kit Reynard
Kittopherson
Klarok
Kogawakenji
Korel Dagh
Kougo
Kris Alexander
Kristi Bjerkaas
Kristofferson
Laimika
Lazy Wolf
Leo
LethargicFox
Louis Lion
Lumble
Mad as A March
Hare
Makoh Dog

Malamutt
Malarwolfe
Malcolm F. Cross
Malec Wolgon
mangowolf
Marc Gold
Marcwolf
Martin Farley
Matt Wills
Matthew Ford
Max Kojote
Max Pitbull
Michael
Morise Anders
Mu Gamma
Myf
Nathan Hopp
NegaImage
Neil McIntosh
Nielas Sinclair
No name
Oh shit my real
name was on here
holy fuck
Omegawolf
Wildpaw
Oscar Landeros
oscar the sergal
oseyeris
Ottah
Peri Llwyn
Phenris
Pinemarten Avatar
Pink Wolf
Pockets
Poi Wong

Pootie Fang
ProwlingPaws
Raito13
Ramuros
Rankine
Ray D.
Redx Wolfski
Rees Cole
Rei Loire
repzzmonster
Reyfar
Rhett
Risus
Riyo
RoflLion
Roger Gilson
Rooth
Ryan
Ryan McKown
sandcat
Shakal Draconis
Shane Elfield
shirou14

Silverfox 361
Silwer
Sirberus Khaos
Skandranon
Rashkae
Skeeter
Sketchy Wolf
SlyFox
Spirit
Stoatmeal
Streaks
Sugi_Quill
sunkawakan
Tame Prince
Tau Switchblade
Thomas
Thorrn
Tidal wolf
Tiger
Tiller Brown
Tom Xepai
TomLeo
tone

Trent Grasse
Trevor Bygland
Trip
Troy Ruggeberg
TuftTip
Tyfle
Tyler Brown
vagabonddiesel
Vaska
Victor Dachs
Viski
Vivian Burning
Vulgus
Wanderer1708
Wigwam
Will Cook
(Midnight Hunter)
wolfeye
Wolfi
Yarac
Ysegrim
Zachary Busto
zleaves

Acknowledgments

Of course, this book has been supported with the help of Patreon and the patrons listed above. In addition, my writing group of Watts Martin, David Cowan, and Ryan Campbell continues to provide support and valuable feedback throughout the writing and editing process. Thanks also to WildeCard, who again helped the tennis matches and language in this book be rendered a bit more realistically.

Thanks to FurPlanet's FuzzWolf and Teiran, who have been fantastic partners to work with in publication and support of this series throughout its life.

As always, Rukis has been more than just an illustrator. Her collaboration on many story points has helped the book along greatly. You can also thank her for including a ligress in the book, because she very much wanted to draw one, and Shona ended up being a pretty important character.

And Kit, Jack, and Kobalt continue to be the best family a fox could ask for. Without their love and encouragement, this book and most of my books would be greatly diminished.

www.ingramcontent.com/pod-product-compliance
Lightning Source LLC
Chambersburg PA
CBHW071340020726
47502CB00001B/190

About the Author

Kyell Gold has won twelve Ursa Major awards and a Cóyotl Award for his stories and novels, and his acclaimed novel "Out of Position" co-won the Rainbow Award for Best Gay Novel of 2009. He helped create RAWR, the first residential furry writing workshop, and has instructed at each of its sessions through 2019.

He lives in California, loves to travel and dine out with his partners (when possible), and can be seen at furry conventions around the world. More information about him and his books is available at http://www.kyellgold.com, and you can follow him on Twitter at @KyellGold.

About the Artist

Rukis lives on a farm, where she spends most of her time working on art, caring for her animals, and hanging out doing tabletop gaming with her friends. She is a huge fan of old school D&D, White Wolf, and Warhammer, as well as studying and collecting exotic fish (Cichlids, mostly) and drinking a lot of Dr. Pepper. Her menagerie includes a rabbit, some fish, two wonderful dogs, and a whole mess of chickens.

She is the author of *Heretic*, the *Off the Beaten Path* trilogy, and *Legacy*, which take place in the world of Red Lantern.

About the Publisher

FurPlanet publishes original works of furry fiction. You can explore their selection at *furplanet.com* and find their e-books at *baddogbooks.com*.